AF472009

About the author

Tony lives in Auckland with his children, pets, and an incredibly understanding (& clairvoyant) wife.

Visit his website at **www.tonyprice.net**

Also by Tony Price

Kicking Out
Moving On

Acknowledgements

This is my first book and writing it took not only many hours of sweat and toil on my behalf, but massive amounts of help and support from others. Thank you to those who read (and re-read) far too many early drafts: Jill & Trevor Price, Malcolm & Christine Attree and Bill Somerville. Thanks also to Alison Brook and Geoff Walker of Penguin Group (NZ) for their advice and encouragement. And special thanks to Mary-Ann Attree for her patience and help with the cover design.

But, as always, my warmest thanks are to my wife, Kiri, for actually believing I might be capable of completing this.

First published 2011
by Starting Gun Books,
Auckland, New Zealand.

National Library of New Zealand Cataloguing-in-Publication Data

Price, Tony, 1965-
Moving on / Tony Price
ISBN 978-0-473-18291-5
I.Title.
NZ823.3—dc 22

Cover design by Mary-Ann Attree
Cover image: Zane Price
Printed by Lightning Source

MOVING ON

TONY PRICE

'Actually I don't remember being born, it must have happened during one of my black outs.'

Jim Morrison

'Sometimes I lie awake at night and ask why me? Then a voice answers - nothing personal, your name just happened to come up.'

Charles M. Schulz

14 September 1999, Tuesday evening

ONE

As I gun the small car around a curve in the road my cell-phone rings softly. I'm running a little late – it was a shit of a day at work – and I guess that it's Sarah calling. Probably wondering where I am. We're supposed to be all going out for dinner, for my daughter's birthday, and I should have been home twenty minutes ago.

I glance across at the little phone, lying on the vacant passenger seat, to see who is calling. At that moment the other car hits me, broadside, right on the driver's side door. It comes careering out of a side street, far too fast to take the corner safely and clearly ignoring the Stop sign it has practically flown through.

I half glimpse a blur of blue as the car punches into mine with a sickeningly loud scream of metal tearing metal. The width of my car is practically halved in an instant and I feel every breath in me abruptly leave.

My car spins a full circle, bouncing over the roadside kerb and on towards the trees and bush alongside. The other car seems to have fused with mine and scrapes and squeals alongside, locked in a grim embrace. Then, abruptly, it breaks free as we reach the trees, rolling away to disappear into the bushes somewhere behind my field of vision.

I didn't see the other driver, nor can I now see the road I have just left. Blood is seeping down my face, blurring my vision. I struggle to breathe and feel nothing much beyond a swaying and spinning inside my head. I may be upside down but I'm really not sure.

I should be scared but oddly realise that I'm more concerned about messing up the birthday dinner than anything else. I want to call home and try to look around the car for my still ringing cell-phone. I can hear it somewhere off in the distance, but all I can see through my haziness is a dim impression of the cars dashboard lights and its splintered windscreen. I try to move, but can't. My body simply won't respond.

With the persistent trilling of the cell-phone beginning to frustrate me, my sight blurs even further before unexpectedly clearing sharply. Now I am outside the car, lying on my back, staring up into the evening sky through the trees. A bicycle wheel is spinning in a tree above me, with a red reflector thing lodged between its spokes which flashes every time the wheel completes a turn. Suddenly the dark shape of a very large man moves into my line of sight and stands there, looming over me. Then he's gone. Darkness falls abruptly and I'm back in my car, pinned in my seat, with blood washing down my face.

That damn cell-phone is still ringing insistently. My chest shudders as I fight for air. I think I hear a voice calling out somewhere nearby. Then the ringing cuts off abruptly. The silence is frightening and I shiver, although I'm not cold.

Pain erupts through my forehead like a bolt of lightning and the darkness descends again, this time enveloping me completely.

14 November 2008, Friday evening

TWO

MARK MITCHELL is frightened. He can't decide what to do next. It's now fairly dark, but he doesn't feel that it's safe to head home quite yet. Steve might still be there.

His cell-phone rings yet again, it's been trilling gently almost every five minutes since he made his escape. Mark stops his bicycle, keeping one foot ready to begin pedaling again quickly – if it becomes necessary – and pulls the small blue object from his pocket.

The display reveals that Liz is calling, yet again. But he doesn't answer. It may not actually be Liz, but his mother instead, using his sister's phone to try and trick him. Or worse, it could be Steve. He lets it ring on and tries to ignore the persistent sound as he pushes it back into his pocket. The ringing frustrates him. He'd like to talk to Liz, but he can't be sure. Maybe he should just turn it off? But what if Jack, or one of his other friends, tries to text him? Mark likes the phone on. It's his link to the outside world. His link to a better world. A place where he doesn't have to deal with his stupid mother, or her toxic boyfriend.

But what to do now? How long should he wait before trying to head home again? He doesn't want to go back there but knows that he eventually must. He's hungry. Night has fallen and he's getting tired. Will Steve be gone, or will he be waiting for him there?

He knows that Steve is very, very angry with him right now. Mark has never seen his mother's latest boyfriend that furious before and he can't decide whether he should be terrified or pleased. Clearly he's struck pay-dirt this time. Steve was so incredibly angry earlier that Mark feels certain that his mum will send Steve packing this time; just ditch him like the dirty dog he is. And Liz had been so excited when he told her. That pleased Mark very much.

He smiles grimly. Steve is a brute. A bear-like bully with an evil temper. Getting Steve out of their lives will fix everything. He's sure of it. His mother will straighten herself out and they'll all be happy again. Without a doubt.

Mark starts cycling again. He doesn't want to stay in one place – just in case Steve is out looking for him. If Steve catches him he'll be in big trouble. Very big trouble.

He turns the corner and starts heading north again, back up along Waterloo Rd. Heading towards home again, but still unsure if he dares to go there quite yet.

All the businesses are closed in this industrial area of Wilton. It's getting late and all the workers are long gone, not just for the evening but for the weekend. Waterloo Rd has a wide greenbelt on one side and Mark cycles on the footpath, looking through the shadows to the trees and the small stream running alongside as he meanders along.

The cell-phone starts to ring again in his pocket. It's probably Liz again, but what if it's not? What if it's Jack? Mark's desire to know is immediate. Almost a compulsion. But he keeps cycling as he reaches one hand into his pocket.

Without warning he suddenly finds himself flying through the air. There is a sickening crunching sound and his right leg feels like it's just been hit by a cricket bat. He registers little more than a flash of blue in the fading light.

Mark Mitchell cries out in pain, fear and surprise as he spins wildly through the air, totally disoriented, spiraling into the greenbelt and darkness.

15 November 2008, Early Saturday morning

THREE

My hospital room smells clean and antiseptic. It's dimly lit and there is a half-drawn curtain around my bed, shielding me from god-only-knows what. Someone has just left the room, I think maybe a nurse, and the door clicking shut behind her has woken me.

Staring through the night gloom at the panelled ceiling above I try to get my head straight. I begin to recall a car accident and wonder hazily if I've been badly hurt.

I can feel crisp white sheets and cotton blankets and can just make out white painted steel tubing visible beyond the bumps my feet present beneath the blankets. Oddly the bed doesn't feel right somehow. It seems too large for standard hospital issue. Too comfy.

I'm pleased to see my feet though and hesitantly try shifting them, careful that I might send pain shooting through my body. But, other than some stiffness down my right side, there's nothing unusual and my legs respond easily. I'm not dancing yet, but I am relieved.

Encouraged, I raise my right hand and check my stomach and chest. Then I bring my left hand up for both to complete the journey to my face. My arms seem to be working fine and my head is still in place, excellent. And it feels like my face is still all there too. Two ears and a nose. Even better. But I think I may be missing a tooth. Damn, that'll be expensive to fix. And I find a bandage of some kind around my head, but it isn't too tight.

Thank god. I'm effectively in one piece.

It's still very dim in the room and I gingerly lift my head to try and see around, discovering that moving makes my head hurt. There is a window at the foot of my bed with patterned curtains drawn over it. Lights from either the road or neon signs glow through the thin material.

I wonder how my family is feeling. I'll have missed little Katherine's fifth birthday dinner, undoubtedly ruining the occasion. I'm annoyed at myself and resolve that Daddy will make it up to her. She'll forgive me, I feel sure.

I have no idea what time it is and can see no clock in the room. I'm disappointed there is no bedside vigil, but I understand. It must be very late and the kids will have school tomorrow. Sarah will come and see me in the morning. And if I only have a few aches and bruises to deal with then I should be discharged fairly quickly tomorrow. We can have Katherine's birthday dinner tonight, or tomorrow night, instead.

Moving my head slowly I look carefully to my left. Damn, but that smarts. Another bed is across the way and there is a sleeping mound beneath the blanket. Shame. There's no such thing as a private room these days. At least he isn't snoring.

Through the gloom I catch sight of two posters on the wall above the other bed. One looks like a fat guy wearing a mask – like the lone ranger. Big letters spell out *The Incredibles* above him. He's not familiar. I narrow my eyes. The other one is more obvious, it's *Batman*. You're kidding me. What on earth is a Batman poster doing on the wall of a hospital room?

Foolishly I try to sit up, but a thunderstorm of pain crashes around inside my head and the darkness washes over me again.

I wake as a nurse draws the curtains back from the window. Its morning and light streams in to show me that the nurse is tall and fair and quite attractive.

'Good morning,' I try to say, but the words come out somewhat higher and thinner than I intended. I cough to try and clear my throat.

The nurse turns and looks at me. She smiles and moves to my bedside, gently laying an open hand lightly against the side of my face. I'm surprised at the intimacy, but I don't pull away. She leans over to look down at me. There is concern and some tenderness in her eyes, but I can't help being distracted by a flash of lacey bra through the uniform buttons. She looks to be barely in her twenties, and probably stops traffic in that uniform.

'How's the head feeling, tough guy?' she asks.

I'm almost lost for words. Is this girl coming on to me? I'm almost old enough to be her father. I must be still asleep and dreaming, but I try to reply anyway.

'It's good…' is all I can manage. My voice again sounds somehow wrong, but I'm quite distracted by the pretty young nurse. I cough again and wince as the pain returns.

'Hmm…' she murmurs, obviously not convinced. Stepping back she checks the chart hanging from the end of my bed. She looks at me again over it, saying nothing, seeming to expect questions or demands that aren't forthcoming. I offer up a winning smile and she appears bemused by this. Returning the chart to its hook she shakes her head just a little as she moves to push the curtains further back from around my bed.

'Are you hungry? The breakfast trolley has already been around but I can get you a little something if you like?' she offers softly.

I try and pull myself up onto one elbow and suddenly realise how hungry I am.

'God, yes, please. What are my chances of steak, egg and chips?'

She frowns, returning to the bedside and motioning me to stay lying down, which I do fairly quickly as my brain is now thumping at my eyeballs from the inside.

'You need more rest, don't try and get up yet,' she says, then pushes a button near the bed-head. A quiet motor whirs softly, raising me into a semi-sitting position. 'And it's No-Can-Do on the heavy cholesterol, young man, but I think I can find you something that may once have been eggs. Will that do?'

Young man? My head is pounding, but I appreciate her sense of humour.

'Sounds good enough,' I respond. Again my voice feels oddly unfamiliar, but I've given up trying to cough the frog out of it. 'Any chance of a coffee? White, no sugar.'

The pretty nurse looks puzzled. Then she shakes her head lightly, leaving the room saying simply, 'Back soon.'

I watch her go and delight in finding the view from behind easily as intoxicating as that from the front. Doesn't every man love a girl in uniform?

Turning back from the door I finally survey the hospital room in full light. My bed is nearest the door with a window facing it. Once again I find myself thinking that it seems to be a pretty damn big bed. Things have changed since I was last in hospital.

The previously sleeping mound in the bed beside mine is now awake too. I'm startled momentarily to see that it's a young boy, probably only about twelve or so. Surely that can't be right. Don't they put kids in a separate ward? He's reading quietly, a large hard-cover book, Harry Potter and the something-in-a-smaller-font-size. I've never heard of it. It seems an awfully big book for a child. The boy has big ears and very short hair, almost shaved. He ignores me and I decide not to try and start a conversation.

Above him, on the wall, are the two posters I'd glimpsed last night. The fat *Incredibles* guy is wearing a red suit while the *Batman* poster is for a movie called '*Batman Begins*' starring Christian Bale. I don't recall seeing that one, it must be an oldie. And what happened to George Clooney; isn't he the current Batman? Mind you, they do keep changing actor. I can't help but think that these are pretty obscure choices of art, really, for a hospital ward.

Then, from the corner of my eye, I catch a glimpse of a young face at the window. Looking over I see a blonde haired boy with a large bandage around his head, staring at me through the window. The boys face is bruised and a little scratched. He looks about nine, or maybe ten, and he seems a little confused.

After a moment I realise that this boy isn't outside the window but in a hospital bed, propped up and staring at me. His eyes widen in surprise and his mouth falls open.

Suddenly I can't breathe and I feel sure my heart has stopped beating. I raise my hand to my head and the boy in the windows reflection mirrors me, gently touching a blonde bang of his own hair that is poking through the bandage.

This isn't possible. I can feel the hair on my fingertips.

I stare in utter shock at my own reflection.

I'm still staring at myself numbly when the nurse returns. But now I'm trembling, as my mind spins and my heart races. I have to drag my eyes away from the window reflection and find myself shrinking down into the bed.

This is crazy. I must be dreaming. How else could this make sense? I look down and stare at my hands. They're small and smooth. Not a hair, hardly a wrinkle. I turn them over and over and slowly, very slowly, shake my head in disbelief. Predictably, even this makes my head throb again. Should you feel pain in a dream?

'Hey there, big fella,' the nurse says lightly. 'I found you a little breakfast, if you're still feeling hungry?'

I can't answer her. My mind has just stopped working. It's numb, frozen like a Popsicle. I just stare at her and blink a few times as if that will clear my thoughts.

'Are you alright, Mark? Is your head hurting? You took a bit of a nasty bump on it, so we can give you a little something to ease the pain if it hurts.'

I still can't respond. Usually I'm a bit hot-headed, you know – act in haste, repent at leisure – that's my normal way, but shock and confusion have me rooted to the spot.

I can smell the warm food from the tray, it actually smells quite good, and I can sense the warmth of the sun through the window. But I've become frightened and cold inside. My chest is tightening and I think I've forgotten how to breathe. My thoughts begin turning in circles. What's going on?

The nurse places the food tray aside and moves to sit on the edge of my bed, quickly checking my pulse, which must be off the chart. Her hands are soft and gentle and they feel very, very real. I notice her faint perfume, she smells even better than the food. What an amazingly realistic hallucination.

I try to relax, to force myself to detach from the shock. It's not easy but I manage to find my voice again. I force the question out cautiously, in a voice that is not my own.

'Where am I?'

'You're at Hawthorne Central Hospital,' she replies, still holding my wrist. Her eyes are watchful and concerned.

'Okay . . . thank you. And, how long have I been here?'

I can see that this is more familiar territory for her. Her voice is gentle, reassuring.

'Since yesterday evening. The chart says you were brought into the ward about 8 pm. You had a pretty bad bike accident. Do you remember?'

'An accident on my bike . . . ?'

Not possible. I was in my car. I haven't ridden in years.

'Yes. You were hit by a car. But you've been very lucky. Apart from a nasty cut on your head and a couple of minor bruises, you seem to be in pretty good shape.'

'Okay . . . thank you.'

I simply don't understand. My mind is reeling.

'I was unconscious, was I?' I ask. 'From the head injury?'

'Initially, yes. When you first came in. You were given a light sedative around midnight.'

That must have been when I woke in the night. The person leaving the room.

'Can you tell me what day it is today, Mark?' she asks.

Mark? Who the hell is Mark? My name is Nick. Then I realise it's a test. She's checking me for concussion. I respond hesitantly. 'Yesterday was Tuesday . . . so today must be Wednesday, right?'

She doesn't answer and a small frown flickers across her face. She tries to hide it.

'And, can you tell me your full name, Mark?'

But Mark's not my name. I'm stymied. I don't know what to say. Should I tell her my real name or make something up? I can't think straight, can't decide what to say, but then it's too late. I've taken too long to respond and her expression tells me she's already reached a conclusion.

This boy is concussed.

'It's okay, Mark,' she says softly. 'You just need a bit more rest. Relax.'

I say nothing. I'm still lost for words. She releases my hand and produces a small pack of little white pills – painkillers, no doubt – and pops two out into her hand.

'Take these now and have a little something to eat. We can talk a bit more about this a little later on. You've had a bit of a knock, but you're going to be just fine.'

My head is pounding so I take the pills without discussion. Then she raises herself from the bed and moves the tray of food onto a mobile trolley that suspends it over the bed, above my outstretched legs, within my reach.

Silently I watch her leave the room to continue her rounds.

Is this where I should now try and pinch myself, to see if I am in a dream? And to try and wake myself up. But I resist the urge. It seems like a stupid thing to do. I just need to work it all through logically. Be sensible and act rationally.

But these things aren't natural for me.

I look over at the boy in the bed beside me. Maybe I should ask him to slap me, see if that snaps me out of this? But he's still engrossed in the huge book. He doesn't even look up.

Obviously I'm hallucinating. In fact – it strikes me like a bullet – I must be in a coma, from the accident, and this is clearly just a bizarre dream. It's incredibly vivid, the most realistic dream experience I've ever had, but it has to be a dream. Surely. How else does a relatively sane, and usually rational, man go from being a fully grown adult with a wife and two children to suddenly become a small unfamiliar child overnight? The boy in the windows reflection looks nothing like I did when I was a child. I'd never been blonde. Never even wanted to be blonde.

Before the accident yesterday I had been driving home from work. It was Tuesday evening, definitely, and it was my daughter's fifth birthday! My name is Nick Davis – and I have a son who is about the same age as the boy I seem to now be. This doesn't make sense.

I look slowly around the hospital room. There's no mirror so I slip out of the bed and move to the window to take a closer look at this boy. My head immediately starts pounding again and I realise quickly that I'm very tender and sore down the outside of my right leg. I'm only wearing a thin hospital gown and I pull it aside. The boy's legs are skinny, hairless and sporting some pretty colourful bruises. My God, but I'm so puny. Curiously I poke one of the bruises and instantly wince. It hurts like hell. I resolve silently not to try that again.

I look up to see the little blond boy in the window following me, mirroring every move. Releasing the gown I edge closer to make out darkening bruises beneath his eyes, scratches and light abrasions across his right cheek. A big bandage, like a roughly open-topped turban, is wrapped with a lean to the right-hand side around the boy's head. There is longish blonde hair sticking out from above and beneath the bandage. I move forward again and notice the boy is missing a tooth. There's a big gap where his left incisor should be. Leaning in closer to the window I open my mouth to reveal the tiny head of a new tooth peeking through the gum inside the gap. An adult tooth, pushing through the baby ones. Good grief. Then I look up slightly and finally recognise something.

I look into my own eyes.

My very familiar eyes stare right back at me from the bruised young face. They are mainly blue, but with an unusual brown mark, a sort of a smudge, just to the right of the iris on my left eye. You wouldn't notice it from a distance, but it's pretty distinctive up close. Without doubt these are the eyes that have looked back at me from every mirror I've gazed into over the last thirty six years. But they're wide and anxious today. And a wee bit bloodshot.

I look around again. The boy in the other bed is still reading, completely ignoring me.

'Hey,' I call out to him. 'What day is it today?'

He doesn't respond. Maybe I'm a ghost and only the nurse can see me?

'Hello,' I try again. 'Can you hear me?'

'Saturday,' he grunts.

'Seriously?'

He ignores me again.

'But what's the date today? September, umm… 18?'

He shakes his head, annoyed, and finally mutters. 'It's November, the 15th.'

No way! That's two months after my car accident. The realisation hits me like a ton of bricks. I must be in a coma. And I've been out for two god-damn months.

My mind reels. Suddenly I feel faint and quickly stagger back to my hospital bed. Now I understand why it seems so big. Because I'm only tiny. Well, the boy that I'm currently seeing out of is only tiny. What the hell is going on? Am I in a coma, having some sort of surreal dream?

Inspiration hits me.

If I'm lying around somewhere, in a coma, then that somewhere has to be Hawthorne Central. I had the car crash only a short distance from home and this hospital is easily the closest and most likely facility that I would have been taken to. There are much bigger hospitals around the country, but they wouldn't need to take me somewhere else. Hawthorne has top-notch intensive care facilities. So clearly I must be lying in this hospital, in its intensive care wing, in a deep coma. It's the only way this makes any sense.

Problem solved.

I'll just go and find myself. Shake myself awake. Get back into my own head. Simple really.

As I start to leave the room the boy speaks again.

'You gonna eat that?'

'What?'

'The eggs. You gonna eat them?'

I almost laugh. Nothing could be further from my mind now. 'Help yourself mate. I've got bigger fish to fry.'

As I shuffle out the door, with my leg feeling quite stiff, I hear him dragging the trolley across to his own bed.

FOUR

There's no one in the hallway and I spot a bank of lifts to my right. My thin hospital gown is loose and exposes me at the back but I don't care. I'm up and I'm moving. I actually feel pretty positive all of a sudden. I haven't forgotten that I'm seeing the world from inside a child's body, but it's not really bothering me anymore. I'm no longer confused. This isn't real; it's a fantasy in my own mind.

According to the signage in the lift Intensive Care is on the first floor, two stops down, so I hit the button and wait patiently. No one joins me for the ride and I pass an elderly couple as I step out of the lift on the first floor. They don't seem to notice me. I'm feeling pretty detached, now that I've accepted my dream-like state, but as I head towards the entrance to Intensive Care I begin to have doubts.

What will I actually do when I find myself in there? Just shake myself awake? What if that doesn't work? I start to feel uncomfortable, but press on regardless.

Slipping through the double-doors I find myself in a small reception area. An elderly nurse quietly taps away on a computer keyboard, updating some poor soul's files. Possibly mine. Hmm, I hope they're looking after me.

The nurse has a weary, lined face and blue-grey hair. She looks close to retirement age. I don't see any sense in randomly wandering from room to room so I walk straight up to her, feeling quite bold. As she looks up from the keyboard her bright, clear eyes assess me quickly. Elderly – yes, but she's plainly not doddery. Instinctively I decide that a small ruse will be appropriate. I'm not sure why.

'Hi there. I'm looking for my Uncle's room. Mum said he was in here and that it would be okay if I came and sat with him for a bit.'

She looks me over carefully, obviously taking in my gown and bandaged head. Her expression is unreadable, but she responds kindly.

'I see, but you really shouldn't be in here on your own young man, and visiting hours don't start till 2 pm. Perhaps you should come back with your Mummy then.'

Bugger. This may be more of a challenge than I thought. From her tone she seems sympathetic, but she must have rules to follow. I opt to lay on the drama a bit.

'I can't. Mum dropped me off. She has to make arrangements for my Auntie's funeral. Is my Uncle in here? Can I sit with him for a while? Please.'

I try to make tears well up in my eyes, but I don't succeed. I'm not that good an actor. She sizes me up again, now a little frustrated. I hold my breath and wait.

'What's your Uncle's name?' she finally asks with a little sigh. I give her my own full name and address.

'Nicolas Walter Davis, of Charles St, in Wilton.'

She taps away on the keyboard, frowns, and then types some more. 'That's D-A-V-I-S, not Davies with an "E"?'

'Definitely Davis. No "E". A bad car accident. Possibly now in a coma?' I prompt.

She frowns and then taps away again, mumbling to herself. Finally she looks up, her expression guarded.

'I'm sorry young man, but we have no records of anyone by that name being admitted to the hospital in the last six months. Nothing even close.'

I'm dumbfounded, unable to respond.

'So what was your name? And what have you done to your head? Perhaps we should find your mother instead?'

How can I not be in here? I think frantically, my head spins with possibilities. I have to be here.

'No, there must be some mistake. Nick Davis has to be here. Maybe he was transferred to another hospital? Where do people in comas get sent?'

'Calm down, young man, I'm sure there's a simple explanation. We'll find him. Everything will be fine.'

It becomes clear to me that she has decided I'm disoriented because of my head injury. Only she has no idea how incredibly disoriented I really am.

Suddenly I notice movement over my shoulder. A male orderly has wandered in and is standing right behind me, blocking my route to the exit. He raises his eyebrows inquiringly to the nurse. She acknowledges him with a small *wait there* gesture and returns her focus to me.

'Where did the accident happen, and when?' she asks.

I get the feeling she's just trying to pacify me and, although the orderly behind me is making me feel oddly uneasy, I like the direction she's heading so I play along.

'Tuesday evening, earlier this week, just up in Wilton. He would have to have been bought here, right?'

'Yes, he would have been bought here. And if he slipped into a coma he would definitely still be here. We're fully equipped for that sort of thing. But I'm afraid no one of that name has come in.'

Her tone is definitive. Nick Davis is not in this hospital.

The orderly behind me shifts his weight and I get an uneasy feeling once again. He's not a big man, but he looms over my pint-sized form. Is he going to grab and hold me?

But then a more horrible thought suddenly occurs to me.

'What if he'd died in the crash? Would he be on your records?'

The nurse looks shocked, but gathers herself quickly. 'Yes, he would. So you relax, young man. Wherever he is he must be alive and well. Maybe you should tell me your name. Perhaps we can track you and your Uncle down some other way?'

She smiles reassuringly, but I hesitate. I don't want to admit to her that I'm actually the Nick Davis she was looking for, and I don't know what this boy Mark's last name is. I start to step away and notice her eyes flick across to the orderly. Damn it, now I'm in trouble. Clearly she thinks I'm a confused patient who has wandered away from my ward – I'm wearing a gown after all – and she plans to have me returned to my bed.

What should I do? Just go back to my bed? I certainly don't fancy being dragged off to the psych ward. I can feel the orderly move slightly closer and I tense up, ready to run. But as my mind spins frantically we are interrupted.

A blue light suddenly starts flashing over the door of a room about half way down the hall, and a soft siren warbles into life from speakers dotted throughout the ward.

For an old woman the nurse reacts instantly. I'm impressed.

She's halfway down the hallway to the room with the flashing light before I've fully registered what is happening. I turn to the orderly who hesitates, trying to decide if he should secure the child or follow the nurse. For a brief moment I consider trying to run away, but come up with a better option.

'I'm okay,' I say to him, 'I'll wait here. You should hurry.'

He says nothing, but points to a nearby chair as he moves away from me and then jogs up the hall. I walk towards the chair and pretend to sit down, but the moment he disappears I take the opportunity to leave.

I trot quickly through the nearest door, finding myself in a stairwell. Lost in thought and just wanting to get away from Intensive Care I head down one flight and come out in the main ground floor lobby. As I begin to head uncertainly towards the lifts a shrill voice calls out.

'Hi Mark! What are you doing here?'

There is a little girl waving at me from the Emergency Room waiting area. She has dark hair, cut in a bob, and looks about eight or nine years old. Probably about Mark's age. She comes out and lightly skips over.

'Funny seeing you here. What are you wearing? My stupid little brother has gone and broken his arm. He fell out of that big tree in the park. You know the one by the old fort thing. Mum's really angry with him 'cause he shouldn't have been out there. They're putting a cast on him now. Hey, what did you do to your head? Does it hurt?'

She doesn't take a breath during the whole discourse and I'm dumbstruck. I have no idea who she is or how she knows me or what she represents in my now very frustrating coma-nightmare. But my lack of response doesn't seem to faze her in the least. She just starts talking again, seemingly choosing topics at random.

'I guess we're not going to be going sailing today, and that's weird. We almost always go sailing on Saturday mornings, you know, on the lake. But since my stupid brother has broken his stupid arm we probably won't go today. Mum's really mad. I haven't seen her this mad since Daddy came home from his last fishing trip. Boy, she was mad that day. I guess you're not going to be sailing today either, are you Mark? Do you have a yacht? Ours is blue, mainly, with some white. Did you do your spelling homework yet? I did most of mine last night. Mum say's if I don't do my homework I'm not allowed to watch TV and there was a really cool movie on last night. Did you see it?'

Fortunately that's where we are cut off by her mother. I haven't said a word. She hasn't taken a breath so I didn't have much of a chance. I half expect her to faint right there in front of me from lack of oxygen.

Anyway, when I see her mother it's me who nearly faints.

The rapidly-talking-girl's mother turns out to be Mrs Sally Taylor, nee McCarthy. I know Sally quite well. She recently married one of my workmates, Ian Taylor. Sarah and I attended their wedding about two months ago. I play golf with Ian.

'Olivia. Who are you talking to? Come back here now.'

Sally clearly isn't in a good mood. I recall that Olivia had warned me, but I didn't really take it in. However it isn't Sally's mood that upsets me, it's her appearance.

The last time I saw Sally she looked healthy and vital and was veritably glowing with the contentment of a newlywed. The Sally I know is an attractive woman in her early thirties, compact and sporty with flowing dark brown hair. Ian's pretty sporty and fit too and they look good together. Not quite Beck's and Posh, but a nice couple.

But this Sally seems considerably older, and the newlywed glow is nowhere to be seen. While she still looks quite physically fit, her hair is cut much shorter and there are tell-tale little age lines creeping across her face. She looks closer to forty than thirty, and seems quite tired and frayed. Much like any parent with small children, really.

And there is a small boy, probably about five, trailing along behind her with his newly plastered arm in a fresh crisp sling. Evidently Olivia's stupid little brother, who recently fell out of a tree. He's the spitting image of my mate Ian. The poor kid.

I can't speak. I'm frozen in place with my mouth hanging wide. I hear Olivia tell her mother that I'm Mark Mitchell and that I'm in her class at school and that she doesn't know how I've hurt my head. Sally asks her if I'm Tracey Mitchell's boy and Olivia says Yes, I think so. Sally looks at me with some distain, frowns, and without speaking ushers her children away as quickly as she can.

I'm utterly stunned.

I just stand there, no longer clear about anything at all. Am I actually dreaming all this, or not? What on earth is Sally doing here? Sally doesn't have kids. She and Ian have only just been married. They can't possibly have kids yet.

What the hell is going on?

Time seems to stand still as the building spins itself around me furiously. I don't know what to do. I've lost my mind, there's no other explanation. This can't be a dream. How can it be? This must be what it's like to go insane.

I start to feel numb.

Then a hand falls on my shoulder. It's the orderly from Intensive Care. He's caught up to me. But I don't try to run, I'm way too confused. I can't think straight. My knees begin to give way and the orderly catches me, lifting me easily to carry against his chest. I don't resist.

Before I know it I'm back upstairs in my hospital bed. The kid with the big ears and the bottomless appetite is glued to his book again and the pretty nurse comes to give me an injection. It must me another sedative as the darkness quickly claims me once again.

I wake up a lot later on to find three women gathered around my bed. Well, two women and a teenage girl to be precise. One is the pretty nurse but I don't know either of the other two. The sun is dipping low outside the window behind the two women who are engaged in some kind of terse discussion. The teenage girl moves along the bedside and looks at me curiously.

She has long, very dark, brown hair tied back in a pony-tail, and fair lightly freckled skin. Her blue eyes are bright and filled with concern, but also puffy and red as though she's been crying. She looks about sixteen or seventeen and is quite attractive in a gangly teenage sort of way. She sits carefully on the bed and lays one hand onto mine. She whispers softly.

'Hey there, Mark. How you doing?'

Her voice is warm and caring and I instinctively feel close to her. It's a nice feeling. But I don't reply. I'm still half asleep, groggy from the sedative, and immediately become even more confused. Who is this girl?

'I thought he'd killed you. I thought you were going to die,' she's still whispering and a tear begins to slide down her face.

The two women are still in deep discussion but I can't seem to focus on their words. The girl beside me starts to get a bit frantic, her hushed tone becomes insistent.

'Mum doesn't believe me. You'll have to tell her. It was Steve, wasn't it? With his car? You've still got the video? Haven't you? Talk to me, Mark. Please.'

I don't know what to say. I'm just lying here, deep within my own private nightmare, and I have no idea what she's talking about or even who she is. Surely I should have snapped out of this by now. It's not possible to fall asleep in the middle of your own dream, is it? I'm so completely muddled that I can't even try to answer her sensibly.

Then the two women seem to reach a conclusion and my nurse turns on her heel and slips out of the room. The remaining woman addresses me sharply.

'I've brought you some clean clothes, Mark. It's time to get dressed and come home.'

This woman is older, taller, with long bottle-blonde hair. She's fairly attractive, but wears too much make-up for my taste. She has a curvy hour-glass figure, and is dressed in a low cut top and short skirt that shows it all off. I immediately, and a little unkindly, decide she looks like a street-walker. And she isn't smiling. Something doesn't feel right here. Beside the entire weird-dream scenario, that is.

'Come on young man, we haven't got all day. Up and dressed please,' the voluptuous blonde women snaps at me. Her words are terse, authoritative, but there is an over-arching air of disillusionment in her tone. As if life hasn't been treating her fairly.

The dark-haired teenager squeezes my hand while giving the blonde woman a reproachful look, but says nothing. Blondie points at a plastic shopping bag on the end of the bed that appears to contain clothes and nods towards it impatiently. My thoughts are still fuzzy and I don't move. Who are these people? The big eared boy in the other bed is trying hard to look like he's not watching but he's clearly intrigued.

The room goes still and quiet for just a moment before a small Asian man, wearing a white doctor's coat, enters briskly. My pretty nurse is hot on his heels.

'Hello there. How is everyone today,' he offers cheerily.

The blonde woman heaves an exasperated sigh and mutters something under her breath. She doesn't look at him but keeps staring firmly at me, nodding silently towards the clothes in the shopping bag again.

The small man tries another, more direct, approach.

'Mrs Mitchell, I'm Dr Huang. Perhaps I could have a word with you about Mark outside?'

I don't understand. She still won't turn to face him, but she does finally respond.

'Is that really necessary? I understand – from your nurse – that he's not badly hurt and that it's all right to finally take him home now.'

'That is certainly possible, Mrs Mitchell. However your son has taken quite a blow and I was hoping we could keep him here for another night to observe his recovery. Trauma to the head like this can sometimes lead to complications.'

Finally she turns to him.

'Thanks anyway, but we can observe him at home. He'll be fine.'

'Mrs Mitchell, with all due respect, Mark has experienced rather severe cranial trauma and has been displaying classic symptoms of concussion. It would be– '

'Look, this is the third time we've come to get him and every time we've been given the run around. Is he well enough to go home yet, or not?'

'I'm sorry?'

'Is he well enough to go home? To be discharged? To leave?'

'He seems to be over the worst– '

'And he's well enough to leave now?'

'He was unconscious for many hours. I would strongly recommend– '

'Yes or No? Is he allowed to leave?'

'Mrs Mitchell, please, its not– '

'Yes or No?'

Now it was Dr Huang's turn to sigh in exasperation. 'Yes,' he replies softly.

The blonde woman immediately turns away from him to stare at me again. This time she points to the plastic bag of clothing and simply raises her eyebrows in demand.

There is silence in the room.

The doctor looks frustrated, the nurse is glaring daggers at the blonde woman and she, in turn, is frowning impatiently at me. My big-eared room-mate is wide-eyed over in his own bed and the teenage girl looks embarrassed.

As my fuzziness clears I finally start to understand the exchange.

The buxom blonde, Mrs Mitchell, just has to be Mark's mother while it seems almost certain that the dark-haired girl is his sister. And somehow I have become Mark Mitchell – the young blonde boy that everyone is discussing.

Okay, that's all fine, but what the hell am I doing inside this small boy? None of it makes any sense.

The girl is still holding my hand and she squeezes it gently again. With her other hand she reaches down the bed and carefully drags the bag of clothes up towards me.

Everything around me is so very, very realistic. But is it a hallucination, or is it somehow real? I'm so confused. I look to the girl. For some reason I feel drawn to her. I'm strangely convinced that she cares for me deeply, yet I don't even know her name. She forces a smile.

'We should get going, Mark. Do you need help getting dressed?' she says softly.

There is depth to her gaze that I hadn't noticed before and I feel a definite sense of safety and rightness beside her. I'm not sure why but I find myself letting go. I just give in and stop trying to understand. Something deep inside tells me that this girl is going to watch out for me. My sister is here to protect me. It's okay to go with her. It's the right thing to do.

Without speaking I slide out of bed and pick up the shopping bag. I take out the underpants and shorts and slip them on without removing my loose-fitting hospital gown. I feel the bruises on my leg tingle as the clothing passes over them. Then I pull a faded red T-shirt out of the bag, remove the gown and slip it over my head. It's a little bit tight over the bandages around my head, but not a problem. I remain barefoot.

'There is some paperwork we will need to complete, Mrs Mitchell,' says Dr Huang.

Without acknowledging this Mark's mother addresses her daughter in a neutral tone. 'Liz, would you take him out to the car please. I'll be there shortly.'

We leave them in an uncomfortable silence.

I feel okay as we start towards the hallway, with only a slight limp from my bruised right leg, but I'm still a bit woozy from the sedative. I hear the others follow us out of the room and stop at the nurse's work-station.

But once we make it to the lift my head begins to pound again and I start to feel a little faint. I haven't eaten for what seems like forever. I instinctively reach out to the girl, Liz, who takes my arm to lend support. Terse discussions start up again behind us.

We ride down in the lift as I wish wistfully for some painkillers. My head is throbbing. We have to stop for a minute as we cross the carpark to prevent the world from spinning away from me again. But we finally make it to an old cream-coloured hatchback. It's already unlocked so Liz helps me into the back seat where I lie down and close my eyes. My head is now pounding like a jackhammer. Neither of us has spoken during the walk and once I collapse on the back seat I actually pass out again.

FIVE

The car is moving as I come around and there is an uncomfortable silence from the front. I can see Liz in the passenger seat and assume that *Mum* is driving.

Everything feels very real in the back seat, not dream-like at all. It's filled with junk, and is lumpy and uncomfortable. I'm lying on what smells like last week's dirty laundry and can hear empty cans and bottles bouncing around the foot wells. The sensations are unlike any other dream I can ever recall having.

Is this a coma-dream? Maybe my injuries from the car crash are a lot more serious than the ones I'm presenting in this dream. Perhaps I'm dying? Could this be some sort of deeply complicated healing process that no one else has ever experienced? Or lived to talk about? I can't make sense of it.

I sit up a little. The sky is darkening as the sun sets and I can tell we're heading towards home. The streets we pass are familiar as I grew up around here, in the suburb of Wilton. I've actually lived here my whole life so know the area intimately, but this evening everything somehow looks a bit different. We miss my usual turn-off and keep heading north, finally turning into Herbert Drive. This road leads towards the more northerly suburbs that are closer to the lake shore and the neighbourhood I grew up in. My parents still live out this way in a big old house my Grandfather built many, many years ago. The car turns again a few blocks short though, into Miller Road and takes us past my old school, Wilton Comprehensive. We turn once more to head north again, up Lorneville Drive, and shortly turn right into a cul-de-sac side street where we pull into the driveway of a small block of three brick and tile units.

Still in silence we disembark from the car and enter the far end unit. It's small and cramped and looks like it hasn't been refurbished in years. Very 1970's.

Liz leads me through to a small room with two single beds. It's tidier than the rest of the house, but also tatty and in some disrepair. My head is still thumping. She helps me onto one of the beds and slips away. When she returns she has a glass of water and a box of painkillers. She gives me two which I accept gratefully. I feel immensely tired yet my mind is whirling with discomfort and disbelief.

What the hell is going on?

'You need to sleep,' Liz murmurs. 'We'll talk about Steve and the video later.' She slips out again and I close my eyes to ease the pounding – and drift away again.

If my big-eared roommate from the hospital is to be believed, then it's Sunday morning when I next awake. Light is blasting in through a gaping tear in the room's curtains directly into my face. I blink and sit up to move clear of the invasive brightness. The pounding has subsided and I now seem to be only suffering a pretty bad headache. And I'm still looking out at the world from inside a small child, damn it. I'm disappointed. I wanted to wake up myself again.

I look around the room. The other single bed is ruffled, looking like it's been slept in. Mark must have to share the room. I wonder if he has an older or younger brother?

The décor of the room is at best shabby, with more than one tear in the old curtains and an unmarked, but clear, dividing line roughly down the middle. The door is in the middle of the interior wall, with the beds on either side, both facing the window.

Jumbled within the boundary in my half of the room is a battered chest of drawers at the foot of the bed, a bookcase, and some boxes with an old acoustic guitar sat on them.

Clearly this has to be Mark's stuff. But none of it is familiar to me at all.

The other side of the room is similar with a larger chest of drawers – painted purple – and a bookcase with a small boom-box and a meagre collection of CDs in it. There's a mirror between the door and the bed-head, where a half dozen brightly coloured stuffed toys are jumbled, and a poster above the bed of a teenage boy-band I've never heard of. It's odd. My immediate impression is girl stuff, not boys.

Looking up over my bed head I find images of skate-boarders and BMX bikes in mid-air, and Eric Clapton playing his beautiful cream Stratocaster. I smile. I'm not the only person who still thinks that Clapton is God.

I stand up, a little unsteadily, and move closer to the other bed. There are a couple of small certificates on the wall below the boy band poster. One is a certificate of achievement for swimming, made out to Elizabeth Mitchell.

Good grief. The boy is sharing a room with his teenage sister? That seems odd, especially in an affluent suburb like Wilton, and it strikes me as somehow disturbing.

Then I notice movement in the mirror before me and spot the blonde boy with the bandage wound around his head peering back at me. He frowns, looking puzzled.

I lean forward for a closer look, and quickly decide I need to see what's under the bandage. I find some kind of clip over the boy's right ear and unwind the bandage slowly and carefully. A piece of sticky gauze is soon revealed on the right side of the boy's forehead so I peel it gently away. There is a shiny red gash with about a dozen stitches, each spaced about half a centimetre apart, running from near the middle of the boy's forehead into his hairline on a slight upward lean. The area around it is heavily bruised, but that's it. I imagine it would have originally bled pretty seriously, but it looks like a clean cut and the stitching seems pretty tidy. Mark Mitchell is going to have quite a nice scar to show the girls when he gets a bit older.

The boy's hair is longish – just touching his shoulders – and very blonde, with just a small patch missing where the doctors must have had to trim it back to complete their work. His nose is small and finely shaped – nothing like my own – but, once again, it is the predominantly blue eyes that hold my attention. They're mine, not Mark's, but definitely, absolutely, unequivocally my eyes. You don't see a brown smudge like the one in my left eye every day. The boy in the mirror smiles crookedly.

I stare hard and long at my new reflection in the mirror. There has to be a reason I'm here, surely? This can't be real, and I don't fancy being insane, so I must be dreaming.

And all dreams have a purpose, don't they? Isn't a dream just your subconscious mind telling you something? Reinforcing some life-lesson? So is that why I'm here? To re-learn some lesson? To understand something deeper about myself?

Who the hell knows?

Looking away from the mirror I take a deep breath. Whatever this revelation turns out to be it had better be something damn good, to be worth going through all of this for.

As I move to venture outside the bedroom I notice two big, galvanized iron bolts are very roughly screwed to the back of the door. One above the door handle and one below it. They certainly aren't professionally attached, and the rough style is more in keeping with a garden shed, but they're secure and I'm intrigued. Why on earth would they be there? Is there something out there – inside the small unit – that I should be wary of? Surely not. I brace myself though, hesitating briefly, and then snatch open the door–

–to find myself facing a short hallway.

There's no crouching lion or sudden drop into a deep, dark ravine. Just a short, dim hallway. Two steps out and to my left is a closed door which I assume to be another bedroom. Immediately to my right the open doorway reveals a cramped combined bathroom and toilet, and the next door up is a laundry that opens into a small, messy kitchen. Directly in front of me is another door that leads to a more open, dimly lit lounge. The door is ajar and I can see Liz watching TV with the sound turned down low.

Liz turns as she hears me enter the room. 'Hey there. How's your head feeling?' she says in a loud whisper.

I look back at the other, closed, bedroom door and assume their mother must be still asleep and that Liz doesn't want to wake her for some reason. Liz is watching me caringly, so I close the hall door quietly and sit down on an old couch across from her. It seems appropriate to play along as best I can so I try to assume the role of Mark Mitchell, at least for now.

'Better than yesterday,' I reply, mimicking her loud whisper as I gesture to my head. 'Do you have any more painkillers though? It's still pretty sore.'

She slips through to the kitchen and returns with two white pills and a glass of water. Her hair is loose now, tousled from sleep, and she's wearing only a thin cotton nightdress. She makes no effort to cover herself as she passes me the pills and water and sits down again, curling her legs up beneath herself on the chair. She's only a teenager but, like her mother, she already has a curvaceously feminine figure that makes her appear older. I immediately feel ashamed for noticing.

Then questions start streaming out of her like a bursting dam. 'What happened, Mark? Was it Steve? Did he do this to you? Do you still have the cell-phone?'

I have no idea what she's talking about and can't possibly answer her. My response is lame.

'I don't know, I don't remember.'

This clearly isn't what she wants to hear and her face begins to redden in annoyance.

'What don't you remember? Do you remember where you went on your bike after Steve came round? Do you remember shooting the video of him before that?'

I'm perplexed. I decide to say as little as possible and just shrug. She's not impressed.

'You took a video. You must remember that. We need to show it to Mum. What's the last thing you do remember? Leaving school on Friday?'

I'm simply not Mark, and I don't have any memory of being Mark at all, ever. So I'm stumped. I look around the room, desperately trying to spot something that might help me respond but nothing leaps out at me.

'I'm sorry, I don't remember anything. I don't know what to tell you,' I finally say.

Her face hardens and then she drops it into her hands in frustration. She sits shaking her head slowly for almost a full minute, muttering softly to herself. When she raises her head again the disappointment is obvious. She practically radiates disillusionment.

'Of course you don't remember. It's not your fault.'

I feel terrible, she's clearly crushed by my lack of memory, but I still can't think of any way to answer her questions. She uncurls herself and slips away into the small bedroom without speaking again. I sit there for a minute wondering what to do next, and switch off the TV. Then I suddenly realise that I'm incredibly hungry.

I search around in the kitchen and find eggs and a few slices of bread and not much else. So I drag out a heavy old frying pan and start to make myself a large plate of French toast.

Liz suddenly appears, watching me curiously. 'What are you doing?' she asks.

'Just making some breakfast.'

She stares at me like I'm an alien. I realise that in her world Mark probably doesn't cook French toast all that often, if ever.

She's dressed now and is clutching a small handbag. 'Let me do that,' she says.

'No, thanks anyway, I'm okay.'

I dip the bread into the beaten egg mixture and gently lower it into the pan with a satisfying sizzle. Liz continues to watch me in undisguised amazement. Then she shakes her head slowly, in disbelief, but doesn't push it further.

'I'm just popping over to the shops,' she says. 'I'll be back soon. You take it easy, okay. You need more rest.'

I just nod and she turns and leaves quietly. I go back to my cooking. I find some instant coffee, boil the jug and then sit down to eat, and to think.

By the time I finish eating I have a plan.

If this is some kind of coma-induced dream then the answers aren't coming to me here, so I must have to get out and go after them. I've decided on where to go first and I'm suddenly feeling quite hyped up. I wonder if the coffee is having some big effect on my small body, or if there's something in the painkillers that is now making me feel wired.

And oddly I wasn't able to eat everything on my plate. Possibly my stomach is smaller that usual today.

I have a plan, but I need to arrange transportation. It's been a long time since I walked anywhere and I see no reason to revert to shanks pony just because I appear to be a small child. I find the keys easily on a small hook in the kitchen.

I'm still dressed in the T-shirt and shorts I'd put on at the hospital yesterday. I spot some worn sneakers by the door that look about Mark's size and slip them on. Then I quietly steal a peek into the other bedroom. Mark's mother, Tracey Mitchell, is in there snoring loudly. The stale smell of alcohol almost overwhelms me and I gain a deeper insight into the life of the Mitchell family. Tracey obviously likes a drink or two, and is practically comatose herself.

Somehow the irony doesn't strike me as amusing.

I quietly slip out the front door and down to the old hatchback. Although I generally prefer a manual vehicle, I'm pleased to note that this car is automatic. Given my current stature I'm not so sure I will be able to reach the pedals, so operating a clutch and shifting gear would be a problem.

Normally I'm over six foot tall. Almost six-two in fact, but at the moment I estimate that I'm little more than four and a half feet tall, so my normal outlook on life is all shot to hell. It's funny how everything seems huge when you're just a little guy.

I work the levers to adjust the seat as far forward as possible. Fortunately, by leaning forward, I find I can work both the accelerator and the brake with my right foot. The stiffness in my leg isn't an issue, but I can barely see over the dashboard and I'm perched right on the front of the seat. It's not ideal, so I go back into the unit and look around. I need a cushion or something similar to gain a bit more height but the ones on the couch look too small. Then I size up the couch again. The foam squabs come away, for cleaning I guess, and are a good shape.

As I pull out two squabs I'm disgusted by what I find beneath, but we don't need to go into detail about that here.

Back in the hatchback I lay one squab on the seat, climb up on it and squeeze the other one in behind me. That's better. I can now see out quite comfortably while still reaching the pedals with my right foot. I'm pleasantly surprised when the old car starts first time and I put it into reverse and crane my neck to back out of the driveway.

Out on the road, as I start to drive away, I look back up the driveway and spot Liz emerging from behind a tree by the unit. She's holding a plastic shopping bag and frowns in shock as she recognises me at the wheel of the car. I smile and give her a casual wave as I accelerate away. I'm still feeling, strangely, quite buoyant. Well and truly in *she'll-be-right* mode. That coffee must have been damn strong.

I drive back the way we came in last night, out of the cul-de-sac, past my old school and down to Herbert Drive where I turn south and head back towards the hospital.

But that isn't my target. I quickly turn right again, setting course for Charles St.

I'm heading home. There will be answers there. There has to be. Apparently it's Sunday, so Sarah and the kids will be home. For sure. And whatever is going on here with me will become immediately clear. Then we can work this all out and get things back to normal. God, it would be great to just wake up and be back to myself.

But even before I make the final turn into Charles St a tightness has crept into my chest. Something isn't right. I'm focused on my driving, but along the way the streets that should be so familiar have seemed quite different in places. Nothing startling, but some of the landmarks just looked a bit unusual. I can't put my finger on it though.

Then I arrive at Charles St.

We've lived here for about six years, moving in a little before Katherine, our youngest, was born. I know the street well and while it's very familiar I immediately find myself trying to work out what looks out-of-place. Why does the Swann's old house look like it's been repainted recently? I don't remember them doing that. And the Collins' place seems somehow larger, or is it darker? Does it have a new roof, or have they cut down a tree outside so you can now see more of the actual house? Which is it?

Then I reach my house.

I was aiming to pull up in the driveway, but I'm startled by what I see. It's definitely my home, but not as I know it. With the loss of concentration my foot slips from the brake pedal, dropping to the accelerator. Frighteningly, the car leaps ahead, bowling a large plastic rubbish bin as it bounces over the kerb, while I fight for control. I actually squeal aloud as I manage to right myself and plant my foot back on the brake. The car ends up nose-deep into a line of shrubs and, once stopped, I sit there shaking. My heart hammers, and visions of the terrible accident I'd only recently endured rush around my head.

But I'm not hurt. I didn't even bang my head again, thank God. I instinctively pull on the handbrake and then open the door, letting myself spill out of the car onto the ground. It takes me a few moments to calm down after the shock of the minor crash, but it's nothing in comparison to the shock I receive when I finally look up at my home.

The hatchback is parked in the middle of a line of shrubs that I recently planted as a future privacy screen along the road frontage. The trouble is that the shrubs are standing almost two metres tall and are full and bushy. These shrubs were only half a metre tall when I left for work on Tuesday morning.

I don't understand it.

I stand up and walk around the car, immediately noticing that the letterbox is different and that my carport has been rebuilt somewhat and closed in to almost make a garage. I stop and clasp my hands around the back of my head, drinking in the changes and quietly freaking out. My head starts to ache again and I feel more and more disoriented.

Stepping forward I look further up the driveway at the house. It's immediately obvious that there are enough subtle changes to it to feel sure that Nick Davis and family are no longer in residence. Sarah's prized flower pots are all gone for a start. There has always been a line of them along the front veranda and if Sarah was living here they'd still be on display.

I stare at the house in utter bewilderment.

Wait. Someone's at home.

I can see a face peering through the front lounge window. A woman. With long brown hair. Sarah? My heart leaps again, but this time in a good way. Maybe it is Sarah. Thank God. I run up the driveway and try to open the door. But it's locked, so I push the bell and start hammering on the door with my fist.

'Sarah!' I call out. 'Sarah, it's me. Open the door.'

The door suddenly swings open. A woman stands there frowning and anxious. She's slim and cute, with long dark hair. Her voice is a little frightened when she speaks.

'Are you alright? I though I heard a bang out here?'

She's looking out over my head, down the driveway to where the noise seemed to come from. Then she turns her big brown eyes down to me. They're filled with surprise and alarm and my heart freezes, my excitement rapidly turning to confusion.

She isn't Sarah.

SIX

I can't speak.

For a moment I was certain I'd found Sarah, but it clearly isn't her. This woman is very similar, about the same age, dark-haired and attractive, but she isn't my Sarah.

She starts to step forward but I'm frozen in surprise and don't move, blocking the way, so she stays in the open doorway. She asks me again, 'Are you alright?'

'You're not Sarah,' I accuse her without thinking.

Quite rightly she's taken aback, but regains her composure much faster than me.

'No, I'm not,' she acknowledges softly. 'Are you alright?' she asks for the third time.

My mind finally starts grinding back into gear.

'Yes,' I manage, 'Yes, I'm fine.'

I stare at her for another moment and then look around at the changes to my home. There seems to be different carpet on the floor beneath her feet and the old brass house number beside the door has been replaced with a shiny silver modern plaque. GRIFFIN RESIDENCE it proclaims ostentatiously.

'Is this your house?' I demand rather bluntly, eyes darting left and right.

She looks at me a little sideways and replies with a perplexed, 'Yes.'

'Do you know Nick Davis, or Sarah Davis? I thought they lived here?'

'No, I'm sorry. I've never heard of them. Are you sure you have the right address?'

'Yes, pretty sure.' My head is spinning. 'Have you lived here long?'

'Only a few years, but–', she breaks off. 'Are you sure you're all right? You look quite pale. What's your name? Maybe I should call your mother?'

I'm actually feeling quite faint. None of this makes sense and I'm still quite shaky from my dreadful parking effort out front. I turn and look down the drive, silently pleased to note that the car isn't visible through the bushy shrubs.

I look up at her again, she's more concerned now than anxious. I don't know her and she is in my home. She doesn't seem to know Mark, and she doesn't know my wife or family so further discussion seems pointless.

'I'm sorry,' I manage to murmur, as I turn and drift back down the driveway. As I make my way down the drive I hear soft footsteps behind me as the woman follows me out to the roadside. She calls out to me to 'wait on a minute' but I don't turn, and then I hear her gasp in surprise when she spots the little car lodged into her shrubs. As she scurries back inside, probably to call the police, I quickly climb back into the drivers' seat. It starts first time again and I'm impressed by its resilience.

My head is still spinning as I carefully back it out of the shrubs, past the overturned rubbish bin and back onto the road. My happy little caffeine buzz is a distant memory as I point the car up the road and drive cautiously away.

I drive around the streets aimlessly, with no clever plans springing to mind. I keep turning it all over in my head, fruitlessly getting nowhere. Nothing I can think of makes any sense – other than the fact that this simply can't be real.

My auto-pilot must come on at some point as I suddenly find myself back at the cul-de-sac and turning into the driveway of the not-so luxurious abode of young Mark Mitchell and family.

And I'm not surprised when his mother springs from the unit's doorway as I pull slowly up the driveway. She might have woken when I drove the car away or maybe Liz got her up, who knows? Clearly she's been waiting for me and she looks furious.

As I come to a stop, parking the car exactly where I took it from, she starts shouting.

'What the hell are you doing? How could you steal my car?' I slide off the seat and out the door, moving forward to meet her. She's still yelling. 'Who the hell taught you how to drive? What do you think you're doing?'

She advances on me as she howls, not seeming to care who hears her business. I try to respond peacefully, standing my ground. 'Hang on a minute, Tracey, the car is fine, just relax.'

Clearly this is a mistake.

'What? How dare you tell me to relax? And who the hell are you calling Tracey?' Her voice becomes shrill. She keeps advancing and I instinctively back-peddle. 'You disappear on your bike and end up in hospital, then you steal my car and disappear again, and now you have the nerve to call me Tracey to my face. How dare you? I'm your mother god-damn it!'

I try to calm her, instinctively hoping there is no real damage from my minor crash. I haven't looked, but the car seems to be running okay.

'I'm sorry, alright. I apologise. The car's fine . . .'

She keeps advancing and I can see she is hell-bent on catching me to either belt me one, or to just make sure I don't run off again. I stop backing up and stand my ground. She reaches me and snatches hold of my right wrist in her left hand. Her right hand is drawn back ready to swing an open-handed slap across my face.

'You took my car?' she snaps. It's both a question and a statement.

'Yes,' I confirm softly. She'd watched me pull up the driveway in it. Wasn't it obvious?

'How? How the bloody hell did you take my car? Who taught you to drive it?'

I suddenly realise she must suspect Liz of helping me in some way. 'No one taught me. It's not hard to drive a car.'

'Bullshit! Don't you lie to me. You're in enough bloody trouble without lying to me. Who taught you to drive it?'

She's right up in my face now, practically frothing with anger. Her right hand remains drawn back and ready to slap me. I find myself getting angry.

'I taught myself. I found the keys in the kitchen and I used cushions from the couch to get high enough to see out the windscreen. It's automatic, so you don't need to be a brain surgeon to drive it. You just need to be able to accelerate and brake. And if you're going to bloody well hit me then get on with it, I could use a few more days in hospital.'

She flushes at that and lowers her hand a bit, but doesn't let me go. She's obviously furious, but is clearly very confused too. I can feel the tension shaking in her through the grip she has on my wrist. Mark probably doesn't normally talk back to her. And it's a fair guess that he's never driven her car before either.

She takes a deep breath and expels it with a snort. She switches to a demanding icy tone.

'Where did you go?'

I reply as evenly as I can. 'Not far. I just needed to get out. Please let go of my hand.'

'Like hell. You'll just bolt again. Where did you go?'

Anger starts to boil up inside me. It's been a hell of a long time since anyone has spoken to me like this. My natural instinct is to go on the offensive when challenged like this so I'm about to open my mouth and let fly when I spot Liz in the doorway of the unit. She's worried and unhappy. For some reason this depresses me and, as quickly as it flared up, I feel my anger at Tracey subside.

But I don't answer her. What could I say? She stares at my face, like she doesn't recognise her own son, and then holds out her hand. She's absolutely livid.

'Keys. Now!'

I pass them over, still saying nothing. I stand my ground defiantly. We eyeball each other for a full minute before she finally releases her grip on my wrist. When she finally speaks again I'm surprised by the bitterness of defeat in her tone.

'Just put the bloody cushions back and go to your room.' She sounds beaten and fixes me with an angry and meaningful glare. 'And Mark, don't you ever steal my car again or I'll call the police and they can sort you out.'

I'm so surprised I instinctively start to apologise.

'I'm sorry, I didn't think, I didn't mean to upset you . . . or anyone. I'm sorry, okay?'

But this doesn't seem to placate her at all, and I'm taken aback when tears suddenly begin to well up in her eyes. The mood swing is unnerving. What on earth brought that on?

Then, surprising us all, a shiny metallic blue SUV turns into the cul-de-sac and starts to rumble up the driveway. It's a new model that I don't recognise, big and sleek with lots of rounded edges. Its exhaust produces a significantly throaty growling sound that surely means it's been modified.

The atmosphere changes dramatically again.

Liz disappears immediately from where she has been watching at the doorway.

Tracey turns her back on the SUV and sucks back the tears. She produces a tissue from nowhere – I'll never figure out how women do that – and quickly wipes her eyes and blows her nose. The tissue disappears again and she is raking her hair with her fingers. She adjusts her clothing and when she turns to face the new vehicle in the driveway she is smiling broadly.

'Get inside,' she speaks out of the side of her now smiling mouth. 'Now.'

Without understanding what is happening I instinctively obey and start to edge towards the open front door. Something odd is going on here and I suddenly feel a protective urge to stay and defend this disturbed woman.

The SUV's excessive rumbling dies and Tracey steps towards the car as the door swings open.

'Hey, baby, I didn't expect you so early today. Have you missed me that much?' Her voice has changed to a sweet sing-song, like she's talking to an infant or a family pet.

The man that emerges from the car is tall and rugged looking with very short cropped black hair. He seems especially tall from my reduced perspective, but he's probably only about the same as my normal six-two. He's bigger though, very solid and bear-like, but without the excess of shaggy hair. He looks like a young, clean-shaven, version of Murray Mexted.

And he seems to be in a very bad mood.

He looks straight at me and practically growls. It's definitely bear-like, and goose-bumps of fear tingle over me. Tracey reaches the car and attempts to embrace him and draw his attention. For whatever reason she wants me to go inside I start to think it might be a good idea. I begin to move again towards the steps but the guy calls out sharply.

'Hold on, kid. I want a word with you!'

I stop dead in my tracks and my stomach clenches in knots. The guy turns to Tracey and speaks a few words softly that I can't hear, and she protests meekly. Then he smiles, murmurs a few more words and gently kisses her forehead. He reaches back into the SUV and produces two bottles of white wine.

'Go on, pretty lady. Take these inside. I'll be up in a minute,' he says more clearly as he passes the bottles over.

She hesitates for a moment and then takes them and backs up a little, smiling at him uncertainly. She tries to sound firm but it's a weak effort. 'Go easy, all right. He's just a kid.'

But he's watching me with hooded eyes as he replies.

'He'll be fine. I just need to clear up a little misunderstanding we've been having.'

There is some apprehension – and, more disturbingly, a little spite – in Tracey's eyes as she brushes past me and moves towards the unit. I'm still standing in the middle of the driveway, stranded like a possum in the head-lights, as he advances on me.

As before with Tracey I stand my ground, but this time I'm frightened. This man is huge from my viewpoint, and he's angry at Mark, at me. Why, I'm really not sure.

I look up the steps into the unit just as he reaches me. Tracey is gone. I'm on my own.

He puts one big hand on my shoulder and roughly guides me backwards – away from the open door, past the hatchback, and out of ear-shot of the unit. He pushes me up against a tree trunk and puts his open left hand on my chest to hold me there. From thumb to little finger it spans my entire chest.

I feel small, really small.

He must be able to feel my heart pounding through my T-shirt as he stands over me and leans in so that I have to almost look straight up to see his face. I'd like to tell you he has bad breath and rotten teeth, but he doesn't. Although his eyes are very, very dark brown, almost black, and give depth to an icy malevolence. His fury at Mark is practically boiling out of every seam and I feel a chill run up my spine. His voice is low and threatening.

'We are going to come to an understanding right now, you worthless piece of shit. You are going to keep your damn nose out of my business, and stop telling your mother lies about me, or I am going to bloody kill you. Do I make myself clear?'

Jesus Christ. Who is this guy?

I'm so frightened I can't speak, so I just nod. He continues. His voice is bitter ice.

'You've caused me nothing but grief in the last few weeks and it's going to stop right bloody now! It's time for you to crawl back into your shell. Do you understand?'

His hand on my chest closes into a fist, drawing up my shirt with it, as he starts to lift me off the ground, raising the fist up under my chin, choking me a little. Scaring me a lot.

Suddenly he produces a broken blue cell-phone from his pocket and waves it in front of my face. There are dried spatters of what can only be blood on it.

'You see this. It's stuffed. So you got nothing. Nothing! And your crappy little bicycle, that's stuffed too. And you're damn well lucky you weren't road-kill out there. So don't you ever mess with me again, okay? And don't you go telling your mother any more bloody lies about me again, you hear me? Or next time you won't survive the god-damn accident. And neither will your prick-teasing little bitch of a sister. You understand?'

I pretty well understand nothing. Other than I'm damn sure I'm never going to do anything that might piss this guy off again. Not if I can help it.

He keeps staring at me. His eyes just lock onto mine and glare intensely while he tightens his grip on my shirt – lifting me a little higher off the ground. I start to struggle but it's hopelessly ineffective. I'm beginning to choke and there's no way I can respond to him, or escape.

Then I start to feel a darkness closing in again.

SEVEN

ELIZABETH MITCHELL can't just stand by and watch anymore. Her mother is in the kitchen. It annoys Liz that she can pretend that Mark will be okay with Steve, or does she really believe that he won't hurt him? Is she really that far gone? Liz hates her mother at that moment, and then she immediately hates herself for thinking that way.

Liz knows she will have to intervene, but the thought terrifies her. Her baby brother is in trouble, yet again. And it's partly her fault. She'd encouraged him to use the cell-phone. She'd encouraged him to try and catch Steve on video, saying something bad about their mother. She'd even tried it herself but without success. She takes a deep breath.

'Leave him alone,' she shouts as she comes out the door and down the steps. Steve doesn't turn. He has Mark up against the tree. His feet are off the ground, kicking wildly. It looks like Steve is trying to strangle him. Liz crosses the driveway quickly.

'I'll call the police,' she threatens.

Still Steve doesn't turn, he's glaring at Mark with such venom that Liz almost backs away. She's seen him angry before but not like this. Liz glances back over her shoulder. There is still no sign of their mother. She reaches out and tries to pull Steve's arm away from her little brother. Her knuckles are as white as her face. She's terrified. She's seen him lash out before.

Steve's grip stays firm on Mark's shirt but he turns his head lazily towards her. Mark's eyes are bulging, his face crimson. He's frightened, struggling for air.

Steve finally speaks. 'This doesn't involve you.'

'Just leave him alone, your hurting him.'

'Go back inside.'

'He's just a kid. Please let him go.'

Steve pauses and a sick smile slides onto his face.

'And what would it be worth to you if I did?'

Liz can't breathe. She releases his arm like it has suddenly become electrified. It isn't the first time he's talked to her like this. She doesn't reply.

'Pretty girl like you. Must be worth something?' he says.

'Just leave him alone, we won't bother you again.'

'You know you want me. And you can have me, anytime. I won't tell your momma.'

'You're sick.'

His grin seems to confirm her assessment. Then he pretends to be wounded. 'Aww,' he says. 'I get knocked down, but I get up again.'

Liz says nothing. She folds her arms across her chest defensively and stands her ground, wishing she felt braver. Finally Steve gives Mark a rough parting shake, banging his already damaged head against the tree trunk before letting go. Mark drops to the ground and coughs, gasping for air.

Steve points at him. 'Remember. You don't fuck with me again, ever. Understand?'

He doesn't wait for an answer. He just swivels on his heel, glancing over at the unit's front door. No one is there but he still lowers his voice as he addresses Liz.

'But you . . . you can fuck with me anytime you like. Just say the word.'

He winks and swaggers away. Neither Liz nor Mark moves for a minute. Mark stares wide-eyed. He seems to be in total disbelief as Steve saunters up the steps and inside.

'Let's get out of here' Liz says as she reaches out and helps him to his feet.

Mark can barely speak. 'And go where?' he manages roughly.

'It doesn't really matter does it, let's just go. It's not safe here.'

Liz takes his hand and pulls him away from the unit, into the small back yard space and towards an old fence. She pulls back a board and slips through with Mark following her silently. They come out in a narrow walkway between the houses and, as they step through, Mark almost trips over a wiry little white dog in his haste. The dog is on the end of a leash and Liz hears her brother mutter an apology to the creepy old man holding the other end as he moves aside to let them pass.

Liz continues up the path and leads Mark into Fraser Park. It's a big sprawling space, acres of mainly open grassed area dotted with clumps of foliage, with a line of tall trees running along the entire street frontage opposite them. She turns right and leads them down towards *the clearing,* a quiet spot hidden under a canopy of overhanging branches amongst the trees where teenage couples slip away to, for a little privacy. She's never been there with her brother before but today it seems necessary. She looks back briefly. Mark is following obediently but he's staring around like he's just stepped into a parallel universe. For crying out loud, what's wrong with him?

Liz notices the old guy with the dog watching them and frowning, looking perplexed. She ignores him and continues to lead her brother away from their poisoned home.

She desperately needs to tidy up her thoughts.

There is always so much to deal with, what with her mother and with school and everything else. She has a way of filing and sorting things in her mind which helps. She tucks the nasty thoughts away and tries not to dwell on them. She pictures lockers, like the ones at school, steel bins with padlocks. She opens the one with her mothers name on and pushes her hate inside it. It's a very full locker. But she's scared to open the one with Steve's name on it. It's newer, but it's already crammed with far too many horrible things.

She can't think straight if she doesn't suppress all this stuff. She thinks they call this compartmentalizing, but that's not important. Tidying up the clutter is. Getting her head straight so she can focus. That's what's important.

She turns her thoughts to Mark. She's concerned that there's something wrong with her little brother. Steve must have really damaged him somehow. She needs to help him – and they need to get rid of Steve. Her focus is clear on this.

Once inside the clearing she watches Mark flop down at the base of a large old tree, wedging himself between the big gnarled roots. Liz sits down in front of him, crossing her legs.

He looks a bit calmer now, but very distracted. It's clear to her that the encounter with Steve has rattled him deeply. And he was already troubled enough beforehand.

'Are you okay? Did Steve hit you?' she asks.

'I'm fine, I think. He just shook me a bit.'

'I'm sorry, Mark, this is all my fault. I'm so sorry.'

Liz feels close to tears now, the horror of the last forty-eight hours starting to catch up with her. She tries again to push it down, wanting to lock it away to deal with later.

She reaches out a hand to him. Mark looks unsure at first and then takes it and squeezes.

'Did he have the cell-phone?' she asks.

'A blue cell-phone? Yes, he did. Why, is it important?'

He sounds cautious. He still seems preoccupied and he isn't making sense. Liz frowns and quickly gets a sick feeling in her stomach as the realisation sinks in.

'Oh God, if he had the cell-phone then he really did run you down. Oh God, oh God.'

Mark frowns hard. He seems to become more confused.

'Steve ran me down?' he asks.

'Of course he did. Don't you remember? What about the video you took? You said it would get rid of him, that Mum would have to listen to us now.'

'What?'

Liz is dumbfounded. He doesn't seem to understand. She looks at him despairingly, searching for recollection in his eyes. But all she sees is the big, stitched-up gash on his forehead.

'Why did you take the damn bandage off? It'll get infected.'

'What?' he says again.

He looks so puzzled. Like he has no idea what's going on.

'You don't remember being run off your bike, do you?' she asks.

He hesitates, thinking carefully before finally replying.

'I'm sorry, Liz, but I don't remember anything.' He points at the stitches in his forehead. 'I don't know what's happened. I can't remember anything about a video, or a cell-phone. I don't understand why Tracey would have to listen to us now.' He pauses, watching her face. 'I think I've lost my memory.'

Her mouth falls open and she gapes at him. Liz can't decide how to process this. It doesn't fit into any of her nice, neat, tidy lockers. The injury to his head. He must have concussion, like the doctor said. Is it possible that he's really lost his memory? Oh crap! This can't be happening.

'You don't remember anything? At all? What's the last thing you do remember?'

He frowns at her, and then shakes his head slowly.

'Nothing. I'm not even sure of who I am, or who anyone is. I don't remember anything at all,' he pauses, uncertain. 'Will you help me . . . please? I don't know what the hell is going on around here.'

'I don't understand. You know who I am, don't you?'

He hesitates again, clearly weighing his words carefully before replying.

'Well, yes, sort of. I mean, I know you're my big sister. Your name is Liz and we share a room, and we have some serious issues with Steve. But that's about all.'

Liz doesn't like this at all. It's not just the supposed amnesia. Mark is also acting oddly, and he's talking funny. Not really strangely, but better somehow. More eloquently. It's so different to his usual grunts and nonsense.

'We should tell Mum, and get her to take you back to the hospital. They said that you needed more rest. This amnesia, it's not a good thing. I think you need a doctor.'

He reacts too quickly, and actually seems to recoil at the suggestion.

'No! No, I don't think that will help. And Tracey–, I mean Mum, wouldn't be happy. And I don't want to upset her any more. I'm okay, I don't want a doctor.'

His eyes implore her to accept this but she's worried. Something's very wrong. She frowns, trying to decide what to do. He's right; they can't go back to their mother. Steve is there, with wine. Mum will be well on her way again already. She'll be useless again within an hour. So they can't go home.

And Liz can't drive and she wouldn't dare to steal her mum's car. Not like Mark had done this morning. How did he do that? But that's not important right now, lock it away for later. What should she do now? How can she help Mark? He doesn't want to go back to the hospital. Okay, she won't make him.

'We need to help you get your memory back then, don't we?' she says.

'Yes,' he replies simply, nodding.

'How? Where do we start?'

'How about with Steve? You could tell me what I did that got him so pissed off.'

Liz feels frustrated by this but what other options does she have? She keeps it brief.

'You told me that you videoed him saying some pretty horrible things about mum. That he was boasting about seeing other women on the side. You said it was perfect.'

'Why did I say that? Why would I video him? And how?'

'Oh come on, you must remember some of this?'

Mark just shakes his head, 'Nope.'

Liz sighs deeply. This isn't good. Then she has an idea.

'Stand up, short-stuff. Let's take a walk.'

'What . . . Why? Where to?'

'We'll try and re-enact Friday evening for you. We'll start at the pub carpark and retrace your steps from there. It might jog your memory. It's worth a try, okay?'

She watches as Mark considers this. She's never seen him concentrate on anything so hard before, other than a video game that is. Finally he starts nodding.

'Okay, good plan. Better than anything I've got,' he says. 'But why the pub carpark?'

'Because that's where you said you took the video.'

Liz doesn't wait for a response. They both stand up and she impulsively hugs him, just to offer a little reassurance. He seems surprised by this but, after a moment, hugs her back.

Then she releases him and turns, setting off back through the park feeling grim and determined. She has two problems to solve and thinks she has found a way to bring them together – nice and neatly into one tidy locker. She can focus on them both at once.

In one hand there is something wrong with her baby brother – his memory seems to be gone. Apparently it's now locked away in a vault that seems deeper and darker than any of her own internal lockers.

And in the other hand is her stupid mother's latest boyfriend – and quite simply everything is wrong with him. She wants him gone. She needs to find a way to get him away from her mother – and away from their family.

Elizabeth Mitchell has made up her mind. Retracing Mark's steps offers her solutions to both of these intense problems. If only it will help Mark to remember.

EIGHT

As we both stand up and brush off the dirt and leaves, Liz suddenly reaches out and hugs me and I'm overcome by a mixture of emotions. I unexpectedly forget my worries. She is warm and soft and actually smells pretty good. The hug briefly makes me feel safe, there is nothing unusual or remotely sexual about it, and I really enjoy it.

But I also feel paternal, I think, and my head starts spinning with protective feelings. I abruptly feel like I should take charge and start fixing things. You know; be the adult and take responsibility. But I'm so very, very confused that I find myself just wanting to snuggle in and let her protect me, to baby me, to mother me. Then I immediately feel ashamed. This girl is only in her teens, and she's apparently now my sister – and Mark's protector.

God, but I'm badly mixed up.

Then she is gone and I have to take a moment to centre myself. She is deep in thought as I catch her up. We're heading back the way we came.

'Liz,' I interrupt, 'where are we going?'

She doesn't stop. She doesn't even slow down.

'Kensington Tavern.'

I know it. The pub in question is about a twenty minute walk west of the cul-de-sac, not much further than walking to the school, but in a different direction.

As we walk I recognise kiddy swings and slides and a small round-about, and a climbing structure roughly shaped like a fort. They seem to have been upgraded since I was a lad. The fort reminds me of Sally Taylor's little boy who must have fallen out of one of the big trees very near here yesterday morning and broken his arm. Poor kid.

I slow down to take a good look around Fraser Park before we turn back into the alley that runs behind Mark's unit.

This park was one of my favorite hang-outs when I was young. I grew up less than two hundred metres from where Liz and I are now. My old family home is at the northern end of Fraser Park – right across the road. As soon as Liz and I had entered the park I could practically hear it calling to me. Come home Nick. Come and visit your old Mum and Dad. Surely my parents will be home and they could help to wake me from this bizarre nightmare. Or perhaps not.

Although part of me wants to slip away from Liz I oddly don't feel comfortable just leaving her – especially after she'd just saved me from being beaten to death by that maniac Steve. And, I can't explain why, but I'm already starting to feel that visiting my parents will be a wash-out too. Just like my visit to Charles St. It's like fate is trying to lead me somewhere specific – as if by some kind of pre-ordained plan. And meeting up with Nick Davis' family doesn't seem to be a part of that arrangement. The cynical part of me already expects that Mum and Dad will have vanished without trace too, just like Sarah and the kids.

Feeling resigned to follow the path of this loosely scripted hallucination I follow Liz through the alleyway and out onto Lorneville Drive. She's moving quickly and seems to be on a mission. Her focus is intense.

I take her hand and try to ease the pace.

'Slow down, Liz, I can't keep up.'

She slows slightly and I let her go, now better able to keep alongside. 'You said before that I took a video of Steve,' I ask. 'Why?'

She seems to contemplate her response carefully.

'Because we need proof to show Mum. Proof that Steve is lying to her, and cheating on her. So that she'll send him packing and get him out of our lives.'

That seems sensible. My limited knowledge of Steve and Tracey's relationship makes it easy to believe that Liz and Mark would be desperate to break them up. And Steve has already made unbelievable advances on Liz – while I was watching, so infidelity seemed probable.

'Okay,' I reply evenly. 'But how?'

'How, what?'

'How did I take the video? With a video camera?'

Her pace falters but she doesn't stop. She looks at me with a deep frown.

'On your cell-phone of course.'

It takes me a moment to think it through. I'm not naturally technically minded and I know that most cell-phones can take photos, and that some of the newer ones can take little movies with audio and picture. But I can't understand how an obviously poor child can have this sort of advanced technology? Liz looks at me, frowning in frustration and pulls a small, bright red, cell-phone out of her pocket.

'Everyone has one,' she says.

Her phone is the same style as the crushed blue one Steve had shown me earlier. As we walk she clicks something, points it at me and tells me to sing a little song or something. I reply simply 'I don't think so' and then she clicks a few more times and turns the phone around. There on the screen is a perfect video image of little blonde Mark frowning and repeating my earlier words. The picture image is sharp and the audio crystal clear.

I can't help but be impressed, both at the technology and at my previously unknown depth of imagination. If this is a fantasy-world playing out deep in my own subconscious then I am astounded by my own creativity. I've only just learned how to text. And neither of my two children own a cell-phone, let alone one capable of video.

I try to focus back on Liz's story about Mark and Steve and the video.

'So Mark took–', I have to cut myself off. I'm Mark, remember. Liz doesn't react overtly, but I spot a flicker of concern. We keep walking and I try again.

'If I'm following this, then I took a video of Steve saying something horrible about, ah, Mum, on my cell-phone.'

'Uh-huh.'

'The broken one that Steve was holding, back under the tree, at the unit.'

'Yep.'

'So the video is gone then. Steve smashed the phone.'

'Umm, no, apparently it's not.'

'I don't understand.'

Liz looks concerned again, like she is trying to decide if she should tell me something. Finally she sighs and says, 'On Friday, when you got home you said you were worried that Steve might have seen you as you ran away from the carpark. You said you'd downloaded a copy of the video at a friend's place before coming home – just in case.'

'Oh. Okay.' It's all I can think to say. Good grief, this is getting complicated. Liz begins to look more troubled.

'But I never got to see it. Mum was out and just as you were about to show me, well, Steve suddenly turned up. He was looking for you and he was really pissed off, so he must have seen you running away from the pub. But then you disappeared on your bike – I think you went out the bedroom window – along with your cell-phone.'

'Okay, and then?'

She takes another moment to gather herself, still walking with her eyes fixed dead ahead. She doesn't seem able to look at me. I'm sure that she's holding back tears.

'You never came home after that. So when Mum got home I tried to tell her about the video, and about Steve going after you, but she didn't believe me. You know she won't listen to anything we tell her about Steve anymore.'

She becomes angry, her cheeks flush and her pace slows. 'So I kept on trying to call you on your cell-phone, but you never answered. It just kept on ringing, and in the end I started getting an out-of-service signal and that got me even more worried. Then later we got a call from the police. You'd had an accident on your bike and were in hospital – alive but unconscious. The police told us that a car was involved. It was a hit and run. Probably a drunk driver.'

'I'm sorry.' I don't understand why, but I feel guilty about everything. Liz continues.

'We visited you in the hospital that evening but you were out cold so we had to come back the next day. Yesterday. We went in the morning but you were sleeping, so we had to go back again. Steve had come around earlier, but he just denied everything. And, of course, Mum believed every word. He said he didn't see you in the carpark, he didn't know anything about any cell-phone video, and he flatly denied going after you. Mum just apologised to him, and told me off for telling lies. She was so pathetic.'

She lowers her head in shame, shaking it slowly in disbelief. 'Do you remember any of this?' she asks.

I try. God help me, but I try to remember. But there's nothing there. 'I remember waking up in the hospital, but nothing before that.'

She says nothing, just frowns in frustration. We keep walking and she picks up the pace again. My head is spinning, trying to make sense of it all. But I can't.

Ten minutes later we arrive at the Kensington Tavern. It hasn't changed much since I last saw it. In fact I can't remember having gone to this pub at all in the last few years, not after Daniel, our first child, was born. It's funny how your life changes completely once you have kids. Sarah and I had never been big drinkers, but our social circle changed significantly post-babies. Social gatherings happened less frequently and usually over dinner at someone's home, rather than down at the pub like we used to.

Liz and I stand in the carpark and survey our surroundings. It's just an ordinary pub carpark. Sealed tar underfoot with a few faded white lines painted here and there to try and provide some order for parking. There aren't many cars here today, with only around ten in evidence.

Liz is staring at me and I realise that she expects me to do something. To try and remember what happened here on Friday evening. I get a little flustered and try to look like I'm making an effort. We're standing in the middle of the parking area so I try turning a slow full circle. I see cars, tarmac, an old fence, fading signage on a run-down pub. Nothing raises any alarm, or draws out any lost memories. If Mark experienced something here recently I'm not feeling it.

I look at Liz and shrug apologetically. 'Sorry. I don't remember anything here,' I tell her.

She looks frustrated again. We stare at each other for a few seconds and she finally shrugs back, turning away.

'Wait, Liz, are you sure this is where it happened?'

She turns back to me, tilting her head in annoyance.

'Of course I am. You said that you'd taken the video at Mum's pub, so it has to be here.'

'Mum's pub?'

She gestures with a sweeping wave of her arm towards the tavern. 'Mum's pub. The Kensington Tavern. Mum's home away from home. She's here more often than she's at home, or at work, or anywhere else. This is where you said.'

I can't think of an adequate response. Mum's pub. It makes my stomach turn.

'And Steve comes here too?' I finally ask, just to say something.

'Of course he does, it's where they met. Where they hang out together. If Mum could have her way they'd get married here – and honeymoon here too.'

Again I struggle to respond. These poor kids. I stare at her. She's just a teenager, a child. And so obviously trying to hold this broken and dysfunctional family together while her alcoholic mother seems hell-bent on letting it fall apart.

My heart goes out to her.

'Come on then,' she says softly and starts to walk away. Her shoulders have slumped a little but her pace is still quick. She has longer legs than me and I have to scurry again to catch up.

'Where to now?' I ask.

'We'll grab a sandwich and head back towards home. That's where you went after taking the video here, after you stopped somewhere and copied it.'

I suddenly realise I'm hungry again and the sandwich plan sounds great. I want a coffee too but know that isn't likely to happen. Suddenly she stops and turns to me.

'You have to keep your eyes open, Mark. You have to remember where you downloaded that video. You said you stopped at a friends place, but which friend? Was it Jack?'

Once again I can't respond. I have absolutely no idea where Mark might have stopped. And, if I'm honest, finding this video actually seems like a pointless exercise. If Tracey didn't believe Liz before then whatever was on that video would have to be incredibly meaningful to turn her against Steve.

But I don't want to upset Liz now, she's trying so hard. I answer the only way I can.

'I don't remember. I mean . . . who's Jack?'

She closes her eyes in frustration and hangs her head.

Forty minutes later we're back at the cul-de-sac, well out of sight of the unit, trying to decide which way to go next. Along the way we looked out for any shops with computers, like an internet café or similar but didn't pass any. There was nothing on route that offered a download service or even just sold computers that Mark could have used. So he had to have used a computer at someone's home, and there was only one obvious possibility that Liz could think of. This kid, Jack.

She claimed to not really know Mark's small circle of friends. She's seen him hanging out with other kids at school, but his best friend is a boy named Jack who is always there beside him, like a shadow.

Oddly, Liz tells me that Mark's other friends never come around to the unit, and Jack's visits are even quite rare. I'm not sure whether this is because there is nothing to do there, since Mark doesn't even have a room to himself they can play in, or whether Tracey's presence is some kind of a deterrent.

We stopped outside Jack's place on our return but saw no visible activity. Jack lived in a very nice house on Lorneville Drive, the street that the cul-de-sac was off. His home was about one hundred metres south of their unit and Mark must walk past Jack's house every day on the way to and from school. I was sent to knock on the door but there was clearly no one at home. I'm not sure what I would have said to this boy if he had been home. He'd probably have thought I was nuts.

'I'm sorry, Liz. This doesn't seem to be helping. Where to from here?'

When she tells me our next destination, the road where Mark was knocked off his bike, an unnatural chill runs through me. I know this road.

Waterloo Rd is a loop road that runs around the back of an industrial estate nearby, and on the western side of Waterloo Rd is a stretch of reserve land. It isn't a park-like reserve like Fraser Park, but a small greenbelt with a little stream running through.

Most days I use this road as a short-cut on my way home from the City Council offices I work at in Hawthorne, as it's quieter after hours and helps avoid two sets of traffic lights.

It is the road I'd been taking when I was broadsided last Tuesday evening.

It's the road I was driven off when I had last been Nick Davis in all my fully-formed adult glory.

NINE

As I try to process this bizarre new development we consider Mark's escape from Steve at the unit.

Clearly it would have been pretty hard to squeeze his bike through the broken fence out behind the unit, so we decide it's more likely that he must have taken off south, past the school, to get out to Waterloo Rd, rather than back-track – and risk Steve catching him – by short-cutting through Fraser Park on his bike.

So we turn around and set off again, back down Lorneville Drive, towards Wilton Comp. We move quickly. Liz is really pushing the pace, obviously intent on this mission turning up something we can use against Steve. There is still so much I don't understand so I try probing Liz with a few little questions.

I start rather blandly.

'So, ummm, what does Mum do for a living?'

She glances uncertainly at me and for a moment I don't think she's going to answer. Then she sighs deeply and responds in a flat tone.

'Mum's a travel agent, but she doesn't work every day.' She pauses, 'Are you sure you don't remember any of this?'

'No, not a thing. Why doesn't she work every day?'

'She just does temp stuff, you know, like when someone else is on holiday or sick.'

This is actually interesting news – as my wife Sarah is also a travel agent. She's back working again now. Part-time only during school hours on week-days, since our youngest, Katherine, started school a year ago. Is this significant somehow? Perhaps I could try to seek out Sarah at her work. I almost get excited, but then remember that today is Sunday in this crazy second-life, so I'll have to wait till tomorrow. And I'll need a car to get there, which might be a bit difficult. I try to probe a little deeper.

'Oh, okay. Which agency, Liz, and where?'

'Umm, I think it's called Modern Travel or something like that, I'm not sure. I think they were just renamed. And she works at different ones all over Hawthorne – there are three of them.'

I've never heard of Modern Travel, so that's no real help. And it isn't the place that Sarah works. It does make me wonder how Tracey, only doing temp work, manages to pay the rent on the unit, which must be a fair bit each month – even if it is a dump, given the nice area it's in. Temp work can't possibly cover it. Perhaps she has other income streams, an inheritance income or maybe alimony, perhaps Tracey is divorced?

'So where does our Dad live?' I ask casually.

But it's a bad move. Liz stiffens immediately and turns to glare at me. It's clear that this question was neither expected, nor welcome. She looks away and won't meet my eyes.

'Why would you ask that?' she finally responds, in a quiet and flat voice.

Damn it. I don't understand. Is their father in prison, or did he run away from them, or is he – God forbid – dead? I choose not to respond and watch her carefully out of the corner of my eye as we continue walking. She eventually looks my way again, but only fleetingly. Her eyes are blank now, hiding a deep sadness. Then she softly asks again, her voice a cracking whisper, 'Why would you ask that?'

I feel terrible. I've struck on something deeply sensitive here. My best guess is that their father is dead. An absent father would evoke some sadness, or anger, but this sort of hollowness could only indicate a total loss. These poor kids.

We walk on in silence.

About twenty five minutes later and we cross a small over-bridge as we turn into Waterloo Rd. Here the area changes from residential to industrial and we look out over a series of long concrete buildings with large roll-a-doors and brightly coloured advertising hoardings as we walk. It's early afternoon on a Sunday and all the businesses are shut up and deserted, much the same as they would be by nightfall most evenings.

We walk along the western side of the road, alongside the greenbelt and the stream. The trees and bush are well established and more often than not you can't even see the stream which is around twenty metres from the road.

Liz suddenly hesitates. 'Look at this,' she says, pointing a little further up the road.

There is a black rubber skid mark on the footpath, and it's surrounded by a neatly spray-painted fluorescent orange rectangle. The skid mark is only about a metre and a half long and stops abruptly. The angle indicates that the tyre the rubber had previously belonged to had come up onto the footpath at about a 45 degree angle. Someone has helpfully sprayed an arrow leading from the road to the orange box in the direction of the skid. We turn to follow the direction of the painted arrow. The grass for a couple of metres forward of the skid is both flattened and partially dug up. There is again a large orange paint line marking the area, running off the grass right across the footpath and onto the road.

'This must be the spot,' she says. 'Look here, you can see where the car's tyre stopped and then here where it dug into the grass and took off again. These must mark the evidence for the police investigation.'

I'm quietly impressed. It's clear that she's right, so we turn our backs on Waterloo Rd and survey the bushes and trees of the greenbelt before us. It's actually quite serene, an attractive little outlook for the businesses facing it across the way.

There is no indication that Mark's bike had been crushed beneath the cars wheels, as I imagine this would have left quite different deep gouges in the grass. So, starting from the side of the road at the highlighted point of impact, I try to imagine how Mark and his bike would have looked sailing through the air.

Then I turn and look over my shoulder. Directly behind me is an intersection, a simple T-junction, where Samsara Place meets Waterloo Rd. The sign is attached to a lamppost just a few metres beyond the fluorescent paint markings.

All of a sudden my stomach clenches and I feel a cold shiver cascade through me. It won't be fully dark for another hour yet, but I have a sudden terrifying vision of a dark shape, a blur of blue flashing through darkness, hurtling towards me and smashing into me, sending me spinning and rolling out into the bushes before me.

In an instant I feel absolutely certain that this is the precise spot where the car had broadsided mine. I begin to feel strangely nauseous as it becomes sharply clear that Mark was run off his bike in *exactly the same place* where this surreal nightmare began for me.

My legs become wobbly and I stagger forward a few steps. A cold darkness overcomes me and I can no longer see. I feel the grass rush up to meet me. Then I'm on my knees and retching. Warm sticky vomit floods out of my mouth and nose as my stomach clenches in furious spasms. I heave again, and again, and realise hazily that Liz is beside me, talking soothingly, apologising and trying to comfort me. Finally I have nothing left to bring up and I roll to one side, breathing deeply and desperate to regain some composure.

My heart is racing as I lie there quivering with visions of darkness, spinning, smashing and pulsing red flashes reeling before me. Somewhere nearby I can distinctly hear a cell-phone ringing. I cover my ears to try and block out the sound, but it won't go away.

Liz is still talking, desperate and worried, but I can't process her words. I try to sit up, blinking rapidly, trying to clear my sight. Liz pulls me up and into her embrace. I'm unable to speak and my vision is blurred. Sucking in a big lung-full of air I sit shivering for another minute or so, as the episode slowly passes. Liz is rubbing my back, making calming noises. The phantom cell-phone's persistent trilling inside my head finally stops. I shake my head, trying to clear my vision, but succeed only in creating another headache.

'I'm sorry, Mark, I'm so sorry. Are you alright?'

Liz's voice breaks through my haze. She is beside herself with guilt and worry. Daylight starts to return as my sight clears and the ground begins to feel firmer, no longer spinning wildly.

'I'm okay. It's not your fault,' I'm finally able to respond. 'We had to come here. You were right. It's okay, relax.'

I sit quietly, breathing heavily for another few minutes before slowly standing up, a little shakily, with Liz's help.

'We should go,' she says. I shake my head carefully.

'No. Not yet. We came for a reason, and I don't think I want to come back, so let's have a look around. Come on.'

But we don't find anything that helps me to understand my bizarre situation.

We do find another spot that the police have sprayed with the orange fluoro-paint and this looks likely to be where Mark had been found, as there are dark patches in the grass that look suspiciously like dried blood.

Shortly after we find this Liz points up into a nearby tree. On a branch above and to the right of the spot where Mark had ended up, there is more orange paint. The painted branch looks bowed and battered. It seems clear that the bike must have ended up in that tree. As I'm looking up at the branch I have another fairly short dizzy spell but I stay on my feet. In my mind I see a glimmer of a bicycle wheel spinning, with red flashes as a little red reflector thing spins past some light source from behind me. It's dark in the vision and everything seems blurry and out of focus. Then I'm back with Liz, looking forlornly around the accident site.

We move back up the grassy strip towards the road. Either the car or the bike, or both, must have been really traveling as the landing-point paint marks are both well back from the impact-point highlighted back on the foot-path.

It seems that Mark was very lucky to have escaped the accident with only a few bruises and the single head gash.

It's only then that I abruptly realise that everything I'm looking at here is wrong. Completely wrong. What have I been thinking? This area should be a mess. Less than a week ago, or even if it had actually been two months now, my car and another tore through here in a violent collision. There should be more obvious damage. Much, much more damage than the few small marks highlighted by the fluro-paint.

It doesn't add up, yet again. It's almost like I never existed at all. My home is no longer mine, the hospital has no record of me coming in after my accident, and now I find that there is no evidence of the car accident itself. Damn it, this is so frustrating.

Liz is watching me. She's obviously concerned. She must be wondering if I'm about to spin out again, but I don't feel ill anymore. Just angry and frustrated.

Was this supposed to have been the meaningful revelation I've been waiting for? It can't be. I don't understand it. I saw nothing that made any sense. So what the hell do I do now?

Feeling discouraged, and a little disgusted by the taste of my own vomit, I look up at Liz and realise that she's actually watching me expectantly. Damn it. She's still desperate to find that video, but I'm going to have to disappoint her. It's simply not going to happen.

'Sorry,' I mumble, 'I still don't remember anything.'

She frowns, and then quickly nods and tries to put on a brave face. She's obviously dejected. But I can't imagine how I can possibly help her find this video. There's no chance that I will ever remember where Mark downloaded it.

I'm not Mark. How could I know?

Without speaking we trudge back up to the footpath on the side of the road and, in the fading light, begin the disillusioning walk back home again.

When we reach Wilton Rd we continue on towards Fraser Park, rather than taking the longer route past the school. As Fraser Park comes into sight up ahead I almost kick myself as I remember I have another idea to check out. But first I need Liz to let me take a little time out. Unfortunately she seems determined to stick with me, especially since my little episode back on Waterloo Rd. And I get the impression she's in no hurry to get back at the unit either. We have no way of knowing if Steve will still be there, or not.

It's simple. I want to take a closer look at my parent's place and see if anything has changed. I'm not going to allow myself the hope that someone will be home but, with luck, something there might help me determine what I need to do to get back to my own reality. I just have to find a way to lose Liz.

We make it to Fraser Park as the sun dips beneath the suburban skyline. We haven't been talking and I'm lost in thought when I become aware of Mark's name being called.

I stir and look around to see a young boy running towards us through the park, calling out as he approaches. Liz stiffens and groans a little.

'Hey Mark, didn't you see us? You walked right past,' the boys says as he catches up. He's smaller than me, with slightly too long dark hair, a biggish nose and braces on his upper teeth. He's pale and slightly flushed from the short run.

I look back over his shoulder and see, dimly through the shadows from the trees, a group of four people at one of the picnic tables. They must be the boy's family. I turn to Liz, eyebrows raised, a question on my face. Her shoulders slump and she rolls her eyes. She doesn't turn to face the boy, but keeps her eyes on mine.

'Hi, Jack,' she says.

Oh. This must be Jack, Mark's best friend.

Jack looks a bit surprised and murmurs, 'Hi, Liz,' then fixes his attention back on me, completely ignoring her. He takes hold of my shirt and begins dragging me away. 'Come and have some chips, there's heaps left still.'

It doesn't seem that he'll take no for an answer, and I quickly realise that Liz hasn't been invited. I look at her again, another unspoken question on my face.

Liz just groans and stands her ground as I'm dragged away. She calls after me.

'Dinner's at seven, Mark. Don't be late.'

I give her a thumbs-up gesture as I'm being hauled along and just catch a glimpse of her turning away, before I shift my attention to this new challenge.

TEN

As we approach I notice that only two people now remain at the picnic table. The two others are drifting away through the trees, heading for the same alleyway as Liz. It's dark under the trees now but they look like a man and a woman.

Once we reach the table I discover a man of about fifty, who is most likely Jack's dad, and a teenage girl who appears to be a little younger than Liz, huddled around a meal of fish and chips. It's pretty dim, but I can still make out that Jack's dad is clean shaven with receding hair while the girl has very long, straight, dark-hair which is covering half her face. He smiles as we approach but she just looks bored and doesn't acknowledge us. They convey a gentle air of prosperity, unlike the dysfunctional unit poor Mark is a part of, but I don't feel like an intruder as I sit down next to Jack on the picnic table's bench seat.

Jack's dad greets me casually.

'Hey there, Mark, shouldn't you be home for dinner by now?'

'We were just on our way,' I reply quickly, 'it's not six-thirty yet is it?'

He looks at his watch, 'Not quite yet, you've got a couple of minutes. Have some chips,' he offers sociably. 'We always seem to get far more than we need.'

Although they seem to have finished eating there is still enough deep fried food in the open wrappings to clog up the arteries of a rugby team. My stomach growls at me. It's very empty from my recent episode, and the foul taste of vomit has faded in my mouth.

'I guess a couple won't spoil my appetite, thank you,' I say as I reach out and start eating. The chips are still moderately warm. As I chew I'm already trying to think of a reason to slip away. I really want to go and check out my parents' place, not make nice with someone else's family. Nor do I feel up to explaining my amnesia story to them so decide quickly to talk as little as possible. And anyway, I can't think of anything to say. It seems clear that Mark must know these people quite well, as they'd welcomed me to their table without fuss, and he is Jack's best friend after all.

Then I suddenly remember that Mark might have downloaded the video at Jack's place and try to work out a way I can ask about it, but Jack speaks first. He leans in and peers at the stitches on my forehead.

'What's happened to your head?'

I lean back to draw away from him a little as I reply. 'I came off my bike. A car hit me on Friday night.'

'Wow! That's awesome! Does it hurt?'

'It did, but not so much now.'

'So why didn't you text me and tell me?'

He produces a small dark blue cell-phone from nowhere and waves it in my face.

'Ahh, I couldn't. My phone got broken in the accident.'

'Aw no, really? Bad one. That's rank. Is your mum gonna get you another?'

'I don't know. We haven't really talked about it.'

The others are both staring at me now too, Jack's dad leans across to try and make out the stitches more clearly in the dimming light.

'That looks quite nasty,' he says, 'are you sure you're okay?'

'I'm fine. It's nothing, just a few stitches. But the bikes a write-off,' I try to sound nonchalant about it all, not wanting to get into a full inquiry.

'Were you really hit by a car?' the girl asks curiously, actually seeming a little impressed.

'Yeah, but I don't remember anything,' I reply, shrugging.

Jack's dad sits back and states the obvious. 'You know it's pretty dangerous to be out on your bike at night, Mark. You really should be a bit more careful. Were you wearing your helmet? It doesn't look like it.'

I hadn't thought of that. Surely Mark should have been wearing a helmet. But strangely, no one has mentioned it before so I simply don't know. I just shrug and stuff another warm chip in my mouth. Jack pipes up to save me.

'Big Doofus is sitting his driving test tomorrow. You should stay off the road. It'll be even more dangerous soon.'

He's gesturing vaguely towards the alleyway where the two others from the table went and, at first, I don't understand but Jack's dad jumps in again, defensively this time.

'Your brother is a good driver, Jack. Please don't be so rude.'

Jack doesn't seem to hear him. 'Maybe you should get your mum to buy you a tank, or a bike that transforms into a helicopter or something so that you can dodge the cars. How cool would that be?'

He looks at me expectantly, but we're clearly not on the same wavelength so I just nod at him, wide-eyed, and thrust another warm chip into my mouth. Suddenly Jack's dad speaks again, changing the subject, taking me by surprise.

'You know, Mark. I've been meaning to thank you for sharing your lunch with Jack last week. It's been very nice of you, we appreciate it.'

I have no idea what to say in reply, so just nod and stuff in another chip. Then Jack's sister chimes in, her tone demeaning. 'You should just let him starve. You make it too easy for him.'

Good grief, what have I walked into here. Their father leaps to my defence.

'Now, now, Katie. That's not very nice of you. Sharing his lunch is a very generous thing to do. Mark's just being a good friend.'

She doesn't back down though, replying quickly and petulantly. 'Jack should just thump the fat twerp and stop giving in so easily. Writing letters to the headmaster isn't going to stop it.'

'That's enough, thank you, young lady. You all know that the headmaster and I are working through this issue appropriately and the situation will be rectified soon. You all need to appreciate that some things have to be handled with a certain delicacy, and just wading in and thumping someone is very rarely the right answer.'

The conversation is bewildering me so I stay quiet.

I think Jack blushes, but it's getting pretty dark so it's hard to tell. Katie, Jack's sister, thankfully lets it go and goes back to looking bored. There's an uncomfortable silence. Jack's dad finally breaks it.

'How's your guitar playing coming along Mark? Are you still practicing?'

Now guitar is something I can do. I've been playing in bands on and off since I was fourteen, so it's nice to hear that Mark was actually getting some lessons. But with no idea of how advanced he is I have to fudge my answer.

'Yeah, its sounding okay, but I think I need to practice a bit more often.'

'Good on you. You keep it up. I'm sure you'll be a Rock Star in no time.'

I mumble 'thanks' as I stuff another warm chip in my mouth and hope that someone will end this gathering soon so I can get over to my parents house quickly.

Then Jack asks, 'Do you wanna go climb the fort?'

Once again I don't really know what to say.

'Ah, umm, sure, but . . . you know, it's getting a bit dark really,' I mumble back. Jack frowns at me in surprise. Then, to my relief, his father starts to tidy up the chip wrappings and I grasp at the opportunity to escape. 'Hey look,' I say hastily, 'I think I should probably be getting home, it must be six-thirty by now and I don't want to get in trouble, do I?'

'Heaven's no, and we should be heading off too,' Jack's dad replies. 'You run along, before it's too dark to see where you're going. And, Mark, we don't want Tracey angry at us, so you make sure you eat all your dinner tonight. Don't go blaming us for the chips if you don't eat all your vegetables.'

I thank them politely for letting me join them, tell Jack I'll see him later and say goodbye quickly, trotting away into the shadows towards the alleyway that runs along behind the unit. I can hear them packing up their dinner wrappings and Katie saying something to her dad, but I can't quite make out the words as I move away.

Then I duck behind a large tree trunk and dart away from them, further up the park, towards the old homestead. I have about thirty minutes before Liz will start worrying.

As I jog along I can't help wondering what the discussion about sharing lunches was all about. Why would Mark share his lunch with Jack? Did he keep losing his? Maybe someone was taking it from him? That might explain the comment about thumping the fat twerp. Perhaps Jack is being bullied? Possibly. It's hard to be sure.

I vaguely feel a little bit sorry for Jack, if he is being bullied, but push those thoughts aside as I find myself standing across the road from the house I grew up in.

My heart leaps as I behold its large, familiar shape looming in the shadows.

Please let there be some answers here.

The old homestead is two storeyed and tall, with white painted verandahs running around the entire frontage. It's a majestic old thing, quite a statement in its day. My Grandfather built it himself when he was young and he and Grandma had raised their family there. My Dad took it over when they passed on. We moved in when I was about four, well before my little brother was born. Dad keeps it immaculate and always insists that I will take over the place when he and Mum pass on too. I've never been that keen as I prefer more modern architecture, but it isn't something worth arguing about with him. You can never change his mind, not on anything.

I stand before it with feelings of both anticipation and dread. There are no lights on, and no cars in the driveway. The house looks cold and empty.

I look down the road, to my left towards the old shops and get a big surprise. The little cinder-block row of four single storey shops are gone. In their place is a huge development of modern day steel and glass. Even in the gloom I can see that it stands four floors high, with what appears to be apartments on the top two levels. Lights are on inside on both upper levels. The first floor is mostly dark and is probably offices while the well-lit-up ground level shops have multiplied substantially.

The development stretches off for well over a hundred metres down Wilton Rd. Brightly lit neon signs reveal that all the big brands are there – including Starbucks and McDonald's, and many more. Our humble old corner diary is nowhere to be seen.

I stare in total disbelief.

Directly opposite the new shopping centre, on the other side of Wilton Rd, and running right up to the section beside my parent's house, is another major development. This one appears to be very similar, but is only two stories high.

Confused, I look up the road and see that all the houses to the right of my parent's house have also been torn down, and that even more development work seems to be going on there. My God, what a mess. Dad will hate this. They're practically surrounded by new developments.

What the hell is this all about?

I try to reconcile what I'm seeing with what I know. It doesn't fit. The only way I can rationalise it is to suggest that my imagination is working overtime. You see, I'm a town planner by trade. I work for the Hawthorne City Council, managing planning consents for all shape and size of building developments right across the city. In my work I review plans for this sort of development every day, ensuring everything fits within the city's guidelines for environmental growth, construction materials and general infrastructure needs. The only way I can comprehend what I'm seeing is to decide that my mind is somehow creating this part of my fantasy-reality based on some plans I must have seen once upon a time.

That has to be it? Surely. Why else would I dream something like this up?

As I stare up and down the road the idea that I might have been brain-damaged in the accident starts to take a hold of me. I don't like it. I feel a little sick.

I tear my eyes away and return my gaze to the dark old house directly opposite me. I take a deep breath, cross the road and stride purposefully up to the front door. The cast iron knocker is incredibly familiar, but much higher up the door than I last remember it. I have to stretch up to reach it and thump it back down against the heavy wooden door.

I knock loudly, three times, and wait.

I can hear the breeze ruffling through the trees behind me, a wind chime being tickled lightly by it along the verandah, and the faint squeak of loose timber somewhere nearby.

There are no immediate neighbours anymore so there are no sounds of TV, or music, or people talking anywhere near by. With building sites on both sides of the house and the park stretching in both directions out front the once grand old house seems very forlorn and lonely.

It stays quiet, and dark. The house is surely empty.

I shuffle along the verandah and try peering in the nearest window, but I can't see much through the net curtains in the darkness. There are veiled shapes that look like familiar furnishings, but there is no movement and no light inside to bring the house to life. I notice that one of the front windows is boarded up. The boarding is tidy and obviously cut to measure, but its mere presence is odd. If the window was broken Dad would never have left it like this. He'd fix it immediately.

I wander down the driveway, but can't tell if the hard, cold concrete has seen any activity recently. Then I get another shock, for where the double garage used to be around the back is now just a blackened mess.

I stare dumbfounded at the dark pile of rotten timber and iron sheets. The garage had been an entirely separate structure from the main homestead, standing about five metres away. Clearly there has been a fire and the garage was razed to the ground. But there are also weeds and grass growing through the pile of black rubbish, so it wasn't a recent thing. The ashy smell of old and damp burnt wood tells me it has been rained on many times. But the weeds growing out of it still have a lot of work to do to completely turn the mound back into earth.

This fire has to have been at least a year ago, if not more, so why hasn't it been cleaned up and the garage rebuilt? It's baffling.

Beyond the former garage I can see the old section next door and, although it is now quite dark, the section is obviously badly overgrown. I'm shocked again. Dad is fanatical about maintaining his vacant section. He has one of those fun ride-on mowers and runs over the section every Sunday morning, rain or shine. Even when I was old enough to take over the job he refused to let me. I think he just enjoyed himself too much.

He's a funny guy, my Dad. Often funny ha-ha, but sometimes a bit of that odd kind of funny too.

I frown at the thought of Dad sitting by idly as that grass grows and grows. Until now I have never seen the section with more that an inch of grass on it. Now the long grass waves in the light breeze and is well over a metre high.

A heavy weight settles into my stomach. Something is very, very wrong here too.

I move to the back door and look for the old flowerpot that has always concealed our family's hidden key. It's a bit of a cliché, we all know, but it's a useful and practical necessity which I had to use more than once as a teenager. But the flowerpot is no longer there, and neither is the key.

I think briefly about breaking a window, but my Dad has on so many occasions drilled his sons about the evils of wanton destruction of property, especially his, that I can't bring myself to do it. For me, breaking anything here would be a crime that no eternal reward could ever forgive.

So I peer through the kitchen windows. Once again I see very little, yet there are enough bits and pieces' lying around to give the impression that someone is still living there. But in my little fantasy-world there is nobody home tonight.

I give up and leave, cutting through Fraser Park, and go back to the unit.

The big SUV isn't in sight when I arrive so I go inside. Liz is in the kitchen and has put together a very yummy smelling Spaghetti Bolognese. I'm impressed.

'Are you okay now?' she asks, 'I thought you might be pretty hungry by now.'

'I am. I'm starving, and that smells great. Is anyone else home?'

'Nope. I'm guessing at the pub. She didn't leave a note.'

'So we won't be waiting for them for dinner?'

'No,' she replies simply, starting to serve.

We eat at the small dining room table in silence. The meal is delicious and I'm grateful that Liz doesn't raise the subject of the video, or our recent meanderings around the streets of Wilton. But I'm feeling a bit depressed and oddly very tired even though it's still quite early.

As I eat my mind spins desperately, trying to conjure up meaningful explanations to all the weird scenes I've encountered since waking up yesterday, but nothing becomes clearer. I can't seem to get past the idea that I'm dreaming all this. And that doesn't really make sense, but it's all I've got.

It's all I can allow myself to believe.

Afterwards Liz retreats to the kitchen to clean up. She doesn't ask me to help so I wander aimlessly over to the TV. Perhaps there'll be a news item about me or something that might help explain my strange situation. I know I'm desperately clutching at straws.

Having just settled myself onto the couch I'm examining the remote control when I hear a car rumbling up the driveway. The distinctive growling comes to a stop outside.

Steve is back.

In a flash Liz is out from the kitchen and peeking through the curtains.

'Mum's with him,' she says in a small voice. 'Come on, let's move.'

She disappears quickly. I'm tired and far too slow and I'm only just rising from the couch when Tracey and Steve stumble through the front door together.

'Hey baby, how's my little man?' Tracey coos.

She's drunk. Badly and very obviously drunk. She looks like she's close to passing out. Steve is drunk too, but he's significantly more alert. His eyes flick around the unit. I'm not sure if he's assessing the room for any dangerous threats, or hoping to find Liz awaiting him in her birthday suit, but he isn't pleased to discover me sitting here. I freeze.

He glowers and closes the door quietly behind himself, flicking the latch to lock it without taking his eyes off mine. An icy fear begins to expand through me, spreading like a creeping virus. I should have moved more quickly, like Liz.

He smiles at me without warmth and hoods his eyes a little, calculating something, and I get a very uneasy feeling. I finally attempt to move and he speaks quietly.

'Stay right there *little man*. Don't move.'

Tracey is wobbling uncertainly on his arm. She'd probably fall over if he let her go.

'It's okay,' she says to no one in particular. 'Everything's good now. Steve's gonna look after us. We're all good.'

It's meaningless babble, but I start to become frightened. I don't like the idea of being looked after by Steve, not at all. Something about him is very wrong.

Steve keeps smiling and gently lets Tracey drop to her knees beside him. He holds on to one arm to keep her from falling down completely and reaches around to cup her face in his other hand. Then he turns it to look up to his.

'Come on darling, I got a need. You gonna help me out?'

He releases her arm and loosens his belt, then unzips his fly, still holding her face cupped in his hand directly in front of his crotch. His need is obvious and I'm horrified.

Tracey is holding the top of his jeans to steady herself. She tries to look towards me but he holds her face tightly so she can't turn her head.

'But Mark's here, I can't . . .'

'Nah, he's gone. It's just you and me, Babe. C'mon.'

Then he releases himself from the confines of his jeans. Tracey accepts his word without resistance and stops trying to turn her head. She reaches up to him with her free hand.

He looks over, staring at me and grinning in triumph. He doesn't speak again, just sneers over with an intense look of conquest. His message is clear. I'm in control here. I own her and I own you. Don't fuck with me.

I feel sick.

ELEVEN

Hoping that that is all he wants me to stick around for I start to move away again. This time he doesn't speak, he just keeps glaring at me as Tracey continues her efforts below. His self-serving grin repulses me as I back away, around behind the couch, and then turn and dart through the kitchen – to avoid them – as I head for the bedroom.

Liz is watching through a crack in the door when I get there. She lets me in, closing the door behind me and slamming both bolts across. Now I'm crystal clear on why those iron bolts are on the door, and who put them there.

'Oh God, Mark. Are you alright?' she asks. Her voice quivers, she's pale and looks like she's about to throw up.

'I'm fine, don't worry about me.' I hesitate, 'Did you see all that?'

She just nods, and then starts to sob quietly. Her voice cracks as she sits on her bed. 'Do you remember now, Mark? Do you remember why we've got to get rid of him? She can't do it. She's useless. She's a useless, selfish bitch . . .'

I go to her and we hold each other as she sobs uncontrollably, the pain and anguish flowing freely from her.

I'm furious. I just want to charge out of the room and lay into Steve. Just punch him and punch him, but I can't. I'm too small. I know he would just laugh and crush me with one swing of his fist. He's easily twice my current size. It's intensely frustrating and I feel helpless, impotent.

As I hold Liz I more fully understand why this family so desperately needs to be rid of him. But what can I do? Tracey is clearly an alcoholic, a weak-willed addict. Someone like that is easily controlled by a perverted bastard like Steve. And no matter how damning any evidence that these children might produce may be I don't think it could be sufficient to sway Tracey's desperate need for his supposed love. Nevertheless I want to comfort Liz so I tell her softly that we'll find that video, that we'll show it to Tracey, that we'll soon be rid of Steve, that everything will be alright.

Sometimes a little white lie is justified, isn't it?

This settles her down a bit and she finally stops crying. I'm still badly shaken myself and look around the room for some form of distraction – as we can both now hear far too much of Steve and Tracey's increasingly intense activity from the lounge.

'Can you turn the radio on or something?' I say. 'We don't need to listen to all that.'

She moves to the little boom-box in her bookcase and pops in a CD. I don't know who the band is, but the woman voice has a rich and soulful tone and the backing music is tight and agreeable. Liz turns the volume up just enough to drown out the noises from the lounge, but not enough to attract attention.

Once again I start to feel very weary and think about climbing into bed. Then I spot a small calendar on Liz's bookcase that I hadn't noticed this morning. The picture is a standard Southern Alps scenic shot but that's not what catches my eye. I reach over and pick it up, bewildered.

The month is showing as November and there is a dark red circle around the 21st. But the year seems to be wrong.

'Liz, what's the date today?' I ask.

'What?'

'The date. Today. Is it November 16th?'

'I'm not sure. Why?'

'It's definitely not September though, is it?'

Her eyes are red from crying, but she's looking at me like I've just turned green and scaly.

'No, it's definitely November,' she says. 'Somewhere around the 15th or 16th.'

She sees the calendar I'm holding and leans over me to check, then points at the dates.

'Yeah, it's the 16th. See, my birthday's next week so it must be the 16th today.'

'Your birthday, really? On the 21st?'

She's frowning heavily now, obviously frustrated with my bizarre questions.

'Yes, Mark. My birthday, I'll be sixteen. You don't remember do you?'

I'm not sure how to answer her for a moment, my mind is reeling. The big-eared boy at the hospital had been right. It is November, not September. But the year showing on this calendar is wrong. It has to be.

It reads 2008 and that's simply not possible.

'So this calendar, everything about it is correct, right?' I ask hesitantly.

She looks at me cautiously, then at the calendar again. She's searching for something unusual on it, for some big glaring mistake, but she can't find one. Finally she meets my eye again and she nods. The calendar is correct.

I don't know what to think.

Apparently it's now 2008. It was September 1999 when I had my car accident on the way home from work. So somehow I've lost nine years. For some reason this bizarre coma-dream reality-show is set nine years in the future.

But why? Why would I dream this?

I must turn white. Liz sits back on her bed and pulls me down to sit beside her. She's worried about me. She must think Mark is losing his mind. Maybe he is?

'Are you okay?' she asks. 'Why would you ask something like that?'

I shake my head, I can't respond.

Suddenly there's a loud thump in the hallway. Steve and Tracey are staggering through to the bedroom. More noises follow and my anger and frustration returns in a rush. What the hell is going on here? How can it possibly be nine years in the future? How can I possibly be experiencing all of this through the eyes of a small child? I turn to Liz again.

'When is my birthday?'

'What?'

I don't ask again. She heard me. She just doesn't understand why I'm asking. After a moments silence she tells me, 'The 11th of June. You're eight. Nearly eight and a half.'

I absorb this, trying to decide if it's significant in any way. Mark is only eight, my God. I thought he seemed a bit older. He was born almost a year after my accident, closer to nine months in fact. How does this help me? It doesn't, it just confuses me more. I still don't understand. Nine years and two months, it seems so random. Why would I project myself into the future? What would be the point?

Suddenly my head hurts again. I'm so tired.

I leave Liz, shuffling over to flop onto Mark's bed, burying my head in the pillow without even kicking off my sneakers.

I'm shattered. I feel completely exhausted. This doesn't make any sense either, to be so damn tired, especially while I think I'm already asleep, or unconscious and dreaming. But perhaps if I just fall asleep again I might wake up in the morning somewhere else. Possibly in a nice clean hospital bed somewhere, with my family around me. Then I could tell them about the weird dreams I'd been having.

Please God, let this just be a dream. Let this just be my wild imagination.

My thoughts spin wildly as I succumb to darkness once again.

Liz shakes me awake early the next morning. Light is just starting to bleed through the tatty curtains and the house is quiet.

'Come on, sleepyhead. Time to get up.'

She's speaking very softly and my chest immediately tightens in fear as I wonder if Steve is still in the unit. I roll over and look up at her, and then around the room. I'm not disoriented at all. In fact, waking up in Mark's bed feels quite natural. But I can't help feeling disappointed. I didn't want to wake up and be Mark Mitchell again today. I wanted to wake up as Nick Davis. I want to be me.

I notice that my shoes are off and realise Liz must have done that for me last night. But I'm still dressed in the same clothes from yesterday. Liz flicks her long loose hair out of her eyes and shakes her head softly.

'You need a shower and clean clothes. Come on, hurry up or we'll be late. You're going to have to walk with me today so we need to get going.'

'Walk where?' I say, still a bit fuzzy from the deep sleep.

'To school of course, dummy. It's Monday, where do you think we'd be going?'

School? She can't be serious. I shake my head slowly. If I'm still stuck inside this perpetual insanity, then school is not going to be in my plans for the day.

'You go on ahead, I'll catch you up.'

'No chance. You get in the shower now please.' She's using a firm, authoritative tone I wasn't introduced to yesterday. 'And be careful with your forehead. I think its okay to rinse it off, but don't go shampooing your hair, alright. Now get moving. Into the shower. Come on!'

Seeing no point in arguing I reluctantly comply and shuffle through to the tiny bathroom. I set the shower running, strip off and step in under warm water. I normally like it steaming hot, but the cooler water is refreshing and wakes me up somewhat.

Afterwards I grab a towel and step back into the bedroom, drying off and looking for some clothes. With the towel around my waist I approach the mirror beside Liz's bed and take another look at my injury. It still makes a bold statement on Mark's forehead. Dark red, puffy and angry. No wonder my head still aches a bit.

But once again I am transfixed by the eyes that look back at me. They're definitely still my eyes.

'Come on, get dressed. We haven't got all day,' Liz whispers loudly, having returned to find me staring at myself in the mirror. She starts to return to the lounge.

'Liz,' I whisper back as loudly as I dare. Seeing my distinctive eyes in the mirror has made me suddenly curious about something. 'Liz, can I ask you something, please?'

She pops her head back into the room, curious. 'What?'

'Umm, do I look any different to you today?'

'What?'

'Do I look any different? You know, physically, since the accident.'

'You're kidding, right?'

'So I look exactly the same then?'

'Of course you do. I mean, other than that gross big cut on your head.'

I cut to the chase. 'And my eyes?'

'What?' she pauses and leans in a little closer, 'Well they're a bit bloodshot, if that's what you mean?'

'But they're not different somehow?'

'No. Of course not. God, just get dressed will you.' And she disappears down the hallway.

I'm not really sure what to make of that. I felt sure that Mark would have had different eyes and that my distinctive brown mark would be a new thing. But apparently it isn't. If Liz is being honest then Mark doesn't look any different, other than the gross head-wound, of course.

I'm a little disappointed.

I shake the thought away and turn to do a quick clothes search, quickly becoming more disappointed. There are several pairs of shorts and some long pants, plus about a dozen faded and tatty T-shirts. Everything looks seriously second-hand and I feel a surge of annoyance. It seems that Tracey must consider a full bottle of wine to be more important than new clothing.

I pull on dark navy shorts and a reasonably weathered green T-shirt with a big faded pair of Rolling Stones lips on the chest. I look over my shoulder at the Eric Clapton poster over the bed. The boy likes a bit of classic rock and blues. Good taste in music. Good on him.

Liz has two pieces of toast waiting for me in the kitchen, along with a couple of painkillers and a tall glass of water.

'Where are Tracey and Steve?' I ask quietly, seeing no one else in the open plan room.

'Steve's long gone, Mum's asleep. As usual.'

While her tone is neutral, I can see the quiet accusation in her eyes. Apparently we're talking in hushed tones just so as not to wake Tracey, again.

'I take it we won't be waking her for a goodbye kiss,' I murmur as I munch my way into the toast. I'm hungry again. A growing boy, some might say.

Liz doesn't laugh.

'Do we have any more toast?' I ask, finishing the first piece quickly. 'And what are my chances of a coffee to go with it?'

'Don't be stupid,' she frowns at me. Then she mutters, 'I need to get ready,' and disappears down the hallway. I finish the toast and shiver a little in the cool, empty room.

I take the painkillers and make myself coffee, but this time with only half the amount that I'd normally use. It tastes weak, but it seems to reduce the kick I get from it, and that's my goal. I make two more bits of toast before Liz reappears, showered and clean, her hair up in the familiar pony tail. She's wearing a simple skirt and top that she's nearly outgrown. Clearly whatever money that comes into the Mitchell household definitely isn't being spent on new clothing – or on food for that matter as the cupboards are almost bare.

'Come on, get your bag and shoes and let's get going,' she directs me.

'Do I have any other shoes than the sneakers I wore yesterday?'

'No. They still fit. They'll do you fine until winter.'

I feel sorry for her, so I don't protest. Mark's sneakers have found their own way back to sit beside the front door and an old black school bag is hung from a hook near them. Liz must have put them there, I guess.

As we leave the house, I start to feel despondent, and a little grumpy. I haven't yet worked out why I'm here, why I'm Mark, what my purpose is. The thought of trudging off to school, especially when I still don't know what it is I need to do to snap myself out of all this, is hard to accept. It seems pointless.

So I decide to take the day off.

'Liz. You know how my memory is all messed up?'

'Yes.'

'I've been thinking. It might be better if I just skip school today and rest. I'm sure my memory will improve tomorrow and I can go back then. Okay?'

'No chance.'

'What?' I'm surprised at her blunt response. 'What about my head? Have you seen this?'

I point at the stitches on my forehead.

'Don't even think about it. If you can drive a car all around town with that, then you must be well enough to go to school today. End of story.'

'Come on, Liz, let's not argue about it. I don't want to upset you. I just don't think that going to school today is the best option for me. You understand?

She rounds on me swiftly and I'm taken by surprise by the fire in her eyes.

'You are going to go to school today, do you understand! There isn't going to be a debate, and there sure as hell won't be any argument. We've talked about this over and over. The only way you and I are going to get out of this hell-hole existence is with a good education, and you don't get a good education by damn well skipping school. So please, *PLEASE,* do not try telling me that school is not the best bloody option for you today, or tomorrow, or any other day – all right! Are we clear on this?'

I'm left temporarily speechless. I hadn't considered for a moment that she'd respond like that. I'd expected her to just mumble 'whatever' and let me go, so I'm stunned. It takes me almost a full minute to find my voice and when I do I find myself instinctively apologising.

'I'm sorry, Liz. I'm . . . you're right, of course. It's just . . . I'm sorry, I'm coming.'

She takes a deep breath and exhales slowly. Without another word we start walking again, down the driveway and across the cul-de-sac.

As we round the next corner we almost run into an older man walking a little dog. I vaguely remember tripping over the same dog yesterday, as Liz and I escaped through the unit's back fence after Steve's visit. The old guy is almost completely bald and somehow seems familiar. He offers an odd smile this time and I once again find myself mumbling an apology as we move aside to get past him. A feeling of being watched makes me glance back to see that he's again stopped where we'd passed him and is looking after us curiously as we move away, just like yesterday. I don't think we've done anything to upset him, and I'm not even sure if he's looking at Liz, who has barely noticed him, or at me.

I put him out of my mind and sidle up to Liz. She's drifting along at a much slower pace than our excursion around Wilton yesterday. Not such an urgent mission today, I suppose.

As we trudge along I try to think of something I can say to convince her to let me play truant from school, just for today. I briefly consider just running away but that seems wrong somehow. It seems cruel. Liz obviously cares for Mark deeply, and just running off would hurt her – and worry her. I search for a better idea. We're more than half-way there already. Forgotten homework? I could tell her I have to nip back home and grab the homework I forgot to bring with me. Would that work? Possibly. But then I finally have an idea that she might actually agree with. I work it through quickly, but we're almost at the southern end of Lorneville Drive, not far from the school, before I think I can make it work.

'Liz, you know how my memory is gone?' I say.

'Mmmm,' she responds cautiously.

'Do you think I should go back to the hospital? You know, see the doctor again?'

She stops walking and rounds on me again, but this time her expression is one of contemplation. She's definitely more open to this suggestion than my previous effort.

'You still can't remember anything?' she asks.

'No. I don't even know what class I'm in at school,' I tell her truthfully.

'Does your head still hurt?'

'Yeah, it's aching pretty bad. Even after those pills.' This isn't quite so truthful.

She stares at me for a bit, considering what to do before responding. 'I don't know. Maybe we should just get you back to school and see if anything there jogs your memory. You seemed okay yesterday.'

'You mean like when I threw up at Waterloo Rd?'

This slows her down. She hesitates for a few moments more and then seems to give in.

'Okay, so maybe we should get you back to the hospital. Come on, I'll walk you back home and we'll wake Mum.'

'You don't need to do that. I can wake her myself when I get there.'

'I'd feel better if– '

But we're suddenly interrupted by a small boy on a bicycle who pulls up on the sidewalk beside us. It's Mark's best friend Jack and he's smiling broadly, his braces flashing.

'Hey, Mark. Walking today, huh?' he says, completely ignoring Liz – who groans. I don't think she cares much for Jack. Sensing an opportunity I seize on it quickly, before Liz can say anything.

'Now you don't have to worry, Liz. Jack can ride back with me. Make sure I get home okay. Then you won't be late for class, will you? And, on his bike, neither will he.'

Liz frowns, starts to say something and then stops, reconsidering. Jack looks puzzled. He doesn't know what we're talking about so I fill him in quickly.

'I have to go back home, so that Mum can take me to the hospital and have my head checked out again. Liz was going to walk me back, but if you come instead – on your bike – then both you guys can still make it to school on time, okay?'

He looks surprised but shrugs without comment. Liz isn't so easily impressed. 'I'm not so sure,' she says.

'Oh, come on Liz, it makes good sense. You don't want to cut class and I can wake Mum when I get home. Jack will make sure I don't get into any trouble on the way back.'

'Jack's going to look after you? You're kidding, right?'

'I'll be fine, don't worry.'

She frowns again and both Jack and I stay sensibly silent. Then she checks her watch and seems to relent. She steps closer and lowers her voice.

'You go straight home. You go straight inside and you wake Mum. You tell her your head hurts and you feel confused and that you can't remember anything. You tell her you want to go back to the hospital to see if they can help. Do you understand?'

I nod. 'Of course.'

'And if I find out that you do anything different, you'll be in trouble, okay?'

'I won't,' I say, lying as convincingly as I can. My acting must be improving somewhat.

'Right then,' she says, although she doesn't look happy.

She casts a disparaging look at Jack, who actually recoils slightly, and then fixes me with another meaningful frown before she finally turns and continues trudging on to school.

I feel a little bad, lying to her like that, but I have more important things to do. I need to check in on my parent's home again, find my family, and get my life back.

TWELVE

I turn to Jack who immediately begins telling me about his morning. His sister had hidden something of his and there had been an argument, blah, blah, blah. My God, this boy can talk. I'm more than a little amazed. He seems to have no interest in why I need to go to the hospital at all. I stare blankly at him for a minute and then start walking back up Lorneville Drive, towards the unit. He walks beside me, pushing the bike. In full daylight I can now see that he's about an inch shorter than Mark, than me – that is, and his clothes, which actually look like a school uniform, are clean and nearly new. He seems well fed and cared for and I surprise myself with a small pang of jealousy.

I don't really know what to say, so I just let him talk and he starts to tell me about his weekend. I continue to be struck by how self-absorbed this child seems to be as he launches into a tale about fishing with his Dad and big brother out on the lake, and about how his Mum had had a fit when he tore his new jacket and also managed to lose his fishing cap.

As he chatters away something reminds me of Liz's quest for the missing video download. I stop walking and interrupt his verbal barrage.

'Jack, were you at home on Friday after school?'

'What do you mean?'

I thought it was a pretty straight-forward question, but re-phrase it anyway. 'After school on Friday, were you at home or were you out somewhere?'

'We went to the bach, like I just said.'

'You have a bach?'

He looks puzzled. 'Yeah, of course.'

Of course, like everyone owns a holiday home. What was I thinking?

'So you went fishing from your bach, not from Wilton Marina?' I say.

'Why would we come back to the marina?'

It's like pulling teeth. 'So, have you been away all weekend?'

'Yeah, fishing. Like I just told you.'

'When did you leave?'

'What? On Friday, you know that.'

'Straight after school?'

'Yeah.'

'So the last time we saw each other was at school on Friday, not after school?'

He's really frowning now. 'Yeah. Why?'

'So I didn't come to your place after school and download a video?'

He doesn't respond to this, just gives me a really weird look. Like I'm cracking up.

I'm just about to press him further when his bike suddenly topples over and crashes to the footpath noisily. Then something pushes me sharply and I find myself sprawling off the kerb and onto the road.

I'm taken by surprise but move quickly, instinctively, rolling back to the safety of the footpath. I'm lucky there were no cars going by or I could have been run over. I look round to find a boy, who looks about ten, laughing at me while another boy, of about the same age, is pushing Jack into a hedge.

I can't believe my eyes. What the hell do these kids think they're doing? I could have been badly hurt, damn it – I could have been killed. I immediately see red.

'What the bloody hell do you think you're doing?' I shout angrily, getting to my feet.

The laughing boy shuts up quickly, more taken aback than anything else. He's taller than me by almost two inches but quite skinny, almost a rake. The other boy turns quickly, releasing Jack and leaving him sticking half out of the hedge.

This lad is bigger again, with at least another inch on the skinny boy and a lot more bulk. You couldn't quite call him fat but he's certainly big and beefy. Beefy rounds on me as the Rake takes a half step back.

'I'm sorry mm, mm . . . Marcus,' Beefy stutters meaningfully, advancing slowly and leaning his head to one side, mocking me. 'Were you spuh, spuh . . . speaking to me?'

Clearly he's pretending to stutter and I don't understand why, but I'm immediately offended. Does Mark usually stutter? I stand my ground, even more annoyed now.

'Pick up the bike and apologise to Jack,' I demand.

Beefy is genuinely surprised. Obviously this isn't the response he was expecting. He stops and eye's me warily. Then theatrically shakes his head, sticks a finger in his ear, pretending he needs to clear it, he hasn't heard me correctly.

'What did you say to me, ass-wipe?'

'You heard me, fat-boy. Pick up the bike and apologise.'

This time Beefy is seriously stunned. He honestly can't believe what he's hearing. His friend is goggle-eyed in disbelief and even Jack is gaping at me like I'd just transformed into the creature from the black lagoon. But Beefy rallies quickly. He takes another half-step towards me, pulling himself to his full height, puffing out his chest. I reset my feet, casually shifting my weight, ready to move quickly.

'You've done it now shit-for-brains. No one calls me fat.'

He starts to reach out to shove me. Big mistake.

I have Beefy tagged as a standard school-yard bully. He looks to be big for his age and is probably used to winning fights without even trying. I'm willing to gamble that his reputation usually precedes him and he normally doesn't have to do any more than just flex and smaller kids will quake and run. And boys like this expect you to run. They prefer it because it's easier. They're usually all bluster and show and they think that size matters. But it doesn't. Technique beats brawn, every time.

And from past experience I've learned that their friends are usually no more than voyeurs. They don't actually want to get involved in anything, but love the entertaining sideshows that occur when they follow their bully buddy around.

I'm as angry as all hell now and my instincts simply take over. Without really considering my recently reduced stature I feel inexplicably confident that I can take Beefy down, and I'm banking on his mate keeping out of it. I've always hated assholes like this guy.

I clench my fists tight, to ensure I don't hurt any of my own fingers, then duck forwards – inside his outstretched arm – and hit him first, with everything I can muster.

All the frustration and anger inside me drives my right fist into his stomach on an upward swing. He isn't ready for it. It's likely that no one he's ever picked on before has ever hit him back, let alone hit him first, and he isn't expecting anything different from me. I can see the over-confidence in his eyes, just before he squeezes them shut and grunts as I drive the air out of his lungs.

He stays on his feet though, bent over double, gasping for air. I shift my weight quickly and swing a left round-house into the side of his face. My fist glances off him just below his eye, and he spins away in a half pirouette, falling into his skinny friend. The Rake pushes him away in shock and Beefy spins back in front of me. I reset my balance quickly, opening my fist to deliver a straight right, using the palm of my hand, into the centre of his face.

I hear his nose break beneath my palm and he flops down onto his backside, then rolls to one side and curls up into the foetal position. He lies there writhing and gasping for air.

I hastily look up at his friend. He's backed up several paces. I glare at him, daring him to have a go too. He doesn't move. He just stands there with his mouth gaping open in total disbelief. I shake out my hands and relax a little.

Jack hasn't moved either. I walk over and reach out, helping him out of the hedge.

'Wow,' he says quietly, and slowly lowers himself to sit down on the footpath. Beefy is still squirming about on the ground, bleeding profusely from his nose and crying piteously as I sit down beside Jack.

'Are you alright?' I ask.

He can't speak, he's clearly in shock. The skinny boy suddenly darts past us all, heading towards the school. He makes no effort to help his fallen buddy. I'm not surprised.

'Do you know these guys?' I ask Jack.

He looks very, very confused and finally nods a little, still unable to speak.

'So what on earth was that all about?' I ask, shaking my hands out again and checking for injury. The palm on my right is a little sore, but nothing's broken. Jack is watching me in awe. Clearly Mark's never been in a fight before. Or, more likely, never won one before.

'Uhh . . . lunch money,' he finally manages.

Then I remember the conversation with his father and sister last evening. Mark had been sharing his lunch. Now I understand. This beefy git must have been stealing Jack's lunch money and his dad was trying to work it all out through the school. His sister thought he should just thump the bully. I look at the poor kid. Even now Jack is still too frightened to move. It's clear that he's never thumped anyone in his life.

Only a few weeks ago I had with my son, Daniel, about bullies. I told him that if someone pushes you, you push them back no matter how big they are. And if they take a swing at you, make sure you hit them back, as hard as you can. My Dad taught me that and it was good advice. I had wanted to pass it on. I can't help wondering if this whole episode has subconsciously found its way into my weird new world because of that conversation with my son. Oddly, I find myself compelled to push the same advice on to this poor frightened boy.

'You know, if there's a next time, you need to do that yourself, okay?' I suggest.

But he just shakes his head. 'I couldn't do that. I could never do that,' he says.

'Maybe not today. But last week I couldn't have done that either, could I?'

'No . . .' He tails off, staring at me, uncomprehending.

'But today I did do it, didn't I?'

'Yeah, you did. Oh wow, but you really did.' His eyes are very wide.

'So that means that you could do it too, you know, if you have to, maybe next week, maybe tomorrow. It's really not that hard, you know.'

'I dunno. Maybe . . . ?'

He isn't convinced, but I can tell he's seeing the possibility, so I press my point. 'Next time someone tries to bully you, you need to stop them yourself. It's a bit scary, but if you stand up to someone like this once, then usually no one will ever try and bully you again. The thing is, even if you lose they usually won't bother you again anyway. But I reckon you wouldn't lose. I reckon you could beat this fat git.' I'm speaking earnestly now, for some reason it seems very important to get through to him. 'Promise me, will you. That next time you'll stand up for yourself and do something to stop them yourself. Will you do that for me? Please?'

He looks down at the overweight bully, who is still crying and bleeding on the ground in front of us, and looks back at me. His eyes are shining now and he smiles.

'You think I could have done that too, don't you?' he asks. 'He didn't even hit you back. I mean, he just fell down. Wow. You think I could have done that.' It's a statement this time and he's obviously warming to the idea. I find myself pleased that he is now a little more ready to believe in himself. Self-confidence is the key.

Then Beefy is suddenly on his feet, but he clearly has no appetite to further the confrontation. He makes a dash for it too, following his skinny friend towards the school.

Finally it dawns on me that it's only a matter of time before a teacher or someone's parent arrives to sort the situation out. Mark would probably get in trouble for this.

Damn it. I don't have time to get caught up in any fallout. I need to visit my parent's house again, find my family, and so on. I try to think quickly. What to do? I can't get stuck here.

'We need to get going, Jack. I've got to get home. You need to get along to school, and quickly, or you'll be late.'

He's not easily convinced. His expression tells me he doesn't fancy going on to school alone now. I try to pacify him and build up a little confidence.

'You'll be fine. Neither of those guys will come near you, I promise. And even if they do, you can sort them out, just like I did. I'm sure you can. And maybe tomorrow I could show you a couple of things that will help. You know there's a reason he didn't hit me back, and there's a reason I didn't hurt my hands, but I can show you those things later. Right now we have to get going, before a teacher comes out here.'

My little speech seems to do the trick and we both finally stand up. I retrieve my school bag as he rights his bike and brushes a few leaves, from the hedge, off himself.

'I'll catch you later, okay,' I say, starting to move away.

'Mark,' he stops me. 'That was really cool, you know. So, thanks, really.' He's looking at me with an almost religious zeal and I become unreasonably embarrassed.

'No worries,' is all I can think to say before I turn and start heading back towards the unit again. I sneak a peek over my shoulder after a few steps and see him back up on his bike, riding slowly on towards the school.

God, what a morning.

I round the corner to the cul-de-sac moments later and stop, uncertain of what to do next. From across the road I can see the old hatchback parked in the driveway outside the unit. Tracey's still at home, probably still sleeping off her latest hangover.

I look about, the streets are deserted. I need to stop and think a bit, catch my breath.

I head for a large Willow tree a couple of houses along and plonk myself down at its base, leaning back against the trunk and closing my eyes. I put my head in my hands and let my mind start to wander over the unbelievable series of events I've been through in the last few days.

What the hell is going on? Is anything here real? Why me?

There has to be some explanation to all this that makes sense, that will suddenly make everything clear, and hopefully release me and allow me to wake up.

It's weird but, on some level, I can't really believe that Mark is a real person, but simply a body I've been loaned to get around in within this nightmare. But that doesn't add up either. How can I explain my feelings for Liz, or even Jack, when they can't really be real either? I just can't make sense of any of it. I'm so confused.

Then suddenly a voice shatters my reverie.

'Mark, my man. Aren't you gonna be late for school?'

The voice is a loud whisper, and very close. I open my eyes and find a bald man kneeling down in front of me. A leash is wrapped around his hand and his small white dog is sniffing at my feet. It's the same old guy that Liz and I had literally run into on the street earlier and I suddenly understand the familiarity I'd felt then. Up close he's the spitting image of Assistant Director Walter Skinner from the X-Files, my favorite TV show. I'm a big Mulder & Scully fan and this man's sudden appearance confuses me. I actually blink to see if I'm hallucinating, but he doesn't vanish. His big, oblong-shaped bald head stays right where it is and he peers at me inquiringly with bright blue eyes through his wire-framed glasses.

Who the hell is this guy? And how does he know Mark?

'Uh, no . . .' I search for something appropriate, 'I hurt my head. I'm off sick today,' I finally reply, pointing at my forehead. The stitched gash proves to be a great distraction.

'Gnarly,' he says, hunching forward. Before I can move he's cupped my chin in his free hand and leans in to stare very closely at the injury. He speaks sympathetically.

'How did you do this? It's wicked.'

'I got hit by a car, last Friday night,' I say, leaning further back into the tree trunk and not-so-subtly trying to pull my face free from his grip.

'No way. True? Not out here, after you left my place?'

That stops me in my tracks. He lets go of my chin and looks concerned, but he's still leaning in over me. How the hell does Mark know this guy?

'I was at your place Friday evening?' I ask.

'Yeah, of course you were. Dude, don't you remember?'

There's something very odd about him, especially the way he talks. It's like he's trying to sound like a teenager, or a stoner, but it doesn't suit him. He's dressed like an average suburban bloke, in jeans and a light jacket, and he has to be at least sixty. His eyes move across my face and down to the bruises on my legs. He leans back on his haunches and glances up and down the street and then back to me.

I'm really not sure what to make of him.

I answer cautiously. 'No. Umm, no. I don't actually. The doctors say I've got a bit of amnesia. That I've lost my memory of some things.'

He's fascinated by this. 'Wow, really. I've heard that can happen sometimes, you know, with a head accident, but I've never actually met someone that it's happened to. What can you remember? Do you remember the accident?'

'Not really. But I was on my bike and I was hit by a car.'

'Whoa, that's scary. You really must have been lucky supreme. And you don't remember anything, you know, about the accident?'

His eyes are locked on mine and, although his gaze shows concern, the intensity of his stare is making me quite uncomfortable. Regardless, I'm curious to understand why Mark had been at his house. Maybe he has the downloaded video that Liz is so keen on?

'I don't remember anything that happened on Friday at all,' I tell him. 'I don't know. Can you, maybe, help me . . . to remember?'

He pauses, considering the request. The dog is still sniffing around my feet. He glances away, back over his shoulder at the unit. He clearly knows where Mark lives and can see Tracey's car in the driveway. But there's no one about.

'Sure,' he eventually replies. 'We can try, can't we? Look, why don't you come on over and we'll see if we can kick-start that brain of yours. Yeah?'

Before I can respond he stands up, looks up and down the road again, and then extends his hand to help me up. Instinctively I wave it away and spring to my feet unaided. He shrugs, smiles, and leads us around the corner – out of the cul-de-sac – and almost immediately into the short drive-way of a beige house just down Lorneville Drive.

THIRTEEN

As we step into the house he slips the lead off the little dog and it darts away to our left towards a kitchen. But he gestures me forward.

'Let's hit the attic, eh. It's always more laid-back.'

The attic? I'm surprised and hesitate. He doesn't seem to notice and moves on, straight ahead towards a door directly opposite the main entranceway.

He flashes me a conspiratorial smile and opens the door inwards, away from us. I can't see inside as its dark and I start to become a little uneasy about where this is leading. He steps through first and lights come on to reveal a short stairway leading upwards.

'Come on, Dude. Shake a leg,' he calls back as he heads up the stairs.

I follow cautiously, stopping halfway up, just far enough into the space that my head clears the floor level and I can see the entire room. From the quick look at the front of the house I'd had on the way in, I guess that this room must be somewhere above the adjoined garage. It appears to be a converted storage space. It's quite large, bigger than I expect, and looks like it runs the entire depth of the garage. There are no windows, and the ceiling on the far side of the room slopes downwards to indicate the canter of the roofline.

To my surprise there is a pinball machine directly in front of me, with a short glass-fronted fridge to its left. The fridge is stacked with soft drinks and above it is a small open bookcase-style cupboard filled with bags of potato chips, biscuits and other snacks.

As I cast my eye around the room I take in a large grey couch, posters of sports stars and rock bands on the sloping ceiling, a huge flat screen TV with a gaming console, and a computer desk directly to the left of the stairwell. Behind the fixtures and fittings the entire room is painted matt black. Lighting comes only from two single spotlights in the centre of the ceiling space. One is trained on the pinball machine, the other on the computer desk.

The man has helped himself to a Coke from the fridge on his way through and is now sitting on the couch, looking back at me a little concerned. The lighting leaves his face semi-shadowed and he looks even more like Skinner from the X-Files than before. I half expect him to call me Mulder and offer me some cryptic advice. But he doesn't.

'Are you coming in then? What's up?' he asks instead.

I stand on the stairwell gazing uncertainly into the window-less room. The computer on the desk raises my interest, in regards to Liz's missing video, but I'm confused by the set-up. My own father has a den, and it's filled with a lot of unusual things, but something about this room's content doesn't feel right. The black painted walls make it feel trendy and cool, but in a juvenile way rather than in a manly den sort-of way.

I also haven't seen enough of the rest of the house to decide if there is a Mrs Assistant Director Skinner living here too. Something feels wrong, but I can't put my finger on it.

The older man is sensing my anxiety.

'Mark? Are you alright? You look confused,' he says.

'I'm okay,' I manage to reply. Taking a deep breath I decide to carry on and try to get some answers. 'I'm okay,' I repeat. 'My head's still pretty sore and I get funny turns now and then.'

He looks concerned and starts to get up from the couch. I raise my hand quickly in a *Stop* gesture.

'No, you stay there, I'm fine.'

Intuitively I seem to prefer that he keeps a little distance but I take a half step up into the weird attic room anyway. It's enough to stop him and he sinks back onto the couch, but he still seems a little tense.

I go to the fridge and select a can of Coke too. At this he visibly relaxes and I decide to play along a little more. I want to find out if Mark did actually download the video here and, if he has, it probably wouldn't be too hard to convince him to make me a copy. Liz would be pleased.

I open the can and step in front of the pinball machine. It's set to operate continuously, without a coin for payment, so I drop my school bag, put the can down, and fire a steel ball up the channel. I test the flippers and wait for him to speak first. I don't have to wait long.

'So what do you remember about Friday Mark? Do you know where the accident happened?' he asks.

His voice is now friendly and relaxing, he's clearly more at ease. I start to loosen up a little too as I watch the pinball whizzing around and answer without looking over at him.

'It happened out on Waterloo Rd, I got knocked into the bushes there.'

He sounds genuinely interested. 'Wow. Really? Into that greenbelt with the stream? And did they stop the driver? Was he drunk?'

I try and recall all the details that Liz had shared with me as we walked around yesterday. 'It was after dark and no-one saw anything. The driver didn't stop,' I say.

'So who found you?'

'A man walking a dog, they said,' I glance over at him, 'It wasn't you was it?'

'Sorry, Dude. Wasn't me,' he smiles, 'I get around, but that area's a bit outside my comfort zone, you know,' he chuckles softly to himself and pauses. 'I guess you probably should have stayed here, like I offered, on Friday evening. I'm sure I said that riding round in the dark is dangerous and, well, look what happened.'

'Yeah, maybe you're right,' I say. The pinball slips past my flippers and I turn to face him as the ball clunks deeply into the machine. Something about the way he's watching me sends an uncomfortable tingling down my spine. The easiness I had been feeling hastily vanishes and, without thinking, I abruptly abandon pretense and just blurt out the question I really want answered. 'Did you download a video from my cell-phone for me on Friday?'

He doesn't seem surprised. 'Yeah, of course,' he smiles proudly. 'You were pretty excited about it, but we didn't check it out yet. Do you want to see if it's worth uploading?'

I don't understand. 'Uploading? What do you mean?'

'To the site,' he's confused too. 'You know. Our website. Surely you remember. We've been working on it for ages.'

He stands up from the couch and moves across to turn on his computer. His bald head skims the low ceiling and for some reason this alarms me, raising small hackles on the back of my neck. There are two stools in front of the desk and from my new point of view I can now see a video camera in the corner behind it.

As he sits down and fiddles with the computer I start to become less and less comfortable. It wasn't until he stood up and moved a little closer that I suddenly now appreciate the potential danger I am in. My mind starts to grasp at unconsidered possibilities.

Nobody knows where I am, and we appear to be alone in the house. I look about the dark, windowless space and suddenly start to feel isolated. What am I doing here?

And then it strikes me that I've run into this man twice before – out on the street – within the last twenty-four hours and at neither time did Liz acknowledge him. So if Liz doesn't know him then how does Mark? This isn't adding up.

I try to compose myself. I want to get the video for Liz and its right here on this man's computer. I just need to ask him to put it on a disk or something. Just be calm, think it through. I handled myself okay against that fat bully. I'll be fine up here.

But something keeps gnawing at me. I've already decided that the video probably won't actually help Liz and Mark in their efforts to discredit Steve. Am I prepared to put myself at risk for it here? Is it that important?

My mind is spinning. Am I in danger here?

Skinner turns his head and smiles at me again, tapping the second stool to indicate I should come over and sit beside him. My heart begins to race as, within the close confines of the attic, I finally recognise the physical mismatch that will occur if he suddenly turns on me. He isn't all that big, but he's an adult and must weigh at least twice what Mark does. If he suddenly attacks there will be no way that I can fight him off with Mark's pint-sized body. I shiver involuntarily at the thought.

I should get out of here.

Glancing to my left I look down the stairs at the open door, and then turn back to the man who is clicking away on his mouse. Is this really a smart place to be?

I don't think so.

Without speaking, I snatch up my school bag and turn and dart quickly down the stairs, through the attic den's doorway and run to the front door. I grab at the handle and pull, but the door won't open. It's locked, and there's no latch or lever to open it. It has a double-sided deadbolt, and can only be opened with a key.

Damn it, I'm scared now. My heart is pounding furiously and I turn to find Skinner emerging from the attic doorway. He looks surprised and anxious.

'Mark? Are you alright? What's up?' he sounds genuinely concerned, but I'm now too far gone, getting close to panic. I just want out. He's been nice so far, and while he seems okay, I don't even know his name. I shouldn't have come in here. I have to think quickly.

'Sorry, I just got claustrophobic. I've been having trouble with confined spaces since the accident and, you know, there are no windows, and, and . . .'

I tail off, frightened, unsure if he's buying any of this. But he tries to sooth me.

'That's cool, Mark. Chill out. Just relax. Maybe you should sit down a minute, take a few deep breaths.'

'You know, I think I'd prefer some fresh air actually, but the door is locked.'

I can feel the blood rushing in my ears. I think I'm going to explode. He pauses, and tilts his head a little, then he says quietly, 'Okay, sure, no worries. We can go chill out in the back garden. It's nice out there, you remember?'

No. I don't remember anything of the sort, and I don't want to sit in the back garden. I'm almost in a full state of panic now. I just want out, and quickly!

'Yeah, I remember, but . . .' I pause, thinking frantically, 'I think I'd rather get going. My mum will probably be looking for me. And I don't want to worry her, do I?'

My galloping heart threatens to leave without me as I await his response. He's watching me carefully, bewildered by my sudden about-face. It isn't until I see his eyes play across my forehead that he seems to relax a little. Then he smiles calmly.

'Of course not, I understand, the last thing we want is your mum getting upset.'

He steps forward and produces a key ring from his pocket like he's performing a magic trick. I back up, away from him, watching as he unlocks the door, opening it.

I slip outside as soon as the crack is wide enough and move quickly away. Once I'm out my relief is palpable. I take a deep breath and feel my heart rate slow considerably. Then I stop and turn to find him standing watching me from doorway.

'You come back anytime, Mark. You know you're always welcome here,' he says. His voice is soft but he wears an unreadable expression. 'See you again soon, I hope.'

Now it's my turn to be surprised, as he seems genuinely upset. Have I misjudged the situation? Something definitely made me uncomfortable in there. Something about the set-up of the attic room, its isolation and his trying-too-hard-to-be-cool vibe. I really don't know what to think so I force a smile and back a few steps up the short driveway, limply waving in farewell. Then I turn and run.

I stop at the entrance of the unit's driveway, a little wobbly, and lean up against the letterbox. The old hatchback is still parked at the far end. Damn, Tracey is still at home. She's probably not working today, just my luck.

But, as I stand there, Tracey abruptly bursts out of the unit. I hear a stream of loud curses as she slams the door behind her and noisily stomps to her car, jumping in and slamming that door too. She's incredibly pissed off about something, that's for sure.

I move quickly, around behind the letterbox and into a bushy tree when it suddenly hits me. She's probably had a call from the school – about me. Oh shit, of course. The bully I took down will have gone onto school, probably straight to the sick bay. He'll have told someone what happened, pointing the finger at Mark Mitchell and his mate Jack. Parents would be called in, explanations required.

Damn, damn, damn. What a mess.

Moments later the little car comes squealing down the driveway in reverse, not slowing as it swings out into the cul-de-sac. I duck further into the tree. I don't want Tracey to see me. I'm not sure how I would explain myself.

The hatchback's engine races as it's slammed into drive and then leaps forward with a shudder. Tracey's face is grim and set. Mark is in big trouble.

I watch Tracey's car round the corner, heading straight for the school, and then step out of the tree. What to do now? Tracey should be gone for a bit, at least. Maybe I'll grab a coffee at the unit and see if that helps to clear my head.

But I'm locked out, and I don't think that Mark is carrying a key. Standing outside the unit I search through Mark's school bag. There are no keys and I throw the bag aside in annoyance.

Fine, now what?

I have no access to the unit, no money on me, and I'm now officially a wanted truant. Could this get any worse?

Once again I try to get my head straight. Tracey will no doubt return soon, looking for Mark. What would she do? Take me to school probably. Make me explain my actions with the bully and the fight. I wonder what type of punishments they use for this sort of thing here in the future, in 2008? I would have been given the strap in my day. I doubt they do that now.

And I've accidentally found the lost video that has caused Mark all this trouble. But it's really odd. I don't understand why he went to that weird man's house to download the video from his cell-phone? He's clearly been there more than once before. But I just can't fathom why Mark would visit him at all. How does he know him?

I quickly decide I can't tell Liz. If Skinner was an approved friend of Mark's then Liz would have said something when they ran into him before. Liz clearly doesn't know him. And, while I don't know what these kids are going to do about Steve, I'm pretty sure that I don't want to go back and get that video. Liz and Mark are just going to have to make do without it.

Standing outside the front door of the unit I start to feel uncomfortable. Skinner definitely knows where Mark lives. He had looked over here earlier and he clearly knows a fair bit about Mark. And, since I won't be found in my classroom at school, then Tracey could return here at anytime too, looking for me. I need to make myself scarce.

FOURTEEN

I start down the driveway, leaving my schoolbag by the steps, and then abruptly stop and turn around. Not that way. Not past Skinner's house. I scurry back up the drive-way and around the back of the unit, through the loose board in the fence and up the alleyway to the rear entrance to Fraser Park. This is better, plenty of open space.

I wander out into the middle of the park, not wanting to leave myself cornered, and finally realise my obvious next move. Mum and Dad's place. My parents' home is just down and across the road. Clearly I'm now meant to go and check it out again.

But just as I'm about to stride out more purposefully I hear a vaguely familiar, and disturbing, rumbling. Looking sharply over at the road I immediately see the big, shiny blue SUV pulling up at the kerb only metres ahead of me.

Steve's SUV.

I frantically duck backwards, towards the base of a large tree, and away from the car. My heart is suddenly racing. I'm instantly ready to run like hell.

Peeking out from behind the tree I see him, stepping out of his car. He's dressed all in black, with dark sunglasses, and – oddly for a warm day – he's wearing gloves. He looks up and down the road quickly, and then turns to survey the park as I hide again behind my tree.

When I look out again he's crossed the road and is walking away from me, down towards the building sites. My instincts tell me to run, just sprint for the clearing or go back to the unit, but my curiosity overtakes my fear. Where is he going?

I peer around the tree again and can't see him. Another tingle of fear runs through me. Oh shit! Has he seen me, and doubled back? I freeze, but then I see movement beyond the branches. Steve's further down the other side of the road, still heading away from me.

I feel like an idiot. He seems to have no idea I'm in the park at all. I watch him slow down and stop. He looks up and down the street again and I quickly duck my head. When I peek out again he's gone. Disappeared. It's then that I realise that he had been standing at the end of my parent's driveway.

I move forward a little and out towards the road and I spot him again. Now he's halfway up the driveway, about to walk up the steps to my parents' front door.

'What the hell?' I say out loud, to no one in particular.

Now I desperately want to see what's going on. I start to cross the road, and then change my mind. The building site on this side of my parent's house is little more than dug up mud and a few location posts, and the site is very open. I'd have nowhere to hide until I reach the tree line of my childhood home. Then I'd be too close, right across the drive from the front door and very exposed. That side of the road isn't a good choice.

Ducking back I jog along through the park, further up the tree line along the side of the road. Most of the trees along here are mature and tall, offering little cover at ground level, so I sprint down to a large bushier one almost directly opposite the driveway and climb like a monkey. I go up about four metres and lay down flat on a large bough that stretches out towards the road. I reach out and pull a bushy branch aside and find myself staring almost straight across the road at my parent's front door.

Steve is hammering on it with a closed fist and I can hear the banging from about twenty-five metres away. He's wearing a balaclava now. There is a car in the driveway. This surprises me more than the balaclava. My visit last night left me feeling that the house was abandoned, but someone is there now. Someone that Steve really wants to talk to.

Steve stops banging, waits about five seconds, and begins banging again. He's ignoring the old iron knocker and making enough noise to wake the dead. Suddenly the door opens while his fist is still in midair.

I can't see the person behind the door. It opens inwards and whoever is behind it has only opened it slightly, with their face well back from the small gap, in the gloom. I sense, more than actually see, a security chain stopping the door from opening further.

Steve starts talking. I can only hear muffled noise from this distance, but it sounds fairly menacing. Mind you, every time I've ever heard Steve speak his voice has sounded menacing, so I may have been imagining it.

There doesn't appear to be much of an exchange in the conversation, Steve seems to be doing all the talking. He doesn't gesture while he talks, as he's planted his hands on either side of the door frame and is leaning in threateningly towards the opening.

In mid-sentence the door starts to close and Steve's left hand slams into it, forcing it back to the full extent of the chain. He pulls a small piece of paper from his pocket and waves it towards the gap in the door. His voice is rising in volume now, but I still can't make out the words. Then he steps back abruptly and violently slams his booted right foot into the door about midway up. I hear wood splinter and break and Steve's voice carries over to me . . . *'Don't you fuck with me!'* That's Steve all right. I know his catch-cry only too well.

The door flies open from the kick and for a split second I see an old woman caught in the sudden light. She's obviously distressed and her long grey hair flies about wildly as she backs away from the door, out of the daylight.

Steve steps up to the now open frame menacingly. He throws the piece of paper inside the house and spits out a few words, pointing at the woman and then at the paper on the floor. I think he is going to hit her, but he backs up then, and looks like he's going to leave.

But suddenly he brings up his right foot and again lashes out at the door, which had started to swing back towards him to close. The door flies back, crashing into something behind it. I hear glass smash and a clatter of small things breaking.

He stops then, giving the old women one final instruction. Pointing his finger at her and snarling in a low tone that doesn't carry. I can easily guess what's being said though.

I release the bushy branch and hug the tree bough desperately, abruptly realising that he is going to now walk straight towards me as he leaves the house.

He obviously isn't in a good mood and I'm terrified he will spot me. I feel pretty sure that hiding up a tree and spying on him would constitute as 'fucking with him' in some way or another and I don't want to be caught.

I can feel beads of sweat break out on my back and neck and forehead. I can't see anything though as my face is turned sideways, pressed hard onto the branch, looking back up the road at his car, trying to keep still and hidden behind the bushy branches.

Then I realise I have no cover at all on my right hand side. I'm looking directly at Steve's car, and it has an open and clear view of me.

I can hear Steve now, his boots loud on the footpath as he turns at the top of the driveway and starts back along the road to his SUV.

He's parked some distance away so that the old woman won't get to see his car, but he really hasn't made much of an effort at concealment, the car is less than one hundred metres from the house. I can even read the license plate from my vantage point, but it's another hundred metres further down the road to the shops and I suppose it won't be easily visible from there.

I think briefly about trying to shimmy quickly down the tree but Steve comes into sight, in the middle of the road about half way back to his car. I stop dead. If I make any sound he will hear me.

I'd once read that people searching for things very rarely look up, but naturally scan their environment at ground level only, just searching at their own height. I desperately want that to be true at this moment. I feel sure that Steve will look around him, as he did on the way in to the house, to ensure he isn't spotted.

I hug the tree bough and lean slightly away from him, trying to make myself invisible, trying to stay completely still. Silently I become grateful I'd chosen to wear the green Rolling Stones T-shirt today. It isn't camouflage, but it's much less obvious than any other colour option.

Steve doesn't stop, but does look around him as he reaches the car. His gaze darts all around, but only at street level, and I remain utterly still. Then he quickly climbs into the oversized vehicle. He starts it up and I almost cry in relief when he floors the car and spins it away in a noisy u-turn. I see him pull off the balaclava and, thankfully, he doesn't look up as he peels away. Regardless, I stay like a statue until he's turned off Wilton Rd further up, just in case he decides to scan his rear view mirror.

Very slowly my heart rate begins to return to normal.

After a minute I sit up, then shimmy backwards to climb down to the ground. My legs are still shaky as I drop the last metre and I fall and roll, lying there for another minute as I try to calm myself and gather my thoughts.

I didn't recognise the old woman, but I only got a fleeting glance. I had been expecting to see my mother there, but feel sure it wasn't her. My parents have always been fastidious dressers, and Mum always wears her hair up in a tight knot around the back of her head. On many women this would look a little severe, and school-marmish, but Mum has a warm face and the style suits her. Frankly I think I've only seen her hair down once or twice in my entire life and can't visualise her any other way.

I stand up and look across at the big old house. The door is now closed and there are no signs of life again. The car is a little red sedan. It looks quite new, but I don't recognise it. Not as a car my parents would own. Dad hates red cars. He thinks they're too flashy. He only ever chooses cars that are dark blue or grey and Mum has always driven a sporty little yellow Triumph convertible. It's her pride and joy.

I stand staring at the house for a full five minutes, only glancing up the road now and then to watch out for Steve. I don't know what to make of the scene I've just witnessed, and I don't know who this person is that's now living in my parent's home. I can't decide whether I should wander over and knock on the door or just stay in the park – out of harm's way. I'm worried that Steve will return. Fear and indecision almost overwhelm me.

Finally I pull myself together and decide to go over. Bite the bullet. Surely my day can't get any worse, can it?

The red sedan is shiny and very modern looking. But I don't recognise the make or model as I stand in the driveway near the bottom of the stairs that lead to the front door.

I look up at the door, it's closed now and I can see a clear footprint mark from the sole of Steve's boot in the paint-work, and it appears to have a reasonable sized crack in it.

The house is silent and I look up and down the street, just as Steve had done only a few minutes earlier. The trees out by the road, and the front of the house itself, obscure any view from this point to, or from, the new shopping centre. Up the other way there is also little to see, with a line of trees beside the driveway almost entirely obscuring the view across to the park and further up the street.

No wonder Steve had felt safe to kick the door in during broad daylight. And with no immediate neighbours, the sound won't have been heard other than by someone directly over in the park, like I had been.

I start up the steps and then stop. I really have no idea what I'm going to say, and somehow doubt the poor old lady inside will actually come to the door if I knock. She must have been terrified when Steve kicked her door in and I'm half expecting the police to turn up any minute.

It's only after much internal deliberation that I decide to try and talk with her, regardless of Steve's very recent frightening visit. If she's living here she may know where my parents have gone to, and I don't think an eight year old boy will be considered a threat. I also figure that any enemy of Steve's must be someone worth befriending.

I step forwards again and reach up to grab the old iron knocker. I bang it three times and wait. Nothing happens. I bang it again, three more times, and wait some more.

Still nothing, no sounds at all are coming from the house. Then I sense, more than see, a shadow darken the window to my left and as I turn it quickly disappears.

The old woman is definitely in there, but she clearly isn't keen on any more visitors.

I wait a little more, she must have seen that I'm just a harmless young boy and should now come out, but the door doesn't move. I reach up and knock again, three more times.

After waiting another minute I decide to try a new approach. I call out.

'Hello . . .' I pause. 'Hello in there. I need to speak with Walter or Helen Davis if they're at home.' I'm shouting as politely as I can. But nothing happens.

'Hello,' I call out again. 'I have a message from their son for them.'

Finally I hear a muffled crunching sound as someone moves towards the door. The old woman must be stepping in something that Steve broke that's still lying on the floor. It sounds like she's walking through broken glass.

'Hello in there,' I call out, a little less loudly this time. 'I'm a friend of Mr and Mrs Davis and I have a message from their son for them. Are they home?'

The bit about a message seemed to have flushed her out a moment ago and I'm hoping it will be enough to get her to open the door.

A voice calls back to me. It's cracking and scared.

'Who are you?'

Good question, I almost reply. Who the hell am I, really?

I answer her as simply as I can. 'I'm Mark Mitchell. I mean you no harm.'

It's an odd thing to say really, given the circumstances, but it's one of those silly family in-jokes we used to use over and over when I was a child. It came to me unconsciously.

We'd picked up the line *I mean you no harm* from a cheesy TV comedy show about a British explorer in Africa. Somehow he, or his short balding sidekick, would manage to use the phase in almost every episode as they stumbled their way around the wilderness running into different native tribes each week. This running gag had always made us laugh – more than was really warranted – and the phrase became entrenched in Davis family speak after Dad used it one day, walking into the house with an axe in his hands in the middle of chopping firewood. Mum had pretended to be scared and Dad had come out with the clunky line. Bobby, my little brother, and I had both cracked up, so much so that little Bobby laughed so hard he actually fell off his chair. After that the phrase had stuck with us. I guess some things simply get ingrained.

'What did you say?' the old woman's voice asks through the door.

I raise my voice a little, assuming she's a bit deaf, and call back, 'My name is Mark Mitchell.'

The door clicks and opens a tiny sliver, I can see the security chain dangling loosely and swinging back and forth. An eye peeks out at me and she speaks again.

'No, not your name, the other bit?'

I reply cautiously. 'I said "I mean you no harm".'

I don't want to frighten her off now. I smile and lift my arms a little, with palms forward to show myself as open and unthreatening. She responds by widening the crack slightly, her face still in the shadow of the door.

'And who did you say you have a message from?'

'I'm looking for Walter and Helen Davis. I have a message for them from their son.'

I can just see her eyes cast a furtive gaze around the street behind me, and then she opens the door a little wider again and says, 'I'm Helen Davis, what is your message?'

I feel like a cannonball has hit me in the chest.

I step backwards involuntarily and lose my footing, stumbling down the steps. I fall awkwardly and land in a heap on the driveway at the bottom of the steps. My heart is suddenly racing furiously and I gape at her in surprise.

The old woman has pinned her long hair up into a knot behind her head and seems much more together than she had barely ten minutes ago. Her hair is almost completely grey and her face significantly more lined than it was when I'd last dropped by to visit.

My mother stands in the doorway looking down at me, suspicious and wary.

FIFTEEN

HELEN DAVIS doesn't know what to think. She has barely calmed down since her last visitors menacing theatrics, and now this. What on earth does this child want?

She looks nervously around the area of street and parkland that is visible from her front door, uncertain if the boy's fall is premeditated and actually a trick to draw her out of the house. But it doesn't make sense. Why bother with a ruse, the door is already broken. She sees nothing threatening and steps out, looking down at the boy watchfully.

'Are you alright young man?' she asks.

The boy looks like he's just had a heart-attack. He's turned ghostly white and is clearly unable to speak. Helen notes that his face is bruised and there seems to be a nasty, stitched-up gash across his forehead. And he's just sitting there, staring at her with huge, bewildered eyes. But she's very curious. He'd called out some strange things.

'You said you had a message for me, from Robert. What is the message?' she asks.

The reply comes quickly and it shocks her. 'Not from Bobby . . . from Nick,' he says.

She feels her face darken immediately as anger and frustration almost overtake her.

'How dare you?' she snaps at the boy, tears welling up in her eyes. 'You can't possibly have a message from my Nick. You have absolutely no right coming here and upsetting me like this.' She's annoyed now, it's just a con. She waves her arm, pointing away up the street. 'Get away from me. Get off my property now before I call the police.'

The boy seems to recoil in surprise. His eyes glaze over for a moment and she watches as he reflects silently over some kind of difficult internal struggle. She checks the street again quickly, double-checking that this isn't some sort of sick ruse. But they are alone and she doesn't feel threatened anymore.

The boy appears deeply baffled, and Helen suddenly realises that he looks familiar. Where has she seen him before? Abruptly the boy starts babbling, pleading rapidly. He hasn't moved from the bottom of the steps.

'I'm sorry, really I am. I don't want to upset you. I just need to talk with you. Things are really complicated, but I'm sure I can explain if you'll just let me. I'm sorry, I didn't mean to say . . . about . . . Nick. Please, I just need to talk with you . . .'

Helen is still angry and cautious, but she relents a little, her heart going out to this obviously frightened and confused little boy. He only looks about eight, just a baby.

'Who did you say you were again?' she asks.

'Mark Mitchell, my name is Mark Mitchell. I live just over there,' he replies, pointing vaguely at the park across the road. 'I'm sure you don't know who I am, but I really need to talk with you about–'

He seems to change his mind mid-sentence, but then quickly starts babbling again.

'I want to talk to you about . . . umm, about the guy who just came and kicked in your door. I know who he is. I want to help you.'

Helen is taken aback. Did this boy actually see that evil man come to her door? She briefly considers how this could help her situation and then she steels herself.

'All right, Mark. Who is he, and what did he want?'

The child finally looks a little surer of himself and climbs up off the ground. He moves up a step, leaning heavily on the railing before responding. He looks so earnest now.

'His name is Steve, and I'm not absolutely certain what he wants, but he tried to kill me last Friday night.'

'Steve who?'

He suddenly loses confidence and it's clear to her that he doesn't really know much at all. She starts to wonder what to do with him. He's clearly disturbed in some way. Perhaps he'd rattled his brain a bit when he received that gash on his head. Should she call an ambulance or try to track down his mother? Mark Mitchell, he'd said. The name is familiar somehow.

But the boy suddenly pulls himself together and uses the old family phrase again.

'That's not important right now. What is important is that you believe I'm a friend and that I really, really do want to help you. I mean you no harm, please believe that.'

Helen is utterly perplexed. Why would he use that old phrase – again? How did he even know it, surely they're not re-running that silly old TV show? And what had he meant earlier by claiming he had a message from Bobby. Her mind is spinning in circles when she finally remembers how she knows this boy.

'But I do know you, don't I? You're Tracey Mitchell's lad. Yes?' she asks.

She's surprised when he looks down, seeming to slump at the mention of Tracey's name. 'Yes,' he confirms weakly. 'Tracey's my Mum. What did she do to upset you?'

Helen isn't sure what to make of that. Is he embarrassed? 'I'm not upset at your mother, and I haven't seen her in years. Why would you ask that?'

The boy shrugs, and then surprises Helen yet again.

'That guy Steve, who just kicked in your door, he's Tracey's boyfriend. He's a psychopath. You need to be very careful around him. He's already tried to kill me once.'

At first she can't decide how to take his claims, they sound desperately naive and childish, but the poor little boy seems so serious. He clearly believes this allegation and, to be fair, he does look pretty battered. Her concern for the boys' well-being kicks in.

'So, how did he go about this then, this attempt to kill you?' she asks. The boy immediately looks relieved and launches into explanation.

'He ran me off the road, while I was riding my bike,' he replies. Then, it seems like an afterthought, he adds, 'Over on Waterloo Rd, near the intersection with Samsara.'

Then he stops, and waits.

Helen is caught off-guard. She knows this place. She knows it very, very well. She walks along there often, too often really, and she stops most times and wanders off the footpath there, into the trees at exactly this spot.

She feels the colour draining from her face and she becomes a little light-headed. Why, oh why, would this strange little boy mention that dreadful, awful place? He's staring at her silently, meaningfully, and she knows it isn't a mistake. He added it deliberately. He knows something. But what? And how?

She glances around beyond him again. Is this some kind of cruel trick? But there's still no one else anywhere in the vicinity. She feels the anger and frustration begin to well up inside her, and then the grief. That ever-present, gnawing grief that just won't leave her alone. She looks down on the boy again. He's watching her face intently, like he's trying to read her mind. His expression is so dreadfully serious, but then he blurs slightly as a tear starts to well in her eye. This makes her angrier and she takes a deep breath to calm herself. And then another. Her eyes narrow before she finally speaks, it's barely a whisper.

'Who . . .' she pauses, trying to find her voice. 'Who . . . are you?'

He looks down, seeming to gather himself carefully. Then he takes a deep breath and meets her eye with a look that is desperately trying to convey so much.

'I'm someone who loves you very much . . . I'm someone who really shouldn't be here . . . and I'm someone who is very, very confused right now.' He inches forward a little, speaking haltingly. 'I said I had a message for you from your son, but it's more than that and . . . well . . . I'm terrified that you won't understand, and that you'll be frightened . . . and that you'll refuse to talk with me anymore.'

He stops, letting his words sink in. Helen realises that her heart has almost stopped beating and a chilling numbness is spiraling through her.

She can't speak, but she holds his eye and the intensity of his gaze stirs something inside of her. Then he continues.

'I'm someone who thinks that I may have crossed a line that shouldn't be crossed . . . and I don't know how to go back and fix things. In a lot of ways . . . I'm as helpless as the eight year old boy you're looking at now.'

He pauses again briefly. Everything about him is pleading for her to understand something. His tone is unbearably captivating, his gaze intense, and she is now utterly entranced. But she doesn't know what it is she needs to see. She doesn't understand.

'I'm not really Mark Mitchell,' he continues softly, 'I don't really know who Mark Mitchell is because . . . all of my memories are someone else's. And all I can remember is my life up until a point where I had a very bad car crash . . . over on Waterloo Rd.'

At the mere mention of this place again she physically shudders and an inkling of understanding begins to shimmer inside her. But he's paused again. She starts to wonder if she's dreaming. This is insanity. He's dredging up the past, but how? Why? The boy swallows hard, taking another deep breath before plowing on.

'And when I woke up I was here . . . inside Mark Mitchell's head . . . almost nine years later . . .'

Every rational thought inside of her is screaming that this just isn't possible. It's a trick. This boy just wants something. He's playing some kind of cruel game.

But she tries to push those thoughts aside. She is desperate to believe. There is something in his tone – in the simple way that he speaks – that is so incredibly familiar.

And his intensity, even the way that he holds his head. All of his mannerisms, so subtle, but so surely his.

Helen feels a tear running down her cheek as he speaks again, this time blurting the words out in a rush of anticipation and joy. He's reading her expression.

'You know who I am, don't you? You can see me in here, can't you? You can see past this face and all this blonde hair. I can feel it. You know it's me, don't you . . . Mum?'

She can find no words, but she has almost given herself over to the inconceivable. The situation is impossible, completely and utterly impossible. Yet here he is, standing right here, before her. Confusion and doubt fight a frantic, and losing, battle inside her against elation and joy. Her eyes are wide. Tears cascade down both cheeks as she softly shakes her head from side to side in small movements of disbelief.

Then the boy abruptly starts to cry. Tears stream down his face too and his little body heaves, racked with misery, but with relief also. He sinks to his knees, sobbing furiously.

Helen steps down to him, sitting quickly and taking the child in her arms. They huddle together on the steps, both weeping uncontrollably as she rocks him gently.

After some time their flow of tears reduces to sniffling and small whimpers as they bring themselves under a little more control. Helen's heart is aching with joy, but she still has doubt. The situation still isn't resolved. She can't begin to comprehend how her eldest son can be with her here, like this. Not like this.

She draws a deep breath to steady herself and wipes salty tears from the boy's face. Then she grips him by the shoulders, extending her arms full length.

'How many cats did we have when you finished school?' she asks.

The boy nods in understanding. He can feel that she believes him, but she needs more proof before daring to really let herself accept the impossible.

Helen waits hopefully as he considers the question. It's not as easy as it sounds. The family had a number of cats over the years and he doesn't want to get it wrong. After a few more moments he answers decisively.

'There were two cats when I was seventeen. A ginger tom called Donkey, and a black puss called Daisy.'

She's more than satisfied by his response. The boy not only knows how old Nick was when he left school, but he's able to supply the correct names as well. All their cats had been given names starting with 'D', to go with their surname Davis. He could have chosen from Delilah, Diddles, or even Dangermouse, but Helen is reasonably certain that these were actually the two that were around when Nick graduated.

She smiles a little and considers another test, knowing that only one other person in the world could answer it correctly. But would she receive the lie, or the truth?

'Ok then,' she says, 'who was it that broke the laundry window?'

He flushes, snorting as he almost laughs. He knows the answer, she can see that immediately. Her heart fills with warmth as she realises he's going to continue the lie.

'It was me,' he says, a knowing twinkle in his eyes.

'Balderdash,' she retorts. 'It was Robert. And you and I both know it, don't we?' She raises her eyebrows defiantly and the boy pauses, now looking solemn.

'Do you promise not to tell Dad?' he asks.

And these words are exactly what she needs to hear to be certain. To be absolutely and irrevocably convinced. She knows her own son. His desire to please his father, to keep peace within the family, is like a shining beacon of light. Only her Nick would do that. A new tear wells up in the corner of her eye as she replies softly.

'I won't tell. I promise.'

'It was Bobby, but Dad would have killed him, he was already on a second warning that week. So I took the blame.'

She doesn't respond to his earnest confession and just stares at the boy for a few seconds longer, suddenly realising that there is even greater evidence already before her.

'They're your eyes, Nicky. I'd know them anywhere,' she whispers softly. She believes, but she doesn't understand. Who could? The situation simply isn't feasible. There can be no rational explanation. She shakes her head again in total bewilderment.

'But this just isn't possible, Nick,' she says. 'You died. We buried you out at Five Rivers Cemetery. You can't be here now.'

Helen Davis watches the boy in front of her turn as white as a sheet. He seems unable to respond.

SIXTEEN

Earlier she told me that I can't be carrying a message from Nick, and it made me wonder. Would she reveal that her son is in a coma and has been for years – or that her boy Nick is fine and well but has moved to another city – or something similar? But she doesn't.

She tells me that I'm dead.

It's not what I want to hear.

I wipe my face self-consciously, turning away from her. It's irrational, but I'm quite embarrassed by the tears. I haven't cried since I was a teenager, but I just can't control it. I try to convince myself that they are tears of relief, since I finally found someone within this nightmare that I can fully reveal myself to. Someone that is real to me. But it's more than that. Finding my mother changes everything.

She rubs my shoulder gently, seeking my attention, and then asks me another question, testing me further.

'How many grandchildren did you give me, Nick?'

I smile, this is an easy one. 'Two,' I answer proudly. 'Daniel Walter Davis and Katherine Mary Davis – respectively aged eight and five when I last saw them.'

She nods a little and gives me a rather funny look, somehow both sad and knowing. 'I think you'd better come inside, don't you? We have a lot to talk about.'

We help each other up and I hold her hand as she guides me through the door, past the wreckage of Steve's visit, and back into the sanctuary that was my childhood home.

Inside the house it is gloomy and dim, not at all how I remember things from all those years ago. I look around and count two of the lounge windows boarded up, significantly reducing the light in the room. The furniture is all very familiar, but looks old, tired and dated. Some of it might be getting close to antique by now, but mostly it's just plain old.

My mother guides me through to the kitchen and I sit down at the old Formica dining table. She busies herself putting on the kettle and preparing the teapot for a brew. I notice she is now using teabags, but still hasn't advanced to making just one cup at a time.

'Would you like a glass of juice, or perhaps a hot chocolate?' she asks.

'Actually, I'd really like a half-strength coffee Mum. I haven't drunk hot chocolate for a very long time.'

She looks over at me then, raising her hands to cup the lower half of her face. It looks like she's about to burst into tears again. She's shaking her head, clearly still reeling in disbelief and more than a little shocked. Her hands tremble slightly so she lowers them, crossing her arms and tucking them under her armpits. I stand up and take her arm, guiding her to the table and sit her down.

'Perhaps I should make the tea, okay? You still have it with just a drop of milk, no sugar?'

She nods, unable to trust her voice.

I quietly make the tea, finding instant coffee for myself in the cupboard where it has always been kept for visitors, along with the sugar. Mum and Dad both drink tea, buckets of it every day, but neither with sugar and both with only a few drops of milk.

I've always been a little amused at how people often turn to tea or coffee in times of stress, like it will somehow wash away their worries. I suppose for many it actually might, but I've always thought of it as just something to distract you while you get your head straight. And it's better than turning to anything stronger.

Soon we are sitting together at the old kitchen table, clasping our mugs in front of us, drawing some kind of strength from the hot drinks. Mum speaks first.

'Tell me again how this all works,' she says, pointing vaguely at me, at Mark.

I sigh deeply and then start talking.

I tell her about driving home from work that Tuesday evening. About how a blue car came flying out of the side street along Waterloo Rd, plowing into my car and forcing us both to spin wildly off the road into the greenbelt.

I tell her about blacking out with blood in my eyes, and about waking up at the hospital some time later – as Mark. And how I had tried to visit Intensive Care to find myself, but couldn't. And how Liz and Tracey had come along the next day – but it was actually last Saturday afternoon, here in 2008, only two days ago – and taken me back to their unit just across the park.

She silently watches me, totally absorbed, never taking her eyes off mine, as I describe how I believed I was in a coma, and that all of this was a dream. I tell her about taking Tracey's car and how I'd gone to Charles St to try and find Sarah and the children. I tell her what I'd found there and about taking the car back to Tracey.

I don't know why, but I don't mention Steve at this point. I don't say anything about Tracey's drinking problems either, as somehow it just doesn't seem relevant.

I go on to tell her about how I'd tried to come and see her and Dad yesterday evening but there was no one home.

'Where is Dad?' I ask.

She doesn't answer immediately, and it's clear that her mind is spinning with information overload. Then she simply replies, 'He's not here Nick, carry on with your story. I believe it will be my turn to tell you a tale soon enough.'

There is some evasiveness in her voice, but I'm too caught up in my own story of desperation and woe to fully register it, so I begin talking again.

I tell her about the wound to Mark's head – my head – and how I believe it came from a bicycle accident at the very same spot as my car crash on Waterloo Rd. My account is getting jumbled up a bit now, I find myself skipping back and forth, and just blurting out whatever comes into my mind. I tell her about the return visit to the accident site with Liz and the powerful physical reaction I had in returning to that place. And I explain how I've covered up my situation with Liz and with others by telling them I have amnesia and pretending to still be Mark, even though I know almost nothing about him.

Mum interrupts me. 'But surely Tracey would have sensed the difference? A mother knows these things Nick. She must know something is wrong with her son?'

It's my turn to be a little evasive. 'I don't think so Mum, Tracey's got a lot going on at the moment and Mark doesn't seem to really be top priority.'

She frowns at this, not really understanding, and I leap quickly back into my story. I tell her about almost going to school earlier, and about how I'd tricked Liz to avoid it and then run into some other boys and got into a fight.

'Who were the other boys?' she asks, interrupting for only the second time.

'I don't know. A couple of bullies and a kid called Jack. Apparently he's Mark's best friend.'

'You mean Jack Thompson?'

'I don't know, Liz never told me his last name.'

'Did he have longish, dark hair – and braces on his teeth?'

'Yes. Do you know him?'

'Hmm, yes. Well, I've seen you with him. I mean I've seen Mark with him, out on your bikes in the park, fooling around.' She smiles curiously at this, but just says, 'Carry on with your story. Tell me everything.'

Suddenly I'm not sure what else to tell her. I realise I don't want to mention my visit to the strange old man's attic and after that I came here, following Steve.

'But that's pretty much it. Somehow I'm here, alive and fully functioning inside the body of an eight year old boy – nine years in the future. So if you can explain this to me, you'd make me pretty damn happy.'

Her eyes are wide. She just shrugs very slowly, in a very exaggerated way. We stare at each other in silence for a moment before I speak again.

'Do you think it might be possible that I am actually . . . you know, dead? And that my soul, or spirit, life-force or whatever, is somehow controlling Mark's body for some reason? For some supernatural purpose that I just can't figure out?'

She frowns. Clearly this sort of discussion is way out of her comfort zone, as it is mine.

'Or is this just a bad dream,' I continue, 'and nothing here is real. Not me. Not Mark. Not you? Should I ask you to pinch me, or slap me or something?'

She stays quiet, contemplating my situation carefully. I stop talking and wait. Finally she responds, gently.

'I don't think that will help, and I don't see any easy answers to any of this, Nick. But I can tell you one thing. Well, two things I suppose. I can tell you that this is not a dream, not as far as I'm concerned. I am real, this house is real and nine years have truly passed since your accident.'

I stare at her, not really sure if I want to comprehend.

'And I'm sorry,' she continues, 'but you need to know that you didn't survive that car accident. You were already gone when the ambulance arrived. They said you would have died almost instantly, your injuries were so severe.'

She pauses. I just sit there, going numb.

'So I don't know where we go to from here, but this definitely is not a dream. My eldest son Nick passed away nine years ago and I have been grieving for you ever since.'

I stay frozen. I feel like my world has just ended.

I look searchingly into my mother's eyes, desperate for her to suddenly laugh and tell me this is all just an elaborate practical joke. Ha-ha, you fell for it. But she doesn't. Her face is grim. She's serious, earnestly sharing in my worst night-mare. Her eyes show deep concern, but she's also confused and unsure. I'm forced to conclude that this is real.

I have to absorb it somehow, but it isn't easy.

I mean, what are the options? What are the alternatives?

If I accept the fact that I'm dead, then I have to be a ghost or something, don't I? I certainly don't feel like a ghost. I feel real, completely real and alive. I have feelings, I feel pain, and I need to eat and drink and sleep, just like a normal living person.

And if I accept that, then it would mean that Mark is real too. He has a mother and a sister, a home – such as it is, and friends too. Mark isn't just a figment of my imagination.

So then, if I am dead, I have to be in possession of Mark's body, like a rogue spirit that has somehow fought its way into his mind and cast him aside, taking over control. That seems incredibly far-fetched, even to me, and I'm right here inside him.

'Mum . . . If I am actually dead, then do you think that it's possible that I'm somehow possessing this boy's body? You know, like a spiritual takeover of some kind?'

She replies cautiously. 'I don't know what to think, honestly I don't. I've never believed in ghosts – or in heaven or hell – or any of that religious or supernatural claptrap, but it would be nice to think that people go somewhere when they die I suppose.' She pauses, anxious and frowning yet again. 'I really don't know.'

We fall into an uneasy silence as I contemplate this. I'm not quite ready to accept being dead, but deep down I've always suspected that I might be, especially since my visit back to the crash site with Liz.

But I just can't understand being Mark.

If I truly am dead then why have I forced myself into the body of a small boy, and why don't I know why I'm here. Surely if I had been a restless spirit, wandering the earth for nine long years, I should have some idea why I chose Mark to inhabit and what I'm supposed to do with him. I mean, if I can remember everything about being me, why can't I remember what I've been up to over the last nine years?

And what the hell has happened to Mark?

Guilt flows through me like an electric current. Have I, in some way, pushed Mark aside – or even killed him – to take control of his body? It doesn't feel right, or fair, and I don't believe that I could bring myself to do something so callous, even if I had been a spirit, or an undead life-force roaming the world looking for redemption, or salvation, or whatever. Taking someone's life just isn't something I think that I could ever do.

My mother has been watching me intently as these thoughts bounce around inside Mark's head and, as if she's been reading my mind, she reaches out and takes my hand.

'If you're in Mark's body now,' she whispers, 'then I'm sure he's somewhere safe. I'm sure he's okay.'

How can she know that's where I got to? It's spooky, but Mum has always been pretty intuitive and I'm not really all that surprised.

'So what do I do, Mum, what happens now?' I ask. She just looks confused and I suddenly remember the one person who I do think may have the answers. My Dad. He has an opinion on everything and has always been a wealth of knowledge whenever we need obscure questions answered. And I'm excited by the prospect of seeing him again. 'When is Dad getting home, Mum? He'll know what to do.'

But my mother hesitates, obviously unsure of how to respond. She turns her head, but I can still see the tears, once again beginning to well up in her eyes, as she finally speaks.

'He won't be coming home, Nick. He left me too, less than two years ago. I'm sorry, Nick. But your father is dead.'

I feel my heart shatter into little pieces.

SEVENTEEN

My father has always been my rock. He is the cornerstone of the family, the foundation that everything else is built upon. He simply can't be dead, it's almost inconceivable.

I sit impassively, trying to take it in as I read the sorrow and anguish in my mother's eyes.

'How . . . I mean when . . . I mean . . . I . . .'

I can't get the words out. My father can't possibly be gone. Surely not?

'I'm sorry Nick.'

Her voice is barely a whisper and we stare at each other, both lost in our own thoughts. Suddenly other terrible possibilities sweep through my mind and I can hear my voice quivering as I finally manage to speak again.

'There's more you need to tell me, isn't there Mum. What on earth has happened over these last nine years? Are Daniel and Katherine alright, and Sarah? And what about Bobby, has he come back?'

'Just relax,' she says. 'They're all still alive, to the best of my knowledge. Let me pour myself another cup of tea and I'll try to fill you in as best I can. This could take a while.'

I'm desperate with impatience when she finally settles in front of me again, with a fresh cup in her hands, and she begins her tale. She starts right back at the time of the car crash, nine long years ago to her, but only just last week to me. I was killed. I need to accept this somehow, but it's hard. Damn hard. I try not to interrupt as she speaks.

'When the police investigated the accident they told us that your car had been run off the road by a drunk driver, in a stolen car, and that he'd somehow managed to flee the scene. To this day they've never caught him.'

'All we know is that he, or she, left blood at the scene, but oddly enough no fingerprints. And, as the stolen car reeked of alcohol, the police somehow concluded that it had been stolen by some idiot who had been drinking, continued drinking, and then plowed into you by accident. Clearly the other driver was injured in the accident, but apparently not badly enough to have to go to hospital, or they would have caught him there.'

Her tone is unforgiving and it's clear that Mum still isn't happy with the investigation, or the conclusion, and the eventual non-result. And a drunk driver leaving no fingerprints seems very odd to me but, for reasons I can't explain, I don't want to discuss the accident so I try to move her on.

'Don't worry about that for now. Tell me about my family, would you, please. If they're alive, where are they?'

She sighs and starts again. 'Sarah is remarried now, and living in Wilton – not far away.'

This news upsets me deeply.

Sarah and I are very happy together and very rarely fight about anything. Just last week we'd toasted fourteen years of relatively blissful harmony, the last twelve of which as man and wife. We're still very much in love, we both actually enjoy our jobs, and we desperately love our kids, reveling in every aspect of watching them grow up. So, obviously, I don't believe her. Sarah just can't be remarried. How could she? Sure, she's an attractive woman and life goes on. And she's only thirty-three, or would have been when I died. But, come on. Was I really that easy to get over?

I feel hurt and betrayed, only vaguely understanding that it's unreasonable and illogical to think that she should mourn me forever. But, with my old life still so very fresh in my mind it hurts intensely to think of her with another man. I struggle desperately as I try to push these painful feelings aside and concentrate on what I am being told. Nevertheless I'm hopelessly unprepared for what she reveals next.

'You didn't know about the pregnancy then, did you?' she asks.

I don't understand. What pregnancy? With both of our kids already at school we're very happy with our lot. Sarah and I have no plans for another child.

I shake my head slowly.

'This may come as a bit of a shock, Nick,' she pauses briefly, 'but Sarah was pregnant.'

I simply can't respond. If I was stunned before I'm in freefall now. Mum continues. 'Sarah was pregnant, at the time of the car crash. You didn't know did you?'

I finally find my voice, but it's very weak. 'No,' I mutter, lost in my own thoughts.

This news suddenly explains so much. In the last week or so Sarah's moods have been off, and her appetite has changed. Having eaten ravenously throughout her previous two pregnancies I should have known. She'd been polishing off everything before her recently, literally piling the food on her plate. Why didn't I see that? And she'd been a little more secretive than usual. She's always a little mysterious, that's a big part of her charm, but she knew something was up and she had been keeping it from me.

But why? Did she want to surprise me, or wasn't she happy? Had she been considering termination?

I look up at my mother sharply. 'So she had the baby?' I ask. My guts clench in dreadful anticipation.

'Yes, Nick. She had the baby. It was a boy, born about eight months after you died. A beautiful, healthy, baby boy. She named him Nicolas Jackson Davis, after both you and her father.'

I let out a huge sigh. I'd been holding my breath and didn't even realise it. 'Wow. Oh. My. God . . .' I try to let it sink in a bit. 'So I have three children, not two. That's why you asked me the question before.'

She nods and I shake my head a little to try and clear the feelings of confusion, anger and guilt. It doesn't help. I have another son, and I wasn't there for him. Or for Sarah.

But my mother chooses not to let me dwell on this and continues on with her tale. As I listen I struggle on the verge of tears. My poor family, they've been through so much.

'After the accident, especially that first year, was very, very hard on everyone. Sure, your insurance company paid out, so money wasn't an issue, but emotionally – it was awful. Everyday life for everyone that knew and loved you just became a horrible mess.'

'Obviously, the kids were devastated. Daniel spent week after week refusing to come out of his room. He got so withdrawn and sullen. And poor wee Katherine, what can I say, she had the worst possible fifth birthday a child can have and, for months after, would just burst out crying whenever anyone said your name, or even if there was a Daddy in the TV program she was watching. No one was allowed to tuck her in at night but Sarah. Both kids became incredibly clingy, as you'd expect, and that became really, really hard on Sarah as she was struggling with her own grief. And with a baby growing inside her.'

Mum stops, clearly upsetting herself all over again as she revisits this tragic time. I wait, my heart in my throat, until she is able to start talking again.

'So anyway, we all got together, Sarah's parents and ourselves, to try and help in every way we possibly could and somehow we all got through to the birth of Baby Nicky. Sarah's parents even moved into Charles St for a while, but it was too cramped. They stayed almost the baby's entire first year. But they just couldn't keep up, they were getting on, you know, they were much older than your Dad and I. And eventually they moved out again, to a rest home. I think that was just before the baby turned one.'

She pauses, softly adding, 'They're both gone too now, Sarah's dad, Jackson, died about eighteen months later and Peggy only six months after that.'

Hearing this I feel terrible, they were good people. I'd always been proud to call them my in-laws. But I can't dwell on their deaths either as Mum's tale isn't over yet, not by a long shot. She moves on quickly, tearing at my heart with every word.

'So, a few months after they'd moved out, Sarah started to . . . umm, get involved with her future new husband. And this, as I'm sure you'll understand, caused a little friction.'

I can't help thinking that the term "involved" is a fairly quaint one for Mum to use, but she's obviously trying to spare my feelings. I mean, dating only eighteen lousy months after my death, what kind of a grieving period is that? Regardless of Mum's old-fashioned attempt to soften the blow, I'm hurt.

And apparently, so too had my Dad been at the time. Mum sighs deeply and continues.

'Your Dad felt strongly that anything less than five years was far too short a time for any widow to grieve properly, especially for his eldest, and his favourite, son.'

I don't react to this, as I tend to agree about the length of mourning. And sadly there has never been any question of favorites in my fathers' eyes – as he barely ever acknowledged my little brothers' existence. I realise this sounds harsh, but understanding my father – and his ways – isn't necessarily the easiest thing. To be fair my Dad was a difficult man. A straight-shooter who only ever saw things his way, and in absolute black and white. He wasn't always the easiest person to please. But I loved him, regardless.

'So, as you'll understand, this meant that things became strained between us. Your father pretty much created an Us-and-Them scenario and he actually forbade me from having any contact with Sarah and the little ones. It was difficult. I didn't know what to do.'

I can see the pain in her eyes. My mother has always been simply incapable of saying no to my father, so I do understand. She isn't spineless, just very accepting. Sometimes too accepting. And she would do almost anything to keep the peace at home. As she continues on I can't help to notice a small hint of pride in her tone.

'But I couldn't keep away entirely, and I don't see this as a betrayal, but . . . I used to find ways to run into them every now and then. Here and there. Around and about. You know how Sarah has always been very organised and scheduled, well, that made it easier. I knew I could run into them at the supermarket on a Thursday afternoon, and you can almost guarantee that the family will eat a take-away dinner either down by the lake, or in the park, most Sunday evenings, so I started taking walks at that time – and bumping into them. And, for a while, that's how I kept in contact.'

The idea of my mother stalking my family almost makes me smile, but I hold it back and nod to encourage her to keep talking. She looks away as she speaks this time.

'And so I got to meet this new man and get to know him a bit. Their . . . umm, relationship seemed to move slowly at first, but it was only a year later, I'd say somewhere around three years after your death, that they became engaged, and then another year after that – it would have been late 2003 – that they married. Your father and I didn't attend the wedding, but we were invited.'

She pauses, but only to steel herself. I sense something even worse is coming.

'Anyway, it was just after the wedding that I found out about their plans . . . for the children. I ran into Sarah shopping and she told me. Well, I guess she felt we should be aware . . . that they had decided that the children were to be legally adopted by Sarah's new husband – and that the entire family would take his surname. She explained, and it does make some sense to me, that they believed that it would help to bind them as a family. To bring them all together for a new beginning. For a fresh start . . .'

She trails off and finally sneaks a peek at my face, looking to gauge my reaction.

I gaze back blankly, feeling completely flattened. Devastated. But this numbness almost immediately gives way to an angry red mist. How could Sarah do that to me? How is it possible that some other man can just walk into my life and not only take my wife from me, but my children too? *Damn him!*

Damn them both! Not only am I easy enough to forget, but apparently I'm easy to erase as well.

I snap. I just can't take it all in. Standing up with a lurch I stomp around the kitchen slamming doors and punching walls, just lashing out wildly.

Nothing is making sense. I'm dead, supposedly. My father is dead too. And I have another child, and my wife has remarried. Not only that, but she's gone and allowed my children to take another man's name. Surely that's not right. Surely a man's surname on his offspring should be sacred, cast in stone. It shouldn't be possible for that to be taken away.

God damn it!

Mum has to settle me down.

'You're so much like your father,' she says. 'Come here and sit down. This all happened many years ago,' she continues with a firm practicality, 'and there's nothing you can do about it now, so please stop wrecking my home.'

I'm still very angry, but I cave in quickly to embarrassment. Grudgingly I sit. I apologise, hanging my head and sighing deeply. 'So what happened then?' I ask. 'I assume the name change happened. So did Dad find out?'

She opens her mouth to speak, but before she can answer another thought crosses my mind and I interrupt.

'Hang on. You haven't told me who he is yet. Do I know this guy?'

She pauses, carefully searching for the right words. 'I'm not sure, but it is possible.' There is a long pause. 'He was Sarah's boss . . . at the travel agency. When they became . . . an item . . . I believe he owned two or three agencies. And now I understand that he runs a national chain of them.'

My head is spinning, 'What's his name, Mum?'

'I realise you won't want to hear this, but he's actually a good man, Nick. He's been very good to Sarah and he treats those children very well. And I'm certain there was nothing going on before you died. I don't think that Sarah would have done that sort of thing.'

'What's his name?' I repeat, more firmly. She sighs.

'Try and stay calm, Nick. His name is Brett Thompson . . .'

But the name means nothing to me, I don't know him. I don't understand why she's being so cautious. Then her final words send me reeling headfirst into another tailspin.

'. . . he's Mark's uncle.'

EIGHTEEN

My mind just goes blank.

Mark's uncle is married to my wife. I can't get my head around it. Mark has an uncle? Sure, why not? And he's married to my wife, to my Sarah. I'm struggling. It seems such a bizarre coincidence. It's almost impossible to absorb.

Brett Thompson. Have I met him? I don't think so. The name doesn't ring any bells. I can't put a face to it.

But I immediately dislike him. More than that, I despise him. I hate him. He's living my life! Sleeping with my wife! Raising my children! I want to tear his heart out.

My mother murmurs something, but I don't hear it, I'm losing focus again. I close my eyes, trying to control my anger. It's not easy. Only a few short days ago I was a happily married, thirty-something adult, with two lovely children. And now where-the-hell am I? Somehow trapped inside an eight year old child with everything upside down. The frustration is overwhelming. I want to just lash out and hit something, anything. I slam my fist down on the table.

'Nick! Calm down, will you please.'

My mothers' voice is firm and I instinctively regret the display. She deserves better, it's not her fault.

'It's okay. I'm sorry. I'm just so . . . so damn . . .'

'Frustrated?'

'Yes, frustrated. I don't understand. None of this makes any sense.'

'No. You're right. It makes no sense at all.'

We stare at each other in silence for some time and I take a few deep breathes.

'You don't know Brett, do you?' she asks.

I shake my head. 'He's Tracey's older brother,' she tells me. I just nod and shrug. 'They live not far from here,' she continues. 'Just over on Lorneville Drive. The children all go to Wilton Comp, just like you. I'm sorry, I mean, like Mark does.' Suddenly she has my full attention. I nod again, now willing her on. 'And I've seen you, or rather Mark, playing in the park with . . . with young Jack.'

Trepidation hits me like a missile. 'Jack? Who's Jack?'

My mother is watching me intently. She almost looks like she's enjoying this torture.

'He was christened Nicolas Jackson Davis,' she says, '. . . and they called him Nicky, for a few months, but it just didn't stick. Little Katherine would cry and Sarah soon became uncomfortable with it too. So they started using his middle name, calling him Jackson, or Jackie and then eventually it just reduced to plain old Jack. Especially after Sarah married Brett and he became Jackson Thompson, it just sounded wrong.'

I can barely breathe. The realisation that I have already crossed paths with my own child chills me to the bone. Mark's little friend, Jack – is my son. A child I never knew I had. A son that I'd never met, until yesterday.

I somehow manage to nod, but I can't speak.

My mother leans back in her chair and watches me with infinite patience as my thoughts reel, trying to catch up.

I picture the boy in my mind, with his big green eyes and straggly dark hair, and the determined angles of his face. We had been face to face only a short time ago, after our run in with those bullies, but it feels like a life-time ago. He wore braces on his teeth and it hits me that he looks quite a bit like Daniel had at that age, but not the same. Daniel has blue eyes, like mine but without the brown mark, and we'd kept his hair much shorter. Jack has Sarah's green eyes and struck me as significantly less confident, lacking Daniel's strong and forceful nature, but none-the-less they looked fairly similar. Then I recall the day before.

My little Katherine. Oh my God. I've met her too, but didn't know it at the time. I shared warm chips with her and Jack in the park only yesterday, but it had been getting dark and I'd been quite distracted. How could I not have recognised her?

My precious baby girl, Katherine, now called Katie, all grown up, and blossoming into a beautiful young woman. Now I can see it. She looks so much like her mother, except for her nose. That's all my fault, and both Katherine and Jack have it. While the long dark hair and slim figure was Sarah's, there is no escaping that they have both inherited the Davis nose. It isn't a bad nose, just a little on the large side. Good for breathing in your mother's fine cooking smells my Dad used to say.

Mum is still watching me and this time I know what she's thinking.

'Yes,' I tell her, without being asked. 'I met both Jack and Katherine yesterday, just briefly. They were having takeaways over in the park.'

'Of course,' she replies. 'It was Sunday yesterday, wasn't it?' We both smile. Sunday night takeaways have been a Davis family tradition all my life. Sometimes we'd splash out on Chinese or Pizza, but we'd most often remain faithful to good old fish and chips, year after year after year. Sarah must be continuing the tradition.

'I didn't recognize them,' I admit, ashamed at myself.

Mum smiles wryly. 'Be fair on yourself, Nick. Katie's changed a lot in the last nine years. I barely recognised her myself when I last caught up with them . . .' she pauses, shaking her head. 'Well, she's not so little anymore, is she?'

'She must be fourteen now. She looked older,' I concede. Then I remember something from the conversation. About the *big doofus*. 'And Daniel, he must be sitting his drivers' licence test today. My God, how is this possible?'

Mum doesn't answer, how can she? Instead she asks another question. 'But wasn't Sarah there too, and Daniel?'

I'm taken by surprise, but I should have thought of it myself. Sunday dinner is a family event, so where were Daniel and Sarah? Then I remember the couple wandering away in the gloom and realise that it wasn't a couple, but my wife and my grown-up son. Daniel would be seventeen now, practically a man. I can't recall much from the glimpse of them in the gloom, but the man had been big, and tall, easily six foot, probably more. My boy. My little boy is no longer a child. My heart wrenches as I try to picture them both again, but I can't. The image is too vague. It had been too dark. I'm so frustrated.

'I saw them leaving, heading home from the park,' I tell her finally. 'It was dark. I didn't recognise them, any of them.' I slump into depression. Mum doesn't respond. 'I can't turn the clock back here, can I?' I ask.

There is a long pause before she speaks.

'No, I don't think you can. What's done is done, and you can't change the past.'

'But that's not fair,' I hear myself whine.

'I'm sorry, Nick. Sometimes life isn't fair.'

'Damn it Mum, that doesn't help,' I fire off, unfairly. She says nothing. I fume a little more, and then calm myself and apologise. 'I'm sorry, I didn't mean that.'

'I know,' she replies. 'It's a lot to take in, isn't it?' I nod slowly. 'Are you hungry?' she asks and I automatically look over to the kitchen clock and realise that hours have flown by. It's already early afternoon.

'Yes,' I reply. 'I'm actually starving.'

Mum rises and begins pottering around the kitchen as I lose myself in thought, trying to remember everything I talked about with Jack and with Katherine. Trying to push aside the realisation that I'd actually met Brett – the bastard who is now married to my wife. Trying to make sense of everything. But nothing adds up. Suddenly I remember that we have skipped over something very important.

'Mum,' I say hesitantly. 'What happened to Dad?'

Her back is to me as she becomes motionless and I watch her shoulders slump at the question. It's obvious that she is steeling herself as she doesn't immediately answer. Without turning around she eventually responds.

'Later,' she says softly. 'We'll talk about that later.'

I want to push her to discuss it now but her body language is clear. She's not ready yet. I wait as she completes laying out sandwiches for us on the old Formica table and brings over a bowl of fruit. We eat in relative silence. I'm again surprised by how hungry I am, and then again by how quickly I become full. My mother is deep in thought.

I'm startled when she abruptly breaks the silence.

'Earlier,' she says, 'you told me that the man who came to my door is Mark's mothers' boyfriend. Was that true?'

I'm momentarily taken aback. I'd almost forgotten about Steve, and how he had kicked the door in earlier. 'Yes,' I reply. 'His name is Steve. He's a bad bastard.'

She doesn't respond. Instead she rises again and sets about brewing more tea. I decide to let her drive the conversation. Clearly something important is on her mind. Finally she faces me and seems to come to a decision. 'I think we need to talk about this Steve chap,' she says.

'What did he want?'

'It's pretty complicated.'

'I'm sure I can keep up.'

She just nods and goes quiet. After a minute she finally speaks again. 'Perhaps we should go sit in your father's den,' she suggests softly. 'It'll be more comfortable in there and . . . well, so much of what I have to tell you concerns your father and his . . .' she sighs, but with a faint smile on her lips, '. . . and his ways.'

I understand. Dad was always a fairly unique man. "His ways" is one of our more polite ways of describing his endearing eccentricities.

She presents me with a fresh, half-strength coffee and I follow her across the house and into my father's den.

As we pass I notice that on almost every wall, and on most of the available surfaces there are framed family photos. I spot Mark's reflection in the glass of one of myself (wearing my first business suit, I think) as I pass. The faces are nothing alike and it leaves me feeling uneasy.

We enter my father's den. The walls are richly panelled wood, traditional and warm, and there is only one window, but the afternoon sun streaming in through it warms the whole room considerably.

The room is crowded with the vast array of oddities and absurdities my father collected during his lifetime. Amongst my favorite items are an elephant's foot umbrella stand near the door, and a beautifully crafted heavy wrought iron coat stand. I smile at the old mounted wild boar's head that hangs over the mock fireplace. I know Mum hates it but I'm pleased she hasn't taken it down since Dad's death. I also know that Dad hid gold coins inside it once as he never really trusted the banks. I wonder if they're still there.

There is so much more. Like the blown-glass artistic fish sculpture and a beautiful antique grandfather clock. A small collection of cavalry swords stand inside a cabinet beside a leather bound series of traditional fictional works displayed, dusty and proud, in the bookcase beside the fireplace.

I'd been in this room, with my Dad, only a few weeks ago, but this time I feel a sense of real sadness as I enter the shrine to his idiosyncrasies. Behind the desk is the exquisite antique pair of mounted Derringer pistols I gave him for his last birthday. He'd loved them immediately and swelled with pride as I repeated their history, with thanks to a full run-down from the enthusiastic antiquities salesman.

Mum and I sit beside each other in the comfy leather bound chairs that face Dad's big old oak desk. It doesn't strike me as unusual that neither of us even consider taking the seat behind the desk. That will always be Dad's seat.

This room so starkly differs from the strange attic den I visited earlier today. Here there is homeliness, a companionable warmth. That attic was just a room trying too hard to be interesting. My father's den is everything Skinner's attic space was not, without even trying. I love this room.

As we snuggle into the welcoming chairs and I take another long look around the room and my eyes fall upon two pictures of me on the wall beside the desk. In one I am about eighteen, dressed in my first grade rugby gear and grinning broadly. While the other is a closer shot of me holding a newly born baby, Daniel. I'm smiling again but in a very different way. I remember the photo being taken and the enormous amount of pride I felt in that moment.

As always it saddens me to see those pictures, because there are no corresponding ones of my little brother, Bobby, anywhere at all in this room.

I turn back to Mum and our eyes lock. We both know what I am thinking and I shrug.

Finally she begins the tale.

NINETEEN

'You've probably noticed all the new developments along the street here, have you?' she asks, pointing north out the window. I nod. 'Right, well these changes all started quite a while back, late 2005, about three years ago, while your father was still alive.'

'What does this have to do with Steve?' I interrupt.

'Quite a bit young man, quite a bit,' she frowns at me, 'so if you'll let me I'll tell you all about it, all right?'

I clam up, mildly chastised, and let her continue.

'They'd already removed the old block of shops across the road and begun building that big, garish new complex when your Dad and I received our first visit from the developers. It would have been mid-winter, 2006. Initially they were very friendly, bringing small gifts and showing us a big bright artist's impression of how they saw the future of this area. And they had some pretty bold visions, with plans that went well beyond redeveloping the shopping centre. Like building a low-rise apartment complex, along the road, just over there.' She points out the window at the building site directly next door with a sour expression. 'But then they unveiled even bigger plans that would stretch the apartment complex for almost three hundred metres further along the road, including this house.' She jerked her thumb back over her shoulder, gesturing towards the other building site on the other side of our historic old home. 'Well, your Dad simply laughed and showed them the door. We never dreamed they would manage to actually buy and remove the ten other houses that used to be along this stretch of the road. Their plan effectively ran opposite the entire length of Fraser Park. It just seemed crazy.'

My mother is frowning and staring wistfully out the window as she speaks. I still don't understand where this can possibly be leading but I stay quiet, listening attentively.

'But they came back, still positive and friendly, and showed us revised plans that included an offer to provide a new home for us within the new apartment complex. We would have to move further down the street, but they would put us into a brand new three bedroom apartment. It was clear that to complete their vision they would need us to sell them this homestead and the section too. You won't be surprised that your father just sent them packing again. He would never, ever consider selling.'

It didn't surprise me at all. My grandfather built the homestead, and to my father it was more than just our home. It was our family's castle. It was his father's legacy. Before he died, my grandfather had been very clear that it was to be retained within our family for generations to come – and the section next door could only ever be built on to house future generations of the Davis family. The homestead wasn't for sale and it never would be.

My mother continued her tale stoically.

'So anyway, then things got a little nastier. The developers got their lawyers out and they managed to find some way to initiate legal action over some petty little historic compliance issue on the title. You'll understand this better than I ever did, but apparently your Grandfather never got the right permits for adding the garage out back, and the developers decided they could use this to stir up trouble. So they came to us and they offered us more money and they increased the three bedroom apartment to four bedrooms, and even tried to throw in a spa pool. But they went and made hints about this compliance thing. I think to try and use it as a little leverage, but all it did was rile up your father some more. Walter was incensed. He hated to be manipulated and he dug his toes in. He got so angry. There was no way he would ever sell our home to those men.'

I could just imagine it. Dad wasn't the sort of man who ever backed down, or changed his mind, on anything. He'd have despised being threatened. And he and Mum could both be pretty bloody-minded when it comes down to it. Stubbornness is a family trait.

I shake my head slowly in wonder as Mum continues.

'But when the four houses up the road, opposite the new shopping centre, were all demolished, things started getting quite heated. Their lawyers got more heavily involved and the un-permitted garage actually became a big issue. And since it seemed that these developers had their fingers in every pie, including people at the City Council, it came to a head. The Council refused to give us a permit for the garage. So your Dad did what only Walter could possibly have done in these circumstances . . .' she pauses, finally turning to face me. Her eyes are moist as she finishes, '. . . he burned down the garage.'

'He did what?' My father had done many odd things in his time, but this was extreme, even for him.

Mum sighs. 'He sent out invites to the developers and to the City Council and the local papers and he set the garage alight. The local paper came, but the Council people didn't, and the developers watched from their building site up the road. He'd already removed all his valuables, and he splashed petrol around inside, and he warned the Fire Department. So once the photographer from the paper was ready he just tossed in a match and we all stood and watched it burn. It was a horrible thing, and it really weighed heavily on his heart, setting fire to something his father had built for the family.'

Tears roll down her cheeks as she revisits the memories.

'Afterwards the lawyers all had to back off, but your Dad was never quite the same. He'd won a small victory over them, but at quite an emotional price. He insisted on leaving the burned pile of wood right where it was, as some kind of a testament, or symbol, of his resolve. And it hasn't been touched since.'

I let the moment settle for a minute, allowing Mum to gather herself again and then quietly interject. 'Are you sure we're not straying a bit far from the subject of Steve here?'

She hushes me with a determined frown and replies fairly bluntly. 'We're getting there. Hold your horses.'

Patience isn't one of my strengths, but I manage to shut up and she moves on again, seemingly in another direction altogether. Her tone is muted.

'About a week later your father found out, through a friend, about your family's change of surname – you know, from Davis to Thompson – and, hearing this . . . shocking revelation, well it really had an appalling effect on him. You see, I never told him. I just couldn't and, as he had effectively disowned them all when Sarah began dating Brett and consistently refused to visit, well . . . he'd had no idea. I'd kept it a secret . . .'

The remorse in her eyes is heart-rending. But I understand why she tried to keep it from him. He would have been agonised. Family was everything to my father and I had been his prodigal son, the perfect child, the light of his life – so it makes sense that, in his eyes, my Daniel was the future of the Davis family.

Please try and understand, I realise this sounds big-headed, but that's simply how it was for Dad. From the day I was born, when my parents were both still teenagers, I was his shadow, his little mini-me, and he was so proud of absolutely everything I ever did. There isn't a single sporting event, or school prize-giving, or important moment in my life I can remember when Dad wasn't right there, beaming proudly, encouraging me and soaking up my achievements. I wasn't really aware of his overt intensity until my little brother was born, when I was eight.

As we grew up I slowly became aware that Dad almost completely ignored little Bobby. I don't believe it was intentional. He was just so damn wrapped up in me. But by the time I was fifteen, and Bobby was seven, it was obvious to all. And no matter how hard Mum and I tried we just couldn't get Dad to notice Bobby's achievements at all. Physically Bobby grew up looking a lot like me, but he was a very different person, to say the least. He was somewhat shy and quiet. Bookish, you might say, and showed very little interest in sports. While his academic record was actually very good, it just wasn't enough to move him out into the limelight of Dad's world view.

So I can only begin to imagine how Dad's world must have crumpled when I died in that car crash. And how overcome he would subsequently have been to find out that my firstborn son, my Daniel, and both of his other grandchildren had taken another man's surname, the Davis family legacy removed. God only knows how he'd react.

Being heavily consumed by family tradition, and a very demonstrative man, my father would have had to make some kind of grand gesture to clearly express his anger.

'What did he do, when he found out?' I ask Mum carefully, dreading the possibilities. She looks at me for a few seconds, another tear slipping down her cheek.

'He blew his top at first – as you can imagine – he was so incredibly angry.' She pauses and I wait while she gathers herself to continue wretchedly once again.

'I'd never seen him so distraught. But he calmed down after a few days and then he just seemed to give up. It's like he just woke up one day and decided he couldn't be bothered anymore. You wouldn't have recognised him, Nick. He just plain died inside.'

She blows her nose and wipes her face, then continues.

'About a week later he suddenly insisted we go back to the lawyer and he changed his will, and the Family Trust deeds. We cut them off completely. Sarah, Daniel, all of them. He wanted to re-align the Family Trust to go to Robert, which was really where it should have been directed after you'd gone, so I agreed and I signed everything too.'

'You didn't have Bobby included in the Trust before?'

'No,' she replies simply. 'After you died Walter changed the Trust to direct all the family assets to be equally shared between Daniel, Katherine and little Nicky – after we passed. Until then it had been directed solely at you. I know it's wrong, but he always insisted that Robert be excluded, because we . . . well, we don't know where he is.'

She looks forlorn and fresh tears well up in her eyes.

I'm surprised and disappointed that Dad had previously excluded Bobby entirely from any inheritance. It's much harsher than I've ever considered.

'You still haven't heard from Bobby?' I ask carefully. She shakes her head softly. 'Not even now? Not ever?' She shakes her head again. She can't meet me eye.

Bobby left early 1992, about a year after Daniel was born. He'd only recently turned twenty. So if he's never been back then he can't have been at my funeral, or at Dad's.

I'm a little crushed when I realise this, but I understand. Bobby never felt truly wanted here and made his escape from Wilton a long time ago. He'd left a brief note – addressed pointedly to only Mum and I – and just disappeared quietly one weekend. We've never even received a postcard from him since. It's such a shame. He was a good kid and, even though there was a big age difference between us, we had been pretty close before he disappeared. I still miss my little brother and love him very much regardless.

Mum fights back tears and charges on. 'But we changed it all again, after your father found out about the full adoption and name change. It still wasn't right, but it was better than we'd had it before, so I agreed.'

She looks at me, ashamed of herself, imploring me for forgiveness. 'I thought I could work on him for a while and have it changed again later to include a share for the children also, because they shouldn't miss out because of something they couldn't control.'

She conjures up a hanky and wipes her eyes, going quiet for a spell. 'So what happened next?' I ask, breaking the silence.

Again she just looks at me, struggling desperately to put her thoughts into words.

'He just gave up. Simply and quietly, sitting in his favorite chair out there in the lounge,' she takes a deep breath, pauses, and then continues slowly. 'It was only a few days later. We'd had another visit from the developer's lawyer that afternoon and he had argued with the man out on the verandah. He wouldn't tell me what they argued about. He just went to his chair and sat down and stared out the window. He wouldn't talk to me, didn't eat his dinner, and so I left him there. You know how he could be . . .'

She's really struggling now, and sniffs back her tears, sighing deeply again.

'In the morning I found him there. He didn't look like he'd moved, and he was cold. His eyes were closed and it seemed like his heart had just stopped beating sometime in the night. When I found out later that the developers had told him they'd found a way to force us to sell, I understood a little more.'

She stops again, barely able to find the words.

'How do you mean?' I ask, dreading what I might hear.

'You need to understand, Nick. He'd lost you, and through his own stubbornness he'd lost Bobby and he'd lost his grandchildren too, and he thought he was going to lose the family homestead as well . . .'

She is crying now. Just sobbing softly and I lean across and hug her and try to comfort her. But I need to know. I need her to tell me how he died.

'What happened, Mum? Was it a heart attack?'

'It was my fault. I'd been having trouble sleeping . . .'

'What do you mean?'

'They would never have been in the house if I'd just been stronger . . .'

'In the house . . . who? What?'

'Don't blame him, Nick. He just couldn't see it any differently . . .'

'What are you saying, Mum? What did he do?'

'The doctor gave me some sleeping pills, but I hardly ever used any of them . . .'

And then I finally understand.

'He died of a broken heart, Nick. You have to think of it like that. He'd lost so much, and he was such a proud man. He just . . . just . . .'

And then neither of us can speak anymore so we just hug and she sobs. I'm overwhelmed with denial. He was such a strong man, so very righteous. How could my father have overdosed on sleeping pills, taken his own life? I don't understand it at all. My mind wanders away, running over all the times he was there for me, replaying all the good memories of my youth, of my entire life. He was my rock. He was always there for me, why couldn't I have been there for him?

I become numb. What feels like hours later I have to rouse myself as Mum finally recovers her composure and seems ready to carry on. But I find it hard to concentrate.

She haltingly explains that they buried Dad out at Five Rivers Cemetery. His grave right alongside my own, a few days after. Sarah and my kids were there, with Brett, and all of Mum and Dad's friends. But not Bobby. They had no way of contacting him.

Then she looks at me intently, her eyes become fierce and determined. 'And so, after all of that,' she says, 'this is where Tracey's boyfriend Steve finally makes it back onto the stage.'

Once again I don't understand, but a sick feeling of dread begins gnawing in my stomach.

'This man, Steve. He told me that he is now representing the developers. This morning was his first visit, but he's promised to drop by again tomorrow evening.'

TWENTY

'I told you we'd get there, didn't I?' she murmurs.

I'm dumbstruck at first, but suddenly find a million questions that I need her to answer immediately. As I open my mouth she abruptly raises a hand to stop me from responding. I'm desperately frustrated, but it's clear that she is determined to tell it her own way, in her own time. I gesture silently, but meaningfully, that she should get to the point. She slips back into her tale.

'For the last eighteen months, since your father passed away, the developers have tried to get me to sell up and move on, and they actually almost succeeded. Obviously I was very upset and, for about six months after, I just refused to talk with them. So, after they'd knocked down all the houses they'd managed to buy up along the road, the developments around here have ground slowly to a standstill.'

She is staring out the window again, speaking in a flat and somber tone.

'To this day I don't know what it was they said to your father but it seems more and more likely that it was nothing more than a big bluff. You know; just some kind of wicked lie, to try and force us into selling up. Once they started visiting again they wouldn't tell me – but they clearly had no legal grounds to force the sale. I spent the following six months politely listening to them and then saying I would think about it. But I didn't think about it at all, I just wanted to annoy them. I wasn't going to sell, not then.'

She turns back to me, her manner sharpens.

'Then odd things started happening. My windows would get broken in the night by someone throwing stones. And then there was a fire. My beautiful car – you remember my Spitfire – it went up in flames, right out there in the driveway. That was heart-breaking too. These people, they've been quite relentless.'

How could I forget Mum's lovingly maintained little yellow convertible? It was a Triumph Spitfire, a classic car from the 70's. No one else was ever allowed to drive it.

A gnawing feeling begins in my stomach as I listen, becoming horrified by my mother's story. In my job at the City Council I saw plenty of evidence of property developers pushing the envelope here and there, but I've never known any that would actually go to the lengths Mum is describing now. Her mood darkens again.

'And the police. They make me so angry. They've been useless, utterly useless. You know they haven't been able to connect anything at all from these things to the developers. Not a thing. So anyway, I had the windows repaired at first, but it just keeps happening so I've given up and now just get them boarded over. It's such a nuisance. And, of course, I had to get a new car. It's nothing exciting, but I have to admit it's actually much easier to drive.'

'And it's red. What's with that?'

Dad hated red cars – just one of his many things – and I'm surprised she'd chosen this colour. She just shrugs at my question with an unreadable expression, and then continues on as if I hadn't spoken.

'I knew it was the developers, but just couldn't prove it, they left no evidence. And they kept on visiting, making new offers, even more generous than before. They were starting to wear me down so I went to Don Jamieson, our family lawyer, to get some advice about actually selling up and moving away.'

I feel myself frown unreasonably. Instinctively I hate the thought of the old family home being sold, but reluctantly I can see the sense of this decision.

'But I can't do it, Nick,' she says.

I try to comfort her. 'I'm sure Dad would understand Mum, I can see why you'd sell.'

'No, you don't understand. It's not that I can't bring myself to sell. It's that I can't. Legally I just can't. Because of the Family Trust.'

'What . . . why not?'

I know that the Family Trust is something my Grandfather set up when he first built this house to ensure it would be kept safe and sound through any future financial crisis. The properties ownership sits in a Trust, which means that the house doesn't actually belong to any individual, but to the Trust – which is legally required to be administered by at least two people who, traditionally, must be members of the Davis family. The Trust stops any one person from selling the house, or using the house as security for a dodgy business venture, and also protects it for the family legally from bankruptcy.

'Surely the Trust passed to you, and the executor of Dad's will, didn't it? I ask.

'Well, yes, it did. But there was a second family member named too. Remember that your father added Robert to the Trust when we changed the deeds around last. I didn't think twice about it then, as it was the right thing to do. But Robert's not here and, without his consent, and without his signature, this house cannot be sold. No matter what.'

I have to smile a little inside. If Dad was looking down on us he'd be laughing now. He would have hated to see the house sold off, end of story.

But then Steve's involvement creeps back up on me and I suddenly feel very anxious. The gnawing in my stomach tightens. 'Steve's come along now,' I say, 'and he's threatening you, isn't he? Oh my God, what did he say? What's he going to do if you won't sell?'

The look on her face chills me to the bone.

Whatever it is has her deeply worried. Dozens of unsettling images run through my mind. This is a man who has actually run a small boy off the road with his car, just to retrieve a video from a cell-phone. And he'd physically threatened that boy – me – afterwards. Not to mention the way he's been tormenting me with his control over Tracey since then. This man has Liz absolutely terrified, enough to drive her to double bolt her bedroom door, and now he's making threats against my sixty-something year old mother.

I ask her again, more firmly this time. 'What did he want, Mum? This guy is bad news. What did he say?'

She doesn't reply. She looks down anxiously and, trembling a little, pulls a folded piece of paper out of her pocket. I recognise it. Steve had thrown it at her through the battered front door this morning. She hands it slowly across to me. There are no words, just a printed image. A photo, not perfect, but clear enough for its purpose.

It shows two children.

It shows a small boy on a bike talking to a teenage girl on the side of the road. This time I recognise them instantly. My stomach knots and I feel the colour drain from my face. The two children are Jack and Katie.

I look up from the image to my mother's face. She's crying again.

Everything comes crashing down around me. Mum doesn't need to speak. The meaning of the image is obvious. I feel physically sick. Steve is threatening to harm my children if Mum doesn't sign the papers to sell the house.

And she can't do it.

I become frantic, and angry, and very, very frustrated.

'What did he say, Mum? What did he say?' I blurt out. 'We have to do something. We can't let him hurt the kids. We need to tell the police. We need to do something.'

Tears are flowing as it all comes streaming out in a rush.

'I know, I know. But it's just so awful. He said that he would hurt them if I didn't sign, but that if I tried to bring in the police he'd kill them. Do you hear me, Nick. If I involve the police he said he would kill them. I don't know what to do. I mean I can sign the document, but that won't fix anything because they'll find out about the Trust, and about Robert. And God knows what they'll do then. They won't believe me. They'll think I'm stalling again, and that horrible man said he would do something to one of the children, and it'll be my fault. It will be my fault and I can't have that, I just couldn't live with that.'

She is sobbing hysterically, tears just streaming down her face. None of this is her fault, but she can't see that. But I don't know what to do either. My mind races as I think of Steve, pursuing one of my children. I imagine him running little Jack off his bike, or abducting Katie and doing God only knows what to her. My heart nearly explodes at this thought and I have to hold back the bile from the back of my throat. A confused rushing sound in my head joins the sickened lurching of my stomach. I start mumbling. 'It's okay, it's okay. We'll work it out. It's okay, it's okay . . .' But my mind is spinning into overdrive. I vaguely understand why she didn't wanted to tell me this earlier, but the realisation of her efforts to spare my feelings doesn't ease my pain now. Damn, damn, damn. The rushing feeling in my head is drowning me, screaming at me to think, to think, think, think! There must be a solution. There has to be a way to fix this.

I try to calm myself and think it out logically, but it's hard. Damn hard. I immediately feel sure that going to the police with only this image as evidence isn't going to be enough. I remember that Steve had been wearing gloves this morning so his fingerprints won't be on it, and I remember that I don't even know Steve's last name. Christ, I don't even know if Steve is really his first name.

But we simply have to get the police involved. I can't see any other choice. There is no way an eight year old boy and a senior citizen can deal with a man like this. Yet we need something more to convince them that he is actually making threats. It would be too easily for him to simply deny all knowledge of both the visit and the picture, and we can't link him to either without proof – like fingerprints.

I look again at the image in my hand. Jack, sitting on his bike, saying something to Katie as she frowns at him. The angle of the photo has caught her slim, but feminine figure. I feel a burning rage ignite inside me as I imagine Steve taking her, and locking her away somewhere. Hurting her, physically . . . and mentally. Or possibly even sexually.

'God, damn it. No!' I shout with all my pent up rage. I slam my fist down onto the armrest of the leather chair. There has to be something we can do.

'When is he coming back, Mum?' I ask. She's still sobbing softly and I feel a stab of horror. She looks so old all of a sudden. Her face is grey with despair. I reach out to her, trying to offer comfort when I feel none myself. We're a wretched pair.

'Tomorrow,' she replies, her voice barely a whisper. 'He said he'd come back tomorrow evening. He didn't say what time exactly.'

'Then we have some time, we can–', I cut myself off abruptly as an idea explodes into my mind. 'We can take a video of him,' I hear myself say. Then I become excited. 'Yes, we need proof, and we know he's coming back, we can take a video of him.'

My mother is staring at me, desperately confused. I try to explain. 'When he comes to the door, we can video him as he's threatening you again. We can take the video to the police. They'd have to do something about it. It's proof.'

She's shaking her head, unsure. 'But, how?' she asks.

'Easy. On a cell-phone. Have you got one?'

'A cell-phone? Why on earth would I want a cell-phone?'

'So you don't have one then?'

'No. I've never seen the need. They're so intrusive.'

'Okay, then we need to get one. And to get organised, and be ready for him.'

'I'm not sure. What if it doesn't work'

'But it has to. I can hide somewhere just inside maybe–'

'I don't know, Nick. It sounds dangerous.'

'No, it doesn't need to be. We have time to plan it out. We can– '

'Let's just give this some more thought, shall we? It doesn't feel right to me.'

'But Mum, it's a– '

'It's getting late. I think we should take a little time out, think this through.'

'What?'

'I think we both need to sleep on this, Nick. I'm just so very, very confused right now. And you being here, like this, well it's been an awfully wonderful fright. But I really don't think I'm up to talking about this any more, not right now, not tonight. I need to think . . .'

I start to push on, 'But Mum, this guy is a grade-A nutcase and he's threatening my kids . . .'

But her expression tells me clearly that there will be no more discussion about this right now. My mother can be like a rock when she decides on something, and her mind is obviously made up. She's looking away again, out the window. The sun is getting low in the sky. When she speaks her voice is softer and sadder somehow.

'You know you've been here all day. Mark's mother will be getting worried about you.'

Worried? No, sadly I can't imagine that. But annoyed or downright furious, that's quite likely. I don't answer her and just shrug. But then I think of Liz, who probably will be worried. I look out at the late afternoon sun and I'm hopelessly torn. I really don't want to go back to the unit, not now, not ever. I feel at home now, right here. There's nothing I need or want back at the unit. But there is Liz, and I start to feel guilty.

'Look, how about I run over and show my face and then come back. There's still so much we need to discuss.'

'I'm really not sure that's a good idea,' my mother replies. 'I'm sure Tracey won't allow it and I don't want you getting in trouble, and I'm actually very tired. It's been a horribly long day, and we both have so much to think about already. And I think I need to make a call to Don Jamieson again, before he goes home for the evening.' She pauses, 'I think you should go home. Take Mark back to his mother.'

I start to protest and then stop myself. I don't want to burden her with how crappy Mark's family life is and – to be fair – my mind is also spinning with far too much information.

And we do have time. Steve isn't coming back for another twenty-four hours. And Mum looks drained, there is very little colour in her and it's clear that the days events have taken their toll. Maybe some time to process all this and work out a really good plan might be for the best.

'I'll come back and see you first thing tomorrow then, okay? We can work it all out then. Make a plan. We can fix this thing, I know we can.'

She nods, grateful that I'm letting go for today, to allow her to recuperate.

'You need to run along now,' she says. 'Before it gets dark. And you go straight back to your home, you understand. I don't want you running around out there after dark. There are a lot of strange people around these days.'

I have to smile. She used to say almost exactly the same thing to Bobby and me when we were kids. I'm still torn, but as a child I was well trained not to argue with this woman. Some things are ingrained, I guess. Every son should know when it is time to stop trying to debate certain things with his mother, so I comply.

We hug long and hard before I go. My mind spins ferociously with all the news. As I leave I hesitate quite a few times, wanting to go back but forcing myself to move forward instead, and I finally trudge down the drive and back across the park.

Sarah is remarried. Dad is dead. I have a third child. Nine years have really passed me by and a psychotic man is threatening to harm my children. How has this happened?

The unit is unlocked when I arrive, but there is no sign of the hatchback. I hear the phone ringing as I step through the door, and hear Liz answer it.

She turns and frowns at me as I enter, but maintains a brief conversation on the phone. Her responses are short and terse and when she hangs up she snaps at me.

'Where the hell have you been? I get home and there's no one here, there's no note, and your school bag's lying around outside. What's going on?'

'Who was on the phone?' I ask.

'Don't try and change the subject, what's been happening?'

I haven't thought at all about what to tell Liz as I walked back across the park. I was too self-absorbed. I wonder if she knows about the fight I had this morning, and I wonder where Tracey is. I suddenly recall that I was supposed to be going to the hospital with Tracey. Did Liz know I hadn't gone? Desperately I try to make up a potentially believable story, but I can't think quickly enough and fail miserably.

'Nothing much has been happening. Tracey dropped me back here earlier, and then she went to the pub. So I –'

'Then why was your bag outside?'

'She didn't leave me a key, so I couldn't get in.'

'Rubbish. Mum wouldn't drop you off and lock you out. And anyway, why wouldn't you use the key in the tree?'

'The key in the . . . what?'

'The key we have hidden in the tree out there,' she says angrily, pointing outside. 'The key that's always been hidden out there for emergencies.'

'Oh,' I feel stupid. Of course there's a hidden key. There's always a hidden key. 'I forgot . . .'

She frowns, shaking her head. 'And then?' she demands.

This isn't going well. 'And, so . . . I went to the park and I've been hanging out over there. I didn't want to come home in case Tracey came back with Steve.'

'You're lying. I looked all around the park for you. Where were you?'

Liz is really upset, and I feel terrible.

'I'm sorry, Liz. I was wandering around a bit. I may have been up near the shops when you came looking. I didn't see you. Please don't be angry.'

But it's obviously too late for that, she's already fuming. She waves a finger at me and starts to shout fiercely.

'Don't tell me not to get angry. You might remember that the last time you disappeared we got a phone call from the police, because you'd been found half dead in a ditch. I think I'm allowed to get a little angry.'

I suddenly feel immense pride for her. Her passion is truly magnificent. She is only fifteen, coping with stresses that no child should have to bear, and her zeal for the safety and well-being of her little brother overwhelms me.

I walk over and hug her. 'I'm sorry, Liz. Thank you for caring,' I mumble into her chest.

It works. I can feel the anger drain out of her. In no time at all the tension is gone and she hugs me back, then she pushes me away both roughly and playfully.

'You dick . . .' she mutters.

I change the subject quickly. 'So who was that on the phone?' I ask.

She takes a deep breath. It's clear she isn't really satisfied with my telling off, but her shoulders slump and she lets it go, for now. Then she sighs heavily.

'That was Brett. He's on his way to pick up Mum from the pub. She passed out . . . again.'

I can't think of an adequate response.

TWENTY-ONE

Liz is in the kitchen preparing dinner when we hear the old hatchback coming up the driveway. I stay sitting on the couch as she goes and opens the door wide, then does the same with the hall door and Tracey's bedroom door, finally stepping away and leaving them all open as in a practised routine. Less than a minute later the man I met briefly in the park yesterday – Jack's step-father, Brett Thompson – comes through the front door with Tracey slumped in an unflattering fireman's lift over his left shoulder. He slips quietly through to the bedroom, quickly emerging without her.

He can't make eye contact with us and we all stay in silence for what seems like a very long time.

'She'll be fine in the morning,' he finally says. 'A good night's sleep will work wonders on her.' He pauses. 'Are you guys alright for dinner?'

'It's under control,' replies Liz.

There is another long awkward silence. I can't help but stare coldly at this man as I see him now in the light of day. He's around six foot and balding, but would have been relatively handsome a few years back. He looks like a lawyer or a stockbroker, comfortable in a business suit.

I'm not sure what we are waiting for him to say or do, but I'm suddenly bubbling with anger inside.

This man is married to my wife. And he erased the Davis surname from my family. Mum had told me earlier that he's a good man, and I try to keep that in mind, but seeing him here now, looking embarrassed and uncomfortable – and knowing who he is – my raw feelings start to quiver with fury.

'Right. Well then,' he mutters uneasily, looking at the floor. 'I guess I'll leave you to it then,' and he starts to move towards the door. Liz doesn't move, or speak.

I'm surprised that he is leaving so quickly, and I find myself overcome with resentment. This is the man who has been sleeping with my wife for the last six or seven years. I see red. I want to knock his block off.

'Hang on,' I cry out as I stand up. 'That's it then? You're just going to dump her and leave? You're just going to go home to your perfect family and pretend this isn't happening? You're going to do nothing?' I'm almost shouting.

He stops in his tracks, and I feel a guilty pleasure from the look of anguish on his face.

'Now look here, Mark,' he says. 'I think you've said and done enough already today, don't you?' His tone is moderate, but there is bitterness just beneath the surface.

'Oh great, so you think this is my fault do you?' I snarl at him. 'You think it's my fault that she drinks herself blind every god-damn day.'

He hangs his head, and then looks up at me. 'No, Mark. That's not your fault. But your actions today haven't helped.'

'Maybe not, Brett. But have you done anything recently to help her? She's your damn sister – and she's screaming out for help. Surely you can see that, or don't you care?'

I'm being unreasonable, I know it, but I'm angry. I just want to find some way to hurt this man. I want to wound him in any way I can for taking my family from me. I want to just step up and punch him and tell him to keep his filthy hands off my wife. It's completely irrational, but as my mother had recently reminded me, life isn't fair.

His response is far too rational for my liking.

'I can see you're upset, Mark. But please try and understand that we're all trying to help your mother. We're doing everything we can.'

Before I can respond Liz suddenly pipes up. 'What do you mean by Mark's actions today? What's he done?'

I cringe. Damn it. Liz doesn't know about the fight.

Brett fills her in. 'He assaulted another student this morning, before school. He broke his nose. The boy's family are, quite rightly, very unhappy. Mark's been suspended. I got a call from the principal's office after, umm . . . after Tracey visited the school this morning and said a few things I think she will regret when she, well . . . when she wakes up tomorrow.'

'He's been suspended?' Liz asks in disbelief.

I try to deflect their attention back to Tracey. Storming past the couch I stand directly in front of Brett, angrily yelling at the top of my voice. 'But what are you doing to help Mum? Have you done anything other than just scrape her up from the pub and dump her into her bed at home. That's not helping, that's just cleaning up an inconvenient mess.' I start poking him in the ribs, still shouting, 'What about getting her into rehab, taking her to the AA, or just tying her up and making her go cold turkey? Have you done any of that? Well, have you? Or are you just too bloody busy playing house with your new family? With your other perfect bloody family, you bastard.'

I'm getting way off track, but I struggle to focus. Leaning forward I shove him as hard as I can, two handed in the lower chest and actually force him back against the wall.

I shout at him some more. 'So what the hell does she have to do before you step in and actually help her? Slit her bloody wrists? Would that get your attention?'

I suddenly step back, heart racing and chest heaving at the exertion. Brett stares at me, completely stunned at both my verbal and physical outburst. Totally lost for words.

I glance over my shoulder and see a similar vision of disbelief on Liz's face.

'Fuck it,' I curse to myself quietly, turning away from him and drop back onto the couch. I'm all shouted out, and the outburst hasn't made me feel any better at all. I know that none of this is Brett's fault, but I'm damned if I'm going to apologise to him, for anything, ever.

Nobody speaks or moves for what seems an eternity until Liz asks, 'So Mark is actually suspended from school then?'

The room is quiet again. I say nothing.

'Yes,' Brett finally replies. 'The boy in question, that Mark assaulted, was Gordon Breckenock.'

'You're kidding. Oh . . .' Liz trails off.

'I wish I was.'

For a few seconds the name means nothing to me but then it hits home with a jolt. Breckenock, the beefy git was a Breckenock. Oh Shit. That bloody family probably owns more than half of Hawthorne. Even the lake is named after them. No wonder Brett had been dancing around trying to sort out the bullying and theft of Jack's lunch money. The Breckenock's are a powerful family.

'For how long?' Liz asks.

'At least until next week. The boy's father is overseas until this weekend. There's nothing we can really do until he returns and we can discuss the matter.'

Liz just nods. I think I've said enough for this evening so I have nothing to add. Brett looks at the floor again. I can hear the kitchen clock ticking, it's so quiet.

'I should probably go then,' Brett eventually mumbles. He shuffles on his feet and almost reaches the door when Liz breaks the silence again.

'Is there any way you could help to get her into, you know, rehab, or something?'

The question hangs in the air, like a bad smell that no one wants to acknowledge. After a short while Brett takes a deep breath and turns back to face us.

'Guys, I am so, so sorry this is happening, but it's just not that easy.' He holds out a hand to stop me from leaping up in response. 'Yes, your mother is an alcoholic, we all know that. But I can only help her if she'll let me. And you need to believe me when I tell you . . . I'm trying.' His eyes are tinged with distress. He takes another deep breath then continues. 'We don't talk about it when you're around, so I understand if you think I'm not doing anything, but I am trying to help her. The thing is . . . she needs to want to help herself, before anything I can offer will make any difference . . . but we're not quite there.'

There is another long, almost deathly, silence. It's so quiet I can hear Tracey's heavy breathing from her bedroom.

'I'm sorry,' he apologises again. 'I do care, and I really am trying to help.'

His expression is grim and sad as he drifts out the door without a goodbye, and without saying anything more. The bastard. He does seem to care, and it's possible he actually might just be a good man. Damn him.

Things would be so much easier to stomach if he was a complete asshole.

In the morning, as I stumble sleepily up the short hallway, Tracey's room is closed up tight. It's unlikely she will emerge before noon. Liz didn't wake me – as I'm not going to school today – and is just about to leave.

'Morning, lazybones,' she says. 'Planning anything educational today?'

'Possibly,' I reply. 'I'm not sure.' I haven't woken up fully yet and don't have a snappy rejoinder ready.

'Well, get your act together and find us that video, okay?'

'Ahh . . . yep. Yes, I will,' I lie, not very smoothly.

'Right, then try and keep out of trouble today. I think you did enough yesterday to last us all for a while.'

'Okay, I promise, no trouble today.'

'And if you go out, remember the key in the tree.'

'Oh, right . . . umm . . . which tree is it again?'

She tips her head to one side and raises an eyebrow significantly, then leads me outside.

'Over there, you loser,' she says, pointing towards a low branch in the big tree at the end of the driveway. I go over and investigate. There is a semi-rusted key hanging on a small nail. I turn to smile and give her the thumbs up, but she's already shuffling away, meandering off to another dreary day at school.

As I make my way back inside I turn and stare at the tree, suddenly realising that it's the same one that Steve backed me up against when I first had the dubious pleasure of meeting him. A shiver passes through me as I remember the moment vividly. Steve had been furious, holding me belligerently. Trying to choke the life out of me. It makes me wonder what he would have done if Liz hadn't interrupted. I try to shake it off, but something about the memory nags at me.

Why was he so angry? Was it really because he thought that Mark might expose his infidelity to Tracey? Would exposing *that* really upset him so much?

I stare at the tree, trying to make sense of it. There must have been more to it. I simply can't believe that Steve would be so annoyed at the possibility of upsetting Tracey. The longer I think about it the clearer it starts to become.

Liz had told me, from Mark's insistence before the accident, that there was something on Mark's video that would upset Tracey, enough to make her dump Steve. But that just doesn't wash. There is no way that Steve cares enough, if at all, about Tracey's feelings to have run Mark over to destroy that video just to be with her. There has to be something else to it. Something else must be captured on the video that Steve doesn't want anyone to see. Something that's important. Something that *really* bothers him.

I slept fitfully last night, worrying about the situation with my mother, and the old homestead, and my kids. And my mind is whirling again now. I have an idea. Maybe there is something else that Mum and I can do. An alternative to lying in wait for Steve later this afternoon. I don't know if it will actually work, but it may help.

And we have to do something.

Leaving the key in the tree where it is I rush back inside to dress and grab a quick breakfast. Around fifteen minutes later I'm ready to go.

I leave Tracey snoring quietly in her room once again.

A few hours later my mother and I are sitting in her shiny little red sedan, parked on Lorneville Drive, just around the corner from Mark's cul-de-sac.

'You understand what you need to do, Mum?' I ask.

She sits nervously in the driver's seat, holding a brand new cell-phone in her hand, shaking her head in disbelief.

'I think so,' she says, still shaking her head – which doesn't fill me with confidence. 'But you might want to just run over it one more time.'

I respond a little irritably. 'Okay, but only once more because we're running out of time. We don't even know if he's home.'

'I really don't know if I like this.'

'I know you don't, but it has to be done. I'm going in, and I'll be out again within twenty minutes, otherwise you know what to do, don't you.'

'I push this button and I call the police.'

'That's right, and you know what to say?'

'Yes, I think so.'

'Okay, then I'm going to go now. Are you ready with your stopwatch?'

'I push this button, right?'

'Yes, that's the one. Are you ready?'

She finally nods and I step out of the car. I hold my wrist up to her window and we both push the buttons on the countdown timers of our new wristwatches. We've been shopping.

Turning away I walk briskly towards my task. As I make my way down the short driveway and see the house again, my heart starts beating more rapidly. I suck in a big breath and approach the front door, ring the bell and then wait.

I look down at my watch, just over nineteen minutes to go until Mum calls the police. There's no answer. I don't know what we'll do if he's not at home.

I ring the bell again, nervous and practically trembling in anticipation. We'd been so busy planning this that I haven't really had a chance to work out what I'm going to say. But there is still no answer. Part of me is a little relieved, but as I reach up to press the bell again, the door clicks and starts to open.

Oh shit. Here we go.

'Mark,' he is taken aback. 'Well hey, what a surprise.'

'Hi there,' I say, smiling at the old man who still looks remarkably like Skinner from the X-Files. 'How are you?'

'I'm fine and well, thank you,' he replies opening the door wider. He steps outside to look out at the street over my head. 'It's nice to see you, Mark.' He's still looking beyond me. 'But shouldn't you be at school right now?'

'I pulled a sickie again. You know – sore head.' I brush my hair up to reveal the slowly healing gash on my forehead once more. 'But Mum's gone to the pub, and Liz is at school, so I thought I'd come and see that video. May I come in?'

He pauses, and then offers me a conspiratorial, and somewhat relieved, smile. 'Very smooth, my man. Okay, since you're here, and I've got nothing else on – why not.'

With my heart pounding in my chest I step through the door. I'm hoping that he won't lock it behind me, but he does, dropping the key into his right hip pocket.

Seventeen minutes until Mum makes the call.

Fortunately Skinner doesn't muck about and leads us directly to the attic door. And he's up the stairs, flicking on the lights as he passes, before I even start to move. There's no sign of the little dog, or of any other human beings.

Once again he leaves the attic door wide open, which I'm pleased about, and I slowly make my way inside and up the stairs. He's already seated in front of the computer and he taps on the stool beside him as I enter the room.

'Take a load off, Dude. Lets check out what you got,' he calls out. His mood is oddly buoyant and he's quickly slipped into stoner talk again. When he opened his door he'd been almost formal, talking like the adult he is. I try not to cringe.

The scene is almost exactly as it had been when I'd hurriedly left him just yesterday morning. A flutter of nervousness runs through me. I'm possibly being a bit naive, but I'm still confused about this old guy, and his motivation for keeping company with an eight year old, but he seems genuinely pleased to see Mark and I don't feel overly threatened. And this time I have back-up. Still, I'm not sure what to make of him.

I can see the computer is warming up, running through its start-up sequence. Although more relaxed this time I really don't want to get too close until I have to, so I move towards the fridge and help myself to a Coke again and lean against the pinball machine. Bright light from the spot-lights gleam off its chrome trimmings. Opening the Coke I wait impatiently as the computer screen ticks over. It seems to take forever.

'Would you like a drink?' I ask politely.

'Why not,' he replies brightly. 'Whatever you're having would be good, thanks.'

I take my time, waiting for the start-up sequence to complete and for him to launch his video viewing program. I check my watch as I move over and sit down on the second stool, passing over an unopened can from the fridge.

Fifteen minutes to go.

'Now,' he mutters quietly to himself. 'If I can just find the right one.'

On the screen he is clicking away through system files to find his video images. He opens a file simply called 'My Images' and reveals half a dozen sub-folders. Each one is a boy's name and my heart nearly stops in my chest. I watch as he clicks on the one called 'Mark' but before the screen changes I spot one a few folders above called 'Jack'.

The series of names on the files has thrown me and I hear myself exclaim softly, 'Oh, fuck!' He looks up, surprised, raising his eyebrows quizzically.

'Good luck,' I blurt. 'You know, finding the right one.'

He blinks at me. Half smiles, and then turns back and starts visually scanning through the files in the folder. My heart sinks. There are dozens of files and they seem to be set up with some kind of code, but he seems to know what he's looking for. I feel sure he'll find the right one, although I'm deeply troubled by how many files there are. Mark must have visited fairly often. And who are the other boys who have folders in his system? My stomach sours as I contemplate the possibilities.

'Here it is, this one,' he says in triumph. As he double-clicks it to open I quickly memorise the code. It seems to be a date, backwards, with 'MMA' added. Easy to remember.

The monitor flickers as the video image starts up and takes over most of the screen. It's a moving shot of the carpark at the pub, taken from the roadside, showing a big metallic blue SUV pulling into a parking space. Steve's car. We can hear traffic noises, and Mark breathing heavily. Mark must have been on his bike while he was taking it as the image suddenly shoots down to give us a view of moving footpath, and then leaps back up so we can see a man emerging from the car. The man is Steve. Then it ends.

'Oh, Dude,' Skinner says. 'That wasn't so cool, was it?'

I'm dumbfounded. 'No,' I concede. It's all I can say.

Is that it? After all this effort and all of Mark's suffering. The video turns out to be less than ten seconds of nothing. I'm bitterly, bitterly disappointed.

'Hmm,' he murmurs. 'Well, shall we kick up the other one?'

'There's another one?' I ask, too quickly, too excited. My heart begins racing again.

'Yeah, there were two on Friday.' His tone softens. 'You really don't remember coming here that day, do you?'

'No, I'm sorry, I don't. I was hoping the video would jog my memory, you know.'

'Its okay, it's cool. Let's see what's on the other one.'

I check my watch. Twelve minutes left.

TWENTY-TWO

Skinner closes the completed video and starts searching through the files again. This time I see it first but hold off in case I'm wrong. There is a second file with the same string of numbers, the same date backwards, but this one ends in 'MMB'. He must simply label multiple daily ones A, B, C and so on; I can now see the pattern amongst the files.

'Here we go, let's try this one,' he says as he double-clicks the one I'd just been looking at with MMB on the end.

Once again the monitor flickers and the new video takes over the screen. We immediately hear voices, quite clearly men talking in deep tones, and the screen is filled with a view of Steve and another man, leaning against the rear of Steve's SUV. Steve is closer, and the other man is older than him, with longer black hair, greying at the fringes and neatly slicked backwards. He's also a big man, fairly solidly built, just like Steve, but not quite as bearish and wears what looks like a fairly expensive suit and tie. There is a vague family resemblance, in the way they stand and the shape of their faces, and I immediately think of him as Steve's big brother. I'm also struck by a feeling that I know him from somewhere, but nothing comes to me clearly.

The two men are hunched together in a conspiratorial way and the angle of the image suggests that Mark is lying beneath, or behind, the next car along in the carpark, aiming the cell-phone upwards at the men.

The conversation is clear and goes like this:

Steve; "I thought your legal eagle had her sorted?"

Brother; "Apparently not. The old bitch is being obstinate and Stanley hasn't been able to work the angles tight enough to force her out. We know her cash funds are solid and the fire and all the breakages really aren't hurting her."

"So what's the problem? She'll crack soon. They always do!"

"We're running out of time for playing around. Each day that bitch holds out now is costing me big money . . . and Jimmy B wants clarity on the apartments urgently, or he may bail out, and I can't have that!"

"So you want me to get involved. Sure, happy to help."

"Yeah, we need to do something about the old bitch, and soon. Stanley has been trying to get her to sign, but everything's just a bit too subtle for the stupid old hag. I don't think she really knows what she's up against. Fact is we need her to bloody sign now."

"OK. So how badly broken do you want her? And does it need to look like an accident?"

"Not broken. Not quite yet. I want you to pay a visit next week, on Monday morning, if she hasn't signed. I want you to get into her head, but less subtle– . . . //

Skinner has stopped the video. 'Dude, I'm not sure what you've got here, but I don't think it's going anywhere good. I reckon we should just delete this one.'

He moves his hand towards the mouse and I explode at him. 'No! Don't you bloody dare!' My heart is hammering.

He pulls his hand back, stopping dead, a look of comical surprise on his face. I'm stunned by what I've heard so far, yet immediately terrified that this strange man might destroy the only copy of it. My plea is desperate.

'I'm sorry. Please, this is very, very important to me. I need to remember what happened on Friday, so I need to see this video. You have to understand.'

There's a deathly silence. He stares at me like I've just grown another head. I take a deep breath and lay my hand on his arm gently, and I beg.

'Please, would you just let it play out, please . . .'

He isn't happy, but my intimate appeal seems to affect him. I leave my hand on his arm until he lightly clicks the mouse to continue playing the video. Steve's brother immediately continues from where he left off.

// . . . – She's got grandchildren locally, she's already lost her husband and son, and I think a visit from you might be enough to move her into signing. I'm sure she'd hate to see one of her grand-kiddies go out like her golden boy did."

"Eh? Not with you!"

"You don't know? Ha! You remember that prick Davis from the council planning office? Back in '99. The one who you had some car trouble with down on Waterloo road?"

"How could I forget, that was almost a royal cock up."

"Yeah, but you lived. In any case, this old bitch is his mother. She was the one rallying the media for any witnesses to come forward. Crying like a baby to anyone who'd listen. Anyway, if the thought of losing more of her offspring isn't enough to get her to sign, we'll just have to take the old bag out and let Stanley go to battle with the estate. I've already got a clean picture of two of them. You can use it to rattle her up."

"No problem. Consider it done. Just say the word and I'll drop by on Monday."

"Thanks, I'll get that picture to you."

"Hmm, so what you doin' for the weekend?"

"Oh you know, a bit of this and that. Sharon's got a few people coming over Saturday, so we'll probably have a few quiet ones and solve all the problems of the world, you know. What about you?"

"I've got a triple banger lined up. A dirty blonde tonight, a horny brunette tomorrow, and a smokin' hot little darkie for Sunday. I am gonna shag myself silly. You should try it sometime."

"You have got to be kidding? You've lined up a hat-trick? Do I know any of these lucky women?"

"Nah, not really. I think you've met the blonde in here before, but the other two are off the record. You know?"

"You mean that old slapper, what's her name; Tina, Tracey? She's the blonde? You still banging that? Oh c'mon man, that's no challenge. You can do better than that old souse."

"Don't knock it big bro, sometimes experience outweighs youth. Tracey may not be the freshest meat at market, but she'll do absolutely anything I tell her. Anytime and anywhere. You can't beat that. And anyway, if you want youth you want to check out the little brown bitch I got lined up for Sunday afternoon. Only eighteen, man, and she goes like a wildcat. Absolutely smoking. It's sweet, man. I might even introduce you when I get bored."

"Shit Steve, you know I'm trying to behave these days. I've got a public image and all that to maintain."

"Hey, no problem, this little bitch can be discrete, as long as you keep her sweet with shiny trinkets and all. You hear me?"

"Hmm, yeah, it's tempting. I'll have to give that a little thought– . . . what the hell is that?"

Then the picture drops to the ground and all we can see is a blur of feet running, flashes of parked cars, and then the video ends suddenly.

I'm shaking so much I just about fall off the stool.

It's no wonder Steve wanted this video destroyed so badly. He wouldn't have cared less about the hat-trick of sexual conquests he was planning, but he would have been very, very worried about all the rest.

This video is powerful evidence of corruption, extortion and even murder.

My own murder.

Steve had already admitted, even boasted, to me of running Mark off his bike, and now it's clear that Steve was also the bastard who drove the car that ran me off the road last week. Or nine years ago, depending on how you look at it. And it wasn't an accident, not from the way they were talking.

I'm too deeply shocked to move.

'Oh. My. God. Sweet Lord in Heaven,' Skinner murmurs softly to himself. We are both still staring blankly at the final fixed frame of the video clip. My mind is whirling as he voices the conclusion I'd also just come to, 'That's why you got run off your bike last Friday night, isn't it?' His eyes are wide with horror. His hand quivers on the mouse as he moves to click the images off his screen when I suddenly come to my senses.

'Don't touch it!' I roar at him, surprising him enough that he lifts his hand from the mouse like it had suddenly become electrified, and he backs away from me a little.

But in a moment he recovers slightly. 'It's okay Mark, you're safe here. I won't let them hurt you again,' he says protectively, his hand still raised. He starts to lower it.

'Just don't touch it,' I command firmly. 'I need that video.'

My tone obviously shocks him and he stops with his hand hovering over the mouse. He blinks rapidly and I can literally see the options running quickly through his mind.

I check my watch again, only eight minutes left.

My time-check concerns him and he frowns as he lays both hands down on his knees, away from the mouse on the desk. I relax marginally. The content of the video has me completely shaken and I'm desperately trying to clear my thoughts and determine my next move.

Dipping a shaky left hand into my pocket I pull out a flash drive USB stick, gently laying it on the table. I try and make my tone reasonable, but firm. 'I need to download that video, and I need it right now. All right?'

'But why, Mark? You can't show *that* to anyone. Those men are clearly dangerous. They'll hurt you again. My God, they could kill you.'

He'd completely dispensed with the stoner dude talk and I'm surprised at how genuinely concerned he seems to be. It's off-putting and more than a little creepy.

'I'll be fine. I just need you to copy that file over to this flash drive and then you can delete it from your system and no one will ever know where I got it from. Okay?'

He shakes his head furiously. He's both anxious and scared. 'No. No, no, no, Mark. I can't do that. One of those men ran you off your bike last week, didn't he? I can't let you put yourself in that sort of danger. I think we should just delete the video and forget we ever saw it.'

I check my watch again, we're down to seven minutes. He sees me and this time asks, 'What are you doing, Mark? Why do you keep checking your watch?'

I take a deep breath. This is it.

'Look, here's the thing. I need that video and there's no way you can talk me out of it. I need a copy of it, and I need it right now,' I pause, taking another deep breath. 'And to be on the safe side I have a friend sitting outside in a car ready to call the cops, in just five minutes, if I don't emerge from this house with what I need. My friend will give the cops this address and tell them that she saw you abduct me from the street and that she can hear screaming coming from inside. That's kidnapping, and they should respond within minutes.'

His mouth hangs open in total disbelief.

I continue. 'So we really need to get moving here. We're almost down to four minutes and I am totally serious about that friend and making that call.'

With eyebrows twitching, his nostrils flare and he opens his mouth and then closes it. This sudden change in the situation has him bewildered. Then his cheeks flush and he starts to become angry. 'Why would you . . . I mean . . . I thought you were my friend, I thought–', but I have to cut him off.

'I'm sorry, but I'm almost out of time.'

He leans back away from me like I am now some form of toxic waste, so I reach out and take control of the mouse. Jamming the flash drive into the computer's USB port I start clicking purposefully.

Mum and I visited a local computer store just hours before and purchased a brand new laptop, lots of connection cables and the flash drive memory stick. The salesman had been quite amused at our questions and quickly demonstrated how to take a video on a cell-phone – which we then bought from him too – and then download it to a computer, and then how to transfer a copy onto a flash drive. He made it look pretty easy and it took him less than thirty seconds to make that final transfer.

I copy the moves I'd watched him make earlier and it only takes me just under a minute to complete. We're now down to just four minutes on my countdown.

As I remove the flash drive from Skinner's computer his demeanour changes. It seems he doesn't like being out of control and he tries to take command of the situation again. He grabs my hand. Our physical differences once again become immediately apparent. His grip is firm. He may be older, but he's still strong enough to hold a child easily.

'Don't do this, Mark. It doesn't have to be like this,' he pleads, half confused and half angry. 'I wouldn't hurt you, Mark. You know that. I'm your friend.'

'Let me go, please. I need to get outside and see my friend within the next three minutes, or you're going to have some serious questions to answer from the police. Neither of us really want that, do we?'

I raise my other wrist and show him the timer counting down. He shakes his head in disbelief, and then turns ugly.

'But this isn't right. How can you treat me like this? I've been so good to you . . . I mean,' he pauses and then lets it all out in a rush. 'When you're feeling down, who cheers you up? I do. And when your good-for-nothing mother is lying drunk in the gutter, who is there to look after you and make sure you're not going hungry? I am. Why would you treat me like this? Why, Mark?'

Only three minutes left and he's still holding my wrist whilst waving his other hand around wildly and getting more and more upset with every word. I try to pull my wrist from his grip, but he holds me firm. My efforts only makes him angrier.

'How dare you try and run away. How dare you threaten me,' he shouts. 'I've been so good to you. I've loved you like no one else could love you, Mark. This isn't right. You need me. You can't do this!'

Trying to pull away again, I keep my fist tightly closed so as not to drop the flash drive. I wrench my arm right around, so that his arm twists uncomfortably, then I heave again, desperately, with all my weight. Abruptly my wrist comes free and I fall backwards, off the stool, scrambling as I scurry away from him.

'No, Mark. Please don't do this,' he calls out tearfully.

I clamber away and down the stairs, thrusting the flash drive deep into my pocket. I look at my watch, there's less than a minute to go. Suddenly he's following me.

I reach the front door, which is locked, and I back up against it as he stumbles down the stairs. We stand and stare at each other across the length of the short hallway. Any cheery stoner-dude affectation is long gone as his face is distorted with sadness and anger. As I press my back to the door he starts to advance slowly, he is clearly furious. His mouth opens and a steady stream of ranting accusation begins to flow from him.

Time is up.

When Mum and I planned this earlier I thought it unlikely we would actually have to call the police, but now I desperately wonder how long it will take them to arrive. If Mum calls now, as she is supposed to do, it may be at least ten minutes, at best, before a patrol car can respond.

As he moves towards me I'm shockingly reminded of my new physical limitations. Being only half of an average man's size this raving lunatic could easily kill me in a lot less than ten minutes if he chose to. Oh Christ, what was I thinking?

Skinner takes another small step forward. 'How could you do this to me?' he continues to rant. He's flushed like a beetroot and his tone quivers between sullen and bitter. His words wash over me like a tsunami of loathing. Obviously he either thinks that I'm bluffing about the friend, that I've lied to him.

Or worse – he just doesn't care.

My watch has well and truly reached zero. Mum will have called the police. I just need to stall him somehow. Play for time. I decide to try a bluff.

'Look, there's still time! There's still a minute to go. If you open the door for me right now then I can stop her from calling the police. Everything will be fine. Okay?'

He falls silent and comes to a halt, two metres away. Glaring at me, he coughs to clear his throat, and folds his arms across his chest. When he speaks his voice is hollow and flat.

'No, there's not. There's no more time, and there's no one out there . . .' he shakes his head slowly, 'and this is now a big, big mess. You stupid, stupid boy.'

The sparkle of excitement I'd seen in his eyes only twenty minutes ago is long gone, as is any concern or sadness he'd previously displayed. Now there is nothing but resentment. His eyes are dull and flat. He shakes himself, a quivering like a dog shaking off water, and an air of determination emerges.

With this newly found resolve he starts to move slowly forward again, grimly. I push back against the unyielding door and damn myself again for not thinking this through properly.

Holding my breath and desperately wishing I was anywhere else, I silently pray that the police will arrive quickly.

TWENTY-THREE

Skinner's words cut through me like ice.

'No one's coming, and no one knows you're here. I'm sorry Mark. You seemed like such a nice young man. I really thought we could be friends. But now you treat me like this, and you get me involved with underworld criminals . . .'

He gestures vaguely towards the computer back in the attic, still moving forward slowly. I press myself harder into the door, willing it to just pop open. My heart pounds furiously. Beads of sweat roll down my forehead.

'I can't let you leave with that video, Mark,' he continues as he inches forward. 'It will raise too many questions and cause too much trouble for us both. I'm so sorry,' he is now less than a metre away, 'but I must have it back.'

Suddenly his right hand whips around to catch my left arm just above the elbow. With a solid tug he pulls me away from the door and spins me down to the floor, face down.

'I don't want to hurt you, Mark. But I must have that video back,' his hand slips down to my wrist and forces my arm up behind my back. 'We have to destroy it, you must understand. Where did you put it?'

With his other hand he reaches around and pats me down, trying to locate the flash drive hidden in my clothing.

I try to wriggle out of his grip, but he's far too strong. I flail vainly with my free right arm and kick out with both legs. My resistance slows and annoys him, but is hopelessly ineffective. I can't break free. I'm trapped.

Then a car horn sounds piercingly behind us.

It's very loud, and very tinny, and it's right outside the door. The horn sounds again and again, peeping furiously and insistently. I'm able to turn my head just enough to look through the slim window that runs vertically down the side of the door. There I see Mum's red sedan in the driveway, its headlights on full and its yellow emergency hazard lights flashing as the horn peeps away continuously.

It's not the police, but at that moment it's – without doubt – the best thing I've ever seen.

Skinner freezes, then abruptly throws himself off me and away from the window, out of sight of the driver. His face is contorted with horror.

His wiry dog suddenly appears from nowhere and starts to bark furiously through the door at the honking car. Skinner looks at me and starts to shuffle sideways down the hall, trying desperately to decide the best course of action. He's acting like the proverbial cornered rat.

'Stay there!' I shout at him over all the noise. 'Don't do anything silly, just open the door now and we can still make this all right. I can stop this. Just open the door.'

He only hesitates momentarily before fumbling in his pocket for his keys and stumbling over to the door. As it unlocks he picks up the yapping animal and tucks it under one arm. Throwing the door open wide he steps aside.

The car's peeping stops immediately, but the lights and flashing hazards stay on.

I bolt quickly outside, through the doorway and stop at the bonnet of the little car. Mum is sitting in the driver's seat holding up the new little cell-phone. I look back. Skinner is trying to peek through the narrow window to see what's going on. He's managed to silence the dog somehow. It's so quiet now I can hear the engine running quietly and the repetitive ticking of the hazard lights.

I scoot around and jump into the passenger seat.

'Did you call the police?' I ask quickly.

'No,' she sobs. 'I'm sorry, but I couldn't make it work. I tried to, but –'

I cut her off, 'It's okay Mum, it's okay. Don't worry, I'm fine,' I tell her quickly, as I check the flash drive is still in my pocket. It is. 'Let's just go, and fast, before he decides to do something stupid.'

She slams it into reverse gear and we literally fly backwards up the short driveway and onto the road. Mum sobs as we drive and my heart is still pounding furiously when we pull up at the old homestead only minutes later.

'Are you okay, Mum?' I ask.

She's white and shaking and clearly not okay. But I'm pretty sure we can fix what ails her with a good strong cup of tea. She doesn't answer, not fully trusting her voice I think, but nods weakly, attempting a small smile.

My hands are shaking a little too, but I can't help feeling some self-satisfaction. Given the difficult circumstances we'd actually managed to retrieve the video and that's what really matters. I reach back, pick up the new laptop and get out of the car, walking around to open my mother's door.

She still hasn't moved.

'Come on, Mum. If you think that was bad wait until you see the video I copied.'

As I help her out the new cell-phone falls out of her lap onto the ground. Picking it up I quickly realise that the key-pad lock is still on. Mum has never used a cell-phone before and, while I had shown her which buttons to push to call the police, I hadn't shown her how to unlock the key-pad. My feeling of satisfaction vanishes as I realise there was no way she could have actually called the police while I was in the house. An involuntary shiver runs down my spine at the thought.

We get ourselves inside, boil the jug and make weak coffee and strong tea while we review the errors we'd made along the way. Mum describes waiting in the car as the longest twenty minutes of her life, and she was stricken with horror when she couldn't make the phone go. Having waited an extra minute after the deadline, she started pushing the cell-phones buttons. But nothing worked. The little screen just kept flashing up a message asking her to enter her password. After a short panic she decided to do the only thing she could think of.

Make a commotion.

She was relieved to learn that her appearance in the driveway actually made a difference. It changed everything inside the house. And, we agree, staying in the car is the best thing Mum could have done. If she'd come to the door and he'd realised Mark's friend was just an old woman things may have worked out quite differently.

But while our outing didn't exactly go like clockwork, we did achieve our goal. We have the video.

Forcing thoughts of Skinner's house aside I move to show Mum the video, and I know it will shock her. But once again we are running low on time.

I fire up the new laptop, just as the salesman had shown me earlier, and click away to open its program for viewing videos. Then I pull out the flash drive and plug it in. There is only one file on it so I don't have to search and, after copying it onto the laptop's hard drive, I double-click it and the video starts to play.

For a couple of seconds we watch the faces on the screen and their mouths move wordlessly. There is no sound.

I panic briefly and then manage to find the laptops volume controls. As I push them up deep voices boom out at us. Thank God for that. We have the video, in its entirety.

I start it again from the beginning.

After the first viewing I look at Mum's face, she's as white as a ghost again. 'It's pretty nasty stuff, isn't it,' I say. There is a pause, and then she responds.

'That man, Steve. He was involved in your accident on Waterloo Rd.' She is as shocked as I was, first time. I can see the realisation in her eyes as she continues to stare at the screen, transfixed. I feel deeply unsettled again myself.

'Would you play it again please, Nick,' she asks quietly, without looking at me. I hit the button again. After the second viewing she nods and clears her throat. 'I've seen that man before. Not the one you call Steve, but the other one. But I'm not sure where.'

'Yeah, he looks familiar to me too. I'll play it again.'

Near the end of the third screening there is a moment when the older man turns slightly and grins fully towards the camera. It's then that a name leaps into my head.

'Cassidy,' I say. 'That's the guy from Cassidy Construction.'

'Yes,' agrees Mum, nodding seriously. 'Richard Cassidy. He's been here. At the start of all the troubles, he gave us the original presentation about what they wanted to do here. Your father laughed at him and threw him out.'

She looks at me. 'His name is on the bottom of the all the Sale and Purchase forms they want me to sign. He's the owner of the property development company.'

No wonder Steve had tried to kill Mark.

'It's all a bit much really, isn't it,' Mum says quietly, shaking her head slowly, trying to take it all in. Another massive understatement. The scale of the situation we are in leaves me numb as I struggle to come to grips with everything the short video has revealed.

In one brief conversation the Cassidy brothers have revealed indisputable proof of their efforts to blackmail Mum into selling them the old homestead. They have as good as confirmed that they are responsible for the window breakages and the car fire, and they've also inferred that they had significant involvement in the car accident nine years ago on Waterloo Rd that ended my life, as such.

But poor little Mark hadn't cared about any of that.

Within this video he had proof that Steve was being unfaithful to Tracey, and he must have believed that it would be enough for her to break up with him, and to get him out of their lives. Who knows? It may have worked. But sadly I doubt it. Tracey can't possibly think he's being faithful to her. Surely not.

But I am impressed that Mark thought to download the video somewhere safe, to ensure it wasn't lost or stolen before he could play it to his Mum. He was a smart kid. It's just sad that it all worked out so badly for him after that.

And, after watching the video, it makes me think that there may be an even greater link between my memories of my accident and the clash between Steve's car and Mark's bike some nine years later. But nothing is clear. I have so much information swirling through my mind right now I can't focus on that mystery. It's more important for Mum and I to use this video somehow, and make sure our family stays safe.

'We need a plan, Mum,' I finally conclude. 'We need a damn good plan.'

'We have to call the police,' she tells me bluntly. 'There's nothing else we can do here. You've already put yourself at enough risk just to get hold of this video. And these men are far, far more dangerous than that strange old man. We need to just give it to the police and let them handle it.'

It's good advice, but not so easily put into action.

'OK then,' I say. 'So we just call up the police, and explain to them that I've returned from the dead, and that before I did that I took this video showing not only who it was that killed me nine years ago, but that the same chap is now threatening to harm my children . . .'

'Well . . . yes,' says Mum, frowning at my sarcasm. 'It does sound a little ludicrous.'

'And while they have me out the back, with the doctors running every test from here to eternity on me, you'll be explaining to them how we retrieved the video from an old man, who is quite likely a paedophile, using nothing but a stopwatch and the flashing hazard lights on your car.'

She puts her hands up in surrender, 'All right then, Nick. What should we do?'

I sigh deeply, my head spinning. 'I don't know.'

So we talk it through, soon establishing what our boundaries are and where our problems lie.

Firstly, we don't want to reveal that Mark has been taken over by the ghost of Mum's dead son. Obviously this will be far too complicated to explain, besides the fact that no one would believe us. And worse, if they did believe us I would be whisked off for probing and analysis by every doctor and scientist in the country, if not the world.

I really don't fancy that.

So to achieve that goal, we need to explain how Mark has come to bring the video to Mum's attention, especially since the Cassidy brother's never used her name, or Nick's, in the video – and given that Mark doesn't actually know her, even though there is a tenuous relationship by marriage.

And I don't want to go to the police with Mum, if it can be helped. I expect that they would separate us for questioning and that would provide more opportunity for one of us to mess up the story and slow things down.

And, of course, Mark is only a child and Helen Davis is neither his parent nor legal guardian. Having to track down Tracey and drag her into the interviews would bring everything to a grinding halt.

We bandy options around for quite a while before finally settling on a very simple strategy. We both agree that keeping close to the truth will be easier to remember, and less likely to trip us up on any lies.

So only Mum will go to the police, specifically to see the chap she'd dealt with before about the car fire and the vandalism. Then the background will be already known and she can get onto the new information much quicker.

Mum will simply tell him that a young boy came to her door early this morning and gave her a copy of the video on a flash drive. He didn't tell her his name, just told her to watch the video and it might help. Then he ran away.

But she didn't have a computer to watch the video on so, desperately hoping that the video would prove valuable, she went out and bought a laptop and watched the video at home. Then she came straight to see them.

We expect the police to press her for a description of the boy and we agree that she should simply tell them that she did recognise him, but doesn't want to reveal his identity as yet. Not until after Steve is behind bars. She's worried that if anything goes wrong the boy may be in danger.

Neither of us are totally convinced we have the story straight, but it's vital that we get the police involved urgently, as Steve had told Mum he would be back later today for her decision and it's now midday.

We talk it through a few more times while we eat a hurried lunch and then Mum jumps in her car, with the flash drive and all her Cassidy Construction papers.

With nothing else that I can do I tuck the laptop under my arm and set off across the park to the unit, seriously trying to decide if I should show the video to Liz, and possibly to Tracey too. But I'm not sure if showing them is such a good idea. If I show Liz, what would she want to do? And what would Tracey make of it?

Fortunately Tracey isn't home, so that simplifies things.

As I retrieve the hidden key from the tree I come to the conclusion that I can't trust Tracey with this information, as yet. She's clearly an alcoholic, and appears to be in love with Steve on some deeply disturbed level, so I can't be sure that she won't go running off and immediately tell Steve about the video.

Whether she would want to show it to him as an accusation of his infidelity, or to try and win favour with him in a pathetic demonstration of her loyalty, I don't know. Perhaps showing her after Steve is safely incarcerated is a better idea, depending on how the police handle things.

The unit is dim and depressing. I drop the laptop on the dining table and go through the place opening all the curtains and windows, to try and let a little light and air in. It doesn't help a lot. Tracey's room is a bomb-site and I decide to leave well enough alone and keep out of there, so I just close the door.

I have a couple of hours to kill before school breaks up and I've already decided that I will walk down and try to meet Jack and Katie as they leave to walk home. I'm nervous that Steve might try something before the deadline. Perhaps arriving at the house with one of Mum's grandchildren in the boot of his car will ensure he gets things sorted tonight. He could do anything, but I don't think this is likely, as the risks became higher for him. I know from the video that he's expected to get a result urgently, but it doesn't make sense to take that sort of risk so soon. I think he will more likely stick with his aggressive scare tactic today and see if that produces the result first. If it doesn't I think he would most likely then try something relatively simple to show he means business. And, with his history of success with cars, that would most probably mean a car accident. I don't believe he'd worry about whether the child lives or dies, just so long as he hit the right one – to make his point. It makes me feel very, very sick inside.

Although, given my current physical limitations, I really don't know what I could do if he chooses to attack either of my children. But, regardless of stature, I'm damn well going to be there to try and protect them if he does do something.

I flop down onto the couch in the lounge and take a few deep breaths trying to clear my head, thankful of an opportunity to relax and think about what I've now learned.

But the peace doesn't last long as I hear a car begin to pull up into the driveway. I'm instantly wary, but it's a small tinny sound. The old hatchback, not Steve's big SUV.

Tracey is coming home.

Thankfully I suddenly remember the brand new laptop, sitting on the dining table where I dropped it as I came in. Out in the open. I jump up, dash across and grab it as I hear her coming up the stairs. I duck back into the kitchen, frantically trying to decide where I can hide it. But the kitchen isn't a smart option for hiding anything, so I scurry through it and down the short hallway. Just as I slide into the bedroom Mark shares with Liz I hear the front door open. I don't have much time, so just drop the laptop onto the bed, throw a few dirty clothes over it, and then I turn and dodge out back into the hall.

TWENTY-FOUR

TRACEY MITCHELL pushes open the front door to her shit-hole of a home despondently. Every time she enters this soulless pit she feels the weight of responsibility descend upon her – and she hates it. She's a beautiful woman, desirable. She knows that she deserves better than this. The unit is a pervasive reminder of the injustice of her life, which has been so unfair. Everything she ever loves either turns to shit, or simply dies. Why does she bother?

She reaches the middle of the lounge and stops. God, but this place is a dump. Suddenly Mark appears out of nowhere, skidding to a halt in the hall doorway. For a moment she is confused. Why is he here? Isn't it a school day? And then she remembers. He's been suspended, for fighting. And not just for scrapping with any damn kid, but with the son of the richest, and most powerful family in this part of the country. Stupid little shit. She can't believe the crap he's put her through in the last few days. It's like he's trying to fuck her life up even more. It's like he's trying to tear her down.

She frowns disparagingly at him.

He just stands there, watching her. She feels like the little bastard is appraising her, taking note of the premature bags under her eyes and the other weary ravages that time has taken on her body. She wants to just scream at him: Yes, look at me, look at what you've done to me. But she doesn't, she hasn't got the energy. And anyway, what good will it do?

She holds a brown bag containing a couple of bottles of cheap red wine. The package comforts her. Gives her strength. She hugs it to her breast. She and the boy watch each other for a long time, neither moving nor speaking. Both seem unsure of what to say, both hoping the other will speak first and set the tone. Finally Tracey speaks.

'So you're back then, are you?'

'I had a couple of things to do. You were still asleep.'

They revert to an uncomfortable silence, still just watching each other warily.

'I could go out again, if you'd prefer?' he offers.

'Do whatever you want, Mark. You always do anyway.'

'Come on, that's not fair. I'm not trying to hurt you.'

She broods on this for a few moments, frowning and glancing down to the floor briefly, and then she looks back up with a reproachful expression.

'Yet somehow you always do,' she mutters as she turns away and moves through to the kitchen, placing her handbag and the wine bottles on the counter. As she starts to open one of the bottles she hears Mark groan. He's followed her.

'Do you really need that?' he asks, accusingly.

The boys tone instantly irritates her, and she's surprised by his brashness. Normally he almost never speaks when she is around. She stops, grimacing, and replies sharply.

'If you're going to keep trying to ruin my life, then I think I'm allowed a small pick-me-up now and then.'

'It's not a pick-me-up, it's a top-up. And it's not now and then, it's all the time! You have a drinking problem.'

She can't believe what she's hearing and she feels the anger rising up within her like a volcano. Then her son unexpectedly adds, more softly, 'Please don't. We need to talk.'

But it's too late. She can't hold back.

'How dare you lecture me on things you don't understand? You have no idea how hard it is to cope with all the problems you create around here. I'm damn well entitled to a glass of wine to help get me through the day, all right?'

She turns away from him, the bottle open, now looking for a clean glass. But the damn child just doesn't seem to know when to shut-the-hell-up anymore.

'No, it's not all right. You need help,' he says. 'Please don't treat me like an idiot. We both know that the wine isn't good for you. That it's not really helping.'

Tracey closes her eyes to try and control her temper. She gets enough of this sort of bull-shit from her bloody brother. Big bloody *My-life-is-so-fucking-perfect* Brett, that prick. She resents him and everything he has, even though she knows she's heavily indebted to him. Has Mark been talking to him? Has Brett been coaching the boy about what to say to really push her buttons? Why can't they all just leave her alone?

Then Mark steps forward and tries a more conciliatory tone. 'It's like you're running away from something. Let Liz and I help. Try talking to us.'

Tracey shakes her head in wonder. She's just wants to shout at him again, tell him to get the fuck out of her face, let it go, but she manages to hold back with some effort. Brett's been in his ear, she's now certain of this. Mark doesn't talk like this.

'I'm not running away from anything. And I don't appreciate you poking your nose in where it's not welcome.'

But her irritation is building, on the rise towards anger. She finds a glass and pours some wine and is relieved when Mark moves away, sitting down at the dining table without speaking. A quick glance reveals dismay and accusation in his eyes so she resolves not to make eye contact with him again. Who needs it?

She takes a deep swig of the sharp dark liquid, gives a tiny shudder and then busies herself pottering around the kitchen. A warming numbness immediately begins to flow through her. God, that feels better. She can feel her mood change like magic, the anger washing away. She takes another healthy sip.

'So what are we having for dinner then, young man,' she asks, almost sweetly, as she forages in the freezer. 'How about sausages?' she says, producing a frozen package and placing it on the counter by the sink. 'That sounds nice.'

She risks another glance towards her son who only offers her a small look of disgust. He doesn't understand though, how can he? He's just a child, he can't possibly appreciate the pressure she is under, how difficult and unforgiving life can be.

A moment of melancholy tears through her. The boy is nothing like his father, too much like her. It's such a shame. Adam had been a good man, a great man. Worthy of her love. But he is gone, torn from her without warning. Lost soon after the boy was born. This damn child is a curse on their family. An unplanned accident. He'd never amount to anything.

'Are you going to see Steve tonight?' Mark suddenly asks.

Oh crap, here we go again. The tone of his voice immediately puts her on edge again. He's become such a self-righteous little shit. Why can't he just go and play in his bloody room? Why these damn children dislike her latest boyfriend so much is an absolute mystery to Tracey. They've never even given him a chance. He's a good man. Why can't they see that?

'Possibly,' she finally replies. 'He has a few things on today and may drop by later.'

She knows it's unlikely but some part of her really wants Mark and Liz to sort out their differences with Steve. She loves him and he loves her. Someday they may actually get married. It would be so much better if everyone would just get along.

'You know, if you tried a little harder you might find you like him. He's a good man,' she says, without looking over, but takes note of Mark's small snort of disbelief. She presses on.

'And I can't believe you'd think that he had anything to do with your accident the other day. He was so worried about you when you went missing. He was out looking for you everywhere.'

But, typically, her son doesn't understand. He misinterprets everything. 'So why did he attack me out there on Sunday afternoon?' Mark asks.

'He didn't attack you, don't be stupid. He just talked to you about running away and scaring everyone. I thought it was decent of him to bother. And he's right about boys needing a firm hand. I'm just not firm enough with you half the time.'

'Oh, come on,' Mark blurts out. 'You're deluded. He's not the good guy you seem to think he is. Why won't you believe Liz and me about Steve? He's just using you!'

Tracey feels the anger return, even through her warm core of numbness. She takes another sip, emptying the glass, trying to stay calm as she refills it. She's even closer to the edge now.

'For Christ's sake, Mark. Don't start all that again. Steve is a good man. I know he's not your dad, and he never could be, but there's no reason for you to keep on after him with all these lies and accusations. He's never done anything to harm you, and he treats me like a queen. And he loves me, so just accept it. He's part of our lives.'

Mark goes quiet again and she sneaks a glance as he silently considers something. She hopes that the silence is a good thing. Maybe she's actually getting through to him? For a moment she lets herself hope that her son will finally accept her newest man. Then her life would be so much easier, and it might even be nice for Mark to accept a father-figure into his life. Having a man around the house would take some of the crushing pressure off of her. Wouldn't it?

'So, how come you're not at work today?' The boy asks, changing the subject.

Tracey snorts derisively; an ugly little sound. She's relieved to no longer be discussing either her drinking or her love-life with her son. But she finds talking about her brother almost as painful as the other subjects. She takes another long, deep swallow before answering somewhat defensively.

'Brett's given me the week off . . . to give me some time to come to terms with my son's accident, and his suspension from school. Fully paid leave, of course. So thank you,' she finishes sarcastically.

She actually isn't that unhappy about it, as going in to work in Brett's bloody travel agency is a grind she can do without. And she feels she's done well to have so eloquently rephrased Brett's directive to *sober up and do something positive with her son*. But she is again surprised when Mark so quickly seems to see through her.

'I take it you've now come to terms with both?' he asks bluntly. She glares at him, instantly annoyed.

'You just mind yourself, little man. You may have recovered from your accident, but if you keep talking to me like that you might just find yourself back in that damn hospital.'

The boy has the good grace to look a little abashed at first, but his expression soon changes to a frown of disgust as her words sink in. He shakes his head, pityingly. Seeing this pushes her over the edge. The little son-of-a-bitch, is he mocking me? She just wants to lash out at him. Knock that stupid look of repugnance off his face.

'How dare you sit there and judge me,' she snarls loudly, feeling her face flush with suppressed rage. 'You've got a damn nerve. Get out, will you. Just get the hell away from me.'

His new look of disbelief infuriates her further and she is suddenly filled with an unbearable shame and self-loathing as the red mist of resentment finally extinguishes reason.

'Go on, piss off. You're nothing but trouble and always have been.' She waves her hand angrily and dismissively, pointing towards the front door. 'Get out! Just go! Leave me alone,' she shouts, snatching up the wine glass and turning away from him.

The boy stays silent behind her back.

She stares angrily around her crappy little kitchen, once again desperate to lose herself within this pitiful existence. Thank Christ she has Steve. She can't bear to think how empty and pathetic her life would be without him.

Tracey Mitchell hears her son rise and quietly slip away, through the lounge and out the front door. She raises her glass and stares sullenly into the dark, blood-like liquid.

TWENTY FIVE

As I leave the unit I can scarcely believe the conversation I've just had with Tracey. There can be no doubt that she is hopelessly and completely deluded about her relationship with Steve. Between all his bullshit, and her drowning herself in booze, she clearly has no idea what he's really up to. No grasp on reality at all. I'm relieved that I decided not to show her the video, at least not yet anyway. Perhaps I shouldn't show her it at all – and just let the police take him away? Maybe it's best not to. If I do show her she'll probably just despise Mark for being right. It seems like a no-win situation.

I try to put her problems out of my mind. Clear my head and focus on the next few hours. School will be out soon and I need to get over there and watch out for my children.

As I start to walk up the cul-de-sac it occurs to me that I will have to walk right past Skinner's place to get to the school. I'm not keen on doing that, and I have plenty of time, so I turn around, head back up the unit's driveway, and climb through the back fence into the park, choosing to take the longer route.

From the park, in the distance, I can see the old homestead and it looks very quiet. I wonder how Mum is getting on with the police. Hopefully they'll be able to use the video and lock Steve away for life.

As I drift along I let my mind wander, trying to make sense of it all, reflecting on what I'd seen in the video. Mum and I had only had time to talk about solving our problems with Steve, and we'd had no time to discuss the other glaring issues.

Like, why me?

I'm convinced that it was Steve that ran my car off the road, but why? Why ram *my car* off the road? What on earth did I ever do to him? I think I know, but it seems so extreme and I have to try and work through it logically.

Cassidy Construction was still fairly new in town, back in 1999, and was cutting a lot of corners in their buildings to save money. In the months before the accident I was in charge of the resource consents for their latest and boldest project to date, and had been finding a lot of things wrong, which caused them some serious delays. I repeatedly declined dozens of planning approvals and Cassidy's people were getting pretty angry about it all. I now can remember Richard himself coming in a couple of times, earlier on in the process, and trying various tactics to try and coerce me into letting some of the problems just go away. But I didn't relent, and I wouldn't take the bribes they offered, obstinately sticking to my guns.

That was my crime, I guess. My big mistake. Being dedicated to my work – and actually caring about the public's safety. The delays would have been costing them a fortune and they must have wanted me out of the way. Whether they intended a long spell in hospital or the permanent solution they achieved, I can't be sure. A chill runs through me.

Today they probably have any number of City Council staff on their bribery payroll, and I hate to think how many sub-standard buildings might have been approved in the last nine years around Hawthorne.

They say that crime doesn't pay, but maybe it does?

But understanding all this doesn't come with a glittering revelation about why I'm back here now. It doesn't explain how I came to be Mark Mitchell overnight. It just makes me angry, and desperate for some kind of revenge. Knowing that Steve will soon be in jail helps a little, but I really lust for something more primitive. I want to return the favour.

As I stroll along the footpath I force myself to push aside these shameful desires. As there is a much larger, more glaring issue to contemplate.

The really big question is: Why on earth am I back here, in Wilton, so many years after I died? And inside the body of a young child? Is there a reason? Have I been sent back to protect my children somehow? But this just makes my head spin.

It's overwhelming.

Upon reaching Miller Road, another familiar street, I turn right, on towards the school. I went to this school as a child, and now so does Mark. Is that a coincidence? And Waterloo Rd – and the intersection with Samsara Place. For some reason Mark had gone to exactly that spot when Steve was chasing him. That I find odd, and I wonder what made him chose that particular stretch of road. Some strange subconscious urge?

Is there must be some kind of connection between the two accidents? I can't decide. After watching the video the similarity of the two accidents on Waterloo Rd has become even more apparent, but I still don't have a clue as to why.

Both accidents were extremely traumatic experiences, at exactly the same place, and in very alike circumstances. But how does Mark's experience – of being run off the road from his bike, which is so very comparable to my own, of being run off exactly the same stretch of road, in exactly the same place – provide an answer to my supernatural predicament?

As I lay bleeding in my car that night, just before I blacked out, I distinctly remember seeing a bicycle wheel spinning in a tree above me. This has to be almost exactly what Mark would have seen as he lay on the grass after being knocked flying from his bike.

Is that spinning bicycle wheel some kind of clue?

I don't know.

Twenty minutes later and I'm hanging around outside the school gates, towards the corner of Lorneville Drive that both Jack and Katie will go past on their way home.

The parents coming to pick up their kids are starting to swarm. There are big SUV's of every type and colour, with people-movers and shiny flash coupes fighting for parking up and down the road. It's bedlam.

I vaguely wonder why so many of these kids need to be picked up, surely a little exercise will be good for them. But over-protective mothers abound and the streets around the school succumb to chaos. I sit myself down on a low concrete wall and wait.

Eventually the school bell rings loudly and a horde of children begin streaming out of every opening in the high brick wall. I relax a little. Steve would have to have super-powers to even pick out Jack or Katie amongst all these kids. I'm struggling with it.

Then I spot a big metallic blue SUV pushing slowly through the jammed-up traffic. It looks terribly familiar and I watch it cruise along in mounting horror. Then another big blue SUV crawls past on the other side of the road and I do a double-take. Quickly standing up on the little concrete wall I spot yet another blue SUV parked further along the road. If Steve is out there he has the perfect cover.

Then I spot Jack.

He's alone, on his bike, looking relieved that the day is over. I've positioned myself well as he is going to ride right past me. As he pulls closer I jump down off the wall into his path and he slams on his brakes, grinning with pleasure.

I grin right back at him. His innocent face is now even more familiar and I want to just run up and hug him, but manage to control myself. My heart is pounding in my chest as I fully realise just how much he does look like Daniel at the same age. A bit scrawnier, but very similar overall. He looks a bit like my little brother Bobby did at that age.

'Hey,' he calls out in delight. 'How you doing?'

'I'm doing just great, Jack. How about you?'

The look on his face tells me that this was a special greeting that I should have returned a specific answer to, but I got it wrong. I feel bad, but he gets over it quickly. He's clearly very pleased to see Mark.

He immediately starts telling me everything that has been going on at school since I've been away, which is only two days, but he's talking like it has been months. In a matter of seconds he's told me about the announcement the principal made to our class about my suspension, and about how Gordie, the beefy Breckenock boy, still wasn't back at school today, and about how the other kids were hoping he would never return.

I nod and smile, only half taking in the excited rambling while I cast my eye about looking for Katherine. He notices and asks me what I'm looking for.

'I'm just looking for your sister,' I reply honestly, but I struggle to come up with a good reason why. Fortunately he's a fairly accepting boy and doesn't ask the question.

'She'll be with Zoe,' is all he says.

'If it's okay with you we'll just wait for a bit and follow her home, okay?'

He's clearly surprised, but just shrugs and starts sharing other exciting school news. He hasn't asked me a question since his opening salvo and I'm actually quite grateful.

But I'm having real trouble spotting Katie. I've only seen her in her grown up teenage form the once in the park, and it had been almost dark, and I hadn't really taken a lot of notice of her. I know she is wearing her hair long, and it's brown and straight, but there are quite a few girls fitting that description pouring out of the school and all around us.

I watch as the cars fight their way in and out of parking spaces, half listening to Jack jabbering away beside me and examining every girl with long brown hair within sight. A girl fitting my description exactly climbs into a big blue SUV a little way down the street and my heart leaps in panic.

I move like a shot and sprint to the car just as it starts to pull out from the kerb. 'Wait,' I yell, banging my hands on the door. A surprised face spins in the window to look at me as the car screeches to a halt.

It isn't Katie, and the girls' window starts to slide down electronically. Her mother leans across and calls out.

'What do you want?'

I back away, apologising.

'My mistake. I'm sorry,' and wave her away.

'What are you doing?' a girl's voice behind me asks.

I spin around to find myself facing Katie, with a cute little blond girl beside her, and Jack just catching us all up.

'What are you doing, Mark?' Katie asks again.

'He's looking for you,' Jack volunteers a little too quickly.

I'm immediately embarrassed at my mistake, while also being stung with surprise by the face I am looking directly into.

My little Katherine, all grown up. Fourteen years old and looking much more mature. She looks so much like her mother.

She is beautiful.

I blush crimson.

Katie's friend, who must be Zoe, bursts out laughing. Jack looks confused. He doesn't understand what he's just said.

'Oh, Katie. Isn't that sweet. Little Mark here was looking for you,' Zoe tilts her head and laughs out loud again.

I must blush darker still, because Katie then flushes too and rolls her eyes. 'Yeah, whatever,' she snaps and starts to walk away, her laughing friend tailing along behind her.

I sigh. 'Nice one Jack,' I say. 'Smooth move.'

He still looks confused. He isn't the most emotionally aware boy that I've ever met. I wonder if I'd been that dim when I was eight. Who remembers?

'Come on, lets get going,' I say, not wanting to lose them.

Katie gives her friend a shove in front of us and the laughing dries up a lot, but not completely.

We manage to walk all the way up Lorneville Drive without incident. If Steve is on the prowl I don't see him, and he doesn't make any move.

Zoe walks with Katie all the way to the kids' house and just keeps on going with her inside. I stand in the driveway and watch Jack stow his bike away. I smile a little to myself as I recognise Sarah's line of prized flower pots along the fence line near the front doorway. This is definitely the home of my former wife, lover and, I had thought, my soul-mate.

'Are you coming in?' Jack asks, surprising me.

I freeze, not having considered this. I've only thought as far as getting them home safely and then heading back to the unit and awaiting Mum's call.

My God, what if Sarah is home?

I look around. There's a shiny silver coupe in the garage. Someone is home. I can't be sure if it is Brett or Sarah's car though. My heart stops beating.

'Umm, I'm not sure, Jack,' I hesitate. 'Do you think it will be okay with your Mum?'

'Yeah,' he says, looking surprised. 'Why wouldn't it be?'

He doesn't correct me, so I become pretty sure that Sarah is inside the house, not Brett.

Oh. My. God. My mind goes blank.

'I don't know, it's just . . .' but I can't think of anything to add. I take a deep breath, trying to steel myself. 'Sure,' I finally say, 'why not?'

As I start moving forward I break out into a cold sweat and my heart starts to hammer furiously in my chest. What the hell am I going to say to her?

The house is warm and inviting. Diametrically opposed to the shit-hole Mark is living in at the unit, just around the corner. As we enter Jack drops his school bag in an open cupboard space by the door and casually kicks off his shoes, so I copy him, and then take in my surroundings.

The entrance opens into an open family-cum-dining area, with the kitchen at the far end to my left. Everything looks new, and clean.

I immediately recognise some of the artwork hanging on the walls, and the various picture frames and knick-knacks that are scattered liberally around the room. Some I'd given to Sarah, while others she'd bought for herself while dragging me around on one or another of her never ending shopping quests. There are fresh flowers in a vase at the centre of the dark oak dining table, but the smell of freshly popped popcorn overwhelms their aroma. Katie and her friend are seated in a corner alcove munching away, and Jack heads straight for them.

Katie snatches the bowl away before he can reach it and he cries out 'Hey, not fair' and leans in to try and take them. 'These are ours,' Katie exclaims. 'Make your own, Jack.' They're struggling over the bowl, snapping at each other, with popcorn starting to fly around the little alcove.

'Hey, you two. Cut it out!' I shout above their cries.

They both freeze, in surprise more than anything, and I suddenly realise what I've done. In the semi-familiar surroundings I've temporarily forgotten who I am and instinctively gone into parent mode, meaning to stop the petty squabble.

I'm really not too sure why it happened. I've been Mark now for what seems an eternity and I've managed to keep it together pretty well – until now. I don't know what it is exactly that has affected me. Perhaps it's that I know these two squabbling children are actually my own? Or maybe it's the partially familiar surroundings?

Jack just looks surprised, but Katie starts to get angry, when I'm startled by a voice from the kitchen to my left.

'Thank you, Mark. You took the words right out of my mouth.'

It's Sarah. The late afternoon sun glows through a window behind her as she steps into the room – and I simply stop breathing.

'Jack, would you step away from your sister please, I have more popcorn about to go into the microwave for you and Mark,' she says evenly. She turns back into the kitchen and Jack moves away from the alcove, screwing his nose up at his sister, saying nothing and taking a seat at the large dining table.

I can't move.

TWENTY-SIX

I just stand there, staring at Sarah's back as she fusses around in the kitchen, preparing another bowl of popcorn. My mouth falls open in awe.

She looks great.

But then she always looked great to me. Even when she put on the extra weight after giving birth to both Daniel and Katherine, and even when she was tired and without make-up, Sarah always looked great.

Don't get me wrong, Sarah is never going to be a cat-walk model, but I'm no film star myself. Never-the-less Sarah is a beautiful woman. Nine years ago, or just last week depending on how you looked at it, Sarah had been slim, of average height, with beautiful long brown hair that she usually wore loose and carefully tousled. She has a warm and open face with stunningly big green eyes and a smile that can melt stone. She has about a million friends and is the warmest, most caring and sharing person I've ever met.

This is my wife of twelve glorious years, whom I met at age twenty-two and married two years later. The woman I've loved with all my heart and soul, who has borne me two – no actually three – wonderful children. The woman I was still very much in love with, and almost unbelievably happy with, up until a few short days ago.

Now everything is so very different, but she isn't.

I watch her moving around the kitchen. Her hair is shorter now, and straighter, but still long, hanging to just below her neckline. It's the same rich-chocolate-brown colour as always and I smile a little. The wonders of modern hair dye.

Her figure is good. She's actually carrying a little less weight than before and she obviously feels comfortable with it, as her clothes are fitting and show off all the appropriate curves. She's in excellent shape for a woman who must now be, I do the math quickly, forty-two years old.

I'm still standing there gaping openly, with my heart hammering, when Katie and Zoe brush past me, leaving the room. Katie looks at me oddly and Zoe is giggling again.

'Maybe it's not you he fancies,' Zoe sniggers as she moves past, looking straight at me, knowing I will hear her. 'Maybe it's actually your Mum.'

I'm physically unable to respond, and it's probably best that I don't, as I'm really not sure what to say. Katie just shakes her head, frowning at the exchange aloofly and keeps on walking.

They disappear up the hallway as Sarah steps out of the kitchen with a fresh bowl of popcorn. She sets it down in front of Jack and says to me, 'Are you hungry, Mark. You'd better be quick,' pointing at Jack tucking heartily into his first handful. I just nod and move forward slowly, sitting down next to him.

Her eyes are still bright and alive, and her skin clear and smooth. I would pick her as mid-thirties easily, not early-forties. She smiles, and then a look of concern comes over her face.

I realise I'm still staring at her and quickly look down at the bowl of popcorn. Although I've completely lost my appetite I reach out and take a handful while I try to get myself together.

'Are you alright Mark, you look a bit pale?' Sarah asks.

'Yes,' I manage weakly, my voice cracking. 'I'm fine.'

She isn't convinced and steps forward, leaning over me and reaching her hand out towards my face. 'May I?' she asks. I'm mesmerized and don't know what she is doing, and then she pushes back my scruffy hair to fully reveal the stitched gash on my forehead. She leaves her hand there, only lightly touching my face, but still managing to send electric shivers of delight through my entire body.

I can't speak.

'So this is the head wound I've heard so much about,' she says softly. 'It looks pretty nasty. Does it still hurt?'

Her perfume is so very, very familiar and the closeness of her body and the touch of her hand has my heart leaping in my chest. The desire to just reach out and pull her to me, to hold her in my arms, and tell her who I am and what has been happening to me in the last few days is overwhelming.

But I swallow it back and croak a weak response, having to cough a little to clear my throat first.

'No,' I sputter. 'No, it's not too bad.'

'Oh, you poor thing,' she says, pulling back. 'So no other injuries then. Just the bad cut?'

I have to clear my throat again.

'Yes, I'm okay. Just the cut. And some bruises.'

Then Jack interrupts, breaking the spell and diverting his mother's attention. 'Mum, can we have some ice cream?'

I open my mouth to remind him to say please, but come to my wits quickly enough to cut myself off. Sarah does it for me.

'Pardon me, Jack. Did you ask something?'

'Ice cream, Mum. Can we have some ice cream?'

'You've forgotten something, young man.'

He actually looks a little confused and I almost groan out load, but then he seems to remember and asks again.

'Please, Mum. Can we have some ice cream, please?'

'That's better, you should remember your manners when you want something, shouldn't you,' she counsels. 'And no, I'm afraid you're not having ice cream before dinner. But you can have an apple if you're still hungry.'

'Aww, Mum,' he whines.

'An apple would be really nice thanks, Mrs. Thompson,' I interject, noticing that Jack has actually finished off all the popcorn already, and also wondering how the new surname would feel as I speak it.

It feels bad.

Sarah snorts a little in surprise. 'That's awfully formal of you, Mark. I don't think you've ever called me Mrs Thompson before. Where did that come from?'

I don't know what to say, so just shrug. She smiles.

'Please call me Sarah, you'll make me feel old otherwise. And Jack, would you like an apple too?'

He gives me a look that clearly says that I've done the wrong thing, and he isn't happy, but then he just shrugs too and dolefully replies, 'Yes, Mum.'

'So how was your day, boys?' Sarah asks brightly as she lifts two apples from the fruit bowl and begins washing them at the sink. And Jack is off.

It's like turning on a tap also, that boy can ramble. Before she finishes washing the fruit, cutting it and presenting it to us he's covered almost everything he'd already told me about on the walk home, and a few things I must have missed.

Sarah nods and murmurs occasionally while he burbles on, her eyes watching him with love and understanding. If she is bored by the mundane quality of the spiel, or frustrated by the frenetic changes in pace and direction she doesn't show it. She listens attentively and I am so proud of them both as I watch.

Sarah is a great mother. She was wonderful with both Daniel and Katherine, seemingly guiding them along effortlessly while I was quicker to temper and would find myself growling at them when they didn't immediately do what I wanted. And I know I've struggled to actually listen to everything Jack has said, as so much of it is, quite frankly, boring and irrelevant. But she is focused and listens intently.

Jack is kind of funny. He so earnestly appraises her of absolutely everything that has gone on in his day I want to laugh a little. It's great to see that my youngest son has a mother he can really talk to, and I'm pleased to know that he's so happy to share his thoughts with her. Hopefully he'll still be willing to share with her like this as he gets older, as we all know how teenage boys close down and cease to communicate.

I'm quietly enjoying the exchange when Sarah suddenly draws me into the conversation, picking up on Jack's mention of the school bully and how things were different today without him around.

'Do you know when you'll be allowed back at school yet, Mark?' she asks.

I've been day-dreaming and need to gather myself before answering. 'Uh, well . . . no. I don't as yet. They said they would need to discuss the situation with the other boy's parents, and then, um, consider things.'

'Oh dear, that all sounds so vague, doesn't it.' She seems a little irritated, 'You know, Mark. I don't condone fighting for the sake of it, but I tend to think you may have actually done the right thing in standing up to that boy, and I want to thank you for helping Jack with a difficult situation.'

I'm surprised. Brett's attitude had seemed quite different. I must flush more than a little as she goes on.

'Now don't get me wrong, I don't think it's often right to sort things out by fighting. But I do know that it had been going on for quite a while. And I don't care if that boy is a Breckenock and his father owns half this town. What he was doing is wrong and it really should have come to a head sooner. So, I guess, well . . . thank you, Mark, for doing what you did.'

I am so proud to have done something that gains her approval that I completely choke up again. A warm feeling spreads through me. I want to boldly reply with a big smile and a *Happy-to-help-you-ma'am* type of response, but I just can't make myself say anything so I simply nod my thanks back to her, blushing yet again.

Then she looks concerned. 'And what did your Mum say about all this? I guess she will be a bit worried with the suspension?'

With some effort I manage to respond wryly. 'Yes, she was pretty angry. I'm not all that popular at home at the moment.'

'Oh dear, well you better behave yourself for a while then. I'm sure your Mum has enough to worry about with you getting hurt on your bike, and now having been suspended from school, don't you?'

'I'm trying to keep a low profile,' I tell her, smiling.

She smiles back, then ends the conversation by turning back to the kitchen and saying loudly, 'Right then, you two, enough chit-chat. I've got to get something organised for dinner, and you boys need to get outside and play. Go on then, off you go.'

I'm immediately dismayed. I want to stay and chat. I want to somehow find a way to ask her all those questions about everything that has gone on in her life over the last nine years. I don't want to go and play, I want answers. I want to talk. But that doesn't seem likely to happen. Jack sighs and quickly bounces out of his chair.

'Do you want to kick goals out back, or shoot a few hoops?'

I don't want to do either, but I can't think of a good enough excuse for just staying where I am. I watch Sarah over his shoulder and realise she has now completely dismissed us. She's rummaging through the pantry and searching the fridge for ideas for dinner. The sight brings an image of Tracey to mind; planning dinner in her kitchen is virtually the same scene that I encountered just a few hours earlier. Only this scene is somehow very, very different. Sarah has no wine glass and the kitchen is immaculately clean and organised. I wonder vaguely if she will produce sausages from the freezer. I doubt it.

Jack and I slip our shoes back on and go out the front door to play a little one-on-one basketball. My heart isn't in it though, and I just can't concentrate. Simply being that close to Sarah and knowing she is just inside the house, right now, is burning a hole in my chest.

Jack is actually quite a good shot, hitting the backboard and scoring almost every time. But I'm not really focused. My head is spinning once again with memories of my wife and visions of her with her new husband. I'm not sure that I'm ready to actually see Sarah and Brett together. I wonder if I'll lose my temper and physically attack him again. It's possible. Actually it's more than possible, it's quite probable.

Suddenly a large shape brushes past me, startling me and charging in towards Jack. I stumble, falling and twisting to see what is happening. A feeling of dread overwhelms me. I expect to see Steve grabbing Jack, tucking him under his arm and running off. Jack squeals in surprise and tries to defend himself, but our attacker isn't Steve.

It's Daniel.

Jack's big brother has burst onto the driveway, bumping us both aside and is now stealing the basketball. He dribbles it backwards, driving Jack away from the hoop and forces him to fall roughly onto his bottom. Then he jumps up, popping a neat shot straight through the hoop.

'Nothing but net,' he announces proudly, and promptly walks away towards the front door leaving us both sprawled on the ground.

'Hey, you big git,' calls Jack, from the ground. 'Bet you can't do that again, when we're actually ready.'

Daniel doesn't even turn around, 'Sorry short stuff. No time to play. Things to do, places to be, you know . . .' he calls over his shoulder, waving airily, a smile in his voice.

'You're just afraid, you big girl's blouse,' calls Jack, trying to goad him into returning. 'You're just scared to take on a couple of little kids.'

Daniel just laughs, keeps walking, and enters the house.

'Big blouse,' shouts Jack loudly as the door closes.

We're both still sitting on the ground where he'd left us and Jack is grinning. I smile too. I'm not sure why having my almost fully grown son knock me to the ground, while my other, younger, son yells abuse at him is funny, but it is and I laugh out loud.

'What?' asks Jack indignantly.

'Nothing,' I'm still laughing a little. 'You're both just funny . . . somehow.'

'Why?' he asks, now a little puzzled.

I shake my head, I can't explain. 'No reason. Forget it.'

He just looks at me, half puzzled and half amused himself. We drag ourselves back to our feet and I decide it's time to head back to the unit.

TWENTY-SEVEN

Having achieved my aim of seeing the two kids home safely I'm keen to see if Mum has called. I also feel pretty strange hanging around at this house, knowing that my wife and children are all inside. I want to go back inside, but I feel like an intruder. It's impossible to describe the feelings running through me.

'I'd better get going Jack, it's dinner time soon and I promised Mum I'd be home early.'

'Oh,' he replies. He looks a little disappointed. 'Do you want me to ask my Mum if you can stay over for dinner here?'

I'm taken by surprise again. My God, just the thought of sitting down to dinner with the entire family, including Brett, sends a shiver of excitement and dread up my spine.

'Um, thanks. But no. Dinner will be waiting for me at home. Maybe another night?'

He just nods, and then asks, 'Are you going to be back at school soon?'

'Hopefully, but it probably won't be until next week.'

'So are you gonna meet me after school again tomorrow?'

That actually sounds pretty good. 'Sure, why not. I doubt I'll have much else to do.'

'Cool,' he says, smiling again now.

'Right, I'd better get going then,' I say, but I want him out of the driveway before I leave. I still have visions in my head of Steve actually turning up and abducting him like I thought he had done just a few minutes ago. 'You should head back inside and do your homework,' I suggest, cringing inside as I think about what I've just said.

'You sound like my Dad,' he says with a wry smile. His words make my heart ache.

'Sorry, that didn't come out right,' I apologise.

'Whatever,' he says, as he pushes his hands into his pockets. 'See you tomorrow then?'

'Absolutely. You have a great day at school, Jack.'

'Ha, Ha, funny guy,' he laughs and turns away.

I watch him re-enter the house, waving as he goes through the door. Then I set off for another fun-filled evening at the unit.

I can hear shouting as I walk up the driveway and my blood runs cold. As I get closer I realise the voices are both female, it sounds like Tracey and Liz. To call it a heated discussion would be a serious understatement. They're blazing away about something.

There's no sign of Steve's SUV, so I make my way up the stairs and quietly open the front door. The volume escalates immediately.

'He's a soul-sucking cheating bastard, Mum. Why can't you see that? He doesn't love you, he's just using you,' Liz shouts as I peek through the opening in the doorway.

I can see them, across the lounge, face to face in front of the dining table, near the entrance to the kitchen. They're both red in the face and are going at it hammer and tongs.

'How dare you stand there and shout at me, I'm your mother god-damn it. You need to show me some respect–'

'But he's bad for you, and you've been drinking more since you started seeing him– '

'Don't you start in on me about that, you don't know– '

'–how hard it all is for you,' Liz finishes for her. 'Yes I do know Mum, and– '

'You! You little shit, you get in here now.'

Tracey has spotted me at the door and is pointing straight at me, redirecting her anger and venom. 'You've got some explaining to do, little man.' She steps aside and points onto the small dining table. 'What the hell is this?'

The laptop is sitting there, all set up and running, with a frozen frame of the video displaying clearly on the screen.

Damn. This isn't what I wanted. I step in to the unit, closing the door behind me. I curse myself for not hiding the laptop better. I should have moved it before I left earlier.

'Where did you get this,' Tracey shouts at me, pointing at the new laptop.

'I shot it on my cell-phone last Friday,' I reply carefully.

'Not the bloody video,' Tracey roars. 'The bloody computer! Where the hell did you get it? Did you steal it?'

Oh shit, I didn't think of that. I have nothing prepared.

'I borrowed if off Uncle Brett,' I lie quickly. 'To help with my homework while I'm suspended.' It's a poor effort, but it's the best I can come up with. Tracey isn't impressed.

'You're lying,' she says coldly. 'I know when you're lying to me. You stole it didn't you?'

'No,' I say sharply. 'It's not stolen. I've borrowed it.'

'That's not really the point though, is it?' Liz interjects. 'It doesn't matter where he got the computer. What's important is what it can show us.'

'Don't you try and change the subject, young lady,' Tracey whirls on her. 'I won't have any son of mine stealing. I can provide for this family!'

'Oh yeah,' this fires up Liz even more, I've never seen her so angry. 'Like you provide us with comfort and safety, and a positive healthy role model. For crying out loud, we have to lock ourselves in that piteously small room you provide for us to share, just so that we can be safe from your adulterous monster of a boyfriend. That's not providing, that's just crap!'

'It's not like that,' Tracey explodes. 'Steve is a good man, he treats me better than any man alive, and even better than my own daughter and son. How dare you try and ruin that for me with these filthy, filthy lies. Damn it, he loves me and it seems that he loves me more than either of you two.'

She swings back to me, pointing her finger accusingly. 'I don't know how you did this, but I'm not impressed and neither will Steve be when he sees it.'

My stomach lurches and I break out into a cold sweat again. 'You haven't called him have you?' I ask urgently.

Tracey sneers in triumph. 'See, look how scared you get, the moment I threaten to expose your lies. You should think about the consequences of your actions, young man, before you go about creating this sort of fake video thingy to stir up trouble.'

Clearly Liz and Tracey have watched the video. However Tracey seems to be in complete denial of everything she must have seen. I ask again, imploring this time.

'It's not a fake. It's very, very real. Now please tell me, have you called Steve?'

Something in my tone dampens her anger a little and she just looks at me, trying to work something out in her head. I vaguely wonder how much of the wine she's consumed by now. Hopefully not both bottles.

Liz has gone quiet too, the potential implications of a call to Steve suddenly hitting home for her too. Tracey stands there in the sudden silence. She seems to be taking notice of the change in Liz and the desperation in my voice.

'What if I have?' she asks quietly, a little confused.

I take a deep breath. 'If you have, then we are all in a lot of danger right now. Steve has already tried to kill me once for that video. It clearly implicates him for some serious criminal activity and he thinks he destroyed it on Friday after he ran me off my bike. If he finds out that a copy still exists I don't think he'll stop at just hurting me this time. This is serious. Have you called him?'

'The video is a fake,' she says flatly. 'This is all just a horrible, terrible lie that you two have created to try and stop me seeing Steve.' She looks sharply back and forth between us. 'You've got to stop this.'

'It's not a fake, Mum,' Liz says softly.

'It's not,' I add. 'That video is real.'

'It's a fake.' Tracey is resolute. 'And even if it wasn't it's just a load of man bullshit. It's just two guys talking crap, just talking themselves up to try and make their lives sound more exciting than they really are. Men do it all the time,' she's getting angry again, 'so I really don't like you trying to turn something like that into something it's not.'

'Oh, for Christ's sake, Mum. It's not just men blowing bullshit,' Liz is heating up again too. 'They obviously think no one's listening, and they're talking about hurting some old woman's grandchildren, let alone the admission of Steve's sleeping around,' she cries out. 'Wake up, won't you!'

'It's not real,' Tracey explodes again. 'I don't believe it, and I won't!'

She abruptly turns and storms into the kitchen, returning moments later with her handbag in one hand and car keys in the other. She's clearly going to run away again, back to the safety of the pub.

I back up quickly against the closed front door. She storms up and stops directly in front of me. Her face is a mask of fury and anguish. She's very close to breaking down altogether. 'Don't go Mum,' I say softly.

I'm terrified that she has already told Steve, but she hasn't yet confirmed either way. And if she hasn't told him yet we can't risk her going out to the pub and running into him there.

'Get out of my way, Mark.'

'No. I think you should stay. We need to talk about this. Running away isn't going to help.'

'Get out of my bloody way, Mark,' louder this time.

I hold my breath. 'Or what, Mum? Are you going to hit me? Are you going to try and split open the stitches Steve gave me?'

'Damn you, my Steve didn't give you those stitches.'

'He did. He ran me off the road. He could have killed me.'

'He was out looking for you, he would never hurt you.' But she's pleading a little now, confused, and desperate to end the confrontation. 'Please, Mark. Get out of my way.'

Liz slides in beside me, also blocking the door. 'No, Mum. We all need to talk.'

Tracey lets out a cry of anguish and spins away from us, back towards the kitchen. Liz ducks quickly through the short hallway, beating her to the back door, locking it and removing the key before Tracey gets there. She pockets the key and we all stand silently for a minute. Then I see the second bottle of wine, still unopened, on the kitchen bench and grab it quickly, ducking back into the lounge to hide it under a couch cushion.

'We all need to talk,' Liz repeats softly as I return to them.

Tracey turns away from her again, her eyes searching the small kitchen for the wine bottle I've only just removed. 'Where is it?' she exclaims angrily.

'You don't need it,' I respond, sitting down at the kitchen table. 'Why don't you come and sit down and we can try and work this all out.'

I motion towards the seat on the far side of the table, furthest from the front door so that I can keep myself between her and escape. The air is thick with tension.

'Damn you all,' she speaks quietly and a little cryptically. Then she stalks through the small kitchen and sits down heavily on the chair I indicated. She buries her face in her hands and starts to softly sob.

This really throws me.

I look over to Liz, who is also shaken by the sight of her sobbing mother, and we exchange a look. For any number of reasons we're pleased that Tracey has stayed, but neither of us really knows what to do now. But Tracey still hasn't confirmed either way if she'd called Steve – so that becomes my priority. Are we safe here?

'Mum,' I ask softly. 'Did you call Steve . . . or not?'

She keeps sobbing, but raises her head slightly, not looking at either of us. She shakes it just a little, and then falls back to her tears and anguish. I look over at Liz, who shakes her head also, confirming for me that we are in agreement that Tracey hasn't actually called Steve. It's a huge relief.

'Maybe we should have a cuppa, and get some dinner going?' I suggest, mainly to break the tension in the room. I'm not hungry at all.

'Yeah, good idea,' Liz approves. 'I'll do it.'

She busies herself in the kitchen putting the jug on to boil and pulling out a frying pan to cook the sausages Tracey defrosted earlier. She starts peeling potatoes and I just sit there trying to decide what to say to Tracey now. There has to be some way to break this deadlock and help her understand that the video is real, and that Steve is not a good guy.

Tracey weeps quietly, saying nothing. It's impossible to tell what she is thinking. I look out the window as twilight falls and try to think, to put myself in Tracey's shoes, but really struggle. She seems so determined, even rigidly fixated, that the video is fake and that Steve is truly in love with her. What can I possibly say that might tear through her delusions?

I start to wonder if Mum has called, but can't bring myself to ask and break the silence. I look at the laptop which continues to show a still-frame of the beginning of the video, with the two men's faces looming above the camera in sharp clarity. Technology seems to have come a long way in the nine years I've been gone – or dead, or in limbo, or whatever.

Liz catches my eye and tries to mouth something at me. I can't tell what. I've never been good with lip-reading. She fidgets her head about and I get the impression she wants me to try talking with Tracey again. Without speaking I shrug and indicate that I don't know what to say. Tracey's relentless weeping has eased to an ongoing snivel and occasional sob. How can I make her understand? What can I possibly say?

But I don't get the chance to say anything as the front door suddenly bursts open and our lives change again, forever.

TWENTY-EIGHT

STEVE CASSIDY hums softly to himself as he strolls casually through Fraser Park. He isn't afraid of pushing boundaries – in fact, he's certain that life is much more fun on the edge. His favorite saying is: *If you're not living on the edge, then you're taking up too much space.* He has no idea who originally said the quote, but he lives by it. It's his creed.

Steve doesn't define people in terms of good or bad. But more in terms of winners and losers. He's a winner. He knows he's a class above the crowd. One of the special ones.

A Superman. Invulnerable. A living God.

But he doesn't flaunt it, he's humble, unassuming. Sure, he's had to do a few things that lesser mortals might recoil from, might not be able to achieve. But Steve isn't a mere mortal. He is chosen. Untouchable.

Steve tries to spin the basketball he carries on his finger. It takes a couple of attempts but he manages a wobbly two second spin. It's good enough to please him, to bring a smile to his lips.

He looks at the ball again, very happy with himself. It's perfect for his needs. The ball has the child's name – *JACK THOMPSON* – marked on it in big, bold letters, with even his phone number alongside in permanent ink. He's pretty sure that Jack is the younger of the old woman's grandsons, but it's academic really. It definitely belongs to one of them. Either way the bitch will recognise it and understand where it came from.

Only minutes earlier Steve parked his SUV over on Lorneville Drive and walked boldly into the Thompson family's front yard to pick up the ball. No one saw him. The ball had just been lying there, along with all sorts of other kiddy crap, and he'd chosen it immediately, as soon as he saw the name written on it. It was exactly what he'd been hoping for.

Then he crossed the road quickly and cut through the alleyway to the park. In retrospect he realised he'd probably parked a bit too close last time he visited the Davis woman, so this time he is being a little less cavalier.

He rolls the ball in his hands and starts to hum again, a little tune that he can't quite remember the name of. He's actually enjoying himself. It's been some time since his brother has asked him to lend a hand like this and he's happy to help. He'd do anything for Richard, absolutely anything. And this really isn't such a big deal. He just needs to frighten her, wind her up so bad that she'll give it away and get the hell out of the middle of their development. Silly old bitch.

He's got this one in the bag, with the crusty old drone already close to giving in. He has absolutely no reason to believe she won't sign and go, especially once he shows her the basketball. When she understands how close he has already been to her precious grand-kiddies she'll sign for sure.

And he's got a nice little buzz on too. He'd stopped off at the pub on the way here – and for two very good reasons.

The first was to enhance any possible alibi he may need. His brother taught him the value of a good alibi, so at the pub he knocked back a few strong ones and made it clear to everyone around that he was off to Tracey's – for a good bang. And he'll go there too, afterwards, to keep things tight. Obviously a little easy sex is also a good reward.

The second reason is that he performs better with a few drinks in him. A mild buzz seems to bring out his natural menace, his inner fury. He's a bad drunk and he knows it, but he doesn't care. He actually likes this about himself. When he's at the pub people are wary of him, they know that after a couple too many he might turn on them, explode violently, without cause. He likes the reputation. It makes him feel that he's better than them, better than the pathetic weaklings he so often encounters in there.

He reaches the tree-line and stops to survey Wilton Rd and the area around the big old house that his brother needs to knock down. It's always so quiet along here. The beautiful new shopping centre further down the road is always buzzing, but the street here is dead. With no houses, bar the old bags, there is almost never anyone in sight. It's perfect.

He takes a deep breath, thinking of his brother, remembering all the times that Richard has been there for him. He's happy to do this for him, he owes him so much. His big brother was there for him many years ago when their father left them, then again when their mother died. And he'd been there when the police were harassing Steve for various crimes over the years, some of which he didn't commit. And he'd helped him with money, with a job, and put a roof over his head. Steve could never repay Richard for everything he'd done for him, but he knows this will help. Getting this old bitch to sign the sale papers will be a major coup. He'll be a hero, once again, to his big brother – and that means a lot to him.

The red sedan is in the driveway across the road, so he knows she's home. Good. It's twilight and the sun has almost set, it's not dark but it's dim enough. He crosses the road quickly, the ball tucked under his arm. Then he stops in the driveway and pulls out his balaclava, slipping it silently over his head. He waits, checking the area again. All is quiet.

It's his lucky balaclava. The same one he wore when he did his first ever job for Richard. Thank God he was able to wash out all the blood. He'd been so young then, so inexperienced, and he'd nearly botched the whole thing. All he had to do was run the guy's car off the road, put him in hospital for a while, but it had gone wrong. The guy went and died on him and Steve had been quite badly hurt too. But Richard got him out of there, got him to a doctor who stitched him up. It ended up okay though, it could have been worse, and they did get away with it. The cops never even had a clue.

That was when Richard really started to take him seriously, stopped looking at him like his baby brother – like a kid who needed to be taken care of – and started treating him like an equal. A partner. It had been a turning point in their relationship, forming an unbreakable bond.

Steve surveys the area again quickly, then takes another deep breath and steels himself. As he moves up the driveway, and up the steps to stand before the door he mentally pumps himself up.

You are the man; No backward steps; Destroy this bitch.

He repeats the phrases inside his head like a mantra. He feels his heart rate increase as the blood starts pumping. It feels good and he loves it, there's nothing better. Not even sex – and he loves that too.

As he did before he ignores the iron knocker and pounds his fist against the door, enjoying the feel as the wood quakes beneath his hand. He can see the crack he made with his boot the day before and smiles beneath his mask.

He's in the zone, he loves this shit.

He waits for only a moment and then pounds on the door again relentlessly. It swings open suddenly, his fist still in mid-air and he pulls up with a start, surprised. Then his eyes widen in disbelief. It's not the old woman.

A bloody cop has answered the door.

The policeman stares back at him in equal surprise. For a moment they're both frozen in shock, but Steve recovers his wits first and suddenly fires the basketball directly at the cops head. The cop is too slow and barely turns his face away as the ball catches him in a solid, glancing blow.

Steve doesn't wait. He turns abruptly and leaps down the steps, onto the driveway and sprints off as quickly as he can. He doesn't look back, but hears the cop shouting, his voice angry. He dashes across the road, into the park and stumbles slightly, almost tripping. As he regains his balance he risks a quick look behind – and almost laughs out loud. The cop is sprawling on the driveway. It looks like he's fallen over his own feet.

Steve keeps running, aiming for the alleyway, to get to his car. As he reaches the alleyway he looks back again, but the cop is chasing now and he's already half way across the park. He won't have time to reach his car, and it'll be too obvious, the cop will see him pulling away, get his plates. He can't allow that, he needs to hide, get the car later.

As he sprints past a broken fence board along the alleyway inspiration hits him. He takes the corner into Lorneville Drive too quickly, catching his arm on the fence. He hears a short ripping sound but keeps moving, there's no time, he can't be caught. A few steps later and he's rounding the corner into the cul-de-sac and then sprinting up the driveway to Tracey's crappy unit. He sees that her car is there, good. That's very good, a guaranteed alibi. She'll tell them he's been there for hours, if he needs her to. He's already feeling confident. They won't catch him. He's too fast, too clever.

He is the chosen one.

As Steve Cassidy dashes up the few steps to Tracey's door he whisks off his balaclava, stuffing it hurriedly back into his pocket. Then he lurches through the door without knocking.

TWENTY-NINE

I just freeze in horror, and my heart stops beating.

Tracey looks up sharply, blinking rapidly, and immediately turns her face away from the door to begin wiping up the tears and running mascara.

From the kitchen Liz can't see the door but reacts instantly to the expressions on our faces. She seems to stop breathing and turns as white as a ghost.

Steve is wearing his all black outfit again, the same one he'd worn yesterday morning at the old homestead. He has the gloves on also and looks a little flushed, like he's been running. His sleeve is slightly torn and there may even be a little blood on it from his arm. His expression is initially relieved but, as he steps quickly into the unit, closing the door behind him, he starts to look wary.

'Hey,' he calls out, a little too cheerily. 'You're home, excellent.'

Tracey almost jumps out of her chair and steps towards him. 'Hey, baby. What a lovely surprise. I wasn't expecting to see you till later on.' But she stops short of going all the way to the door. She steps across in front of me, leaning her hip against the back of the couch.

'Are you all right, Sweetie,' he asks, sounding convincingly concerned. 'Have you been crying? What's the matter?'

'Oh, you know. Nothing really,' she tries to lie. 'Just a sad moment.' I can sense her trying to smile and make light of the tear-stained mess her face is in. He isn't buying it though.

'Something's happened, hasn't it? Is everyone okay? Where's Liz?' he asks.

'She's fine. She's just in the kitchen,' Tracey replies and, as if on cue, Liz manages to drop a spatula onto the floor, making enough noise to confirm where she is. 'Everyone's fine. I was just having a moment.'

She's a terrible liar. I'd never have believed her and Steve doesn't either. 'No, everything's not just fine,' he says, a little edgy now, immediately concerned that Tracey's tears may be a threat to him somehow. 'Something's going on here and I think I should know about it.'

He steps further into the room, all the time watching Tracey and I for clues to the unusual behaviour.

As he walks forward to her she shifts her position from beside the couch to block his path. Then it comes to me. She's trying to stop him from seeing the laptop. Shit. In my horror I forgot about it being there. My heart finally kick-starts again, racing furiously in dread.

I must subconsciously look at the laptop on the table as Steve senses something and steps further forward to look around Tracey. I move too quickly to slap the laptop's screen down and he's immediately intrigued.

'What was that?' he asks, almost politely, but with a cold tone. A wave of ice cold terror washes through me.

'It's just a school project,' I reply, my voice quivering. I start to gather up the laptop and wish desperately that it would just vanish somehow into thin air.

'Cool,' he says forebodingly, pushing Tracey gently aside and advancing on me. 'I'd be really interested to see that. What's it about?'

'It's nothing really,' Tracey quickly interjects. 'Just kid's stuff. You wouldn't like it, you know, just math and science and stuff.' She reaches out and tries to take his arm, noticing the tear and the blood. 'Oh, Steve. You're bleeding, look here.'

He looks back at her briefly, then at the arm. 'It's nothing . . . really. It's just a scratch. I'm not worried about it. I'm more interested in Mark's homework.'

He pulls his arm easily from her grip and leans in over me.

'I'm really, really, interested to see what Mark's school project is all about.'

His eyes are unfathomable and I wonder why he is here. Has he been to visit Mum? Clearly the police haven't caught up with him yet. I struggle to mask my terror. If he sees the video there's going to be trouble. He'll probably drag me outside and beat me senseless, if he stops there.

Suddenly he snatches the laptop from my grip, smiling in a leering sort of triumph. Tracey makes a half-hearted attempt to get it off him, but he lifts it over his head so it almost touches the ceiling and turns on his heel. He walks back to the couch and sits down facing us, opening the small computer and sitting it on his knees. Neither Liz nor I have moved from where we were when he burst in the door, and now Tracey is rooted to the spot also. Her expression is a mask of uncertainty.

Then Steve's face turns crimson, and not with embarrassment. He stares at the screen, which proudly displays the silent image of himself and his big brother. He looks up at me, then at Tracey, his eyes flashing with anger.

'It's not what it looks like, Darling,' begs Tracey softly. 'I don't know how they did it but it's obviously a fake. They probably dubbed it on a special computer somehow. You know how these things are these days– '

'Be quiet!' he snaps.

The silence that follows is instantaneous and toxic.

He clicks a button and the deep voices from the video fill the room. Liz must have turned the volume up earlier and it's loud, and very clear. Steve's recorded voice is light and friendly, very unlike the tone he has just shared with us.

We listen to the whole thing before Steve looks up at me with fire in his eyes and says, 'Is that it? Is that everything?'

I'm scared stiff. I can't speak, but I manage a very small nod. He starts to play it again, shaking his head slowly from side to side with every word, but he stops it as soon as the images on screen stop talking about Mum and the property development issues and start into his wild weekend plans.

There is silence again for a short time as he continues to stare at the screen, brooding. Then Tracey speaks again. She sounds desperate, and the words flood out rapidly.

'It's not true, is it? None of it is true. I told them that it was just men talking crap, like they do when they're at the pub, trying to impress their mates. I told them there was no way you would do that to me, that there was no way you would cheat on me like that. You love me too much to do that, I told them, and I know that men like to talk tough with their mates, you know, just talk up their conquests– '

'Shut up, damn you!' he bellows at her.

There is silence again.

Tracey looks confused. Liz mirrors my own pale mask of terror. Steve is fuming. We watch him thinking frantically, trying to work something out. His eyes flicker from the screen, to me, to Tracey. His face has changed from crimson to a deeper, darker red. I've never seen anger so intense.

Other that the gentle bubble of boiling potatoes and the soft sizzle of sausages from the kitchen there is silence. Then his eyes fix on mine and something seems to click for him.

'You gave this to the old lady, didn't you?' he asks quietly. My look of surprise gives me away and I don't need to respond. I feel the colour drain out of my face.

'Shit,' is all he says.

'Steve, what do you mean?' Tracey suddenly comes to life again. 'Why would you ask something like– '

'Shut the hell up, will you!' he shouts at her. 'I need to bloody think!'

She goes silent and looks round at me, a look of dawning horror on her face. It's far too late for understanding now, I think uncharitably.

Liz stands wide-eyed in the kitchen. She still hasn't moved or spoken. I turn my head slightly when I see her reaching out towards the telephone. It's a basic touch-tone cordless phone and she takes the handset up silently.

Steve is still sitting on the couch, thinking furiously, drumming his fingers on the edge of the laptops keypad, his lips moving as he curses silently.

Tracey backs up a little to the wall at the edge of the kitchen and I see her very slight reaction to the quiet beeps that come from behind her as Liz dials the phone. It's just a half turning of the head and a slight raising of the eyebrows, but I see it, and so does Steve.

'What the . . .' he snarls, tossing the laptop onto the couch, leaping up out of the chair and charging to the kitchen. He brushes Tracey's attempt to block his way aside and comes face to face with Liz who has the telephone handset in her hand, desperately trying to dial 111 silently.

Steve grabs her by the wrist, snatching the handset from her with his other hand. 'No you bloody don't,' he growls.

He jams his finger onto the *End Call* button and drops the handset to the ground. Then he raises his booted foot and stomps the phone repeatedly into little pieces.

He's still holding Liz's wrist and he uses this to pull her abruptly and viciously out of the kitchen, sending her sailing between Tracey and I, across the lounge, to bounce off a couch and fall to the floor, cruelly banging her head on the wall as she goes down.

Everything happens so fast after that.

It's nothing like what you see in the movies. There is no slow motion, there are no split-seconds to think and respond in the most valiant and heroic ways. Steve's movements are just scary and fast and violent.

Tracey steps forward to try and help Liz and he punches her. Brutally, and without warning. He just turns slightly, leans back and punches her directly in the face, driving his body forward with the blow to maximize the impact. His fist drives straight ahead, striking her in the cheek, just to the side of her nose and slightly below her left eye.

She doesn't see it coming, and she never has a chance. Folding like a wet paper bag she flies backwards, hitting the floor behind the couch limp and unconscious.

I still haven't moved, and when I try to I don't get far. He spins on his heel as I begin to stand and he back-slaps me across the temple, sending me flying over the dining table and onto the floor near the kitchen entrance.

I black out momentarily, I think.

When I raise myself from the floor my head is pounding again, worse than when I'd woken up only a few days earlier, and my sight is blurry. Steve has his back to me, struggling with Liz. I can hardly think straight, but I know I need to move, and quickly, there's a real chance I could die here.

And I don't want to die again, not so soon.

I manage to scramble a little way into the kitchen and look back to see if Steve has noticed. He hasn't. But I'm horrified by what I see from this slightly different angle.

Steve has Liz half tied up and is struggling to get her feet bound. She kicks wildly, her bare legs flying around beneath her short skirt, but he's managed to gag her already and her hands are hidden behind her back, I assume they're bound too.

What terrifies me most is that he's humming. Not very tunefully, but he's definitely humming softly, in a measured and playful, whistle-while-you-work sort of way. He actually seems to be having fun.

I need to help Liz. I can't just run away.

So I need a weapon. Desperately I look around the kitchen. A big knife. That will do it. I grab wildly at the cutlery drawer and it's a bad mistake. I'm so scared I pull the whole thing out. Forks and spoons spill all over the floor, making a terrific din.

Steve spins at the sound, annoyed to find that I'm neither unconscious nor dead, and that I'm attempting to get away. He starts to rise and Liz's thrashing foot catches him in the thigh.

He grabs her foot and looks back at me, momentarily undecided as to dealing with me now or completely securing Liz first. The look on his face terrifies me.

I think about the moments of fear I'd had trying to escape from Skinner earlier and they pale in comparison. The old guy may have been creepy, but Steve wears his menace like a badge of honour and terror courses through me.

I feel sick in my stomach as I do it, but I run.

I sprint out of the kitchen, down the short hall and into Liz and Mark's bedroom. I slam the door behind me and throw both bolts across as quickly as I can.

It's very dim in the room, but still not fully dark, and I look around wildly for an idea. I see the window that Mark had apparently escaped out of before, the last time Steve came looking for him. Dashing over I wrench it open, as wide as it will go. It would be easy to jump out and run off, but something makes me stay. I really should get out and try to find help, but I just can't leave Liz . . . or Tracey for that matter.

It feels wrong, and cowardly.

Then there is a loud bang behind me.

'Fuck,' Steve's voice reaches me through the thin door. 'You're not getting away this time, damn you,' he snarls and the door shudders as he throws himself against it.

I watch in horror as the screws from the upper bolt pop out. The door isn't going to last long.

Looking down I see Mark's wooden cricket bat at the foot of his bed and, as I look back up, another screw comes flying out of its place as the door shudders again. I snatch up the bat and leap quickly up onto Mark's bed, just turning in time as the door swings violently open. Small pieces of splintered wood fly through the air as the door crashes against the side of the bed I am standing on.

Steve storms into the room, growling like a bear.

THIRTY

Steve heads straight for the wide open window, as I hoped. Now I am behind him, hidden from view by the open door, and standing on the bed so that we're at the same height.

He reaches the window and looks out briefly, swears and steps back slightly, starting to turn around. It's then that I step forward, still on the bed, and swing the cricket bat with my entire body twisting into the blow.

The bat starts from around behind my head, parallel with my shoulders, and swings through almost 360 degrees, gathering power and momentum as it flies. I may only have the body of a small child, but I'm angry and I'm afraid and I swing that bat like my life depends on it – as it probably does.

Steve never sees it coming either. He has no chance to react as the bat smashes into his right temple, ironically exactly where Mark's stitches are on his forehead. I'm worried for a fraction of a second that the bat will break, but it holds together and Steve's forehead takes the full impact.

He doesn't crumple quite the same as Tracey had, but he does go down. He staggers back from the blow and falls backwards into Liz's bookcase, spilling the contents all over the place. A flow of bright red blood erupts from the spot where I've hit him and he grunts loudly before slumping over and flopping limply to the floor.

I step down from the bed and stand there, considering hitting him again. He's down, but is he out? I stand over him with the bat raised, ready to strike again if he moves at all, but he doesn't. I'm breathing heavily. My heart racing ferociously.

I back out of the room, watching Steve's body on the floor, praying he is dead – and then I feel faint.

I begin struggling for breath and my vision tunnels. It feels like I'm going to black out again.

I've never really hurt anyone before. I mean sure, I've been in a few fights and I'm certainly not a pacifist, but never have I been involved in anything like this.

With my knees about to give way I hear struggling and muffled shouting behind me and remember Liz, and Tracey.

Turning I can see Tracey still lying prone, exactly where she fell after Steve's single punch, and Liz's bound feet sticking out from behind the couch just beyond. Taking a deep breath I manage to steady myself and then stagger over, dropping the bat beside the couch as I reach Liz. Her eyes are wide with terror, which changes rapidly to surprise when she sees me standing over her instead of Steve.

'It's okay, Liz. He's down and out. I think I may have killed him,' I say shakily, as I try to move in closer to remove her gag and untie her. Steve has done a thorough job on the bindings of both and the gag is hard to loosen, especially as my hands are now profoundly trembling. 'Let me just get you untied, then you can help me with Tracey. I think she may be badly hurt,' I talk softly, trying to calm myself also.

A small spasm of coldness lances through me suddenly when Liz's eyes fly wide as she looks up over my shoulder. I just stop, staring at her eyes in dismay. I see terror there.

Then I am flying through the air.

For the second time I travel sharply over the kitchen table, this time slamming into the wall just outside the small kitchen area. I roll in the air and my head and back cannon into the wall and I fall, finishing up sitting on the floor.

Everything goes dark, I've almost blacked out.

Unable to resist I feel myself being hauled to my feet, and then up and into the air. I'm swung around like a doll, shaken violently, my body numb and limp.

My vision suddenly returns, just in time to glimpse the blood-soaked face of Steve Cassidy snarling into mine from only inches away.

Then I see his fist come flying at me from behind his right ear and everything goes abruptly black once more.

A cold splash of water brings me around.

My sight is very hazy and I can feel blood mixed with the water running down my face. It feels like the stitched up gash on my forehead has reopened. As my focus starts to return, I quickly understand why.

Steve had thumped me in the face, hard. He was probably a bit upset about the gash I'd opened up on his forehead with the cricket bat – and now he is standing in front of me with an empty bucket in his hand. Water and blood continue to drip down my nose.

'That's better, you little piece of shit,' he sneers at me. 'I want you to see this. I want you awake while you and your precious bitch of a mother die.'

He steps back and I can now see that I'm in the kitchen, on the floor, propped up against the doorframe that leads to the small laundry and the back door. He points behind me.

'It's locked,' he advises me coldly. 'And don't think about running to your room. It's all blocked up now, and anyway, I don't think you're gonna be running anywhere right now. Your ass is mine and I'm gonna watch it fry.'

I don't understand. Everything is so fuzzy. But he smiles in an evil way and I can see that he's roughly strapped up his head, with what looks like a torn up towel, to stem the bleeding. His black shirt is sticky with his own blood and it seems to me that he's slipped well and truly beyond the edge of reason. Although he thankfully isn't humming anymore.

I can't move. I don't seem to be tied up, but my body isn't responding at all. My arms lie weakly by my side and my head lolls about. I'm having trouble seeing him and start to black out again. The darkness is welcoming.

But another cold splash of water rains over me and I'm back on the kitchen floor again. 'Oh no you don't, ass-wipe. You're staying awake for this show.'

He steps back again. He seems pleased to have gained my attention once more. He smiles without mirth, but it seems that he wants to chat.

'I seem to recall telling you just the other day to keep your damn nose out of my business, did I not?'

The question is obviously rhetorical, but I don't think I can speak anyway.

'And I told you to stop telling lies and to keep out of my bloody way, didn't I?'

Again I fail to respond.

'But you didn't, did you? So you, you obsessive little piece of shit, are gonna get yourself and your stupid god-damn mother toasted. And,' he pauses for effect, 'I'm gonna have to take your lovely sister with me, for a little insurance . . . and fun.' His voice seems to get louder and more intense with each word. A wild madness dances behind his eyes. He spits the next words out with intense loathing.

'Because of you, giving that bloody video to that old bitch, who must have given it to the god-damn cops, I am now gonna have to disappear,' he shouts. Then he roars, 'and I'm not fucking happy about it!'

When he stops to take a few breaths I notice the sound. It's a spitting and popping sound and it seems to be coming from somewhere just behind him. He must see my eyes flicker in that direction and he looks over his left shoulder briefly before displaying a sneering, gloating smile as he turns back to me.

'And if I'm going to have to suffer then you, you little dirt-bag, are going to have to suffer a whole hell-of-a-lot more,' he snarls. The popping and spitting suddenly turns into a whoomph sound and a jet of flames bursts up from behind his left shoulder.

'Woo-hoo. Now we have lift-off.' Then he stands up to check the progress of the flames to ensure he isn't going to get burned before turning back to me, smiling even more savagely.

'Did you know . . .' he intones in a mock-serious presenter's voice. 'That by far and away the largest cause of fires in the home is from unattended cooking? It's incredible really, just how many people put too much cooking oil in with their sausages, and then they turn the heat up too high, and then they leave the room to watch TV, leaving the sausages all alone and unattended.' He pauses, a mix of self-satisfaction and loathing on his face. 'And would you be surprised to hear that it's not uncommon for an alcoholic to fall asleep in front of the TV, while they should be attending to the sausages that they're overcooking in the kitchen.' He shakes his head in mock amazement. 'It's just shocking how these sorts of tragic accidents happen every day. Shocking!'

I can't move. My mind is screaming at me to get up and run. To get up and get the hell out of there before the burning fat explodes further and globs of flaming oil and sausage start splattering themselves around the room.

But my body isn't responding. I can't tell if it's broken or if it has just shut down, but I can't make myself move. My focus starts to fade, my vision blurs and my head lolls as I start to black out again.

'Damn it,' Steve yells at me. 'I want you awake! Do you hear me,' he cries out as his open palm slaps me hard across the face. My head snaps up and my eyes open wide again.

I'm conscious, but only just.

I blink rapidly to clear my sight and see Steve stepping back again, smiling. He says something softly like 'that's better' and then suddenly he lurches to his left and his arm whips out looking for support. It finds the handle of the flaming frying pan, slapping it down and launching the contents of the burning pan into the air.

Blazing oil and chunks of cremated sausage rain through the air across the small kitchen. Steve must have practically filled the pan with oil before turning the heat up full as the spray of burning liquid is like watching a volcano erupt.

Flames scatter over almost every surface on the opposite side of the kitchen and Steve is doused liberally.

He goes down on one knee, screaming.

His head, back and both arms immediately leap with flames and he roars like a stuck pig. Lashing out wildly he tries to brush the flames from his hair, only succeeding in spreading them further, and then down onto his face.

He tries to throw himself clear of the burning kitchen area and slams his back into the small counter that divides the kitchen from the dining area, and then falls back onto the kitchen floor, ablaze and howling.

I see that my sneaker is on fire, and though my mind desperately orders my body into motion it still won't move. Again my vision starts to blur and I feel the heat from the flames drying the water and blood on my face.

Then I see her.

Tracey is standing at the other end of the kitchen, a confused look of disgust, horror and madness on her face. She's holding the cricket bat and watching Steve lurching and struggling to put out the flames on his body. The bat is alight too, just a small patch of flames near the very tip.

Steve starts to rise and turn towards her. I'm not sure if he actually sees her there, I think the flames on his head have blinded him, and again he doesn't see it coming.

Tracey snarls, like a lioness, and draws the bat back up and over her shoulder, completely impervious to the flaming tip. She screams manically and swings the bat in an overhead arc, landing it squarely on top of Steve's head. He lurches again and his knees give out, toppling him back down to the burning floor of the kitchen. He lies across it now, his feet at the base of the stove and his head near the entrance to the dining area.

My vision starts to fade once more and I feel the darkness coming yet again.

Tracey steps forward for a second time, into the entrance of the burning kitchen. She is screaming something unintelligible, to me anyway, and she raises the bat and swings it viciously down onto Steve's prone head.

I black out, only for a moment, I think.

My eyes open again, for the final time, and there is Tracey – hitting the burning lump on the kitchen floor again and again and again. Smoke is starting to fill the room.

Then she stops, staggering backwards to prop herself up on the kitchen table. She throws down the burning cricket bat and looks through the haze at me. Tears are streaming down her face, she's sobbing uncontrollably.

Our eyes meet, and hold for a brief moment, and then the darkness envelopes me completely, once again.

THIRTY ONE

My hospital room smells clean and antiseptic. It's dimly lit and there is a half-drawn curtain around my bed, shielding me from god-only-knows what. Someone has just left the room, I think maybe a nurse, and the door clicking shut behind her has woken me.

Staring through the gloom at the panelled ceiling above I try to get my head straight. I struggle to remember what happened and wonder hazily if I've been badly hurt.

It's still very dim in the room and I gingerly lift my head to try and see around. A half-drawn curtain obscures everything to my left, but the muted sound of soft snoring reaches me through it. I'm not alone.

Straight ahead I can see a window beyond the foot of my bed with patterned curtains drawn over it. Dawns soft light glows through the thin material. Moving my head very slowly I look carefully to my right. The movement hurts like hell.

There is an empty chair in the far right corner of the room, beside the door. Then, further around to my right, as I grimace from the pain the movement produces, I find another two chairs, directly to my right, nearest to the bed-head. The chair closest to me is occupied.

The girl in the chair has long very dark-brown hair tied back in a pony-tail, and fair lightly freckled skin. Her blue eyes are closed at first, but suddenly spring open as though some sixth sense has alerted her to my awakening.

Her eyes are puffy and red. She looks like she's been crying, a lot. She's quite attractive in a gangly teenage sort of way and I'd have guessed her age to be about seventeen.

But I know better.

'Hey there, Mark,' she whispers. 'How you doing?'

I try to speak, but can only manage a weak croak. I cough a little to clear my throat, and then hoarsely whisper back.

'I feel great. How 'bout you?'

She smiles at this, and a tear runs down her cheek. 'Fantastic,' she lies. 'Never better.' She pauses, and then asks, 'You sleep well?'

'Like a rock,' I try to smile back, but my head is throbbing and the smile must look pretty crooked. I move a little to try and sit up, pushing myself up onto my right elbow. That hurts too. In fact as I move my little body starts to ache from head to toe. I flex my fingers and move my legs up and down. Nothing seems broken. I try to touch my face and feel big bandages across my nose and forehead.

'It's just your head . . . again,' Liz confirms. 'The doctor said that you'll probably have a bad concussion, and you've lost a bit of blood, and your nose is broken, but they don't think anything else is, or, you know, ruptured inside either . . . and you don't have any burns.' She pauses, looking at me in disbelief. 'You've been awfully lucky . . . again.'

I half smile, gently touching my nose and grimacing at the pain. 'You know, I don't feel all that lucky,'

'You don't know the half of it,' she whispers.

'Then tell me. Please.' I wait, but she frowns, looking undecided. 'What happened after I passed out?' I ask.

We're interrupted by the door swinging open. A man enters. I had expected a nurse, but it isn't. Brett Thompson stands there, looking awkward and a little surprised. He was aiming to take the seat by the door, before he noticed that I am awake. He turns and comes quietly over, whispering softly.

'Hey, Mark. How are you feeling?'

I want to be angry at him, just for being who he is. I want to tell him to piss off and get the hell away from me. But I don't have the energy.

'Pretty sore,' I reply instead.

He looks tired, but offers a faint smile none the less. 'Do you know where you are?'

It's the concussion test, all over again. 'Hawthorne Central,' I reply flatly. He nods, showing some relief.

'And do you remember what happened?'

We're still talking in whispers. Obviously we don't want to wake my room-mate. I take my time to consider my response. 'Some things . . . but . . . I'm not too sure.'

'Okay, that's understandable.' He sits down in the vacant chair next to Liz. 'What do you remember?' he asks cautiously. Instead of answering him I ask my own question.

'Did Steve get away?'

There is a moment's silence. Brett glances at Liz, clearly unsure what to say. Panic spreads through me like wildfire. If he got away we're all still in danger. We need to hide.

But Brett finally answers. 'No,' he says flatly. 'There was a fire. I'm afraid Steve didn't make it out of the unit.'

'So he's dead?'

Liz looks down at the floor. Brett can't meet my eye but he nods slowly, confirming that Steve died in the fire. I mull on that for a moment or two. I had thought the news might make me happy, or even a little righteous, but it doesn't. It makes me numb. It could have been me.

Then panic hits me again.

'Where's Tracey? Is she okay? Was she hurt?'

Immediately Brett starts nodding frantically and Liz looks up with wide eyes. 'Your Mum's okay, Mark,' Brett says quickly. 'Take it easy, she's all right.'

'Where is she then?' I ask.

Liz motions to the soft snoring sound behind me, coming from the other bed behind the curtain.

'She's sleeping, back over there.'

I relax a little. Steve is dead, and both Tracey and Liz are alive, and relatively unharmed. That's good enough, for now.

'So what happened after I passed out?' I ask in a whisper.

Liz looks to Brett, silently seeking permission. He frowns at first but then nods gently. Liz faces me again.

'We don't really know much,' she explains in a quiet voice. 'After Steve knocked you away from me, when you were trying to untie me, he came back and finished tying me up, and then took me outside and bundled me into the back of Mum's car.'

I immediately have a horrific vision of Steve, with Liz all tied up, in the back seat of the old hatchback. What might he have done to her? I search her eyes desperately but she doesn't seem overly traumatized. I get the impression that Steve hadn't had enough time to seize any opportunity, so to speak, while she was bound. Liz carries on.

'I was wedged into the foot-well in the back, and I could barely move, and then he made a call on his cell-phone and he disappeared. Back inside, I guess. I couldn't see anything and I couldn't get free . . . So anyway, after a while Mum suddenly turned up. She pulled me out and untied me. And that's when I saw you again, you were lying unconscious on the lawn near the tree and the unit was on fire, almost completely ablaze. Mum and I, we just, you know, huddled together with you, and then the firemen arrived, and then the police. It was chaotic . . .'

She has to take a deep breath as the memories flood back. Brett shifts uncomfortably in his chair but says nothing. Her voice is barely a whisper as she continues.

'So then, well, you know, all the neighbours start turning up to watch and there are firemen running everywhere with hoses and stuff. And there's lights flashing and water spraying and everyone's shouting . . . Then all three of us got loaded into an ambulance and bought here. They whisked you away real quick and then Mum and I got looked at, and then we came here, to this room. And Brett turned up too, at some point.'

'I was actually at the fire, at the unit . . .' he mumbles softly. 'I followed the ambulance.'

Liz glances at him, and nods. There is an awkward silence before she speaks again.

'Mum's pretty messed up, Mark. She's hardly spoken a word since the fire. Her face is a mess. She managed to sign all the forms to get you in here, but I think she's in shock or something. They let her have that bed, but she's been adamant that she doesn't want to be admitted properly so they can treat her more. I'm pretty worried . . .'

I understand her concern, but I'm kind of relieved to know that she's here with us, sleeping, rather than off somewhere else looking for some liquid comfort.

After a few moments of silence, and an odd shuffling of his feet under his chair, Brett has a question for me.

'Are you able to tell us what happened inside, Mark? There are so many questions, and the police will want to know later. Do you know how the fire started?'

Immediately I wonder what Tracey has told them. Had she said anything at all? Would she have acknowledged beating Steve with the cricket bat? She could find herself in a lot of trouble if our stories don't match up. My God, would the police try to make a case against her for Steve's death? Murder? Or even manslaughter? She'd be jailed. Surely they wouldn't charge her. It had clearly been self-defense, the way I saw it. But then, Tracey is a known alcoholic, and a little unstable, so they might look at her somewhat differently.

'You know, I'm actually pretty tired,' I eventually respond. 'I don't really feel up to talking about all this right now. I think I should get some more rest.'

I lie down and groan a little, closing my eyes to really hammer home my point. I need some time to think.

I hear Brett sigh in frustration as I roll over, turning my back to them. No one else speaks as I keep my eyes closed and try to wish away the pain in my head.

After a minute or so I hear someone get up and leave the room again. I'm pretty sure it's Brett. But I stay where I am, quietly contemplating everything they told me, and actually find myself starting to drift back to sleep before a sharper thought suddenly crosses my mind.

I'm not dead.

I'm still alive, and still in Mark's body.

I've just been knocked unconscious – again. So why wasn't I knocked out of Mark's head . . . and Mark returned to this body? If this was a movie where the hero took a head knock and did a body-swap, or if I had fallen into a coma-dream like I originally thought I had, a punch like the one Steve delivered me in the kitchen last night would surely be enough of a trigger to return me, or the movie hero, to our point of origin.

So why am I still here?

I really can't be sure, but I wonder if there might be some connection between the car crash, where I apparently died, and the bike accident where Mark had been traumatically injured. Somehow the two events seem to be linked, and one possibility – that is suddenly more obvious now – is the independent significant blows to our heads.

But that can't be it. I'm still here.

I've already accepted that this is not a dream and, while I've given some thought to having been a ghost – that has somehow invaded this poor boy's mind and taken over his body, I just can't accept it. I feel more permanent than that. Almost too comfortable within this body, if that makes any sense. And I'm also quite certain that I still have something of Mark here inside my mind, inside his head. It's not something I can put my finger on, but I can sort of feel him within me.

That must mean something . . . surely.

Suddenly the curtain between the hospital beds is pulled aside. Tracey is sitting up on the bed, the sheets cast off. She's fully dressed, and quite filthy with soot. Above and behind her I notice a poster on the wall. Not Batman this time, but some brightly coloured cartoon fish and the words *Finding Nemo*. Isn't Captain Nemo a Jules Verne thing?

Tracey looks dreadful. She has no bandages on her face, but her left hand and right forearm are both neatly wrapped up. Minor burns I guess, from the fire.

But her face is the real tragedy. The entire left hand side of it is a black, purple and yellow swollen mess. If I was trying to be positive, I'd point out that her nose doesn't appear to be damaged and that she can still see quite well out her right eye. But the left is squeezed shut and I imagine she will probably need some serious dental work.

She looks awful, and very tired, and desperately sad. Her bloodshot eyes are devoid of any joy.

I sit up a little as Tracey steps over to sit on the edge of my bed, turning her head away a little so that I can only see the right side. She doesn't seem able to look me in the eye and she murmurs out of the side of her mouth.

'You . . . okay?'

No wonder she's barely spoken since the fire. She must be in agony. The muscles in her face are locked up and I get the strong impression that her jaw is probably broken.

'Oh, Mum. Your face. Is anything broken?' I say.

She probably would have snorted at me, if she could have. Her right eye swivels across, finally looking at me.

'You . . . need . . .' she swallows hard, struggling to get each word out, '. . . a mirror.'

I frown and it hurts. I haven't really thought about my own face and suddenly understand that it can't be much better looking than hers. I touch the bandage across my nose again self-consciously. Liz sniffs loudly, she is crying again. I look back at Tracey. She's trying to speak again, and with great difficulty. I lean forward to catch her words.

'. . . you . . . remember?' is all I hear, but I understand from her look of desperation.

I think carefully before I respond, glancing around to confirm that Brett is no longer in the room with us.

She wants to know if I remember what happened back at the unit. She wants to know if I remember watching her bludgeon Steve with the cricket bat while he burned.

I start to shake my head, but receive a jolt of pain for my efforts. 'No,' I answer quietly instead, knowing it's what she needs to hear. 'No, I don't remember anything after Steve hit me.'

She responds with a very forced smile and a gentle nod. I think I've guessed correctly although I'm not immediately sure why she wants me to have amnesia again. Is she concerned that I will have a terrifying memory that will forever scar Mark's view of his mother? Or is she more worried about how the police will view her actions in the heat of the moment? I decide to give her the benefit of the doubt.

'What happened after that, Mum?' I ask carefully.

She watches me for a long moment and then motions weakly at her face before pointing to Liz. She wants Liz to tell the story, and I suddenly realise that they must have rehearsed it earlier, while I was unconscious. But why hadn't Liz covered this portion of the tale earlier? Was it because Brett was here?

Liz looks from me to Tracey, frowning and seeking silent confirmation of how much she should actually share with me. Had they previously agreed not to tell me anything? I mean, Mark is only eight years old.

As Tracey nods and waves her hand in a get-on-with-it gesture I once again suspect that it's important to Tracey that we all have the same story, probably for when the police start interviewing us later. Liz gazes down; thinking about her words, before leaning in to look me in the eye.

'Steve was a very bad man, Mark. You remember that?' she asks. I give a tiny nod and she continues. 'Mum told me that he'd knocked you out in the kitchen when she came to. She said that he had set the kitchen on fire, and it seemed like he was going to leave you in there.' She shudders and draws a deep breath. 'Mum was frightened. She said he was saying some pretty horrible things to you.'

She pauses momentarily and I impatiently encourage her to carry on. So far we seem to be following a surprisingly truthful version of events.

'So she picked up your cricket bat and hit him with it. And he hit his head on the bench as he fell down . . . and was knocked out. Mum dragged you outside first, and found me in the car, then she went back into the unit and tried to drag Steve out . . . but he was too heavy.'

And there it is.

Just a small lie, or two, to cover her excessive rage – to protect us from the possibility of Tracey going to jail. I feel no pity for Steve, still just numbness, and, although I know better, I will easily repeat this lie to the police if need be. I'm certain Steve could have made it out of that flat alive if Tracey had smothered the flames and helped him, but she hadn't. If she had, God only knows where we would all be now.

I nod slightly again, and lie back into the bed.

'Wow,' I breathe softly, playing along. 'Okay,' I pause, and then say to Tracey. 'Thanks, Mum.'

A small tear slides from her good eye and she turns away from me. She wipes it up before turning back and laying her hand on my chest.

'Rest . . . now,' is all she can manage. Then she stands up and moves towards the door, signalling Liz to follow her. They leave quietly and I stare up at the ceiling panels, wondering where my strange new existence is going to lead me now.

THIRTY-TWO

About an hour later, after a nurse has bought me some breakfast, there is a gentle knock on the door. Neither Brett nor Tracey has returned, but Liz is with me. She rises from her seat at my bedside and slips out. There is a soft murmur of voices and I wait for something to happen. Moments later Liz returns, followed by an immaculately dressed woman sporting a very familiar knot of grey hair on the back of her head.

I'm surprised, but also very pleased. Liz looks worried. She's never met Helen Davis before.

My bed has already been raised so I'm in an upright sitting position now and I turn sideways, smiling to greet my new visitor as she and Liz draw chairs up to the side of the bed.

'Hi, Helen. It's nice to see you looking so well.'

She has been watching me intently since she entered the room and becomes obviously relieved at my welcome. Not just because I am alive and relatively unscathed – but because I am clearly still her boy, Nick, inside. She can tell. A mother knows these things, she'd told me recently.

She smiles back. 'Hi, Mark. How are you feeling?'

I suddenly realise how difficult this is going to be. After we run through the accepted pleasantries, we will have to somehow communicate while Liz listens in. I try to clear my thoughts and remember what we've agreed previously as our actual relationship so far.

'I'm fine, thanks, Helen. A little sore, but I'm really pleased you made the effort to come and visit.'

And I am pleased. I'm also very curious. I've been thinking about last night a lot and wondering why Steve had turned up so suddenly. What on earth happened with the police? Had Steve even gone back to the old homestead?

'How could I not come and thank you for everything you've done for me, and for my family, young man. You're quite the hero, you know,' she smiles again.

Liz is following the exchange intently, trying to work out how Helen fits in. She's a smart kid, but I don't think she's actually connected Mum with the video as yet.

'But I didn't do anything really,' I actually manage to blush a little. 'All I did was bring you the video. You put it all together and went to the police.'

I worry that I may be laying it out a little too boldly for our audience, but Helen plays along nicely.

'And you did the right thing. I'm so glad you were in the right place the other day to see Steve harassing me, and I'm so glad you decided to do the right thing and help me out.'

We both stop there and just look at each other. We're on the same wavelength and it makes me feel warm inside. I try to remind myself that I mustn't call her Mum, but Helen instead. Mind you, she has it tougher – trying to chat with a small blonde boy while knowing that Nick, your eldest son, is actually inside his head. She's doing really well.

But Liz isn't with us and politely interrupts.

'Umm, I'm sorry, I don't mean to be rude, but . . . who are you, and what are you two talking about?'

I almost laugh out loud, but manage to hold it back. I open my mouth to reply, but Helen interjects.

'I'm sorry. You're Elizabeth, aren't you?'

Liz nods. 'Liz,' she says.

'All right, Liz. I'm Helen Davis, your wee cousin Jack's grandmother.' Liz frowns, still not understanding.

'My late son, Nick Davis, was your Aunt Sarah's first husband. Before Sarah married your Uncle Brett. My son was Daniel, Katherine and young Jack's father.'

You can see recognition slowly dawning in Liz's face. But Helen continues before she can speak again.

'You have a very brave little brother here. He took a video of two very bad men – Steve and Richard Cassidy. I think you know, I'm sorry . . . you knew Steve?'

Liz nods again and Helen continues.

'That video contained references to some very nasty criminal activity the pair were involved in . . . and, quite by chance, Mark was in the park across from my home when this Steve chap came by Monday morning to pay me a visit. He watched Steve threaten me and realised that I was the *old lady* they referred to in the video. I'm very fortunate that he decided to come and see me yesterday and show me the video, which I was able to take to the police.'

'But . . . hang on,' Liz stops her. 'Mark didn't know where the video was, he'd forgotten.' She looks at me with a furrowed brow and asks, 'Where was it, when did you get it? And why didn't you tell me?' She looks hurt.

I feel terrible – and worse, without mentioning Skinner – which I really don't want to do – I have no plausible answer.

'I'm sorry Liz,' I begin, thinking furiously, 'I sort of remembered and then got it from a friend's place yesterday. I was going to show you it on the laptop when you got home from school. But either you or Mum found it first and played it before I had the chance. Who found it?'

She doesn't look convinced and I plead to her with my eyes not to press it any further, at least not in front of Helen. She's still frowning heavily when she replies.

'I found it, on your bed, when I was picking up your dirty laundry . . . I wondered where the laptop came from and switched it on to see if I could work out whose it was.'

She looks at me meaningfully, and then glances at Helen and back to me. She's a smart girl and I cross my fingers in hope that she won't press the ownership issue. Helen and I never discussed it. But Helen leaps in to defend me.

'It's my laptop. I loaned it to Mark after he gave me a copy of the video. He said he wanted to show you the video too but had no means to do so.'

I stay silent and Liz seems to accept the answer.

'Okay,' she says, turning back to me. 'So all I could find on it was one solitary file. Just the video. There was nothing else on it at all – like it had been wiped completely clean, you know, other than that video.'

'It's brand new,' I explain. 'Helen bought it specially. She didn't have a computer when I went to see her.'

'Oh,' she says simply, accepting this also. 'And so,' she continues, 'I played the video and . . . wow! It was everything you'd said you had recorded . . . and more. So I played it a few times and tried to decide what to do. I probably should have waited till you got home, but I got so excited I showed it to Mum when she turned up,' she hangs her head now, regretting her actions. 'If I'd waited this may all have turned out differently. Steve might never have needed to see the video, and you and I might have been able to convince Mum to stop seeing him,' she pauses again, tears starting to well up in her eyes. 'I should have waited, shouldn't I?'

I try to console her. 'It doesn't matter Liz. We all make mistakes, and I made plenty myself in the last few days. Nothing that happened last night was your fault, or mine, or Mum's. Steve's the only one at fault here.'

Helen chimes in, surprising me. 'You know, if you hadn't played your mother that video then Steve may have got clean away, and we'd all still be in danger right now. In a way we all have a lot to thank you for, as well as Mark.'

'What do you mean?' I ask, not understanding.

She looks at me and explains as if to a child, which I guess I actually still am. 'What happened in your home last night was horrible Mark, but, because of it, Steve can no longer hurt you or either of our families again.'

She takes a deep breath, and frowns. 'I probably shouldn't say too much, but the police actually weren't being a lot of help. You see, after Mark left me the video I went to the police, as you know . . . but they did very little. It took them half the afternoon just to organise a computer to play the video on, and once they'd seen it, there were streams of people running back and forth offering opinions on what it all might mean, and the legal ramifications.'

She sighs, shaking her head before continuing. 'It took hours just to convince them that people were in real danger and that Steve was going to come back and visit me that evening. They asked so many questions, all the same ones, over and over, but finally they started to organise for a few officers to come home with me to try to catch Steve in the act. But not with much enthusiasm I might add.'

'So by the time we got back home it was very late in the afternoon. Two police officers had followed me and parked their car down by the shops. We'd only been inside for a few minutes, and we were still expecting the detective and another officer to arrive any time, when there was a banging on the door. After that it was like a scene from the keystone cops.'

She shakes her head in frustration. 'Steve was at the door, but he got away. One of the policemen gave chase, but lost him in the park. And then it got worse . . .'

She looks at me, embarrassed, and I immediately realise what she is going to say, because we'd never discussed it, we'd been so intent on other things.

'I didn't know where you lived, so I couldn't call. I ran inside and grabbed the phone book, but there were no Mitchell's listed anywhere close by in Wilton, so I called Directory Services and they confirmed that they did have a listing for Tracey Mitchell, but wouldn't give me any details as she's ex-directory. And I begged and I pleaded, but they refused and hung up on me.'

With Helen close to tears Liz pipes up.

'The number's not listed. We were getting a lot of crank calls from people about Mum's, umm . . . drinking, so she changed it and had them block the new number from the directory. I don't think even Uncle Brett has the new one . . .'

I feel terrible. I should have found the phone number and given it to Helen. It's my mistake.

But Helen just nods and resumes her story.

'And so then the police started to take things a little more seriously, but again it took them a while to get going. They didn't seem to think you were in any danger, and I would think that Steve had probably started the fire before they even sent someone to Brett and Sarah's house to try and obtain your address. When I heard all the sirens from across the park soon after, I got really scared. I didn't know whether something was happening at Sarah's – or somewhere else. It was horrible, just horrible.'

Liz looks confused again. 'Why would something be happening at Aunt Sarah's place?' she asks.

'Oh, I'm sorry. It's quite complicated,' Helen replies gently, 'but Steve was blackmailing me and threatening to hurt my grandchildren. I thought he might have gone there to act on the threat after finding the police at my home.'

'Ohhh . . .' she says. 'But he'd come to our place . . .'

There is a short silence which is suddenly broken by noises from the hallway outside. Tracey bustles into the room, still looking haunted and sullen. Following close behind her is a tall, lanky woman whose eyes quickly dart around the room taking everything in. Right behind her is a uniformed policewoman.

Tracey eyes Helen suspiciously and then moves past us all to sit on the spare bed. The lanky woman appraises us silently for a moment and then speaks.

'Good morning. I'm Detective Inspector Dowd. I'm going to need a few minutes of your time.'

By the time the police leave, almost two hours later, my head is spinning and throbbing, but I think we covered everything without any mistakes and without having to reveal the visit to Skinner. This is a subject I'm still determined to keep quiet if I can.

In this regard Helen simply claimed ignorance. She maintained no knowledge of where the video was before I brought it to her yesterday morning, and I just refused to tell. I'm a small, injured boy – and I played on that, sticking firmly with blandly saying that I got the video from a friend. And I wouldn't tell who the friend was because I promised not to tell. The detective eventually gave up and moved on.

We were interrupted by a reporter at one point, but the uniformed policewoman thankfully shooed him away. I imagine the whole incident will be big news later today.

And Brett turned up again to interrupt briefly. He talked with Tracey out in the hall, but I don't think the conversation went well. Tracey returned to the room looking even more defeated than before. It's a disturbing sight. What little hope that existed in her train-wreck of a life before has been shattered. It's obvious too that Liz is desperately worried about how she is going to handle all this.

After the police depart Helen slips away and returns to the room with sandwiches and muffins from the hospital cafeteria. Liz and I tuck in greedily. She even has a large milkshake for Tracey that is grudgingly accepted.

'So what are your plans, Tracey,' Helen asks thoughtfully as we fly into the food. 'Where will you go tonight?'

It's clear that Liz and Tracey can't stay sitting around at the hospital again, they're both exhausted and clearly need some serious rest. I'm probably able to stay in another night, but doubt that Tracey will want that. She doesn't seem to like hospitals very much, I'm not clear why. I wonder if she has insurance that might cover temporary accommodation, but I doubt it. She is probably now very seriously broke.

Tracey just shrugs. She has no idea what to do. Her eyes are blank. Helen speaks softly.

'I know it may seem a little odd to some people, but you need to appreciate just how incredibly grateful I am to Mark for the very brave thing he did in bringing me that video . . . and in light of that, although I will fully understand if you say no, I would be very pleased if you'd allow me to put you all up for a few nights, while you get back on your feet.'

There is silence. Helen glances at me expectantly. Immediately I find the idea of moving back into the old homestead immensely appealing. To be able to live in familiar surroundings may help me to cope better with being Mark. At least while we figure out what to do next.

I look from Helen, to Liz, to Tracey. Liz seems puzzled. Tracey is numb and lost and remains silent.

I quickly throw out my opinion. 'I think it's a great idea. Don't you Liz?'

But she's wary. I can tell she is wondering why on earth this old lady would invite us into her home so readily. She doesn't know us at all. I try to encourage her.

'Surely you think it'd be okay to stay a few days with Jack's grandmother, don't you, Liz. It's a big house. We'd get a room each,' I suggest positively. She flushes a little, I'm not sure why, and still looks uncertain so I persist doggedly. 'And it's in our school zone, and really handy to everything, and . . . well, we've got nowhere else to go, have we?'

Tracey shifts and seems to come out of her trance. With some difficulty she murmurs one word. 'Brett's . . .' But she doesn't look happy about it. I wonder if she'll ever feel happy about anything ever again.

Liz visibly blanches at this. Again I don't understand why. Maybe she doesn't get on with Katherine, or with Sarah? Whatever goes through her mind it results in a quick response.

'No,' she says firmly. 'I think we should accept Mrs Davis's kind offer.'

'Me too,' I chip in immediately. 'It's a very generous offer. We should accept it quickly, before she changes her mind.'

Even though it hurts my face I grin hopefully.

Tracey looks blankly from me to Liz and her shoulders slump in bitter resignation. It seems pretty obvious that she doesn't want to go to Brett's. She turns to Helen and nods, with a twisted attempt at a polite smile and softly murmurs.

'Yes . . . Thanks.'

'Well then, that's settled,' exclaims Helen. 'Thank you for accepting. You'll be doing me a great honour.'

I abruptly swing my legs out of the bed. 'Shall we get going then?' I ask. All three faces turn and frown at me.

But it doesn't take long to convince the ladies that I don't need further hospitalisation, especially Tracey. The doctors put up a similar fuss to the last time I'd been discharged early, but we leave anyway.

As the Mitchell family escaped from the unit with little more than the clothes on our backs – although Tracey apparently did go back into the burning unit, but only managed to retrieve her purse – Helen and Liz make a quick trip down the road to buy some new clothes before we go. Mine have been ruined by my own blood, yet again, and various other things, while both ladies also need something clean to change into.

It's late-afternoon when we finally arrive at the old homestead. Tracey, Liz and I – in the old hatchback, which survived the blaze – follow Helen in her shiny red sedan.

There are reporters waiting outside, but only one from the local paper and one from TVNZ with a cameraman. We scramble inside quickly, with a camera following our movement, and Helen stops only to advise them that we have no comment at this time. Tracey shields her face but both Liz and I are a little awe-struck and must provide them with some usable footage before we finally dash inside.

Neither Tracey nor Liz has ever been to the old homestead before and, while Liz is fairly wide-eyed, Tracey fails to appear at all impressed by the old houses grandeur. She only pauses briefly to stare vacantly at an old photo on the wall, one of Bobby and me together, probably taken less than a month before he left Wilton and disappeared. She makes no comment though and Helen leads us all upstairs.

Tracey is shown to the guest bedroom, which has its own ensuite, and we leave her to crawl straight into bed. I'm certain she will be snoring within minutes. I'm just glad she chose to stay and not to run away to the pub.

I'm oddly excited and get a bit carried away, without much thought for who I'm supposed to be. I take Liz by the hand and lead her forwards.

'This will be your room,' I say with a flourish as I open the door to Bobby's old bedroom. Her puzzled expression reminds me quickly to stop and think a bit harder. How does Mark know which room is which? But she doesn't say anything, fortunately. She looks into the room and smiles shyly. It's smaller than my old bedroom, but it has been neatly refurbished since I last looked in and is clean and simply decorated.

Helen is behind us now and gestures Liz in.

'I'm sure you'll be comfortable in here. The sheets are fresh on and you'll find towels in the bathroom down the hall,' she points the way. 'I think you should rest up a little now though. You've had a pretty tough time of it all.'

'Yes,' Liz admits. 'A shower and a nap sound fantastic.'

Leaving her to it I open the door to my old bedroom and almost fall over in shock.

The last time I visited, the room had been relatively plain, with all my old things packed away in boxes, should I ever decide that I want to come and take them away.

But it's very different now. It's packed with images from every aspect of my life – framed certificates of various achievements, my old rugby uniform, my favorite cricket cap, even artwork from my primary school years, and more and more photos all over the walls.

I shudder. It feels like a shrine.

A voice behind me speaks softly.

'Your father did all this . . . just after the car accident. It seemed to help him deal with his grief so I didn't try to stop him.' Helen sighs, 'Not that I could have, even if I'd wanted to.'

Gazing around the room in amazement I hear the shower start up in the bathroom and I'm glad that Liz didn't see this.

'He loved you so very much, Nick. Probably too much, if that's possible.'

Almost overwhelmed, I struggle to respond. 'Oh God, Mum. This is actually a little creepy.'

'No, please,' she sounds sad. 'It's not creepy. It's just your father's way of keeping his dreams alive. I'm not saying its right, but, well . . .' and she tails off, obviously unsure how to explain further. I back out of the room, pulling the door closed.

'We'll need to take it all down,' I say, trying to make light of it. 'I can't sleep in there with so many pictures of, you know, me, staring at me. I wouldn't be . . . comfortable. You understand?'

She just stares at me, struggling with her emotions. She looks both elated and despondent somehow.

'But not right now,' I say, taking her by the hand and leading her towards the stairs. 'I think we could both use a cuppa, don't you?'

As we pass by the guest bedroom the unmistakable sound of Tracey's snoring drifts through the door. Soon Liz will be crashed out in her new bedroom also. I'm grateful of the chance to sit down and talk with Helen for a while, unobserved. There is still so much we need to discuss.

But as we reach the bottom step a soft, yet deep and very firm voice stops us in our tracks.

'Hello there, you two,' the voice is vaguely familiar, but the tone is not at all as warm as the words might suggest. 'Now that you have your houseguests settled, I wonder if you both might spare me a few minutes to discuss a couple of pressing issues.'

Richard Cassidy stands in the hall doorway. He's wearing latex gloves and holds a large pistol which is pointing directly at me.

THIRTY-THREE

RICHARD CASSIDY was furious earlier, but he's more composed now. He's had a bit of time to reflect on everything and it's clear that he needs to re-establish control himself. That way there can be no further mistakes. No more foul-ups.

But time is against him.

He watches as the old woman almost has a heart attack. Now wouldn't that be ironic, after everything he's been through if she just dropped dead right here and now. But he doesn't laugh or smile, he's determined to betray no emotion while he gets this done.

The boy takes her hand and she steadies herself, she's still as white as a sheet.

Richard sighs, allowing himself to display a little impatience. While he waits for them to grasp the situation he adjusts his tie slightly and smoothes a little lint off his formal grey suit. He holds the gun casually in his right hand. His quiet poise is intended to disconcert.

Once he's confident he has their undivided attention he waves the gun to indicate that he wants them to move down the hallway. He speaks moderately.

'Down this way please, where we can have a little more privacy.' The boy glances about quickly, clearly thinking about running, or perhaps considering grabbing something and throwing it at him. Richard addresses him firmly.

'Don't even think it. I will gun you down before you make two steps, and then I'll shoot the old lady, before going upstairs to deal with your mother and sister.' He glares at the boy icily, raising the gun so they can both see the silencer protruding from its barrel more clearly.

'And with this on, even those nosey reporters outside won't hear a thing. So just behave, and everyone will get a reasonably happy ending. You understand?'

The boy just stares at him, now clearly too frightened to move or to speak. 'Good, thank you,' he says politely. 'Now then, down this way please, to the old boy's fascinating den where we can talk a little more.'

Helen leads the way as Richard steps back from the doorway to ensure no one can try anything stupid. He's pretty confident they won't, but he always plays it safe. You don't get to be as successful as he is if you don't cover all your bases. Smart thinking always wins.

Inside the wood panelled den he lets them sit down on the leather chairs in front of the big oak desk. Locking the door behind them he moves across the room to seat himself in the larger chair behind the desk. He lays the gun to rest on the big white blotter, but leaves his hand on it, ready to lift and fire quickly if it becomes necessary.

The woman can't meet his eye, but the damn boy seems to be appraising him, taking in his obvious resemblance to his younger brother. This annoys him and he glares at the boy with the same very dark brown, almost-black, unfathomable eyes as Steve. The boy initially stares back, but eventually blinks in resignation when they both clearly hear the shower stop running above. Richard can see the feeling of guilt passing through the boy and it pleases him.

'Okay,' Richard says. 'Here's how it's going to work. I am going to ask you a few very simple questions. If you answer them honestly I will quietly slip away and everyone will remain alive and well.'

He pauses dramatically, to let that sink in before continuing. 'But if I think you're not being honest with me, someone is going to get hurt, and it won't be me, I can assure you. Are we clear on the rules?'

Both of them just nod quickly. That's good. It makes him feel more comfortable. He's the one in control here.

'Okay, first question,' he says. 'How many more copies of that bloody video are there?'

They look at each other immediately and he frowns. He's good at reading people, that's how he's become so successful. Reading people and managing them – and cutting a few corners here and there. The boy speaks without turning back to face him, instead holding eye contact with the old woman. Richard knows immediately that he's lying.

'We don't know. The police have it. They could have made any number of copies.'

Richard frowns angrily, raising the gun quickly to point it at the boys head. 'Okay, smart-arse. I'll give you that one for free, but don't you try and give me any more bullshit answers. I don't have a lot of patience for smart-mouths.'

The boy turns deathly pale and the old woman closes her eyes, afraid to look. Still holding the gun up Richard reaches into a pocket with his other hand and produces the flash drive that Helen had given to the police. He lays it gently on the table and lowers the gun beside it.

'The police will soon find that they've mislaid this – and that the two copies they've made so far have been accidentally deleted.' He pauses for effect.

'Then they'll find that their official transcript records have disappeared too – and that they now have no record of this video ever existing.'

Richard looks directly at the smart-mouthed boy. 'The original copy you had on your cell-phone is long since destroyed, and the copy you had on Mrs Davis' laptop was ruined in the fire,' he pauses again dramatically.

'What I want you to tell me right now is whether there are any other copies in existence, anywhere at all.'

He lapses into a watchful silence. Their expressions will tell him everything he needs to know. The boy is thinking hard and he looks over at the woman who is clearly terrified and is fidgeting nervously. He's convinced that the boy won't dare to be clever and try lying again.

'I doubt it,' the boy finally says. 'There was another copy but I'm pretty sure it will have been destroyed by now too.'

'Explain,' Richard says bluntly.

The boy swallows hard, it's obvious that he's mentally scrambling again, and then he takes a deep breath. There is guilt and shame written all over his face.

'I downloaded the video at an old man's place before Steve ran me down and took my cell-phone. I got the copy you have there from his computer, but when he saw it he freaked out and was going to delete it. I'm pretty sure he will have by now.'

Richard doesn't understand, but the boy's expression, and the tone of his voice has him convinced that this is the truth. He keeps his own face impassive, issuing a sharp and simple demand. 'Name and Address.'

The boy takes another deep breath. He can't meet Richard's eye but he still seems to be telling the truth.

'I don't know his name, or the number of the house, but it's on Lorneville Drive, just south of the cul-de-sac. About three houses down, on the same side. It's beige.' There is a pause, and the boy closes his eyes before adding, 'This old man, he looks just like that guy Skinner from the X-Files. Clean shaven, solid, bald, with wire glasses.'

Richard frowns as he tries to make sense of the reference. He used to watch that old show, but it hasn't been on in years. How would this kid know an actor from the X-Files? It's weird, but irrelevant.

'I need a number,' he demands, pushing his annoyance away. The boy looks lost, but suddenly the old woman joins the conversation.

'Two-twenty-three,' she says flatly and quietly. The boy looks at her in wonder before slowly nodding to himself. Richard believes her, she's obviously terrified.

'So who is he?' he asks. 'And does anyone else live there?'

They glance at each other, clearly unsure how to respond. The boy flushes ever so slightly. He's embarrassed about this old guy for some reason. But he's given him up fairly easily, so it's not a truly close relationship. When the boy responds he's again unable to meet Richard's eye.

'He's just a friend. He lives alone, with just a small dog.'

Richard stares hard at him, unblinking, trying to fit it all together. Young boy, old man, embarrassment. It's an unlikely pairing. One that he knows they didn't reveal to the police or his inside man would have mentioned it. He swivels his eyes without moving to study the old woman, there's something off there too. Then it comes to him. A paedophile. The old bastard had been grooming the boy. That's why he's still under the radar. The idea of it makes Richard silently recoil inside but he keeps a straight face.

'Right then,' he says, nodding slowly. 'You're doing well, I believe you.' He pauses briefly. 'Now, second question. How did my brother die?'

He almost enjoys the shock and horror on their faces at his bluntness. He doesn't expect an honest answer here, but has to take this opportunity to understand. When Steve had called him he'd been almost nonsensical, and Richard had been unable to convince him to just walk away, to leave them and scarper. Clearly his little brother had pushed his luck just a little too far, but what did really happen?

The boy looks terrified. He may actually tell the truth.

'He was trying to kill us,' he says carefully. 'He caught us watching the video. He was going to set fire to the unit using burning cooking oil on the stove. He was going to leave Mum and me to die and take my sister Liz, but Mum hit him with my cricket bat. When he fell over he banged his head and knocked himself out. And he knocked the burning frying pan off the stove too. Mum couldn't drag him out, he was too heavy, and she was injured too – by him. We were lucky to get out alive.'

Richard assesses this as part-truth and part-lie. The boy's eyes flickered when he talked about Steve knocking himself out. Christ almighty, his brother had been overpowered by a drunken souse with a kid's cricket bat. He shakes his head slowly and purses his lips. He stares at the boy for a very long time, flicking his index finger with his thumb repeatedly. The latex glove giving off an odd shushing sound. He loses focus momentarily as memories of his little brother fly through his head. Growing up. Getting in trouble. Celebrating. Good times and bad. He forces the images aside. Not now, there's no time. He must stay on task. Focus.

There is no longer any noise from above. The girl must have gone to bed. All he can hear is the ticking of the ostentatious antique clock and the old woman's laboured breathing.

Richard takes a deep breath and continues.

'Question three,' he shifts his gaze to the old woman. She physically recoils at its intensity. 'Who the hell is Robert Davis?'

They both gasp softly in shock, it's almost comical. He pulls open a draw on the desk and removes a manilla folder labelled simply *The Trust*, laying it down beside the gun.

'I had some time while I've been waiting for you in here and, if you'll pardon the intrusion, I looked around a bit. I found this. It's truly fascinating.'

He allows a measure of annoyance to creep into his voice. 'You don't have full control of the Family Trust, do you? You can't actually sell the house, even if you want to. Why the hell didn't you tell us this?'

The old woman doesn't speak for a long time, but he watches as a flush slowly moves across her face. He's managed to upset her and she's actually getting angry. Finally, in halting defiance, she responds.

'I didn't tell your people because I don't want to sell. It didn't seem important at the time whether I could have or not. And that hasn't changed. I still have no intention of selling you this house.'

Her face is grim and set, her brow furrowed. Now the boy is fidgeting. Obviously frightened that this will end badly. Richard leans back in his chair and chuckles softly. Clearly they are not on the same page. He will need to regain control, frighten the old woman back into submission.

'Oh, you silly old bint,' he says evenly. 'You have absolutely no idea what you're dealing with here, have you?' Then he stands suddenly and slams both fists down onto the blotter, making the gun jump an inch into the air. He doesn't shout though, he adopts a more threatening snarl. 'We are not playing games any more, you daft hag. People have died, and more will follow – if necessary. Let me be clear with you, I will not lose everything I have invested here to a primary school child and a doddery pensioner, damn it. You will sell to me, or you will die! Do you understand?'

Glaring at her malevolently he believes that he's achieved his aim perfectly. Not only did his carefully controlled outburst get their absolute attention, but they're both pushing themselves as far back into their chairs as they can manage, drawing away in terror. It's too easy.

Trying hard not to smile, he deliberately takes a deep breath to let them think that he needs to regain his poise. Then he releases it slowly and sits back down, adjusting his suit and tie. Once he's settled, and has re-established eye contact, he asks carefully. 'So where exactly is,' he pauses, opening the folder theatrically and pretending to refer to one of the deed documents, '. . . this Robert Charles Davis at the moment?'

Now the woman looks embarrassed and he doesn't understand why. Is Robert a paedophile too? What's going on with this family? Her hands tremble and her face turns even whiter. He's certain that this response will be truthful as she looks up to meet his eyes.

'I don't know,' she says quietly. 'If I did know I might have seriously considered selling to you. If Robert was willing.'

'Why don't you know? You're his mother aren't you?'

She flushes. The old woman is clearly ashamed, but of what? This Robert character simply has to be another son. But what on earth is she so embarrassed about? Is he in prison? Richard is very surprised, and incredibly annoyed, when the damn boy suddenly interrupts.

'He left a long time ago, and he doesn't keep–'

'Shut the hell up, damn you,' Richard snaps abruptly, standing up again and leaning over the desk to point a wavering finger in his face. 'I'm talking to the old lady and I'm damned if I need any more smart answers from you!'

The boy closes his eyes and sinks back into his chair, terrified and contrite. Richard briefly considers tying him up and gagging him, but decides against it. Too much trouble. His intimidation is working. The boy won't bother him again. He composes himself and sits down again.

'Well,' he demands of the old woman. She seems to grit her teeth, and her reply is heavy with reluctance.

'Robert hasn't been home, or in contact, for over sixteen years. He and his father didn't get on very well and he just up and left one day. I have absolutely no idea where he is . . .' She fixes him with an accusing glare, '. . . and he probably doesn't even know that his father and brother are dead.'

He watches her carefully, the anger and hostility are genuine, and so is the guilt and embarrassment. He's quite easily convinced that she's telling the truth, unless she is one hell of an actor and he doesn't think she is. He nods slowly.

'Right then,' he says quietly. 'We'll get someone to sign on his behalf, with a witness to confirm that it's truly Robert Charles Davis's signature. We can do that.'

He starts to work it through step-by-step. There are still a few loose ends. Eventually he'll need to find and silence this Robert chap, but for now he just needs to clear up all the video evidence and get himself clear of any police investigations. And he needs to resolve the sale of this property, and urgently. Time is against him, so he can't afford to wait until everything blows over. It's not ideal, but he can make it work. He's tidied away bigger issues, worse messes. If only Steve had listened to him when they last talked, damn it. But he can't let himself think of Steve right now, there will be time to deal with that wound later. These people will pay for what they did to him. This god-damn interfering boy, and that stupid drunken slut, will die, and soon, that's for certain. He forces himself to focus on immediate issues.

'Okay,' he says finally, 'here's how this is going to work.' He pauses, re-running it all once again in his head before he tells them. He's fairly pleased with his solution. It's like solving a very difficult cryptic puzzle.

'I'm going to leave you in peace for now, but I'll be back in two hours. And when I get back,' he points at the old woman, 'you are going to sign a new sale document, re-drawn to take into consideration Robert's inclusion in your Family Trust.'

He nods to himself, this is going to work. It just has to. 'Robert will have already signed it, and so will our witness. It'll be for the same fair price we've agreed on, so nobody will be suspicious. However the apartment we had offered won't be included. It'll be just a straight cash purchase.'

He pauses, watching for the old woman's reaction. She's not happy. She just stares at him grimly. He expects nothing else and continues unfazed.

'First thing tomorrow you will take it to your lawyer and tell him that Robert turned up unexpectedly and agreed to sell, and that he's doing well for himself and doesn't want any of the proceeds.' He pauses, realising he's almost missed something. 'I'll have a document for that too. And . . . that he's gone off again. Just a flying visit, you understand?'

The old woman still doesn't move or say anything, and Richard continues unperturbed.

'Settlement will be in ten days time. By that day you will have packed up and pissed off and we will never see each other again,' he pauses, mainly for effect. 'And if you try and do anything stupid that might upset these plans – in any way – I will make you very, very remorseful.'

Richard Cassidy slips his gloved hand into another pocket and produces a piece of folded paper, which he opens and drops on the table before his captive audience.

It is a duplicate of the picture he gave Steve to show the old woman a few days ago.

A picture of the old woman's grandchildren.

THIRTY-FOUR

Helen and I stare at the image of Katie and Jack in horror.

'You may have found yourself a nice new family here, but I'm guessing that blood remains thicker than water,' Richard advises evenly. 'You wouldn't want anything bad to happen to either of these lovely children now, would you?'

Helen is at boiling point and I'm not far off, but the combination of the picture, the gun, and his confident and imperious manner keep us both silent and in our seats. Helen and Richard lock eyes before he finally speaks again.

'I'll take your silence to be understanding, and acceptance.'

Still Helen says nothing, and Richard rises quietly.

'I will be back in two hours,' he says. 'And in that time you two will do absolutely nothing,' he pauses, and I'm sure it's just to be dramatic. 'You will just sit quietly here, or take yourself off for a little nap, but you will not make any effort to contact either the police, or any family, or the media. No one at all. Do I make myself clear?'

We both just stare at him, without moving or speaking. Suddenly he leans forward and, adopting the same threatening snarl as he'd used earlier, repeats;

'Do I make myself clear?'

This time we both acknowledge him, meekly and in unison. 'Yes.' We're clear.

'Very good,' he says, returning to his usual flat and authoritative tone. 'Think hard about it all, both of you. If you do anything stupid in that time . . . people will get hurt. People you care about. And the more stupid the thing that you might consider doing is . . . then the worse off those people will be. Once again, are we clear?'

We both nod immediately this time, not wanting to rile him further. He doesn't speak again. He quietly leaves the room, closing the door softly behind him. Helen and I sit rigidly, holding our collective breaths and listening for his departure. But we hear nothing more.

Finally leaving my chair I move to the window. As I look out across the empty section next door I can just make out a grey suited figure wading through the long grass towards the building site across the way. He keeps low and vanishes into the site quickly.

Richard Cassidy is gone. For now.

'Oh, my sweet lord,' Helen whispers. 'I thought it was all over. I thought that he would be caught by the police or just disappear forever. This simply isn't possible, I mean, how can he do this? What kind of a man would do this?'

Tears well up in her eyes and I go back to the seat and hold her. I want to offer comfort, but I once again feel very small, and insignificant.

'It's going to be alright,' I say without confidence. 'We'll work this all out. Everything is going to be okay.'

'It's not going to be okay, Nick. It's not and we both know it,' she sobs. 'A man like that, he won't just take the house and walk away. He'll kill us, and probably those poor women upstairs too. He won't want to leave anything behind that might incriminate him. He's too careful. He won't just let us walk away.' She's frightened and shaking and tears are streaming down her face. 'He'll come back and he'll get my signature and then he'll kill us all, and set a fire or something to cover it all up. And he'll have an alibi, and he'll get away with it. Dear lord, did you see his eyes? He's not worried about hurting people, or killing people. He's not afraid of anything. He's a monster . . .' she breaks down, weeping uncontrollably.

I don't know what to say. I'm in shock myself. I had also thought our troubles were all over – but the sudden appearance of this man, right here in our home, chills me to the bone. I'm at a complete loss.

'Look, Mum. I don't think he will hurt us. Once he has the house he'll have everything he wants. He has no reason to hurt anyone after that,' I try to calm her, but I'm struggling to believe the words myself.

'No he won't, Nick. He'll have loose ends. You and I, we know what he's done – and we know what he's going to go and do right now. He's going to hurt that old man. He might even kill him. We need to do something, to stop him.'

She's right. I know it and I feel terrible, but what can we do. We can't call the police, that's obvious. He had the flash drive, so he must have someone on the inside. I'm absolutely convinced that if we call the police then Richard will find out. And if that happens then something terrible might happen to one of my children. It's not an acceptable gamble. Helen seems to understand this too.

'We can't go to the police though, can we?' she asks, once again as if she's read my mind.

'No, we can't. He'll find out. We have to take his threat on the kids seriously.'

'But what about that old man, who had the video, around on Lorneville Drive?'

'We can't help him,' I say flatly.

'We could phone him and warn him.'

I think about it, but just can't accept it. 'I don't think so. Besides the fact that we don't even know his name – if Richard finds out we did that he could do anything, just to teach us a lesson. We can't call him, or anyone else, it's just too big a risk.'

She stares at me long and hard, and then slowly nods. Neither of us like it, but Skinner is on his own. I feel sick in the stomach. Regardless of whatever he may or may not have done to the children in this neighbourhood, no one deserves a visit from Richard Cassidy.

'Then we should call Sarah and Brett, and tell them to take the kids away somewhere, to get away and hide,' Helen suggests with more enthusiasm.

I like this idea a whole lot better and almost immediately agree, but have to force myself to stop and think it through. It seems like such a short-term solution, and how would Sarah and Brett react?

'No, that won't work,' I say. 'They'll probably just call the police themselves. Then we'd be back at pissing off Richard again and we don't want that. We need to come up with something better. We need to stop him somehow.'

She looks at me as if I've gone mad. 'But we can't . . .'

'But we have to. Just think about it. He's on his own now, he must be. At least as far as doing the really bad stuff goes. I mean, Steve was obviously his go-to guy for the dirty work. For threatening people, or hurting them. You saw the video. He wouldn't have come here himself today if he had someone else he could trust to fix this all for him.'

In part I'm still trying to convince myself as I continue.

'Obviously Richard doesn't want to have to run away and start all over, or go to jail. So he will come back tonight – and when he does, all we have to do is stop him, and make sure he's caught in the act, and he'll get locked up. And if he's in prison with no one to do his dirty work on the outside, we'll all be safe. It'll be over.'

Helen doesn't look convinced, but I'm actually starting to persuade myself. 'Look, we can't call the police, can we?' She shakes her head. 'And if we do nothing and you just sign the document and we do as he tells us – then he'll come back. Maybe not until after the sale is completed, but he will come back. And he'll tidy up all his loose ends.'

I pause meaningfully and she doesn't disagree.

'So we have no other choice. We have to try and capture him ourselves. If we don't, well . . . we're all dead anyway.'

She looks mortified, but nods imperceptibly. It's settled, we have to do something. All we need is a good enough plan.

My gaze flits around the room, searching for inspiration.

And then it comes to me. We can do this.

* * *

The wait for Richard's return is interminable.

Helen still doesn't seem completely convinced by my idea, but has conceded that she can think of no other way to resolve our problem. So we worked hard in the time we had and, while it is far from foolproof, we're agreed on a way in which we can capture Richard ourselves when he returns. It's risky, but we have very few options.

We rummaged through Dad's things in the den until we found what we need. Then I checked again that Tracey and Liz were both sleeping soundly above us before slipping awkwardly into my hiding place.

Now we wait.

The kitchen clock ticks away slowly while Helen fidgets nervously at the kitchen table.

Almost exactly two hours after he departed silently we hear the back door open quietly. Richard is punctual, a man of his word. I'm stiff already and Helen is clearly tense.

I hear the back door click quietly shut and the soft fall of his shoes on the kitchen linoleum. Helen will be in plain sight at the kitchen table as he enters the house, as we planned. He steps into the kitchen and just into my line of sight. He's wearing the latex gloves again and his eyes shift quickly around, taking in everything.

'Where's the boy?' he asks Helen quietly.

'Resting. Upstairs in his room,' she replies coldly.

He doesn't speak, or move, taking this in. Then he snaps at her, 'Don't move,' and backs away towards the rear entrance he just came in through. Damn, I think frantically, and my stomach turns in a knot. Where's he going? He's supposed to walk into the kitchen and go directly up to Helen at the table. It's going wrong already.

He moves out of my sight and Helen's expression changes to concern, touched with fear. She's watching him back away and trying desperately to decide what to do.

'Do you want to sort this out or not?' she challenges him boldly. Then she immediately blanches as he does something I cannot see. My guess is that he's pointed the gun at her from the look of horror on her face.

'Be quiet,' he tells her. I can only just hear the words. 'And don't move,' he repeats.

A bead of sweat trickles down my forehead as my heart absolutely hammers in my chest. I can see Helen sitting rigidly at the kitchen table, pale as a ghost, no longer fidgeting at all. But I can hear nothing.

Richard has disappeared.

I shut my eyes and focus all my being onto my hearing, to try and establish just where he's gone to. My stomach feels like it's filled with acid, I'm so nervous.

The homestead is old, but it's sturdily built and very few floorboards creak. The carpet is still pretty thick and I can hear no movement at all. Richard might be anywhere.

I wait, trying to be quiet, and this waiting is even more excruciating than before.

After about three or four very, very long minutes I hear a sound behind me. I hold my breath and look ever-so-slowly over my shoulder. My vision is very limited by the thin gap in the louver doors of the pantry I am hiding inside.

I can barely move for fear of tipping over a box of cereal or can of beans and giving away my position. I can only turn enough to glimpse him with peripheral vision. He's in the lounge, looking up the stairs. He's holding the gun at waist height in his right hand, with the silencer on.

It's a coldly menacing image.

Closing my eyes I pray he won't go up and check that everyone is safely tucked away in bed, as Helen had told him. I'm still holding my breath. My heart continues to pound uncontrollably and I open my eyes to see Helen watching him carefully, the look on her face as neutral as she can manage. The silence is eternal. Then he starts to move into the kitchen. I almost breathe a sigh of relief, but he's right outside the pantry door so I remain like a statue.

He pauses there, glancing back over his shoulder to reconfirm the angle of the view to the road outside. Fortunately the reporters have left. I'm sure they'll be back tomorrow, but for now all is quiet out front. Richard seems happy enough and edges lightly forward, past my hiding place to stand by the kitchen table with his back to me. He looks over his shoulder again, and then turns back to Helen.

'I'm pleased,' he says quietly. 'We don't need anything stupid to happen now, do we?'

He slides the gun into a holster under his left armpit and his hand returns holding a small bundle of folded paper which he opens out and places on the table in front of her. Then he produces a pen and holds it out to her.

'Just sign where the big yellow stickers indicate.'

She glares at him, with both anger and despair in her eyes. 'What did you do to the old man?' she asks.

He doesn't move or answer her for a long moment, and then he responds simply in his haunting flat tone.

'Just sign the document.'

I'm waiting for her to put pen to paper. This is my cue, when we agree he will be most distracted and relaxed. But she just stares at him, unmoving.

'Did you kill him?' she asks.

Richard's instincts are sharp. He won't answer such a blunt question directly, if at all. But after a short period of trying to stare each other down he finally responds.

'That's not the way I do business. But I did drop by, to visit. You should thank me. I don't think he will be so . . . *friendly* . . . with any more small children in the area.'

Helen doesn't speak, but her eyes close and her face shows a desperate resignation. She seems to have reached a crucial decision. Shaking her head slowly she takes the pen. As she bends over the table and begins to scrawl her signature Richard visibly relaxes and I make my move.

I step out of the pantry, raise one arm straight out in front of me, and point the antique Derringer single-shot pistol I hold directly at Richard's back. I stand slightly side on and keep my left arm down by my side, staring determinedly down the gun's short barrel.

Richard hears the door open behind him and swings around, quick as a cat, drawing his weapon and returning my pose. Helen stands up, taking a half-step away.

Richard freezes when he sees me, quickly taking in the situation. He's mirroring me, the gun in his right hand with arm outstretched full length, standing side-on, staring down his arm and the barrel of his significantly superior firearm.

Then he snorts and laughs derisively. I must look like a joke to him. Here I stand, an eight year old boy brandishing a tiny antique pistol. He will have seen this gun and its matching partner in Dad's den earlier and, we have to assume, may even have examined the pair at some length. If you're a firearms collector, the two Derringers from the den would be irresistible and beautiful, and even if you're not a fan of weaponry these little pistols are quite fascinating.

'You know, kid,' he says slowly and evenly. 'This really isn't funny, or smart.'

'Drop your gun,' I order in reply.

He gapes at me, stunned that I could even suggest anything so ludicrous. He makes an overly-dramatic show of blinking, mocking me, pretending that I must be an illusion, and then he laughs again.

'You do realise, little man, that your teeny little pop-gun there would barely scratch me, if it has any ammunition – which I doubt – and if it actually works – which I also doubt – and if you could actually hit me with your hand shaking as much as it is,' he pauses, and the smile fades from his lips. 'I'll say it again, this isn't smart, so put that pathetic little pop-gun down and let's all get on with moving on.'

'This gun works. And it's loaded. And I'm certain I can hit you from here,' I say with an authority I certainly don't feel. 'So drop your gun.' My hand *is* shaking a bit, but I stand my ground and hold my pose, aiming the little Derringer at the breadth of his chest.

THIRTY-FIVE

Richard suddenly looks over my shoulder, at something behind me, and feigns surprise. I'm ready for it, I've anticipated it, but still I almost look. There's nothing behind me and we both know it. He gives a little nod in a small show of acknowledgement that I wasn't fooled. We both hold our ground, right arms outstretched, in a Mexican stand-off.

When he moves though, he's quick, faster than I anticipated. I'm surprised by both his agility and speed, but not his purpose. He suddenly reaches out with his left hand, barely flicking his eyes away from my gaze, and snatches Helen from where she is standing, pulling her in front of him as a human shield. She lets out a small cry of surprise and his left hand comes up across her mouth to stifle the sound.

Now he's standing square on to me, his face peering over Helen's right shoulder, looking once more down his arm and the barrel of the silenced automatic firearm. His left arm crosses over Helen's shoulder and her body leaving only his arms and head exposed to my aim. There is no way I can safely fire the little Derringer now without a very high probability of hitting Helen. Richard smiles yet again.

'All right, kid,' he leers at me. 'Show's over. Put the pop-gun down carefully so it doesn't go off by accident.'

I look back at him, defeat in my eyes, and then at Helen who looks terrified but resigned to what is going to happen next. I swallow hard and take a deep breath.

'Don't hurt her,' I say. 'We'll do what you say. Please don't hurt her.'

I start to lower myself to the ground, staying side-on to him so he can't see my left hand. I moved agonisingly slowly, intent on keeping his attention on both me and the little Derringer in my right hand.

'Please don't hurt her,' I repeat. 'We mean you no harm,' I say as my right hand reaches the floor and the tiny gun touches the linoleum.

He frowns at this, as it's really a pretty odd thing to say. While he's distracted Helen quickly raises the second little Derringer pistol that she has been hiding in her skirt pocket.

Placing it immediately against Richard's right wrist she pulls the trigger.

I'd like to tell you that the gunshot is deafening, but it isn't. In fact I'm just pleased that there is a gunshot at all, but it's a bit of an anticlimax in terms of volume. The old Derringer only gives off a reasonably loud pop, but it produces a satisfying cry of pain and surprise from Richard.

Blood sprays from his shattered wrist across the kitchen cupboards and his gun drops away from his now badly injured hand. Richard groans angrily, in surprise and disbelief, and then falls to his knees clutching the bleeding wrist to his chest, moaning in pain.

I'm stunned. My plan has actually worked, but perhaps a little too well.

I dash forward and snatch up Richard's fallen weapon and turn it on him, then step away to ensure he can't lunge over and disarm me. But that doesn't seem likely. He's writhing on the floor, cursing and moaning, with blood spurting from the severed artery in his wrist.

Damn, I didn't expect this. He's bleeding furiously. Our desire was simply to disarm him, to get the gun out of his hand. But this is turning into a real mess.

I knew that the Derringers worked and had been pleased to find that Dad still had the ammunition I gave him locked away safely. But we had to work with the fact that these little pistols are seriously short-range weapons and dreadfully inaccurate. If I had pulled the trigger on my Derringer it would have fired, but there was no guarantee I could have actually hit him from any distance. Richard had read the situation very well.

So a point blank attack became the only real option, and for that to work one of us had to be able to draw a gun on him at extreme close quarters. Helen came up with the idea of getting him to use her as a human shield so she could get close enough.

I just had to distract him, and it worked, but a little too well. I never considered that the little gun might actually fire a shot strong enough to blow Richard's wrist this badly open – and now here he is, bleeding profusely all over the kitchen. His efforts to stem the flow are failing badly.

'Quick, Mum. We'd better call an ambulance,' I say.

When she doesn't reply I look over at her anxiously. I'm surprised to find a look of grim determination on her otherwise pale and frightened face. She looks back at me slowly, the little Derringer still grasped firmly in her left hand.

'You do it, Nick,' she says calmly. 'Give me his gun. I'll watch over him.'

She holds out a reasonably steady hand for the weapon. She's acting strangely but I put it down to shock. Richard is still struggling unsuccessfully to stem the flow. He's swearing and groaning and tries to stand up, but he's getting weaker by the moment. He's losing a lot of blood very quickly.

'Get a . . . ambu– . . . lance, damn it . . . hurry.'

I hand her the big gun and backtrack into the lounge where the phone sits on a small table near the door. Picking up the receiver I start to dial, but the line is dead. There's no signal. I hurry back to the kitchen.

'It's dead, the lines been cut.'

'Yes, I thought it might be,' she says softly.

Richard looks up in surprise. 'It's not cut, you– ', he looks at Helen with dawning realisation. 'You bitch . . .'

Now I'm really confused.

Richard starts to try and get up again, but he's white as a sheet and his strength is almost gone. He slips in his own blood, falling back to the floor to sit with his back up against a cabinet.

'Where's your cell-phone, Mum. We need to call an ambulance,' I say urgently.

Helen is as still as a statue, holding the gun out in front of her to cover Richard in case he actually manages to stand. She says nothing at first, just shakes her head slowly.

'I don't remember where I put it, Nick,' she says. 'It could be anywhere.'

'Oh, shit,' I reply. 'I'd better wake Liz, she has a cell-phone.'

I start to move again and Helen suddenly turns on me. 'No. Not yet. Just another minute. To be sure.'

I stop in confusion and stare at her, and then at Richard. He's blinking rapidly and swaying where he sits, and he understands. But it takes me another few seconds to fully grasp Helen's intentions.

'Oh, my God, Mum,' I say softly. 'You cut the phone line yourself, didn't you? You're going to let him bleed. You planned it this way. You, but . . . but . . .'

She turns away from me, resuming her stance with the big gun out in front of her and eyes locked firmly on the man slowly dying on her kitchen floor.

'We didn't start this. But it's going to end here.'

'But, Mum– ', I start, but she cuts me off.

'Don't say anything, please. This is hard enough as it is.' She takes a deep breath, holds it in and then exhales slowly. 'Just remember . . . This man is responsible for your own death, and for your father's,' she says, beginning to sob quietly. 'And he won't just give up, will he? He as good as admitted to killing that poor old man, and he would hurt little Jack or Katie if he needed to. He isn't going to just go away.' She pauses, wiping away a fat tear. 'A mother has to protect her family, Nick. It's what we do.'

Immediately the image of Tracey bludgeoning Steve's inert, burning form with the cricket bat springs into my mind. Is that what Tracey was doing, protecting her family?

I try to refocus. Richard slumps further, his face now grey and his eyes glazing. Blood continues to pump out of him rapidly despite his now feeble efforts to stem the flow.

'He's not a good man, and we both know it,' she continues on, weeping openly as she talks. 'He's an evil man and even if we got him arrested it wouldn't end there. You know that, I know you do. Please understand. I simply can't let him leave here, knowing that he'll always be a threat to my grandchildren. Knowing he'll come back and try to kill you . . . again. I can't live with that, so there really is only one choice, and it's a simple one.' She pauses and looks directly at me. I can see the pain in her eyes. 'It's either him, or it's us.'

I can't speak. To say that I'm staggered would be an understatement. This just can't be the same woman who raised me to believe that all life is precious.

Or can it? When push comes to shove, I have to wonder if she is right, and that this is the right thing to do. But just standing there, watching this man die, it doesn't feel right.

Oddly, it doesn't feel all that wrong either.

I look down at the man bleeding to death on our kitchen floor. He's slumped completely now and the blood flow is easing to a trickle. I feel sick in my stomach and shudder. It's a shocking thing to have to watch. His face becomes still and lifeless. It's almost over.

'I should go and call someone,' I say flatly.

'Yes,' she replies. 'I think it's time now.'

She drops to her knees, placing the gun gently on the linoleum floor and starts to weep uncontrollably into her hands. I watch for a few seconds, my mind going numb.

Then a siren in the distance begins to wail, and then another, their different pitches and intensity telling me that multiple emergency services are in motion.

Suddenly my brain snaps into gear. The police are coming. We have to make this right – whether Helen's actions have been right or wrong, I somehow have to ensure that she doesn't suffer any further from this man's deeds.

I go and kneel down beside her, 'Mum,' I say, thinking quickly. 'I'm pretty sure I remember watching him cut the phone line, here in the lounge, just before he left earlier. Do you remember that?'

She looks up. Her eyes are red-rimmed and very wet. She looks confused, lost. I don't think she's even registered the sirens. It's obvious she hasn't given any thought to what happens now.

'Is that how you remember it?' I ask, leading her gently.

Comprehension starts to dawn in her eyes. She nods. 'Yes,' she says finally.

'He used one of the kitchen knives and cut the wire over there,' I say, pointing to the table with the phone on it.

'Yes,' she says again, still nodding. 'But he cut it over there, nearer the door,' she corrects my assumption.

'Okay,' I say. 'And we never planned to shoot his wrist. That just happened when he surprised us by taking you as a shield.' I pause to think a bit. 'We just had a gun each . . . and our plan was to stand apart to ensure he couldn't shoot both of us. And you just hadn't had a chance to get yours out yet, it all happened so fast,' I blurt out.

'Yes,' she says. She's heard the sirens now and is looking past me, out the window to the street, waiting for flashing lights to appear. 'As I remember it you came out of the pantry and he snatched me up before I could step away. And I meant to shoot him in the hand so he would just drop the gun, but my old hands were shaking so badly.'

'Perfect, and what do we know about the old man? Anything?'

'I think we'll have to confess to that if they connect the deaths, assuming he is dead too,' she says miserably.

'Fair enough,' I agree. It will complicate everything, but it's better than Helen being arrested for pre-meditated murder. 'So why did it take us so long to call someone?'

'Hmm, I don't know,' she frowns, worried now, and understanding that the delay might mean the difference between self-defense, manslaughter, or even murder.

'I think we should simply call it shock,' I suggest. 'I mean, I'm an eight year old boy, and you're just a frail old woman.' I smile at her for the first time that afternoon, 'And we've both had quite a series of extremely nasty shocks, haven't we?'

She thinks on this for a few seconds before finally agreeing, 'Yes,' she says. 'We just curled up together and shielded our faces and ears from the horrible things he was saying and the horrible noises.'

'Okay. They'll be here soon. Are you ready?' I asked.

'Do you think we should wake our houseguests?' Helen asks unexpectedly, her voice full of concern.

I smile and almost laugh. Liz and Tracey have slept through the whole thing. Even the not-so-thunderous pop of the Derringer and Richard's death-throe moaning hasn't woken them. 'Maybe not quite yet,' I reply. 'They need their sleep and it looks like it's going to be another long evening.'

I leave her then, slipping quietly outside, intent on meeting the police as they arrive. But there's no one there. The sirens aren't converging on the old homestead. Instead they seem to be coming from the Park.

As I reach the road I understand. The action is actually a few streets over, beyond the park. There is a thick black pall of smoke rising from what must be a burning house, roughly south of where I stand.

Without needing to look more closely I know immediately that the smoke will be coming from a beige house on Lorneville Drive, just a few doors down from the cul-de-sac.

Clearly Richard did pay a visit to Skinner before he came to see us.

THIRTY-SIX

The next few days are a blur.

Liz went into a state of suspended disbelief after being awoken that evening, and Tracey, well – let's just say that Tracey hasn't been coping at all well. Brett's had to carry her home from the pub again already and she seems to be on a path to oblivion. I've asked Helen to talk with Brett and try to find some way to help her, but it's all a bit difficult with the police and the media interest shining so brightly on us all right now. Hopefully everything will die down soon and we can try to really help her.

After Richard's demise in Helen's kitchen, the police eventually arrived to barrage us with another mountain of questions. Fortunately, as an eight year old boy I was spared most of the interrogations, but when I did have to speak to them, with Tracey listening in mounting horror, I tried to keep my answers short and vague, and where possible a little ambiguous.

Poor Helen took the brunt of the questioning onslaught, but held firm to her version of events, and maintained excuses of age and frailty when the lines of questioning cut too close to the bone. The police have yet to officially decide if they are going to prosecute either Tracey for Steve's demise in the fire, or Helen for actually shooting Richard. The media seem to be behind us but that doesn't guarantee exoneration. However, positively, while we await this decision, both women are free without bail.

It might have been a lot worse if Richard had actually managed to destroy every copy of the video, but fortunately he didn't. Detective Dowd made a copy of the video at the police station that she didn't log, which he missed. This proved to be the last one available as they found no flash drive on Richard when they took his body away.

We've all only just been able to move back into the old homestead after spending a couple of very cramped and awkward nights at Brett and Sarah's place while the homestead was treated as a crime scene. Tracey was very keen to escape from Brett's home, as was I, and this time accepted Helen's offer to stay without hesitation. I think Brett and Sarah are quite grateful too, as there had been a few uncomfortable moments.

And, thankfully, Helen has been granted permission to begin organising refurbishments in her kitchen. Partly to erase the physical evidence of the horror that unfolded there, but more so to help to erase our memories of the event.

I'm not sure that will ever be possible though.

Today, however, has been very eventful and, with the wind in my hair and a flash new bicycle carrying me forward, I'm almost enjoying myself as I ride towards Waterloo Rd.

The bike is a shiny metallic red colour with racing stripes, and it has a futuristic-looking light on the front. Helen bought it for me about an hour ago – and it's true what they say about riding a bike, you never forget. And if I'm honest I'm actually enjoying the breeze in my hair and the fading sunlight on my back. Even with my face still bruised and tender, the feeling is quite liberating after everything I've been through recently.

I'm almost enjoying myself, but not quite.

My thoughts are too cluttered and my conscience too heavy to allow true joy – as I now have a reasonable theory about how I came to be Mark Mitchell, but I'm not yet truly comfortable with it. So I'm heading back to *the place* to try and test it out.

It's late in the day, as Friday evening begins to turn from dusk into night. Tomorrow morning I will have been Mark Mitchell for a week – if I'm still in here tomorrow.

I'm on my own. Somehow it feels more appropriate. And, while I don't know what I expect, I'm hopeful that returning to the place where our two worlds seem to have so violently converged will help me to *look inside myself.*

I need to find a way to purge myself of the guilt that I feel about Mark. I may be wrong, but I think that this is what I need to do now.

As I turn the final corner into Waterloo Rd the sun dips amongst the trees to my right. Soon I arrive at the point where fluorescent orange paint still boldly marks the side-walk.

My feelings of ease start to ebb away as I contemplate what I am going to do next. I have a plan, but I'm far from certain that it's a good one. It's a bit bizarre really and, as is my way, it isn't very well thought out. But I am a man of action, and I can't just sit around and wonder.

I need to act.

You see, earlier today, Helen and I went to visit a clairvoyant, a psychic.

Let's be clear, this is an absolute first for any Davis that I know of. We've always been a family of serious skeptics, but my situation here is pretty unique and this visit seemed more appropriate than any other options we considered.

Helen and I have discussed my situation endlessly over the last few days, whenever we found ourselves alone. But I need answers, and we weren't getting anywhere. So we had to try something, anything. We considered approaching either a doctor or a scientist with my situation but it made us both feel uncomfortable. I don't want to be probed – nor do I want to be exposed – so we had to look to alternatives.

And who else claims to have expertise in the field of people that are, or should be, deceased? So we decided to try a visit to a psychic, or a clairvoyant or medium, or any kind of ghost-whisperer. We had to try something.

Yesterday neither of us had any idea of what to expect, or even where to find someone like that, so Helen called around her friends. I'm still surprised that so many of them seemed to know of at least one type of psychic and they all shared strong opinions on the quality of their abilities. It's my guess that older folk, by virtue of their advancing years, simply know more dead people and are keener to try to make contact with them.

Two of Helen's friends separately recommended the same clairvoyant to us. She works out of a small crystal shop about twenty minutes drive out of Wilton, on the northern shores of Lake Breckenock. One friend described her as both accurate and concise. The other just said she was lovely.

We managed to make an appointment at short notice, and actually joked about why she hadn't been expecting us already. Davis humour – not to be underestimated in times of trouble.

And so it was that late this morning we parked Helen's car across the road from this clairvoyant's shop, which is nestled amongst a quiet little row of touristy-type ventures in the tiny village of Bluff Creek. The *Crystal Heart* and other shops all share spectacular views out over the lake, across the main road.

The little settlement is quiet and sunny, with only a gentle breeze disturbing the shade-giving trees we park under. It's an idyllic scene.

The shop itself is small and filled with crystals, rocks, candles and other things I can only describe loosely as hippie stuff. Wind chimes and incense, indoor water features, dolphin music and meditation tapes along with books on star signs, tarot cards, and more.

There are two women behind the counter, both dressed in matching deep-purple, uniform-style, polo shirts with a small insignia promoting the shop's name on their chests. Modern and stylish, like a chain store operation. The dark haired woman is good-looking and seems quite middle-class-normal while the other one is a little less conventional. Younger, in her late teens, and sporting a nose-stud and brightly dyed red hair.

Helen announces our appointment, pre-payment is quickly and efficiently taken, and then the dark-haired woman leads us through a plain wooden door into a small back room where I am instantly disappointed.

The room is well lit, fresh and simply furnished with a small table and chairs that would look at home in any office. The images on the walls are contemporary, depicting tranquil ocean scenes with sunlight sparkling off either dolphins or whales. There is no crystal ball and nothing hazy or mysterious about the room. And it is empty.

I had been half-hoping to meet a classic gypsy crone with big gold earrings, a colourful head scarf and an embroidered waistcoat, but she is nowhere to be found.

The woman who led us through from the shop gestures to the chairs in front of the table. We sit down as she closes the door and then moves to sit down in front of us, across the table. I exchange a surprised look with Helen.

This is our psychic?

She's in her mid-to-late twenties, an attractive brunette with very dark brown eyes, and wears little make-up or jewellery. She looks like she'd be right at home at any school's PTA meeting. My preconceptions are crushed.

'Good morning,' she speaks softly. 'I'm Lily. Is there anything in particular you'd like to talk about today?'

Helen and I exchange looks again. We'd discussed what we are hoping to discover on the drive out here, but suddenly realise we didn't really talk about how we were going to approach the situation. Neither of us speaks as we try to figure out where to start, and how much to say, without revealing any of our secrets.

Still looking at me, Helen finally says, 'Well it's a bit unusual really . . . but, umm, I don't know where to start. I guess I'm trying to . . . reach my . . . son.' She pauses, frowning. 'I'm sorry, I – um – we've never been to a clairvoyant before. What do you need from us?'

I turn to find Lily inspecting my bruised and battered face, not looking at Helen. Her gaze is even, relaxed. A hint of a half-smile touches her lips as she continues to watch me.

'But your son isn't the one who is missing, is he?' she asks cryptically, without looking away from my face. I sense, rather than see, Helen's jaw drop as Lily draws our attention in a heartbeat. Neither of us is able to reply.

'I get the feeling he's already found you,' she continues quietly, finally looking away from me, to Helen. 'It's another that you've misplaced, and you want to reach him if you can. Am I on the right track here?'

She is, albeit a little cryptically, very much on the right track. We both want to know where Mark is. Is he still inside his own body somewhere, repressed somehow, or is he dead. Gone. Forever. We have no idea if a clairvoyant can actually help us to answer this, yet I'm already stunned by this ladies opening remarks.

'Well . . . Yes,' Helen manages to respond, uncertainly. 'But how do you know that?'

Lily just shrugs slightly. 'It's what I do,' she replies, turning her gaze briefly to me and then back to Helen.

'Your young friend here is troubled,' she stops, gathering her thoughts. 'I know the booking was for you, but I'm being directed to this young man,' she pauses, and then focuses her gaze on me intently again. 'He's amiss somehow, almost . . . like,' she pauses again, her brow furrowed. 'Almost like . . .' she repeats, stopping. 'I'm receiving a feeling like the breaking down of a barrier,' she tilts her head and thinks for a moment then resumes after seconds that seem like minutes. 'It's like you've washed away time itself . . . and emerged fresh and new. It's such a strong feeling. Does this mean something to you?' It's the first time she's spoken to me directly.

I don't know how to reply. The words are so cryptic, but I feel like she's seized upon my feelings and my situation perfectly. I take a long slow breath and say simply, 'Yes.'

She nods. 'I'm being told to tell you that you're not alone. That you're not the first,' she seems to speak without really understanding her own words. 'Your situation is very rare, but not unique.' She pauses, reflecting inwardly. 'Do you understand?'

I really don't, but I feel strangely compelled to nod and I manage to respond with another weak, 'Yes,' again.

'And you feel guilt, enormous guilt. But you shouldn't,' she pauses, tilting her head to the other side now. She looks across at Helen briefly, then back to me. 'I'm sensing another child. He was the one misplaced, but he was due to move on. I'm being told to assure you that he is content now. He's happy. And what happened to him was not your doing.'

Her dark brown eyes are fathomless as they bore into mine, imploring that I understand this mysterious revelation.

'This other child was a victim, but not of your doing, and he was ready to pass on. He's with his father now, a joyous reunion. But he's already preparing to start over again. Soon, but not close. A new life. Better. An easier road.'

She frowns again, shakes her head slightly and asks, 'Is this meaning something to you? I'm sorry if I'm rambling, but the message is coming through strong and clear, but it's unusual. Can you relate to what I'm saying?'

I look at Helen. She is white as a sheet and she nods. We both know Lily is talking about Mark. How she's doing this we don't understand, but the message is coming through clearly to us too. I hesitate and quietly ask.

'He's not coming back then, is he?'

Lily doesn't hesitate. 'No, he's not coming back. He never knew his father and is so glad to be with him. But he's moving forward, and will be reborn again soon. His passing to the spirit world was not your fault.'

She closes her eyes briefly, taking a deep breath, appearing to centre herself. 'I believe that you should relax and enjoy the opportunities before you. That you should let go of the past and look to the future. Just accept. Enjoy. Relax,' she pauses yet again. 'And forgive. It's important that you embrace forgiveness. Let go of the anger. No good can come from being angry all the time. Forgive, but don't forget. Just let the past go.'

Immediately, thoughts of Brett Thompson and his possession of my family spring to mind. 'Okay,' I say lamely.

But she isn't finished with me. 'And there are other children involved. I'm sensing a young adult, and two other children – like yourself,' she stops, looking at me uncertainly. 'You must try not to interfere. I need to reinforce that the children are in good hands, trust in that,' she pauses, a little bemused. 'You must trust their mother to provide for them. Do you understand this?' The look on her face tells me she is more confused about the message than I am.

In good hands, she said. Are Daniel, Katie and Jack really in good hands? I suppose they are. 'I guess so,' I reply.

It's incredible. We have told Lily absolutely nothing about ourselves, only Helen's name to make the booking, and I'm astounded at how easily the words seem to flow from her, and how easy it is to relate these words to our current situations. Then a thought strikes me.

'May I ask . . .' I blurt, '. . . who is telling you this?'

But the question doesn't trouble her at all. 'I'm sorry, that's not clear to me,' she replies simply, shaking her head.

'Oh,' is all I can say, feeling a little thwarted.

She sits back in her chair a little and switches her focus to Helen. 'I do have a message for you too, but not from your son I'm afraid. This is from a man. An older man,' she pauses, focusing inwardly again. 'He's showing me an axe. But he tells me he means you no harm. Does this mean something to you?'

Helen nearly falls off her chair. She grips the table in surprise. 'Walter?' she says. I can't believe my ears either. How can this woman know that phrase?

Lily continues. 'I'm feeling immense pride from Walter, for both you and this boy, although he makes me feel that he's referring to *my boy*, not necessarily this boy.' She pauses, frowning, obviously quite puzzled again by her own words, then shrugs slightly and presses on.

'He says that he's proud of your decisiveness, and your commitment, and your actions. He couldn't be prouder, he's practically glowing.' Very oddly she actually squints a little as she says this. 'He says that you did the right thing, every time. He's so happy. He misses being with you, with you both. But he's watching, all the time. Looking in, he says.'

Helen chokes a little on these words, and although I don't recognise them she obviously does. Looking in. It means something to her. She clears her throat and speaks, 'He has two sons, would you remind him.'

Lily nods, not so much to Helen's words, but to whatever she can see or hear being played out within her mind. This is really weird, but fiercely compelling. I'm entranced.

'He knows, he knows,' she repeats. 'He knows, and he's so sorry for how he treated him, but he's watching over him too. Your baby is fine,' she pauses, gathering herself. 'He tells me that your baby is successful, very happy, and well. And he may not be lost for good. Time is on your side.'

There is a moment's silence as Helen and I try to absorb everything. She simply has to be referring to Bobby, Mum's youngest child, her baby. He's well and happy somewhere. That's good, I'm so relieved. Helen is close to tears.

'I'm afraid your time is almost up,' Lily advises politely, 'but I do have a final message for you,' she says, turning back to look at me. Her eyes lock onto mine, transfixing me, somehow seeing right inside me. Her gaze is almost hypnotic as she leans forward a little, drawing me in further.

I can hardly breathe. I'm totally captivated.

'Return to the place and relive the moment,' she finally advises, somewhat obscurely. 'Look inside yourself . . . Nothing will change, but things will be clearer,' she concludes decisively. Then she draws a deep breath, releasing the hold she has over me and smiles, with genuine warmth, and sits back in her chair.

I feel sure she has no real idea what her final words may mean but I think that I might. I look over at Helen. She's stunned too, and I can tell instantly that she doesn't want it to end there. Small tears are welling in her eyes.

'Is there any more you can tell us,' she asks hesitantly. 'Is there anything more coming from Walter?'

'I'm sorry, no,' Lily's response is sympathetic. 'There is no more. Not today.'

'We can pay. Money's not an issue,' Helen blurts quickly, sounding slightly desperate.

Lily's smile is again warm, but her words are firm. 'I'm sorry. It's not about money. That's simply all I'm receiving,' she pauses and smiles again, ending the discussion gently but firmly with: 'There's nothing more for me to tell you at the moment. Kushti bok.'

Intrigued by the unfamiliar words I ask, 'Pardon me?'

'Kushti bok,' she repeats. 'It means, Good Luck.'

I wait for further clarification, but she simply maintains the warm smile. I suddenly realise that this is her way of ending the session cleanly and that the words are merely a distraction to help to move people along. Fair enough. Some of Lily's visitors must be very lonely and desperate and want to stay and talk practically forever. It must be hard on her.

I stand quietly and take Helen's hand, thanking Lily sincerely before leading my mother back through the crystal shop. The girl with the bright red hair offers a pleasant smile of farewell as we pass, but doesn't try to sell us anything.

We spend almost an hour at a small café just down the road while Helen composes herself over a large pot of tea. She isn't in a fit state to drive home straight after. The few words from Dad have really surprised her, but in a good way. We talk through everything we heard and fairly readily agree on many of the key points Lily made.

While she didn't specifically answer all our questions – and to be fair we only asked one – she gave us a lot to think about.

We do agree that she told us that Mark is going to be re-born, to a new life, and will not return to his past-life's body.

So Mark is going to be reincarnated. This gets me really thinking.

THIRTY-SEVEN

And so my simple plan came together and I have *returned to the place* – the intersection of Waterloo Rd and Samsara Place – just as Lily advised.

I climb off the flash new bike and survey the area around me. Over the road the long concrete industrial buildings are once again deserted for the day. Their large roll-a-doors shut tight and the advertising hoardings dim as the shadows rise across them. The workers from the area are all now well on their way home to their families.

I stand on the western side of Waterloo Rd, beneath the lamppost which bears the Samsara Place sign that points back across the road and directly up the now quiet and dim industrial way. Behind me are the greenbelt and stream, and the trees and bush where both Mark and I have previously ended up following our separate traumatic accidents.

I turn a full circle, slowly, taking in my surroundings, and then stop and close my eyes tight. Lily's words about *reliving the moment,* and *looking inside myself,* swirl about in my mind as I try to remember anything I can about either of those two accidents.

I remember driving along this road, and the flash of a blue car, and the sickening lurch as my car was shunted forcefully across the footpath and into the trees. These are my recollect-ions, Nick's memory.

But I'm sure that I have some limited recall from Mark's point of view also. A hazy thought of lying on the grass, looking up – with the silhouette of a man standing over me, and flashes from the reflectors on a bicycle's wheel spinning above.

I am convinced that this short blur of memory is actually Mark's, and not my own.

But somehow I saw it, and I remember it.

Somehow, this has to be the link between us.

So here I stand, at the exact spot where the two accidents occurred, at roughly the same time of day, and – unlike the last time I visited here with Liz – I'm experiencing no physical reaction. No nausea, nothing extraordinary.

Not yet, anyway.

I get back on the bike.

It's almost fully dark as I ride further up Waterloo Rd and then stop and turn about fifty metres from the signpost I had been standing under.

I take a deep breath and start peddling, as fast as I can, back along the road towards the signpost. My heart begins racing in anticipation. I pump my legs furiously, wanting to get up as much speed as possible before I reach the spot. The road flashes beneath me, the sidewalk and greenbelt speed past to my left and the low industrial buildings loom in the darkness to my right. My hair flies back in the breeze and the bikes new tires hum loudly on the road surface. My heart rate increases as I pump the pedals feverishly.

I look up to see the entrance to Samsara Place appearing just ahead. There are no cars. Other than my low-flying bicycle the road is deserted.

I keep pedaling furiously as I speed past the signpost, then I turn my head to glance briefly up the side road – where Steve's SUV must have come from – and pull the bike violently to its left, bouncing it up and over the footpath directly over the bright orange paint marks and onto the greenbelt.

Without braking I throw myself off the bike, instinctively closing my eyes and raising my arms over my already battered face to protect my head – and then hit the ground and roll, tumbling into the bushes. I hear the bike clatter as it flies forward into a bush and I gasp for air as the breath is knocked out of me from the impact with the ground.

I stop rolling and end up on my back, my feet pointing towards the stream, away from the road. I lie there momentarily dazed, adrenaline pumping through me, eyes still closed but wide awake and trying to soak up the experience.

Air returns to my lungs in a frenzied rush.

I lie on the grass, eyes closed, imagining the dark trees above, listening and waiting.

As my heart beats to a new and frantic rhythm I begin to picture what Mark must have experienced as Steve's SUV bounced him off the sidewalk and into these trees.

I hear a muffled cell-phone ringing somewhere nearby and then the image of a bicycle wheel spinning above comes into view, but it's much clearer than before. Bright lights sparkle red flashes through the hazy gloom, off the reflectors on the spinning wheel, until the silhouette of a man steps in to stand over me.

My heart races in terror. It's Steve.

He bends over me, roughly searching in my pockets. His face is dark and angry. The moving shadows of the trees play across him.

I'm petrified.

Abruptly he stands up, triumphant, cursing at me and holding something. He waves it in my face, scaring me further.

The little blue cell-phone, still persistently ringing.

I can't see the display but I know it's Liz calling, trying to track me down. Tears well into my eyes as I realise what serious trouble I'm in. My body is wracked with tremors of panic and I start to cry and beg . . . please don't, I didn't meant to, please, I'm sorry . . . as I anticipate Steve's terrifying reprisal.

Through my tears I see him draw his fist back. My heart is still racing, and it lurches and I can't breathe. I'm overcome with a sense of finality. I somehow know the blow is coming, but I can't move. Then a dog barks nearby and a man's voice calls out.

Steve hesitates only for a second, then suddenly lashes down sharply and violently to smash the cell-phone against my forehead.

The ringing ceases abruptly and thankfully I feel no pain, but the vision in my head blurs and flickers like a flame about to be extinguished in a breeze.

And yet again I feel darkness envelope me completely.

I sit up abruptly, once again gripped by nausea, and spill the contents of my stomach onto the grass beside me. My body is suddenly racked with cold shivers and spasms, which slowly pass. I lie back down, rolling away from the vomit, wiping tears from my cheeks and instinctively reach to check my injured forehead. It isn't bleeding.

It takes a few minutes for my heart rate to slow and for my mind to clear and start to work adequately again. I keep my eyes shut tight as I try to digest all this.

What I saw was definitely Mark's memory. Not mine, but clearly the last moments of Mark's short life. I recall once again the words, *return . . . relive . . . look inside yourself*, that Lily's had so hypnotically delivered. *Nothing will change, but things will be clearer*. I try to absorb this, along with my new experiences.

Evidently, some parts of Mark's memories are in my head too. They have to be, but somewhere deep down in my subconscious. Deep down in our shared subconscious.

And now I'm convinced. I know how I got here, inside Mark's body. It should be unbelievable, but I believe.

It was Lily's words about Mark being re-born that helped Helen and I form this theory, but neither of us were comfortable with it. Frankly, it seems rather far-fetched.

But this isn't a dream, and I'm certain also that I've never been a ghost. I'm convinced that all of this is real.

And our theory held up when we worked out the dates. There is some sense to it, obscure as the idea may be.

Mark was born almost exactly nine months after the date I died. This calculation is fact. Based on this, our theory is simply that my life-force, or soul, moved from my old body – at my moment of death – to immediately seek and enter a new body at its moment of conception.

Mark Mitchell's conception. Mark's newly created human form. This is essentially an act of reincarnation.

But is this how reincarnation works? I think so.

Maybe it isn't the way an organised religion that believes in reincarnation might consider or promote it. And I don't think that it happens like this to everyone that dies, but I imagine it may only happen to those that meet untimely deaths.

Helen and I can't prove anything, with only my one example to offer, but the dates work out for me.

This means that I, Nick Davis, am Mark's past-life. His previous incarnation on earth. And, therefore, the freshest past-life within the subconscious mind of his young being.

So Mark grew up with me, or rather with my previous life's memories, already inside of him. Deep, deep down in his subconscious somewhere.

Is it so hard to believe that each of us might carry memories from our prior life-cycles down deep in our subconscious minds? Honestly, before all this I would have scoffed. But who really knows. Some people believe.

And now I, too, am a believer.

But then, when Mark suffered his traumatic accident on the same stretch of road, in very similar circumstances to the one that actually ended my life – something jolted my past-life memories, or life-force, up from his subconscious to seize control of the boy's young body. Effectively expelling Mark's consciousness. Either crushing, or ejecting, his life-force and moving him onward to the spirit world, as Lily so delicately put it. I don't really understand how this works.

How could this happen? Who knows? I'm no psychologist, or scientist. But I believe, now, that anything is possible. I'm here aren't I? How can I argue against it? Who knows, really, what such severe psychological trauma can do to a person.

And why did it happen? Again I don't know. Was it fate, or karma, or something to do with unfinished business? Did God himself intervene? Am I, perhaps, being given an opportunity to right the wrongs of my untimely death, or is it just a phenomenal freak of nature? A supernatural glitch? I don't think anyone can truly give a definitive explanation for what has happened to me, but Lily's words about Mark being *misplaced* and *due to pass on* make it seem almost pre-destined.

Helen and I even discussed those people who attempt to access past-lives through hypnosis, and that makes me wonder too. I vaguely recall seeing a documentary on TV once where hypnosis supposedly drew out other voices and personalities when these people's subconscious minds were plumbed. At the time the documentary had been over-hyped and was hard to believe. I wasn't convinced then, but today – I've become more open-minded. I am my own living, breathing example.

I believe in reincarnation now.

I open my eyes and finally sit up, very slowly, still shaky from my unnatural experience. Looking around I realise I'm still quite some distance from where the orange paint indicates that Mark had landed. He must have been really flying when he came off his bike. And my new bike is lodged, at ground level, into a bush a few metres in front of me. Not up a tree.

Steve must have hit the poor kid damn hard.

The poor kid. Guilt floods through me.

A small part of me was hoping that Lily's advice to *return to the place, relive the moments* might restore Mark to his body – and let him live the rest of his life. But it hasn't. The thought of it had been terrifying me, but it seemed only fair.

It seemed like the right thing to do.

But Mark is gone, forever. He isn't coming back.

Lily also told me that this wasn't my fault, and that nothing could be changed. But, while being able to relive Mark's final moments has convinced me that I had already been inside his subconscious, it doesn't ease my burden.

I simple have to trust now that Mark is soon to move on again. If Lily is to be believed then he will be back in our world soon. Somewhere better. Somewhere he will live an easier and happier life.

I guess that's some consolation, isn't it?

But the Mark Mitchell that his mother, sister and friends all knew regrettably no longer exists in this life-cycle.

I stand up and take a few slow deep breaths' to clear my head. Then I pull the bike out of the bushes. It isn't damaged and neither am I, not with anything physically new anyway, so I climb back onto it and slowly start to pedal back to the old homestead.

Back to my new life – and family.

30 November 2008, late Sunday afternoon.

THIRTY-EIGHT

The Sunday evening takeaway-dinner-in-the-park is a long-held Davis family tradition. Usually fun, but not always joyful, with siblings often bickering.

The gathering this evening is no different, but I'm pretty happy none-the-less.

Katie and Jack provide the bickering, but I'm more curious about the quiet interplay between Daniel and Liz. She's wearing her hair down, which is unusual, and with a little touch of make-up and a fitted top that shows off her god-given curves, she looks much more mature than her very recently-turned sixteen years.

She sat down first and Daniel moved pretty quickly to take the seat beside her. The flirting isn't open and obvious but the small blushes and sneaky smiles are making me a little uncomfortable. And I can see that Sarah is feeling the same way. I'm torn, and seriously confused about what is appropriate for me to be feeling. My eldest son is casually chatting up a pretty girl – a girl who I have now oddly become accustomed to thinking of as my sister. And while I feel some pride at my son having become such a smooth talker, I also feel somewhat protective of my sister's honour.

Could this be any more complex?

I think about throwing a chip at them to break it up – surely that would be acceptable from an eight year old – but I restrain myself, trying to be mature about it.

It isn't easy.

Helen arranged the gathering and we now have the entire Thompson family with us at the same bench in Fraser Park at which I'd first stumbled across them. But this time the sun is still shining down on us and I can see all their features clearly. Only Tracey is missing. We assume she's down the pub, but as usual she didn't leave a note.

Some things aren't going to change quickly.

Jack is sitting immediately to my left on the park bench, beside Brett and then Sarah. Across the table from me are Helen, Katie and then Daniel and Liz.

Seeing Brett with Sarah is hard. I continue to struggle with my feelings about Brett, but it does seem that he might actually be one of the good guys. I feel rushes of anger whenever he touches Sarah, and I know I shouldn't hate him. But it's not that simple. I'm working on it.

I glance over at Helen and smile. She smiles back and winks – relief in her eyes. Our nightmare is finally fading.

Thankfully, the police investigations are over now and, thanks to many factors – including the video; the physical evidence and witness testimonies; not to mention other reports of intimidation and corruption by the Cassidy brothers that have started to emerge – the police have decided not to prosecute either Tracey or Helen. Both Cassidy brothers' deaths have finally, and fortunately, been accepted as self-defence.

A little disturbingly the police have never connected us with the mysterious disappearance of the old man who I still think looked remarkably like Skinner from the X-Files.

Media reports indicate that no bodies were found in the ruins of his house, which was very badly damaged by the fire. My best guess is that the old guy packed up and skipped town within minutes of Helen and I evacuating his driveway. Finding the house empty, Richard must have torched it to both send Skinner a message and to destroy his computer files. If Skinner's smart he'll arrange for lawyers to sort out the mess for him and just stay away.

Helen and I both feel quite guilty about what happened to him, but it's not like we had a lot of choice.

I'm a little lost in my own thoughts, so I don't hear the joke Jack tells that makes Katie snort her lemonade across the table in surprise. Helen tries hard not to smile as Brett admonishes them both for displaying such poor manners in company. Katie blushes in embarrassment as Jack mumbles a weak apology and then looks at me and rolls his eyes.

I roll my eyes back at him, smiling. Yes, we have some guilt about Skinner, but we will learn to live with it.

I also have to learn to live with going to school again each day since my suspension was recently lifted.

It turns out that the Breckenock boy's father, James, was a major investor in Cassidy Construction and it seems pretty certain that he is actually the *Jimmy B* that Richard referred to in the video. Mind you, with his battalion of lawyers, I doubt they will ever be able to successfully prosecute him for whatever part he played in the whole mess. But, with the scandal damaging the Breckenock family reputation, they have withdrawn their complaint over my assault, just to calm the waters.

So this means I now have no excuse not to go to school. The simplicity of the lessons is driving me crazy, but there is no more bullying and even the bigger children give me a fairly wide berth. Mind you, I have to admit that I'm actually finding the sports activities quite a lot of fun. Starting over again in a young, fit body does have some advantages.

And after school I've found that Mark is always welcome at the Thompson residence, so I've been dropping by to hang out there most afternoons. Although it is pretty strange being there, especially when the kids start bickering. I try not to interfere, but it's not easy.

And I am very glad to be here – and able to watch my children grow up. Even if it is from a highly unusual perspective. Yes, I'd prefer to still be Nick Davis, but I'm slowly coming to grips with being Mark Mitchell now and I'm determined to enjoy myself as fully as possible.

Nevertheless, while I'm thankful of the second chance this incredible turn of fate has handed me, I'm still profoundly troubled that it came at the expense of another.

And a child at that.

I wish I could change things, but I can't. It's out of my hands. Mark has moved on. So must I.

I do know that Helen has been back to visit Lily already. She just wants to talk to Dad, and to try and find out more about Bobby. The visits make me wonder why Dad hasn't been reborn yet. Or would he not be able to watch over us if he has already been reincarnated? I mean, is it possible for a soul to be communicating through someone like Lily, and yet also be reborn into a new life? Or can a medium, or clairvoyant, only receive messages from a soul that is between assignments?

I'm damned if I know. Every time I think about it there seem to be more questions than answers.

Helen is being somewhat secretive about the visits, a little embarrassed about wanting to communicate with Dad, but who can blame her.

Who wouldn't do the same in her situation?

I look again at the faces around the bench.

Helen seems content as she silently watches Katie debate something earnestly with Brett. Jack interrupts the discussion to share his opinion, earning himself a reproachful look from his sister. Meanwhile Daniel is trying his best to look cool and indifferent as Liz plays with her hair and whispers something to him. He flushes slightly at whatever it is she says. Sarah still has one eye on them and frowns at the teenage byplay. Then Jack laughs at something I again don't hear properly and elbows me roughly in the ribs. I frown and shove him back. He laughs again and starts repeatedly poking me in the ribs with both hands, before Brett leans over to break up the minor altercation.

I feel good. With the problems of the Cassidy brothers behind us I'm now starting to look forward to my strange new future. And while there is much of my old life I will miss as a father and husband, it feels good to know that I will be able to move ahead while still holding on to so many of the most important things from my past.

I suddenly realise that Helen is watching me gaze quietly around the group, a wee smile on her face. Then she winks at me again and I try hard to hold back the small tear of happiness that begins to creep into my eye.

* * *

Also available by Tony Price

KICKING OUT

For 20 year old Lily MacDonald, aside from the death of her mother when she was only a child, growing up in the small town of Hawthorne, New Zealand has been relatively idyllic – until the day her safe and carefree world is torn apart by the detonation of a bomb in her work-place. Friends and colleagues perish and Lily's life begins to spiral out of control as she fears that a psychopath is targeting her. Her initial terror quickly turns to desperation when events become darker and more bizarre as Lily is also forced to battle with a psychic gift awakening inside her . . .

www.ingramcontent.com/pod-product-compliance
Ingram Content Group UK Ltd.
Pitfield, Milton Keynes, MK11 3LW, UK
UKHW040022200726
13854UKWH00001B/312

9 780473 182915